Also by Pete McCormack
Shelby

UNDERSTANDING KEN

UNDERSTANDING **KEN**

PETE McCORMACK

DOUGLAS & McINTYRE VANCOUVER TORONTO

Douglas & McIntyre Ltd.
1615 Venables Street
Vancouver, B.C
V5L 2H1

The publisher gratefully acknowledges the assistance of the
Canada Council for the Arts and of the British Columbia
Ministry of Tourism, Small Business and Culture. The
publisher also acknowledges the financial support of the
Government of Canada through the Book Publishing Industry
Development Program for our publishing activities.

Canadian Cataloguing in Publication Data

McCormack, Pete, 1965-
Understanding Ken
ISBN 1-55054-268-0
I. Title.
PS8575.C68U52 1998   C813'.54   C98-931509-6
PR9199.3.M4238U52 1998

Book design by Michael Solomon
Cover photograph by Brett Simms
Printed and bound in Canada by Webcom

For my family, of course, and a few others.

When I was a kid, I prayed for enough talent to be a pro hockey player. — **Don Cherry**

PRE-GAME SKATE

I remember exactly when it happened. Everybody was in the neighbour's basement shouting and screaming. They were all watching this playoff series between the Montreal Canadiens and the Chicago Black Hawks. Bobby Hull. Jean Béliveau. Stan Mikita. Yvan Cournoyer. Best players in the world. I was sitting on the stairs with a few other kids, peering at the TV set through the railing.

It was a miracle.

There was this goalie for Montreal who would stand up and lean on his stick when the puck was in the other team's end. Just like God he'd stand there watching.

Everyone was talking about this new guy. Where'd he come from? Nobody knew. How could he be so good? Nobody knew.

That was Ken Dryden.

Seventh game of a seven-game series for the Stanley Cup. The Montreal Canadiens are leading 3-2 over the Chicago Black Hawks in Chicago in the dying minutes. The dying minutes are when the game is almost dead. Ken makes a save on one side of the net and is way out of the play. The puck scoots across the crease to Jim Pappin. Pappin has a whole open net. Four feet high. Six feet wide. To tie the game. Think about it. It's impossible to miss an open net. You'd have to be a total loser.

Pappin shoots.

Pappin puts his arms in the air to celebrate the goal.

That's when the goalie pad came out of nowhere. That pad

swallowed up the puck like water down the bathtub drain. That pad broke Jim Pappin's heart and all the Black Hawks' hearts and my brother's heart.

That was the pad of Ken Dryden.

The greatest goalie in the history of the world.

*

Montreal Canadiens.

They were it.

There was no chance of me ever liking any other team. Every other team can go die in a plane crash for all I care. I don't want them to suffer. They just don't matter.

My favourite player after Ken? Yvan Cournoyer. He's the fastest skater in the world. They call him the Roadrunner—like that cartoon. But Cournoyer would catch that cartoon Roadrunner in about twelve seconds. You can barely follow Cournoyer on the TV set when he starts skating. He skates right off the screen. Watch him next time. He's on the screen. *Boom.* They lose him. Gone. The only time they keep him on the screen is when he has the puck. The puck slows Cournoyer down just enough for the cameraman to keep his job.

There's a kid who lives down the street from me—actually down the street, around a corner, past my school, down a hill and then up a hill. Right there. He has the same name as the Roadrunner but they say it Corn-oy-er, not Corn-why-ay. Imagine having the same name as the Roadrunner and saying it differently! After having to sometimes watch the Vancouver Canucks instead of the Montreal Canadiens on Hockey Night in Canada because we live in British Columbia, that's the dumbest thing I've ever heard.

*

My dad's a doctor. I stay with him on weekends. He's building on to his house in the middle of winter. The front room is wide open. There's a big sheet of clear plastic hanging from the roof that drops down where the wall used to be. It flaps in the wind but keeps most of the snow out. That's the main thing. Keeping the snow out of the front room. Yesterday when I woke up there was a glass of water on the kitchen counter. It was frozen. That's how cold it is. That's as cold as an arena.

My dad is building a new downstairs, too. After they pour the cement we might fill the downstairs with water before the walls are built and let it freeze over so we'd have an indoor hockey arena. That's what my dad said. Imagine that. An arena in your own house.

Right now it's a mess, though, downstairs and upstairs. Sawdust and wood and tools everywhere. My dad's got all kinds of tools: drill presses, table saws, band saws, lathes. We can barely get in the door. And when you do, you drag all the sawdust upstairs on your wet boots and it makes a big mess. There's almost no place in the house where you can't find sawdust. Even in the fridge. Even in the jam and the butter.

My dad doesn't care about the mess and neither do I. It would make my mom's head fall off. It's probably the reason they're not together. They should be together. They will be together. Probably after the hockey season. They like each other, that's for sure. That's why they scream at each other so much. If you don't like someone, you scream once and never talk to them again. If you love someone, you scream all the time and keep coming back. I don't know why they have to have boyfriends and girlfriends when it's each other they like. That's like wanting to play hockey and buying a soccer ball.

It would be perfect if we had a rink downstairs in my dad's house. Dad says you gotta play three hours a day if you want to make pro. That's what Bobby Orr said, too. I'm making a rink in the yard at my mom's place where I live. That's what I did Friday after school before my dad picked me up to go to his house for the weekend. I've already got the plastic down. That's how you make a rink. You get a whole bunch of garbage bags. It doesn't matter what colour they are—black or green. Plus I've got a couple of huge sheets of plastic. And what you do is tack 'em into the frozen dirt. You just tack 'em in. Get a big area covered and make sure the plastic doesn't leak. Then you get the hose out and pour water on the plastic and it freezes. You do that for a few nights in a row and *bang*, you've got yourself a rink.

*

The tryouts for the Trail Peewee Smoke Eater Rep team start on Tuesday night. I can't wait. The rep team is the team made up of the best peewees in Trail. We go out and play the rep teams from all the other cities around. The guys that don't make the rep team end up playing in the house league, where the games have no meaning. If you can't make the rep team there's no way you'll ever make pro. That's all there is to it.

My dad says I could make the rep team with a broken leg.

No way.

I know that because I cut my foot this summer. I was goofing around on our stairs outside my mom's house and

I jumped off like I was Superman and landed right on a broken Coke bottle. I've never seen so much blood in my whole life. It was pouring out of my foot and onto the grass like Niagara Falls. Inside my foot you could see all the fatty white stuff. My sister screamed out for my older brother, who was watching the football game on TV. He came out on the porch and looked at my foot from about five miles away. He said it wasn't cut off and he'd come back at the end of the third quarter. Wasn't cut off! It was almost cut in half right down the middle. My mom was at work so the neighbours had to take me to the hospital emergency with my foot in a bucket.

I don't know if my brother came out at the end of the third quarter or not. What I do know is it took fourteen stitches to close up the hole and I spent the summer with my foot in a plastic bag, staring at everyone else swimming in Champion Lake. I'd sit there thinking about the hockey season and Ken and the Roadrunner and Montreal winning the Stanley Cup. Cournoyer batted the puck right out of the air to score the winning goal in game six. Just like a baseball player. If I close my eyes I can see it perfectly. Tony O in the Chicago net didn't even move.

One thing's for sure, if the tryouts for the peewee reps had been in the summer, I wouldn't have made the team. Not even the Roadrunner could make the peewee rep team with a bag on his foot. But my legs feel pretty good right now. That's what matters. That's why I'm pretty sure I'll be the second-best player at the tryouts.

I read it in the paper. It's on the radio, too. It's everywhere.

Ken's not dead. Ken's not traded. Ken didn't get his legs chewed off.

After three years and two Stanley Cups and beating the Russians...

Ken Dryden quit hockey.

It says in the paper he wants to be a lawyer.

What about the Montreal Canadiens?

What about Cournoyer?

Who will play goal? *Bunny Larocque?*

You can't win with a goalie named Bunny.

I feel like I've been butt-ended in the gut a million times.

Last year with Ken the Montreal Canadiens were so good they only lost ten games and won the Stanley Cup. After they won, me and my friend ran outside to celebrate. We were jumping up and down on the grass and he elbowed me in the face and we were laughing our heads off and there was blood everywhere and it was exactly the same colour as the Montreal Canadiens away shirts and everything was perfect.

What's going to happen now?

How could Ken do this? Who would pick anything over hockey, especially when you're the best in the world? Sure, some kids at my school don't play, but they're total losers. Hockey isn't like choosing where you want to live. I live with my mom. I live with my dad. One or the other. But with hockey? You play. Period. Quit? I wouldn't even say that for a joke to my dad. What would we do every Saturday morning if it wasn't for hockey? Ski? Up the hill. Down the hill. That doesn't make any sense. There's no Skiing Night in Canada. There's no skiing cards. Who ever heard of trading a Jean-Claude Killy card? You wouldn't get a Gary Doak for that. I traded a Bobby Orr card for twelve steelies once. Now I'd do anything to have that Bobby Orr card back. He's the best defenceman in the world. He's the best but I like Serge Savard more. Sometimes when I get on the ice I do a Savardian Spinorama and feel just like him. It's weird, but you make a move and you swear for just a second you're the same person.

And then Dryden quits.

It's unbelievable.

"Dad, how could Ken do this?"

"He can do whatever he wants."

"He *quit* hockey, Dad. We're all depending on him!"

"I'm trying to watch the golf!"

"Dad, what about the Roadrunner!"

"What are you talking about?"

"Dad! Ken quit!"

"I'm trying to watch the f---ing golf!"

My dad can't even talk about it.

Me and my dad are serious about hockey. I remember when Montreal lost to the New York Rangers in the quarter-finals two years ago. I cried like a pig. I couldn't help it. That's how serious I am.

Last year I was playing peewee pup rep, but the peewee reps—they're older than the peewee pups—they brought me up to play for a game. I was the youngest on the whole team by a mile. We were playing on the big rink. That's where the Trail Smoke Eaters play. They were the last team from Canada to win the world championships. And there I was, on the big ice in the warmup, a peewee pup skating around with the peewees. Then the game started and I sat down on the bench and waited for my chance.

I sat there the whole first period. Twenty minutes stop time. Sitting there getting freezing feet. That's what happens when you don't play. The second period came and went and I was still on the bench. By then I was the youngest player and the coldest player. Me and the spare goalie just sitting there. We didn't look at each other. I was pretty close to crying. The third period came and I was still sitting there. Just staring out at the game like when you watch it on TV, except I was freezing.

Then I had this feeling. I can pretty much tell certain things. Some things I can't tell, some things I can. But I could tell something. I turned around and I saw my dad climbing down in the stands and I thought, Uh-oh. Sometimes he gets that same look when I help him and it doesn't go so smooth as it could—like cutting a piece of plywood on the table saw downstairs. Sometimes I move the wood too much. He says, "Five cents worth of work and fifty cents worth of damage," but he never pays me the five cents.

My dad had that same look on his face coming down from the stands. I lifted my shoulder pads up and hid my head. I looked back out of the corner of my eye and I saw him leaning over the wire behind the bench. He looked at the coach and said, "You're a f---ing asshole!" louder than the person who announces the goals at the Montreal

Forum. All the kids looked at me and they were thinking, And you're a f---ing asshole like your dad. That was it for me with the peewees last year.

And that's how serious my dad is.

This year I'm peewee all the way. My dad says this year will be different. He says that f---ing prick was a lousy coach and he won't be coaching this year, anyway. He says this year we'll have a great team if we go with two lines. We'll probably win the West Kootenay Championships, then we'll play the best team from the East Kootenays to decide who's the best in all the Kootenays. When we beat them we'll be the Kootenay champions and go to the B.C. Championships and play all the best teams in B.C., which means one of those Vancouver teams with really big players. Penticton has big players, too. Those teams are stocked. That's what my dad says.

I figure I'll be the second-best player on the team this year. I'll probably get the second-most goals, the second-most assists and the second-most points. My dad thinks I'm the best player. I think you'd have to go to Mongolia to find someone other than my dad who thinks that. Everyone knows who the best player on the team is. He's the best in the whole Kootenays. Maybe anywhere. My dad says he's a year older than me and my dad says I've got the smarts for the game and I'm a better stick-handler. I am a pretty good stick-handler as far as stick-handlers go. But the best player is the best player. That's why they call him that. He knows his hockey, too. He's the only player that can touch me on hockey facts. When we go on road trips to Castlegar or Nelson—an hour, two hours—we sit in the back of the team bus and quiz each other. Once I asked him who got the most penalty minutes in the NHL in 1969. He knew. He even knew how many penalty minutes he got. He knew so fast I didn't even know if I was the best at hockey facts any more. For sure I'm the second best. While we're in the back of the bus quizzing each other, the rest of the players sit up at the front and talk about crap that doesn't matter. I don't even know what they talk about. Crap, that's all.

So I'd say I'm the best stick-handler and the best at hockey facts. But I'm not the best player. That's one of the reasons people don't like me. If you're the best player, they love you. If you're the second-best player, you can forget it.

*

I live with my mom so my dad picks me up for hockey. He drives down from Rossland through Trail up to Montrose to pick me up and then back down to Trail for the game and then back up to Montrose to drop me off. It's not too far but I wouldn't want to walk it. Then my dad has to drive home on his own afterwards. Sometimes when he goes away or gets mad, the best player's dad comes and picks me up in his Cadillac. He's about the only parent who doesn't hate me.

Sometimes me and my dad drop by the best player's house and sit in the kitchen. I feel funny when I'm there— like we weren't invited. My dad likes to drop in on people without calling. My mom never does that. One thing is good, my dad doesn't yell at the best player's house. If the best player is around I might go into his room for a little while. He's got a picture of Bobby Orr in there. I don't get mad about it. It's his room. He likes the Bruins. After a while I go back into the kitchen, where my dad talks to the best player's mom and dad. The best player's dad is nice except he smokes and I can barely breathe in his Cadillac and it's too cold to open the window.

My mom won't drive me to hockey. She hates hockey. She hates the sound of it on TV, too, and the sound of my skates being thrown down the stairs when we lose. Some of my teammates that know her—I don't know how they know her because she never comes to games—some say she's a hippie. The only thing we do that's weird like a hippie is eat yogurt. Other than that I think it's just because my parents are split up.

My mom's boyfriend won't drive me to hockey either. He doesn't hate hockey. He hates me. I'm not kidding. Hates my guts. He's never smiled at me once. He says the Russians are way better hockey players than the Canadians. The Canadians are dirty and they dump the puck into the corner and chase it like dogs. That's what he says. But who won the series of the century with thirty-four seconds left? Ha-ha.

I think he should move to Russia if he likes them so much. If he moved there my dad would move back home in about three weeks and he wouldn't have to drive seven miles then six miles and back again to take me to hockey—and then back home on his own. A lot of things would be better if my mom's boyfriend moved to Russia.

When my dad comes to pick me up, my mom's boyfriend's never here. My dad gets here and he screams at my mom for about forty-five minutes. It's just lucky he comes early, otherwise we'd be forty-five minutes late for the game. My mom might scream too but mostly I can't hear her over my dad. My dad is the loudest person I know. He's loud at home. Loud at the rink.

I don't know what they scream about. I sit on the steps
with my hockey equipment and wait or take shots against
the garage or the street-hockey net. If it's really cold I wait
downstairs and maybe take shots there. When my dad's
done he drives me to hockey and asks me if it wouldn't be
better if I lived with him. He thinks it would be. He's probably right, seeing as we both love hockey. I sometimes say
yes just so he'll stop talking about it. It's quieter at my
mom's, that's all. Plus I think kids like me better here in
Montrose.

Of all the things I like to do, most of all I like to go
downstairs in the basement by myself. The roof isn't too
high and the floor is shiny cement just like the ice at the
Forum in Montreal. I get my hockey stick and a tennis ball
and I pretend I'm playing for the Montreal Canadiens. I'll
write down the points I've scored and it'll be the last game
of the year and I'll be behind the top scorer by four points
and I'll get five points to win the scoring title. Maybe the
last point is an assist, probably from behind the net or
maybe off a face-off. I'll pretend I'm Danny Gallivan. He's
the Montreal Canadiens' commentator, best in the world. I
go super-fast, like this:

*The young rookie on the face-off against Esposito. Eight
seconds to go in the third period. The crowd's all buzzy. Big
Espo'll be looking just to tie up the young rookie. Here's
the face-off. The puck is dropped. The young rookie wins
it clean right back to Cournoyer. Cournoyer shoots!
Rebound! A cannonading drive! Scores! Oh, my goodness,
we've got a hockey game on our hands! Have we got a
game on our hands? We've got a game on our hands! Well,*

jumpin' jillickers, that kid's makin' a believer out of me.

Espo can't believe it. "Gee, kid," he says. "That's the best face-off I've ever seen."

I say, "Thanks, Mr. Esposito, and you were pretty darn good against the Russians."

Esposito says, "Hey, call me Phil."

And then when Phil turns around I trip him just like Bobby Clarke would.

The fans, the newspapers, everybody's wondering if I'm for real. I show them. I always show them. I keep trying, keep pushing, and when you keep trying, everything goes the way it should. Not just at the rink, either. With your parents, too. When you keep trying you'll be skating by the crease and a rebound comes out right on your stick and the net is wide open. That's what happens when you keep trying. You get what they call getting a few breaks. Sometimes I cut around the defenceman and stuff it right in the short side. Sometimes I score on a deflection. That's the thing. You just never know what kind of goal you're going to score to win the Stanley Cup. But if you keep trying, you make people believe in you. It's good to have a few people believing in you. If people believe in you and you end up in a slump, they'll stick by you. But if they don't believe in you and you end up in a slump, they'll send you to the minors before you can even get your sweater off.

*

Even though I'm not the coach, I can pretty much tell who's going to make the Trail Peewee Rep team. Still, it's a fish in your pants while you wait for the piece of paper to be posted. They don't write down the guys who got cut. They write down who made the team. There's a few surprises but you pretty much know.

I was about a third of the way down the list. The best player's name was right before mine. We were the first two forwards. That's a pretty good place to be. Now I'm just wondering who's going to be on my line. My dad gets so mad when I get stuck with the crummiest wingers. Some players score maybe every forty-seven games and they don't take the man, either. My dad says those players shouldn't even show up for the games. My dad thinks the rep team should go with two lines. Get the two best lines and keep going. We don't have enough depth for a third line. That's what my dad says. He's right, too. Two lines would be fine by me. All that ice time.

We have a good power play. That's when the other team gets a penalty and me and the best player go out on the ice together. It's pretty unusual if we don't score. You just have to want to score. You have to want to score more than anything.

The coach of this year's peewee rep team is missing the tips of a couple of fingers. They got bitten off in a brawl when he played for the Trail Smoke Eaters about a hundred years ago. A big pile-up. Both teams and the goalies jumped off the bench to join in. Gloves off. Sticks flying. No helmets. Next thing Coach knew, two fingers were gone. They never found out who bit 'em off. There were no fingers at the bottom of the pile. Whoever it was must've eaten them. Some people even think it was someone from his own team. About twenty people had blood on their faces so you couldn't tell. You can't blame anyone. Once somebody's hand gets in your mouth and starts yanking, most anybody would bite down.

Coach was a pretty good player. I heard he could've

gone pro until he got his knee all busted up. He's got a big-league nose, too. It's so flat he could bite a wall. If you ask him about the top of his pinkie and that other finger being bitten off, he says, "Hey, it coulda been an eye."

I asked Coach about Dryden quitting. He said, "Ah, college boy."

*

A season can go about a hundred different ways. I didn't know what this season would be like for the Trail Smoke Eater Peewee Reps, but it started off a couple of weeks ago against Castlegar, and it started pretty good. We tripled them 6-2. We have the best player and the biggest player in the whole Kootenays. I'm the second-best player. I got a goal and an assist. That's a pretty good start.

After the game my dad told me a few things about what I did right and wrong. That's when I really started to think about Dryden quitting the Canadiens. Then I got a blueberry sundae from the Dairy Queen and I couldn't stop swirling the blueberries into the ice cream. We were driving home from Castlegar and it was really snowing hard so my dad wasn't going too fast. It was dark out when we got to Blueberry Corner. Blueberry Corner is a street that turns off the highway in the middle of nowhere on the way back from Castlegar. That's where I saw a gold Mustang bike lit up by the headlights of my dad's car. It was stuck in a snowbank on the side of the highway.

"Dad," I said, "I just saw a gold bike in that snowbank there."

"What?"

"Over there. A gold bike. Stuck in the snowbank. It looked all bent up."

25

It was dark out and snowing and winter and nine o'clock at night. You don't ride a Mustang in the middle of winter on a highway in Canada. That's a fact you just know.

I don't remember what my dad said, but right then we passed a big diesel truck on the side of the road with its lights flashing. Lights all dirty from mud and blurry through the snow. My dad pulled the car over in front of the truck, which had about forty wheels. I had a strange feeling in my gut.

"Wait here," my dad said. He got out of the car. He was wearing his sheepskin jacket with the white furry collar. I saw him walk away, hunched over against the blizzard. My dad sometimes gets a little crazy but the thing is, he knows what to do when there's something wrong. That's what doctors learn in school. How to know what stuff to do and what's going on. Like when we're in the car and he sees someone crossing the road who doesn't look so good, he'll say, "He's an alcoholic."

I say, "How can you tell?"

My dad says, "After a while you just know these things."

While I was sitting in the car, a cop car drove up and a cop with a hat got out. I watched until he disappeared into the blizzard too.

When my dad came back to the car, he was pale like the snow on his shoulders. His face looked even more sunken where he'd broken his cheek a couple of Christmases ago, like an old wrinkled lunch bag.

"What happened, Dad?"

My dad put his hand on my shoulder like he really loved

me. He thinks I'm about the best hockey player ever. He says I'm heads up, which means I use my head. He's pretty sure I can make pro. It's hard, though. You gotta play three hours a day. You gotta make junior by about fourteen.

My dad said, "A boy was hit on his bike."

"That gold bike I saw?"

My dad nodded.

"What was he doing out on a bike so late?"

My dad shrugged. My dad isn't much of a shrugger.

I said, "Is he dead?"

My dad nodded. "Yeah, he's dead." Then we drove off again.

*

After the weekend my dad almost always drives me home. My mom doesn't even meet him halfway. I have to say she hardly drives me anywhere at all. Her and her boyfriend will not take me to hockey. It's only about thirteen minutes to the Cominco Arena in Trail and fifteen minutes back. Of course they'd have to stay for the game too. You can forget that. They'd rather eat purple health-food vegetables and after that go into the front room and listen to classical music. They sit in there after dinner and me and my sister do the dishes while my mom's boyfriend's youngest son sits at the table trying to finish his dinner. He eats about as slow as a dead kid. He sits at the table with his food in his mouth, a big clump of food in each cheek, way after everybody's gone. While we're eating, his dad just says, "Come on, *eat!*" and sometimes pushes on the back of his head. Then his son takes a couple of quick chews, but anyone with a brain as big as a Brussels sprout can tell it's not helping. He just doesn't know how to chew, that's all.

27

I feel sorry for him trying to push the food down. Sometimes I make him laugh and it's pretty funny. He smiles and his face goes all red like a tomato. He doesn't cry about it, either. That's pretty good for a little guy.

Every dinnertime my dad phones me. The black phone is right there up on the wall by the table. My older sister answers it because of where she sits. She talks for about two seconds and then says, "Dad wants to talk to you." Her and my dad don't get along so well. She likes clean dishes and Dad's dishes can sit in the sink until you get used to them being there. Plus when my sister visits my dad on the weekend she has to go to the rink with us all the time and watch me play hockey. I can't remember the last weekend my sister went to my dad's. She likes my mom a lot more, and my mom's boyfriend. My mom's boyfriend doesn't like me and I don't like him. He doesn't know anything about me. He knows all the outside stuff, that's it. Late for dinner. Bringing dirt into the house. Whacking balls against the wall. He doesn't know the rest. He doesn't know about my statistics downstairs. I'd never tell him about that.

I take the phone from my sister while everybody's eating right there, and my dad says, "Have you told them you want to come live with me yet?"

I look back at the table and see nobody talking and my brother and my sister and my mom's boyfriend's oldest son who's always working on cars and his youngest son with big clumps of food in his mouth and I say, "No." I say it like I'm saying no to a different question. Then I answer a few more questions and then I hang up and my mom says, "What did your father want?"

"He just wanted to see how I was doing." I say that every time. I can pretty much tell what will make my mom and dad get along best with each other so I figure out what the best thing to say is. What'll make them fight the littlest amount before they get back together.

The other day me and my sister were fighting while we were washing the dishes and my mom's boyfriend came in and slapped me around a few times to tell me to shut up. There's not much you can do when that happens. You cover up for a second or so. When you can tell that's not helping, you just go down like Muhammad Ali when Smokin' Joe hit him with a left hook at Madison Square Garden. You don't float like a butterfly. You sit down like a bag of cement and stay there figuring it out. You figure out a lot of things really fast sometimes. I was sitting there and I figured out I can't even tell my dad what happened, because if I tell my dad, my dad will kill my mom's boyfriend. My dad's got a pretty bad temper and legs like Superman and he hates my mom's boyfriend's guts. He's hated him ever since the split-up. My dad would be happy to kill him. So you just sit there and decide not to tell him.

*

The dead kid on the bike was Hobey Barker. I couldn't believe it when I heard that. The reason my dad didn't tell me at first was because the kid used to be a friend of mine back in Rossland when I was five. He was more my best friend's friend. I didn't like Hobey like a best friend. Why do you like the Montreal Canadiens instead of the Toronto Maple Leafs? Because they're about two thousand three hundred and twelve times better. With people it's different. With people sometimes you just like one more than the other.

With Hobey I just liked it more when he wasn't hanging around with me and my best friend. He wasn't a sniveller or chicken. He wasn't anything. He wasn't much into looking for bones or caves. He didn't play street hockey, either. He used to carry a wallet in the back pocket of his brown corduroys. That's what I remember. Why would anyone carry a wallet around when you haven't got any loot? That's what I can't figure out.

Hobey had short dark hair and dark skin and a mole on his cheek and black eyes. He had the same face as Oliver in the movie except Oliver had blonde hair and light skin and blue eyes.

After Hobey got hit I asked my dad if Hobey looked happy or sad. My dad said he couldn't even recognize him. He was too munched. That's what happens when a diesel hits you. He must have been riding his gold bike with his banana seat right across the highway in the dark. Then *boom*. When my dad looked he found Hobey's wallet in his back pocket, just where it always was.

Maybe that's why he had a wallet when we were little. Maybe even way back then he knew that one day they'd need his wallet to know who he was. But how could you know? Maybe he did. Maybe that's why Hobey never seemed too happy. Maybe he thought, What's the point? I'm going to be munched by that diesel anyway.

*

On the weekend we won our first game against a house team. A house team is a bunch of guys in the older division who didn't make the rep team. So the house teams in the older division play the rep team in the younger division. That was us. We won 4-2.

My dad wasn't too happy with the way I played. Afterwards we didn't get any jelly donuts from Rosa at the City Bakery. Those donuts are good, too. Sometimes after a Saturday game we'll buy six or twelve of them. Me and my dad will eat them all. If you get 'em right after the game, they're still hot. I can eat about five of 'em—more. You put your mouth over the hole and suck out all the jelly. And when you eat the donut part you can turn it into dough in your mouth. It feels perfect like that.

After the game my dad was driving up the hill to his place and yelling at me. He yells at me but he loves me. That's how I know yelling doesn't mean anything. I'm trying to get my mom to understand that. It's just words. Nobody else buys me CCM Super Tack skates. Those are the best skates in the world. Cournoyer uses them. You can read the label on his skates in that picture when he's hugging Paul Henderson after beating the Russians.

My dad yells because he knows his hockey and he takes it seriously.

"You gotta take the f---ing man! It looks like you're fishing for trout out there! Dangling your goddamn stick, staring at the puck. Don't stare at the puck. Take the f---ing man! You're not a goddamn kid! You're ten years old!"

That's what he said after the game. Sometimes when he yells I cry. Sometimes I just sit there. I don't know exactly what play he was talking about this time, but it must have happened. No one gets that mad about something that doesn't happen. Hitler, maybe. When the guy with the puck comes skating at you, you have to look him square in the shoulders. If you look at the puck? Man, before you know it you're backchecking again and everybody's yelling at you.

I like being at my dad's for the weekend. It's all hockey. Hockey cards. Hockey magazines. Hockey games. Hockey practices. Hockey Night in Canada right after the Bugs Bunny/Roadrunner Hour. I love Bugs Bunny. I love that big, giant rooster Foghorn Leghorn, too—and Porky Pig and Sylvester and the Tasmanian Devil. But Roadrunner and Coyote? I hate those two. I wish one of those big, brown rocks would fall on both of them and it would just say THE END and then we could get back to Bugs Bunny. With all the money Coyote spends on ACME equipment he should just go to a restaurant and order roast roadrunner for dinner.

*

The Trail Peewee Reps looked pretty good last night when we beat Nelson. We doubled them 6-3 and I got a goal and two assists. The best player got three goals. I got the winning goal—that's the fourth goal—and the best player got a goal when they pulled the goalie. I didn't even get on the ice with the goalie pulled. I just sat on the bench staring at that big open net. With an open net, I would have scored for sure. Then we both would have had two goals, plus I got the winning goal like I said.

My dad was pretty pissed off with the wingers I was playing with. He said they're too small, they can't skate and they can't pass and they've got no guts. That doesn't leave too much. He said if I had a good winger I would have had five assists. One time I had the puck behind our own goal and I heard my dad scream, "Bend your f---ing legs!" So I bent them a little farther and took off just like Cournoyer. Before I knew it I had gone end to end and was skating around one of their defencemen at their blueline and I fell into the goal with the puck and the goalie and about three pounds of snow. When I got up my dad was already down at that end too.

There he was yelling at the referee, "That was tripping, four eyes! You're teaching the kids to lie!"

Then the referee gave me a penalty for charging the goalie.

My dad couldn't believe it. "F---ing homer!" That's what he yelled. And the ref was a homer, too. Every call went for the home team.

I couldn't believe my dad beat me down to the other end of the arena.

When he was a kid he was the fastest runner in England. I've seen his medals. About forty of 'em. He keeps them in this old box and sometimes I take them out and look at them. Long jump. Hundred-yard run. Two-hundred-yard run. He's got calf muscles twice as big as Popeye's arms. I'm not kidding. He would've made pro if he'd got a little help but when my dad was four his dad got TB and died. I'm not sure what TB is but it makes you die just like that, and before you know it you've got no dad. They sent my dad away to an orphanage because his mom didn't have any money. Then there was a war and a whole city went up in flames and then he became a doctor and after that he became my dad.

It's good to have a dad. If you don't have one there's no way you can make pro. That's too bad but that's just the way it is.

*

The thing about having a doctor for a dad is, doctors are pretty important at hockey games. Whenever somebody gets hurt my dad goes out on the ice and says, "Yeah, he's hurt." Whenever a teammate gets hurt we all gather around him while the other team skates around in their own end, waiting. If the player gets up and skates off, the crowd claps and we all bang our sticks on the ice. If you want to get hurt, hockey's a pretty good place to do it. At least when you get up the crowd cheers for you.

I've got some stitches in my face right now. I was skating into the other team's end and a guy backhanded a puck and it flew up in the air and hit me right below my eye and cut me and there was blood on the ice. I didn't stop playing. Not for one shift. I played the whole game with blood on my cheek and I got two goals. Like Rocket Richard when he scored on Sugar Jim Henry back when all the photographs were black and white. My dad said it was pretty good that I kept playing. He says most of the players would have gone home before the game was over. Dad and I went home after the game and he got out his medical bag and gave me a needle with some stuff and then he sewed in a couple of stitches. It was pretty cool because I could touch my cheek and it felt all numb. When you feel numb like that all you want to do is touch it.

That night I felt numb thinking about Dryden. It was okay at first. Montreal won their first two games of the season. Then they lost to the Toronto Maple Leafs. After that they lost to the Atlanta Flames. The Atlanta Flames! An expansion team! They've only been in the league for two years.

How could he quit?

What about all the people that would kill themselves to play one shift on Hockey Night in Canada?

I would.

My dad's the team doctor of the Rossland Junior Warriors. They're a junior team. Junior is about as old as you get before you get married. The guys have moustaches and all that. They've got a skate sharpener in the dressing room, and the coach of the junior team sharpens my skates like a razor blade. One day I'm going to play for the Rossland Junior Warriors. They hang all their gear up overnight in their own stalls. Some of those guys are going to play pro. They could play pro right now.

When my dad and their coach start talking hockey, you can't believe how much they know. My dad says some of those players could stop on a dime and give you nine cents change. He says some of them have million-dollar legs and two-cent brains.

They gave my dad a team jacket that says "Doc" on the sleeve. He never wears it. He wears his sheepskin jacket with a collar and he looks like Charlie Rich if Charlie Rich had fallen off a roof.

The good thing about being the team doctor is, he gets into the games for free and I go in with him. It's pretty good when you get in for free. There's a big crowd and they grab onto the wire behind the net and start pulling and pushing and the whole arena shakes. When the Trail Junior Smokies come up the road to play against Rossland, you better get your tickets early, otherwise you'll be sitting at home listening to the radio.

On Saturday night this guy on the Trail team got tripped up and went face first into the goal post at about two hundred and twelve miles an hour. The net didn't even move and the crowd didn't either and there was blood all over the ice. Dad said his nose was trying to get to know his ear a little better. He wasn't kidding. This guy's nose moved about two inches away from the middle of his face. You never realize how right a nose looks where it is until you see it somewhere else.

They took the guy to the dressing room and I went too. I was watching while they stuck all this stuff up his nose to stop the blood. The old trainer with a big red nose of his own was helping my dad and laughing and saying the junior player looked like Leapin' Lou Fontomato back in the fifties after Gordie Howe knocked Leapin' Lou's nose halfway across his face. The trainer said Gordie just kept punching him and punching him. Even the players on the bench could hear the sound of Lou's face breaking.

With Q-tips and kleenex stuffed up his broken nose, the Trail player just sat there with his head tilted back and his eyes running like Niagara Falls. After a while they sent him to the hospital. My dad told me later that they put his nose back pretty much to where it was just before he ran into the goal post. I didn't know a nose could move like that. Most kids don't. That's why it's good if your dad's a doctor. He'll tell you stuff like that.

*

On Monday, back in Montrose where I live with my mom, I got in trouble again with my teacher. I was yapping and she said, "I can always tell when you've been at your father's for the weekend."

I said, "How?"

"You always come back out of control."

I knew she'd been talking to my mom again. My mom says the same thing. She tells my teacher that and my teacher says it to me. My mom says I'm just like my father.

This time I said to my teacher, "So was I there this week-end?"

My teacher looked at me like she was frozen. She said, "No...no you weren't."

I said, "Yes, I was!" and the whole class laughed. I didn't. Not until the class laughed, anyway. You can't help it when everyone else is laughing.

Next thing I knew, I was sitting outside the principal's office with a note in my hand, staring at the picture of the Queen and wondering how the Montreal Canadiens were ever going to get by without Dryden. They win some, then they lose some. It's enough to make you crazy. You can't count on anything any more thanks to Dryden. I try not to think about it. I've got other things I have to think about. Like the outdoor rink I'm making.

Every night last week I took the garden hose out of the basement, hooked it up to the outside tap and poured water all over the plastic that I'd tacked into the yard. A big spread of plastic. Perfect size for an outdoor rink. It takes about an hour to flood the whole area. It's freezing out and it's hard to see because there's no light except from the porch. I don't care about that. I'll freeze if I have to. I dream about waking up in the morning and skating before school. That's what warms me up. That's what Gordie Howe did.

After I've flooded the yard in the dark, I drain all the water out of the hose and take it back downstairs so it won't freeze overnight and crack. Then I lie in bed and dream about skating on my rink three hours a day. That's what Bobby Orr did. All the great players did it. That's what I want to do more than anything.

And every morning I wake up and it's still dark out and I put on my boots and a tuque and my long underwear under my jeans and my Montreal Canadiens shirt under my hockey jacket. I put my skates over my shoulder and I have my hockey stick ready. Then I go outside to see my rink.

Puddles.

Nothing but little puddles with bits of thin ice and plastic everywhere. I'm thinking maybe the plastic is leaking on me. Or maybe it's just not cold enough—but man, is it cold out there when I'm pouring the water. Last night I had to blowtorch the tap to unfreeze it. That's how cold it was. I think the plastic is the problem. I gotta fix that.

My dad phoned every night this week to ask me if I'd told my mom that I want to go live with him. I'm beginning to hate that phone. The way it hangs on the wall there, all black and staring, while my mom's boyfriend's son just sits there with big clumps of food in both cheeks and nobody really says much except my sister. She talks about school and I think, Who cares? Montreal is losing and this phone keeps staring at me. I jump when it rings now. I know it's my dad.

He says, "Have you told your mom yet?"

I say, "No," just like that.

Mom would be pretty upset if I told her I want to live with my dad. It's not like she did anything wrong. It's not like I even want to. I guess it'd be pretty good with hockey and all, and they wouldn't have to worry about driving me, and Dad wouldn't come here and yell when he picks me up. That would probably make them get back together faster. Maybe even before the hockey season is over. Plus I make a lot more milkshakes at my dad's house. All you need is ice cream and a blender. You just put it all in and blend it up and you've got yourself a milkshake. My dad lets me practise my high jump, too. That's the track sport I do at school. I'm pretty good. He built me a high-jump bar with posts with holes in them and we set it up at the end of his bed. You just run through his bedroom door and over the bar and land on the bed. If you make it you move it up another inch.

But the best thing is, I have a place to practise my slapshot and my wrist shot and my snap shot. Even my backhand. I just line up about seventeen pucks on the floor and shoot 'em against my dad's bed as fast as I can. The high-jump stand with the bar across it is just like a goal. If I miss the bed I get a black mark on the wall but my dad doesn't care. There's hundreds of them. Mickey Redmond and his brother Dick used to practise their shot downstairs in their basement in Ontario, where if you tried to make a rink outdoors it would freeze the first night. They'd set up glass milk bottles and just fire away, smashing them all. Their mom would clean up the mess the next day.

That's why they made pro.

*

I got in big trouble at home because my sister kept saying I like a girl in my class who is pretty fat. I don't have anything against this fat girl but I don't like her either. It's funny, sometimes I find myself liking people that nobody else likes. There's one girl all the girls hate. Even the teacher doesn't like her. But I like her. I think about sniffing her like a dog. I don't know why I'm like that. On the way home from school when I pass her house I think I'd like to visit her and just look at her eyes. She's got eyes like a cat except they're brown like a chestnut. But as for the fat girl in my class, who like I said is pretty fat, I have nothing against her. But I don't love her, that's for sure. That was my sister's big mistake. Saying I loved her.

I ran home at lunch before my sister got there. I opened the door with the key and then I put the key back and went inside and locked the door and waited behind the door. When my sister came in I jumped her from behind like I was playing for the Philadelphia Flyers. I jumped her and started to choke her. She pretty much knew about then that she shouldn't have said what she said.

I got in big trouble for that one. I was putting a two-by-four rim around the plastic in the yard to keep the water in on my rink when my mom's boyfriend came outside. He started saying something about what happened and he stepped down on the two-by-four with his foot while my fingers were under it and said, "You better goddamn listen to me."

I didn't look at him but I was thinking, I could get you killed. I felt so mad at myself knowing I'd never tell my dad anything about it.

After that we had dinner and my dad phoned again and I said, "No," like I always do. Then I phoned the radio station and found out the Montreal Canadiens lost 5-0 to the St. Louis Blues. Five-nothing! How can you win with a goalie named Bunny! Montreal's other goalie is Wayne Thomas. Two first names. It might as well be Frank Fred. I don't know which one played. It doesn't make any difference. Montreal didn't even score. They've given up thanks to Dryden.

When we play Castlegar this Saturday, their goalie is going to wish his dad got a flat tire and they never made it to the game. I'm glad we're playing them at home in Trail. I don't really want to drive past Blueberry Corner again. Sometimes I wonder what Hobey was thinking just as that diesel came. I guess we're like electricity and when you get hit hard enough, the hit unplugs you. All that electricity just shoots out your mouth. Then you're dead.

*

Every time my dad picks me up, you can hear him and my mom yelling all the way down the street. The neighbours can hear it too. In the winter when they yell I go outside and take shots on the net. Me and my dog Rex—actually he's my older brother's dog but he kind of belongs to everybody. Having a dog like Rex really helps when you play street hockey, because if you miss the net he chases the tennis ball for you. Everybody wants Rex to come when we play hockey. You can knock that ball into the meanest neighbour's yard or under a car or into a bush with thorns or in a snowbank and Rex'll get it every time. You could shoot it all the way down to Trail and he'd get it. He just waits until someone misses the net and he runs a thousand miles an hour and snaps it up in his mouth. He drops it for you, too. All you have to do is put the blade of your stick above his head and he opens his mouth. He's been there for all my Stanley Cups downstairs pretty much. He's about the smartest dog in the world.

The thing about Rex, though, is he chases cars. That's his dumb side. I guess everybody has a dumb side. That's why he's got a gimped leg and he's blind in his left eye. It's all glossy and smoky like a marble. I don't know what he's

41

thinking. With a ball he can put it in his mouth, but what's he going to do with a car?

Once I was riding on my bike to pick up the mail and Rex took off onto the highway to chase a car. He ended up going right under it. I thought he was a goner. If you can believe it, Rex came out the other side and he ran back to me. I was screaming and Rex was yelping. I grabbed him and hugged him and I guess he must've been hurt because when I petted his tail he growled at me like, If you do that again I'm going to have to put some holes in your skin. Rex never growls at me. I didn't pet him there again. I just took him home and let him have some food while I practised my shot. I made sure I didn't miss the net because he was in no mood for chasing balls.

*

Coach asked me if I was up to being an assistant captain. That's when they put an A on your hockey sweater like Cournoyer has on his. I said yeah and Coach said, Okay. That was it.

It's good being assistant captain because I don't have any friends on the team. They all live in Trail and I live in Montrose so we go to different schools. I guess the best player is a friend but I don't call him up or anything. They made him captain, which is good. The best player should be the captain. They put a C on his shirt.

The thing about being assistant captain is, you get to yap at the referee. The other assistant captain is one of those guys that grew way too fast. He weighs about a hundred and eighty pounds. I weigh a hundred. Cournoyer only weighs one sixty-five. That's it. Five foot seven and a hundred and sixty-five pounds. But this kid on our team? He's as tall as my dad. Everybody says, "Woo, he's a big boy. What do they feed him?" Most rep teams have some guy that grew way too fast. You have to watch out for those guys because their bodies are a lot bigger than their brains.

Sometimes the big boy gets out of control and starts hitting everything, and before you know it he gets so confused he might just plough you into the boards, too, even though you're on his team. If he ploughs you into the boards and you're not ready, you'll be flattened and it's pretty much for sure that my dad will have to come onto the ice and say, "Yeah, he's hurt. He got ploughed by the big boy."

When you're that big you can really shoot, too. He's a defenceman and sometimes the puck goes back to the point and I rush to the net because I love deflections. I get there in the slot—that's right in front of the net. I think, Come on, big boy, give me a slapshot right along the ice and I'll deflect that puck right into the corner of the net. I get my stick on the ice and no one is going to stop me from deflecting that puck—maybe through the goalie's legs, maybe in the far corner, maybe even in the top corner. Then the big boy winds up like he's on a golf course and before you know it all you can do is duck, because his shot is eight feet high and a hundred miles an hour and twenty feet wide of the net and if it hits you, you're as good as dead. After he's done it, all you can do is stare at him. You can't say anything. You just stare and think, Wow, you're sure big and dumb. I'm hoping that being assistant captain will make him think a little more and maybe keep his shot down. Coach tells him but as soon as he winds up I think he forgets everything.

So like I said, it's me, the best player and the big boy. The parents can hate me and hate my dad, but that A on my sweater says, No matter what you want to think, I'm the second-best player and, no matter what, I have to do anything to help the team win. That's all there is to it.

I'll do it, too.

*

I'm scoring. That's for sure. I scored two goals on Saturday morning and two more on Sunday morning against Nelson. We're beating everybody. Next week we're going to Spokane for two games and we'll be billeted out with the kids from that team.

I like playing against the Americans. Their arenas are a lot newer than ours and the teams have good uniforms and most of the kids wear Super Tack skates and Jofa gloves and McDonald's are everywhere.

Oh, man, did my dad get mad this weekend. He always buys me the best equipment. I've got Super Tack skates and super-light shin pads. They're made out of astronaut foam. He doesn't mind. He says I work hard, I should get good equipment.

I wore my equipment to the game on Saturday morning. I was out in the driveway shooting pieces of ice against the wall of the garage while I was waiting for him. I was thinking about getting that rink ready. I'll get my three hours a day in and they'll all know it when the playoffs roll around. So my dad came out of the house in his jeans and his sheepskin jacket and somehow I must have left my hockey gloves on the bumper of his car. When we got to the game, no gloves. They must be on the hill somewhere, stuck in a snowbank. See you in the spring.

My dad said, "You stupid piece of shit! You don't

respect anything!" It was pretty dumb. I make him yell way more than anybody. The best player had an old pair of gloves that he lent me. They weren't as nice as my gloves but they were pretty worked in so I didn't have any trouble stick-handling.

It's crazy how often I forget my hockey equipment. Every time I start looking for something and I remember I hung them up somewhere else or I know I've forgotten them, my throat gets all dry like I swallowed sawdust. I always forget my garter belt. With your garter belt gone you can still tape your hockey socks up. They fall down and your thigh gets a little cold but at least you can fake it. I played without shoulder pads a couple of times, too. Once I left a shin pad behind. That's harder to fake. You have to stick something in there or you can say goodbye to your leg. If you forget a skate, the first thing people will say if you try to fake it is "Look, that kid's got a shoe on."

I don't know why I always forget stuff. I think I've got my mind on Dryden too much. Doesn't he know what he's doing? Doesn't he care about the Montreal Canadiens? They're not even in first place. I read in the paper he's playing recreational hockey! He's not even playing goal! Meanwhile, the Montreal Canadiens lost to the Detroit Red Wings. But Dryden just does what he wants and it doesn't matter who gets hurt.

*

Everything's weird around home this week. My mom's boyfriend hasn't been around at all but both his sons are still here. He's got another house so I guess he's staying there. I don't care where he's staying. He can live in China for all I care.

I was in my mom's bedroom the other morning and he was there in his boxer shorts. I couldn't even look at him. I was polite and all but the truth is, it made me feel like a dog when it eats grass. I kept thinking about my dad. My dad has girlfriends sometimes, too, but not like my mom's boyfriend. You can pretty much tell my dad would trade in his girlfriends for my mom in about two seconds.

My dad's got a new young girlfriend. She's pretty nice to me. I guess women are just nicer than men. That's why men fish and women don't. Men put that hook out there and when the fish isn't ready, *whammo*! It doesn't matter if it hurts like an axe in the head. Look at Dryden. He's ruined a whole winter for everybody. My dad at least tries to make you laugh. He doesn't wear clothes too much and he does this funny dance sometimes or a funny voice. Or he'll say something about some hockey player. It'll make you laugh. My mom's boyfriend is about as funny as not making the rep team and knowing you'll never make pro.

Anyway, he's away and my mom doesn't seem in any mood to hear I left the hose out and it froze. I'm not in any mood to tell her, either. I just taped up the crack with electrician's tape so I could keep trying to get this rink going. I should have a rink by now. I doubled the layers of plastic but so far nothing. Friends of ours that own a farm in Rossland had an outdoor rink last year. It was so good. You just skate around and around when everything is quiet and dark and all you can hear is the wind and your skate blades cutting into the ice and the sound of the puck on your stick and you can think about scoring and winning the Stanley Cup—or the B.C. Championships. That's what I'll be doing here soon, too, when I get this rink done. Just skating and thinking. Then I can forget about Dryden.

*

On Wednesday one of the guys in my class farted when the teacher left the room. It was so loud we all knew who it was. I bet he tried to make it a silent one but there's nothing you can do when it doesn't want to be silent. You can squeeze but it'll come out as loud as it wants. Everybody turned and looked at him and he looked like a beet root. The whole class—even the girls who never talk and the smartest guy—they all got up from their desks and moved to the outside of the room. The guy who farted put his head straight down on his desk, buried in his arms, and didn't move. That's exactly how the room was when the teacher came back. She got pretty mad. What were we supposed to do? That's what I'd like to know. Sit around his fart?

After we sat back down, the kid that farted still wouldn't lift his head up. He just stayed like that until lunchtime and then he never came back to school in the afternoon. Too bad, he's a pretty good street-hockey goaltender, and we had to play the whole lunchtime and after school without him.

The thing about farting is I've never heard a girl fart. My dad farts. Free as a dog. He doesn't even think about it. No guys do. They just do it. On the hockey bus, in the dressing room, playing street hockey. My mom? Never. If you're just with guys and you let one go like the guy in my class, nobody would care. Maybe you make a joke or something. But all the rules change when you fart around girls. That was that guy's big mistake.

*

The peewee rep team took a bus to Spokane in the United

States of America. It takes about three hours to get down there. Except for Hockey Night in Canada and the Bugs Bunny/Roadrunner Hour, the United States of America is where all the good TV comes from. You go over the border and then you get to Colville and things start to get a little bigger and a little brighter. A long time ago I bought a GI Joe there with Kung Fu grip. You couldn't even get Kung Fu grip in Canada.

By the time you get to Spokane you really know you're not in Canada. K mart is as big as a hockey arena and they've got this announcer there just as loud as the announcer guy at the Montreal Forum and he's telling you what to buy. On the street you can't even see the front end of some of the cars there. That's how long they are. We saw a car with horns on the front end. It looked like a bull.

They've got a sign at one of their restaurants. It's about a mile high. It's this giant boy with big overalls holding up a hamburger with a big patty and big lettuce and big cheese and big ketchup, and I think onions, too. I'm not sure about the onions. They just call it Big Boy Restaurant. It's a perfect name. It makes me think of the big boy on our team but this big boy is as tall as the smokestacks up on the hill in Trail.

We ate lunch at an Arby's roast-beef sandwich place and it was pretty good. Women in the United States of America have the biggest bums in the world. Especially at Arby's. You can't believe it. Guys have big guts down there, but the women's bums are bigger. As wide as the bus we drove down in and in bright colours—pink, green, dark blue, pale blue, red, orange, yellow. Those bums are just like two giant balloons squished together. I haven't seen one but they'd have to have special toilets for those bums. I'd bet on it.

When I see bums like that I feel just like I do when someone gets a brush cut. You just want to go feel it but you never do. Sometimes you do with a brush cut. There was a family who got brush cuts in school last year because of lice. Even the sisters. I actually felt one of their heads. But with these bums you can only wonder.

We knocked off the Spokane Americans 7-3 on Saturday afternoon. It was all tied up at three in the third period when the best player got a goal while we were short-handed. I blocked a shot just like Don Awrey and the puck bounced off my shin pad all the way to centre ice and the best player just took off. He deked the Spokane goalie out of his underwear and slipped it in the corner. The best player's dad takes care of all the statistics and I didn't even get an assist on that goal. I blocked the shot and got a bruise but no assist. I should've got an assist. I touched the puck. The bruise proves it.

After the game we all got billeted out and my billet was the big boy of their team—not as big as our assistant captain big boy, but big enough to know he could go mental and skate straight into the boards for no reason and you just might be in the way. He had black glasses and he breathed through his nose all the time like he was snoring but he was wide awake. I think, like our big boy, his brain is too small for his head. It's not his fault. That's how big boys are.

My billet's mom was super-big, too, and super-nice. I couldn't stop staring at her. It was pretty cool. Arms as big as my mom's thighs and thighs as big as those hoops that dolphins jump through at the aquarium. I'm not kidding. And she had one of those Arby's roast-beef sandwich bums, too. You don't find bums like that in Canada. You can look but you just don't.

In their big house they had big food in a big kitchen with big Cokes. For dinner we had brontosaurus steaks and bright yellow corn on the cob as big as a rolling pin and mountains of mashed potatoes with golden butter and thick gravy flowing everywhere. For dessert we had chocolate pudding with whipped cream and angel-food cake with ice cream. Then we all went into their big front room and my billet's mom sat her big bum on the big couch and we all watched a big TV.

I bet if I ate two thousand Arby's roast-beef sandwiches I still wouldn't get a bum like that. How could I? I don't have enough skin.

That night, me and her son slept in bunk beds and I was on the top bunk and I felt my ribs and my pigeon chest. I was wondering what it must be like to lie in bed and be that big. That's when the bedroom door opened. It was the big boy's mom.

She said, "Are my little men okay? Do you need a snack?"

I was so full I could barely talk. I said no but thanks for having me over.

Her son said yes and she brought him a bowl of Count Chocula cereal in bed! Count Chocula! At my dad's we don't even eat breakfast, or we might have pancakes. At my mom's you get granola or a grapefruit and hopefully just enough brown sugar to kill the taste. It's not like that in the United States of America. In the United States of

America you get Count Chocula in bed!

I woke up in the night. I had to find out about how big their toilets were. I snuck upstairs and pushed open one door. It was the dad's office. It had a big oak desk and there was a big moose head on the wall looking right at me. I jumped about forty feet.

The next door was a bathroom. I don't know if it was the bathroom the mom used, but the toilet was just the same as ours at home. About the size of a basketball hoop. The seat had a pink plastic cover. It was padded. Not much. I tried it out. That's when my eyes bulged. Hanging from the shower curtain rod was the biggest pair of underwear in the history of the world. Like a giant white flag. The elastic was wider than hockey tape. That elastic could slingshot you and a buddy all the way back across the border to Canada. I could feel my heart beating like crazy but I stood up and touched them. I had to. They felt just like normal underwear but I felt all funny.

Then I sniffed 'em.

I don't know why. I just did.

They didn't smell like anything either, but I felt even more funny.

*

As long as my dad's getting along with Coach, I don't think about Dryden too much or worry about Cournoyer. He must be hurting, though. He's gotta be.

Coach and the best player's dad and my dad were standing in the lobby of the arena talking when I came into the arena with my American billet. I liked seeing them just talking because you never know when my dad is going to blow up around the arena and tell maybe a half-dozen people to f---off. He's pretty good around the best player's dad, though—and Coach. At one game my dad was swearing about something and one of the Italian mothers of one of the players who has no talent and no drive told my dad he shouldn't yell and swear so much. My dad told her to f---off. After that he got in an argument with her husband and told him to f---off. On the drive home he told me the Italian woman was a religious nut who shouldn't go to hockey games. He yelled at me for not taking the man, too. I started crying and he yelled at me even louder. My dad doesn't believe in God and I guess I don't either. I was having dinner at my mom's and I said I didn't believe in God and then I asked my mom's boyfriend if he believed in God. He said, "Yes, I do," like he was really mad about something. That was all he said. I don't know if my mom believes in God. I bet if I asked her she'd say she doesn't know. My sister believes in God, I think. She goes to church sometimes with friends that live down the street. When she told her friend that I don't believe in God, her friend couldn't believe it. But she better believe it because that's the way it is.

At home my dad was still yelling. Finally his new young girlfriend with the headband, who is about twenty years younger, told him to stop picking on me. He yelled at her, too, but she didn't back down so he stopped picking on me. She's pretty nice that way. It doesn't seem to bother her when he yells. She says, "Leave him alone, he's just a kid."

My dad's new young girlfriend has a dog she calls Ted, even though Ted's a girl. She has a camera, too, and she showed me how to take photographs. She gave me her old Kodak Brownie. It's a little brown square camera. It's easy. You just line up the picture and push the button and you've got yourself some photos. I took some shots of the snow and the hockey game on TV. I got a shot of Cournoyer on the ice but it's blurry.

My dad's girlfriend isn't there all the time but when she's there I find my dad's a little happier. My dad misses my mom so much, I think his new young girlfriend helps him not think about it. She makes health-food cookies and they're pretty good as far as health food goes—a little dry but you can wash them down with all kinds of milkshakes. She'll put anything in a milkshake! Dates. Cantaloupe. Even wheat germ. She paints, too, like my mom but not as good. Mostly just a bunch of colours painted on a board in a way that makes no sense. Then she gives them a title that doesn't mean anything.

*

I threw up all night at my billet's house in Spokane. A whole bunch of that Arby's roast-beef sandwich came up after I went back to bed. His mom was pretty good about it. I'm pretty sure it didn't have anything to do with the underwear. A couple other players on the team were sick too. I played the next day but my legs wouldn't move. The best player got four goals and we squeezed by 6-4. I got a goal but it wasn't a Cournoyer goal. I just shot the puck out from behind the net and it went in off the goalie. That's what they call a garbage goal.

You're supposed to go home on the team bus after the game, but because I was sick I went home with my dad. That was good. One thing I don't like to do is shower after the game. Some kids shower, some don't. I don't like going into a shower with all the other boys. Some of them are pretty hairy already. I don't have one scrap of hair, except on my head. On my head I have the longest hair on the team. My dad says Italian boys mature a lot earlier than everyone else. But he says they stop growing after they're fifteen and their sisters grow sideways.

I don't like being naked in there. I'd rather keep my gonch on, pull on my jeans and go home. All the guys on the team that shower have dinks that stick out, and some of them are pretty big, too. One of the boys said I had a tuque on my dink. I looked around and I noticed my dink was the only dink with a tuque. I felt strange about that so I put on my gonch and pulled up my jeans and packed my bag pretty fast.

In the car, after my dad stopped yelling, I asked him why I had the only dink with a tuque.

"Because you were born in England," he said. "That's what boys in England have."

"Why?"

"That's just the way it is."

I said, "What about boys in the United States of America?"

He said, "What am I? The FBI?"

Then I asked him if I'd always have one and he said, "I guess you could get it cut off."

I didn't ask any questions after that. I just wish I didn't have one. I don't mind having the longest hair on the team but the only tuque I can do without. I'd bet Cournoyer doesn't have a tuque. I don't even want to think about Dryden.

*

I remember every goal that won the Stanley Cup that first year with Ken Dryden. Montreal was losing 2-0 in the second period of the seventh game of the series. They looked like goners. That's when Jacques Lemaire wound up for a slapshot from about two miles away—from centre ice! The Chicago goalie was Phil Esposito's brother Tony. Tony O just muffed it. Like a girl throwing a baseball left-handed. Nobody else has ever said this but I think Tony O was asleep. I'm not kidding. You couldn't tell because he had a mask on but every time I see the replay he just looks like you do when you're sitting in a chair and you fall asleep and your head snaps up. After that, the Pocket Rocket scored two goals and Montreal tripped up the Black Hawks 3-2 for the Stanley Cup.

Oh, man, I bet Espo cried. I would have cried. I would have taken him down to the City Bakery and bought him twelve thousand and twenty-four jelly donuts fresh out of the oven. I would have said, "Rosa, this is Tony O and he's had a bad night. Load up the truck."

The last time I talked about that goal by Lemaire, my older brother stuffed me in a sleeping bag and tied it up like a sack of potatoes. He does that every time. Then I have to put my mouth against the zipper to get enough air. He won't let me out until I say that Stan Mikita is better than Yvan Corn-head. That's what he makes me call Cournoyer. It's a lie that Mikita's better but after about two hours I can't breathe so I cross everything and just say it. He thinks I'm serious.

But that's the way it goes. Sometimes hockey doesn't even go right. The year after Espo fell asleep in goal and Montreal won the Cup, the New York Rangers beat Montreal in the quarter-finals. I cried for about two hours. My older brother says it was two weeks but it wasn't. I was mad for two weeks but I only cried for two hours. Two hours and a little bit the next morning. That was the year my dad picked me up in the middle of the school week and took me away to school in Rossland. I knew something wasn't right when he picked me up. That's why I slipped down in the car seat like a turtle so nobody would see me when we left.

For a little while, it was pretty good going to school in Rossland. The teacher let us draw a lot so I drew goalies. Then one day I looked up and my mom was there in the doorway with two policemen and we walked down the hallway and they put me in a police car. I don't remember what we said in the car. I think I just stared out the window. Sometimes I swear I don't know what to do. I don't remember what my mom said. She wasn't mad. She just sat there all tired. The next thing I knew I was back in school in Montrose. The year after that, like I said, Cournoyer batted the puck out of the air like Johnny Bench and Montreal won the Stanley Cup again.

*

Dryden or no Dryden, this is the year for the Trail Peewee Smoke Eater Reps. I can feel it. December's looking like a pretty good month. We're playing against Cranbrook in a couple of weeks. That's the best team from the East Kootenays. If we beat them it'll pretty much show that we're the best team in the Kootenays. If you win the Kootenays you go to the B.C. Championships. So I'm looking forward to walloping Cranbrook. After that it's a Christmas tournament in Penticton. What a month.

I figure now that it's December the weather will get cold enough that my outdoor rink will freeze up as soon as I pour the water down. Then I'll skate every morning before school all by myself. My mom got some more big sheets of plastic and I think they'll help. I was tacking them in after school yesterday when I got the phone call that there was a street-hockey game going on. My hands were freezing so I was happy to leave the rink for a while.

The street-hockey game was perfect. I scored about sixteen goals from everywhere. It was 22-all and getting too dark to see when the other goalie said he had to go home or his dad would get out the strap. He started to take his net home and I said, "Come on, man! Next goal wins!" Nobody in Canada can refuse that. So he put down his net and we started playing for next goal wins. There were a couple of close calls. Rex was waiting and waiting for a ball to miss the net and the goalie was yelling, "I gotta go! I gotta go!" I had the ball on a bad angle in the driveway and I wound up like Cournoyer and let a slapshot go. It was pretty dark out and the goalie didn't even see it. He was still yelling, "I gotta go! I gotta—"

Gotta was the last thing he said.

Next thing we knew he was down on the road. He wasn't screaming. When you get your fingers slashed you scream and if it's bad you swing your stick and maybe swear at the guy who slashed you or maybe even get in a fight. If you get it in the shins, same thing. The only time you moan and say nothing is when you get it in the balls. For the first few seconds you don't feel anything but you know it's coming. Then *boom*, you're on the ground like Jerry Quarry when Muhammad Ali made his comeback.

We all ran around in a circle and said, "You okay? You

okay?" He never answered. You never answer when you get it in the balls. You can't.

My shot hit him so hard in the balls his nose was bleeding.

Nobody there had ever seen that before—not from getting it in the balls. No one could believe it. They were all saying, "Look at that. You made his nose bleed."

One of our guys put the ball in their empty net and said, "We win! We win!"

We all said, "Shut up, you idiot," because that's an idiot thing to do when someone gets it square in the balls. The goalie was rolling around on the road until he rolled into the net and then the net fell on him and Rex started barking.

In the end his dad had to come and carry him home. He picked him up just like my dad picked up our old dog, Nugget, when we were taking him to the vet to be put down. I carried their net home for them and then I came back and got my net. I know the goalie was late home, but if his dad gave him the belt after he'd already been hit in the balls and it made his nose bleed, he's no dad in my books.

My dad's never given me the belt. He yells a lot but that's it. My dad doesn't wear a belt. Sometimes he doesn't even wear pants.

We called the game a tie.

We had to. That way nobody was happy.

*

December didn't start as well as I'd hoped. I got tripped on a breakaway on Saturday morning and the referee gave me a penalty shot. That's when you take the puck at centre ice all by yourself and get a free shot on the goalie. It's just like

Showdown in the NHL on Hockey Night in Canada. It's not as exciting as the Stanley Cup finals or overtime, but other than that it's the most exciting thing you can get to do.

I was awarded the penalty shot at the beginning of the third period. The game was all tied up. It was a perfect chance to score a big goal. The pressure was on, just like I like it. I skated from my own blueline to where the puck was waiting for me at centre ice.

As soon as I pushed the puck ahead I knew I was in trouble. It just took off on the clean ice. I skated about a hundred and twelve miles an hour after it but I didn't catch up. It went right to the goalie. I was so mad that I ploughed right into the goalie and knocked him flying. Then I got up and hit my stick over the crossbar of the goal and the referee gave me a penalty for unsportsmanlike conduct. The team we were playing against laughed their heads off and my team hated me. Their team scored while I was in the penalty box and then Coach benched me for the rest of the period. We were toppled 5-3. It was our first loss of the season. If anybody thought I was the best player on the team before that, I'd pretty much changed their minds.

My dad had smoke coming out his ears when the game was over, just like Yosemite Sam. We got some donuts and he threw them in the car. I didn't eat one. He said he wasn't mad about the penalty shot—that could happen to anyone. He was mad about the two periods before that. He said it looked like I was dreaming out there. I didn't tell him but he was right. I couldn't stop remembering how me and my friends used to go bat fishing in the summer. What happens is, when the weather warms up you go out under the streetlight where all the moths are and bats start flying around. After that all you need is a fishing net and a fishing rod with a fly on it. You start flicking that fly towards the streetlight. The bats go for the flies just like fish do. Last summer a bat flew right towards me and then over my head. I've heard that if they get their claws into you they go crazy and you get a bat all caught up in your hair. People say they're only fruit bats but don't kid yourself. Given the chance, they'll go for a vein in your neck.

That's what I was thinking about for the first two periods. After that I missed the penalty shot and Coach sat me on the pine. That's why my dad threw the donuts at me and I don't blame him. If he wasn't there, I would've thrown them at myself.

My dad didn't even let me change out of my equipment when we got home. We went straight to public skating at the arena in Rossland. I had to go to public skating in my equipment! I worked on my turns in the corner while everybody else skated around in their jeans and the music blared out of the loudspeaker. I knew some of the kids who were skating around from when I lived in Rossland. I never looked at them but I know they were looking at me because I could feel it in my face. Then the music would stop and the announcer would say, "Skate the other way." The music would start again but I'd just stay in the corner of the rink in my equipment, doing turns and stops. I was thinking, Man, I have to get my outdoor rink made because this is no way to get three hours on the ice a day.

If I get a penalty shot again I'm going to pretend I'm injured. I'll lie on the ice just like the big boy does. The crowd will clap and the players will bang their sticks as they take me off the ice. Maybe on a stretcher. Then the best player will have to take the shot. He'll score, no doubt about it.

*

We bused all the way to Cranbrook. It's a long way. Coach gave us a pep talk before the game. He said none of the other games mattered worth a hill of beans any more. He said quitters never win and winners never quit. He said that this was the biggest game of the season. He said it's not how many fights you win or lose, it's how many you show up for. When a guy only has eight full fingers counting his thumbs, you listen to him. He said if we can beat these guys it'll show everybody we have a good chance of going to the B.C. Championships.

Cranbrook has a pretty big team but we've got the big boy and we've got the best player. They've got one player who's about as fast as Cournoyer but you can stop him if you look square in his shoulders. If you watch the puck he'll stick-handle by you like Pete Mahovlich did against the Russians. I've got a picture of that on my wall. You can see the defenceman looking for his shorts. We've got one player who's about as fast as Cournoyer, too, but as soon as he gets to the other end of the rink he doesn't know what to do. He goes so fast he goes right by the goalie and into the boards. I'm not that fast so I have to stick-handle more. If I stick-handle too much when I should shoot, my dad sometimes yells, "Stop dipsy-doodling and shoot the f---ing puck!" That's one of the things you'll hear him yell when you're at the games. He's right, though. If you dipsy-doodle too much you get knocked over, you get no shot on goal, the coach is yelling at you, the team thinks you're a hog and you're backchecking again. The parents all hate me too. They yell, "Hog!" when I have the puck. With a big team like Cranbrook you shouldn't dipsy-doodle at all.

In the first period the best player gave me a pass from behind the net but I didn't have my stick on the ice and I missed it. I heard my dad yell, "Keep your f---ing stick on the ice!" even before he yelled it. Then he yelled, "Keep your f---ing stick on the ice!" It was pretty much what I thought he'd say. I turned around to backcheck and I glanced up at him out of the corner of my eye. My dad was pacing and for some reason he reminded me of Old Yeller when Old Yeller had rabies and they were just about to shoot him. The puck came back to me and I would have had a breakaway but I missed it because I was still thinking about the rabies. My dad yelled, "Get your f---ing head in the game!" That wasn't exactly what I thought he'd yell but it was pretty close.

In the second period I was crosschecked right in the chin. That's all I remember about the second period. It knocked me flying. I got up but I don't remember where I went. My lip puffed up and it reminded me of the time I got poison ivy a couple of summers ago. I used to go down the mountain bank behind my mom's house and collect bones. If you know where to look it's like a museum down there. The mountain is dusty and rocky with some trees but no water so I figure a lot of animals die of thirst down there in the summer. That's why I always take a water bottle with me. I don't want to end up like one of those bones.

My bone collection was one of the best around. I had a jaw of something prehistoric like a diplodocus. It was about two feet long. About the size of a two-month-old triceratops. Just one side of the jaw, with big flat teeth perfect for grinding bark and leaves. I had some bird bones, too. You wouldn't believe how small the ribs of a bird are—like toothpicks but round. I had a deer jaw. I had the skull of some sort of big rodent. Maybe a prehistoric skunk or some kind of crazy rat. Me and my friend even found an old bear head once but it wasn't all bone yet. Man, it stunk like the dump and there were flies all over it. We couldn't figure out how it got its head knocked off. Maybe a fight with another bear who was still around. We buried it in the ground so all the meat would come off it. Then we took off. Problem was, after that we could never remember where we buried it.

One year me and my brother moved away with my dad to Vancouver, right after my parents split up. I guess my mom didn't understand much about bones because when we moved back from Vancouver she'd thrown them all out. That was the end of my bone collection.

It was down that hill that I must have rolled in some poison ivy. I got so much poison ivy I had to go to the hospital. I had it everywhere—even on places that were covered up, like my tuque. In the hospital the nurse would dip these pads in milk and then lay them on my face. They were pretty soothing. She'd leave them there for a while and then change them.

One morning I woke up and I couldn't see. I thought I was blind like Helen Keller. I was pretty scared. My eyes were so puffed up my eyelashes were gone—sucked right inside my head. My sister came to visit me. She went into my hospital room and saw this blind kid with a watermelon head and went back to the desk to tell them they'd sent her to the wrong room. But it was me.

The day I got out, my mom bought me a hat like Gilligan's, but it was made out of jeans and it had a Canadian flag sewn on it. I put it on my head. You couldn't even recognize me. It was like putting a hat on a watermelon. If you ever try that, you'll see how stupid it looks.

With the crosscheck I took in the chin against Cranbrook, my dad said one inch higher and I would have looked like Bobby Clarke. Bobby Clarke is missing his two front teeth. Most pro hockey players are. Sixty-nine percent. I figure I'll be missing mine by bantam. I don't care. My mom would have a fit but my dad says Bobby Clarke's the hardest-working hockey player in the world. Tough son-of-a-bitch, too. That's what my dad says.

I was pretty mad after that crosscheck. I got two goals in the third period and we clipped them 7-4. The best player got two goals, too. We were pretty happy in the dressing room. After the game I heard my dad talking to Coach and the best player's dad. They were huddled together with a couple of other dads hanging around. I heard my dad say if we had a decent third line we'd have a chance at winning the provincials. That's all of British Columbia. One of the dads whose kid is on the third line was standing there. I took a beeline to the pop machine and pretended I was thinking about which pop to buy. Still, my dad's right. We don't have much of a third line.

*

I duck-taped all the holes in the plastic of my outdoor rink. Duck tape will stop the leaking. That's why they call it duck tape. My mom bought me two rolls. It took about two hundred pieces to tape all the garbage bags together and all the big plastic sheets. I put duck tape over every single nail I tacked into the frozen ground. The ground actually isn't frozen any more. It's still cold but it's getting mushy from all the water. You have to dry off the plastic before you stick the duck tape down. If you get the sticky side of the duck tape wet, you might as well use banana peels for all the sticking you can do.

After that was done I put a bunch more two-by-fours at the slopy end of the rink to help dam the water. By then I was covered in dirt and soaked and frozen but I didn't care. Staring at the rink just waiting for the water to freeze, I didn't care about anything. I figured something else out, too. Every part of the plastic has to be under water if you're going to have a rink. All you have to do is get that first film of ice all over the yard. It can be as thin as paper. It doesn't matter. Get one clean film of ice. After that just keep adding water. I figure one week—five days even. Five cold nights and you've got yourself a rink. It'll be perfect and I'll skate three hours a day.

When I get that first film frozen I'm going to paint a big Montreal Canadiens emblem on it. Just like at the Montreal Forum. I've drawn it about two million times. Plus, I've got a Montreal shirt I can look at if I forget. I'll never forget. It's got a number twelve on the back and my mom said she'd sew a C on the front of it. Why not? Cournoyer will be the captain when the Pocket Rocket with his grey hair packs it in. That's the hockey shirt I wear for street hockey. It's even got the lace to tighten up around the collar. They don't have that lace on hockey shirts any more. Not since Don Awrey got in a fight with Marc Tardif, sat on him, dug his knees into Tardif's arms just like my older brother does before he dangles spit in my face. Awrey was sitting on him and he just reached down and yanked the lace tight around Tardif's neck until Tardif passed out. Awrey choked him so much Tardif decided to go play in the World Hockey Association with Bobby Hull. The WHA is the other hockey league. It's about half as good as the NHL. They said Bobby Hull jumped to the WHA because of the money. That's what I read. Nope. He went there because his goalie Tony Esposito was sleeping on that goal by Lemaire. That's why Hull jumped to the WHA. No one would leave the NHL for money.

*

Christmas looks like it might have a chance to be perfect this year. My mom's boyfriend isn't going to be there so we won't have to worry about him or his son who can't chew or his other son who only cares about cars. It's just going to be my mom, my brother, my sister, me and Rex and that'll be it, right?

Wrong!

My dad's coming over for Christmas dinner with us. I don't know what that's all about but I've got an idea. If I can just stop the yelling and get my dad to stay over, I don't think he'll leave. All he has to do is stay over and then be funny in the morning with one of his silly dances. It'll be so great. We'll all laugh. Then my mom will forget about her boyfriend.

This is our first Christmas together since I was a kid. Even the last Christmas we had together before they split up we didn't have together. That was when we all lived in Rossland. We had so much snow that year we had to dig our way out of the house. I'm not kidding. It was a tunnel like an igloo. The icicles that were hanging from the roof were about ten feet long. If one broke when you walked underneath, it would go right through you, just like a tyrannosaurus rex tooth.

The day before our last Christmas together my dad was shovelling the snow off the roof when he started to slide. You know how that is. You might as well wave goodbye right there. It's not like sliding into second base where you stop. This is going downhill. My dad didn't stop until he fell off the roof and landed on the rock wall in the back yard. My best friend, Flipper—we called him Flipper because he laughed just like that dolphin Flipper, like a baby tommy gun—he was looking out his verandah window and he saw my dad fall off the roof. But Flipper was so short he couldn't see down enough from his window to see my dad land. So Flipper went and told his mom he saw Doc flying. That's what he called my dad. Doc. But my dad wasn't flying. He was falling. And the big difference between flying and falling is the landing—and the blood on the snow.

My dad looked like Henry Cooper after the fifth round of his fight with Muhammad Ali. His eyes were like half a hockey puck had been stuck underneath them and his cheek was smashed in and his arm was broken. All that snow and he landed on the rock wall. We went to visit him on Christmas Day but he was groggy from painkillers. That was our last Christmas together. By the time everybody in the town figured out you better tie a rope around the chimney and then around yourself when you want to shovel snow off the roof, my mom and dad were splitting up.

Me and my dad fall off everything. The year before my

dad fell, I fell about two hundred and twelve feet out of the chairlift at the ski hill and broke my back. That's all I remember. The summer after that I fell out of a treehouse. It was about a mile high. My brother and my dad built it. It had a window and a shelf and you could just sit there the whole day and think about anything. My dad said I wasn't supposed to go up there but I went up there anyway. The last step that was nailed to the tree decided to go for a jump and I went with it. Next thing all my friends are standing around my parents' bed staring at me. I broke my wrist on that fall.

But that's a long time ago now. This Christmas all my dad has to do is load up his car with presents and come over.

I'll be waiting. We'll all be waiting.

I wouldn't be surprised if he stayed.

*

Bunny Larocque is the Montreal Canadiens' goalie, and he must be bowlegged because every shot goes through his legs. A bowlegged goalie is about as useful as a one-legged soccer player. I asked my dad what makes someone bowlegged and he said rickets. It's from a lack of vitamin D. My dad said you get vitamin D from fish and the sun. Well, there's no sun in the Montreal Forum so I took four of my frozen fish that I caught last year in Beaver Creek. I took them out of my mom's freezer. Four speckled trout about eight inches long—pan-size, already cleaned. I put them in a plastic bag and then in a shoebox and sent them to the Montreal Forum. I just put: *For Bunny. Cook in frying pan with butter. Eat before next game against Boston. Good Luck. P.S. Get some sun.* I hope it helps.

All I can do is think about how much I hate Dryden for doing this. He played for three years on the best team in the world. He didn't even have an injury. Look at Bobby Orr. He's not Montreal but he's still the best defenceman in the world. He's got no cartridge in his knees any more. He has to keep his hockey socks on to stop his legs from falling off. Every summer Bobby Orr has about two dozen operations on his knees. But he keeps playing. He keeps playing because that's what's right. Dryden wins the Stanley Cup and then quits. Why? Because people don't matter to Dryden. Probably never have.

*

My mom thinks I should see a counsellor. She's been saying that since I wrote FUCK KEN with my finger where the dirt on her car was. She asked me if I knew what it meant. I said it means Fuck him. Man, was she mad. She says she thinks I'm angry and I need someone to talk to. That's what she says when I'm not angry. When I am angry, like when Bunny Larocque lets in two goals through his legs and I start screaming, then she says, "You're a spiteful little boy." I'm not sure what spiteful means.

When I get my hockey stick out and start swinging around the TV set because my sister wants to change the channel and the Montreal Canadiens are losing to the Boston Bruins, my mom says, "You're just like your father." How could I be? He doesn't care about Montreal! He couldn't care less that Dryden quit! Anyway, I'd never hit my sister with a stick. I'd choke her, like when she said I loved that fat girl but I didn't. With a choke you know how far to go. With a punch or a stick you never know.

My dad in secret tells me to be good to my mom. I try,

but I still make her mad. My dad never says I'm like my mother. I guess I'm not like girls at all. Except that one time last summer when I cut my foot and I was all alone at home in Montrose because everybody went to the lake. I had that plastic bag on my foot and I don't know why but I started putting on my sister's clothes, and my mom's clothes too. I was pretty scared and my heart was beating right in my forehead but it felt pretty good. I looked in the mirror and I don't know why but it all felt soft and good. That's all I know about that.

My mom and my older sister are exactly the same. They talk about a bunch of things that don't matter. They both hate hockey.

My dad never says anything bad about my mom. Not one word. Except maybe when he screams at her. My dad screams the most at people he loves the most. Me and my mom are tied for first. That's why Christmas has a chance this year. If my mom and dad can get together and laugh, I'll work so hard at hockey my dad'll never have to yell again.

When my mom gets so mad her lip sweats—this only happened once and I don't want to talk about it—she says, "You're just like your f---ing father!" That's the only time she swore. It wasn't even my fault. We lost the hockey game and when I got home I threw my skates down the stairs. How was I supposed to know my sister was playing with Barbies at the bottom of the stairs? I said, "I'm not a mind reader!" That was two years ago and you can't even see the scar any more. I always take a look now before I throw my skates down the stairs. I put my skate guards on first. I shoot for carpet. I don't even do it any more. When you look before you throw, what's the point?

*

I don't know why I went to the counsellor. For my mom, I guess. The counsellor chews his nails right down to the bottom like a rabbit. He stinks like old cigarettes. My dad says people that bite their nails are hiding their feelings. Sometimes I wish my dad would bite his nails.

The counsellor was nice enough but he didn't know anything. He said we were just getting together to work a few things out. I didn't say a word. I sat on the chair on my hands like I had a detention. He asked me how I felt about my mom and dad getting a divorce. I thought maybe I didn't hear him but that's what he said. I sat there wondering how someone could be so stupid to not know how getting a divorce makes you feel. I'm the only kid in class whose family is getting divorced and every kid hates you when they find out about it. Parents hate you, too. Then you never see your parents together.

The counsellor couldn't figure out how that makes me feel. Even Rex the dog knows how that feels. When I get sad he comes and sits right next to me. He doesn't ask any questions. He doesn't have any papers on his wall saying how smart he is. He doesn't even have a wall to put papers on. He just knows. He comes over and I hear his collar jingle and that's that.

I thought about answering the counsellor. It seemed like he really wanted me to answer. Then I thought that if he doesn't know how divorce makes everybody feel, but Rex does, there was no point in me saying anything.

*

The last week before Christmas holidays my dad called every night at dinnertime to see if I had told Mom I was going to live with him. I could have killed that phone. I'd give it one good highstick and break it into a thousand pieces. I couldn't even tell him how good Christmas was going to go, either. Not with everybody there.

Other than that, everything was going perfect. I was scoring like crazy. I was pretty happy. Why shouldn't I be? My dad'll be coming home for Christmas. And after Christmas there's a big hockey tournament in Penticton. Not only that, things are working out at school. We've got this sports competition where you try to win what's called an Award of Excellence. That's the best you can get. That's what I got last year. I'll get it this year too. You have to broad jump and sprint and hang from a bar and run a mile under a certain time. A whole bunch of stuff. Some people get a silver or a bronze. Why even change into your gym shorts for that?

One girl—I don't know what she eats but whatever it is she must eat a lot of it—she didn't even get a bronze! She got a participation pin. She wears it around, too, on her jacket. Wearing that participation pin is like walking around with a Fig Newton squished into the bum of your jeans. She did that once. All day. Nobody told her. She couldn't even feel it when she sat down. If I sat on a Fig Newton, I'm pretty sure I'd feel it.

She can't hang from a chin-up bar at all. The teacher made her try. Her time on the chin-up bar was zero seconds. Zero!

One kid told the teacher to put a Big Turk chocolate bar above the chin-up bar and she'd hang there until the Vancouver Canucks won the Stanley Cup. It was pretty mean but it was still funny. The teacher tried not to laugh but she did. We all did. The Vancouver Canucks will never win the Stanley Cup!

When this girl with the participation pin tried to pull herself up on the bar she didn't even budge. She hung there with her feet on the ground and her face went all red until it was the same colour as her hair. She has about two hundred and twelve million freckles and red hair and a red face. If you were timing it you'd have to go like this, "Ready. Set. Stop!"

I just wish she wouldn't wear that participation pin. I want to tell her, "Take it off! Take it off! Pretend you don't care!"

But she wears it and there's nothing I can do.

And after school, if things aren't going good for me? I just go downstairs and make up goals like you wouldn't believe. You should've seen the one I scored last night. It would've made your eyes bulge. I took a pass from Cournoyer and dragged Bobby Orr on my back and deked Gerry Cheevers and popped a backhand in the top corner to win the Stanley Cup in five games. I did a big victory dance and the whole team mobbed me. Cheevers couldn't even look at me.

*

The day before Christmas my mom asked me why I liked hockey so much. Everything was looking good between her and Dad so I didn't want to make her mad. Still, it was a dumb question. That's why I didn't answer. When I didn't answer she asked me if I was mad. I said, "Mom, it's hockey. That's why."

Then she asked me if I wanted to see that counsellor.

I just looked at her.

She said, "It'll help you with your anger."

"Mom, hockey players are supposed to be angry. Nobody sends Bobby Clarke to a counsellor."

My mom said, "Maybe somebody should."

"It's not supposed to be cricket," I said. "If you weren't supposed to get slashed and lose teeth, they wouldn't give you a stick. If you weren't supposed to hit someone, they wouldn't make boards."

My mom said, "God that's a spiteful sport."

Before it got ugly, I decided to take my mom downstairs to teach her how to take shots—you know, one player shooting and one player playing goal—so she could see how fun it is. She barely tried. She held the hockey stick with one hand. I showed her all my stats, all my pictures, all the games I'd made up. I put her in net. I even gave her a mask and told her about Jacques Plante. She was terrible. I didn't raise one shot. I told her where I was going to shoot. How many saves did she make? Zero. She said she couldn't breathe in the mask. There were two holes right where her mouth was. I don't know what she was breathing out of. Gills, maybe. She tried to hold the stick with the baseball glove! "Mom! The blocker!" We were laughing. It's pretty funny seeing your mom laugh with a goalie mask on.

*

Christmas Day finally came. I got a perfect train set. You wouldn't believe it. The son of one of my mom's friends sold my mom his old train set: this huge plywood board with a train track all around it and fake grass and trees, little houses, even a mountain that the track goes through. My mom must have stuck the board in the room downstairs when I was playing street hockey last night.

I didn't get the train set until the end of the Christmas presents. This was before my dad came over for dinner. My older brother hands out all the gifts. He said, "Go downstairs and look in that room." We all went down: my mom, my brother, my sister. I thought it might be a hockey net or a table-hockey game but we've already got both of those. Our table-hockey game has every team except Atlanta and the New York Islanders. You put the little puck in the clock that arches over top. It drops onto the ice for a face-off and you've got yourself a tournament.

But this train set? Man, it's just like real life except smaller. I was thinking I could put an outdoor rink by one of the fake houses. I'd make it perfect. A little piece of plastic from a garbage bag. The size of a hockey card. Glue that down. After that you paint some lacquer on the plastic and you've got an outdoor rink all year round, right there on your train set. I wanted to put a creek in, too, right by the part of the train set that looks like the place I go creek fishing every day in the summer. That's where I caught the fish for Bunny. I get on my bike with my pole and I ride up to Beaver Creek, by the sawmill, where you can smell the wood burning all the time. I go creek fishing all day. I know exactly how to do it. You get right in the water so the fish think your legs are a couple of trees. They'll swim right by when they think that. No fish ever got in trouble swimming by a tree. When you're in the water with them they don't even think there might be a hook on that fly. Then *boom*. Before you know it you've got three or four speckled trout hanging on a stick and ready for cleaning. You can clean a trout just like that. You slice off its head, cut it down the middle and pull out all its guts, kidneys and the rest of it.

Sometimes I imagine if a trout was fishing for humans how that trout would do it. If I was a trout I'd use a Big Mac just like you get in the United States of America. I'd put it on a picnic table with a big hook inside, maybe put some Cheezies and a 7UP nearby so the human you're trying to catch doesn't look too close at the Big Mac. As soon as that human took a bite, *whammo*! Man, that must be scary. One minute you're going to have a Big Mac and some french fries, next minute you're being pulled all over the beach by a fish you can't even see. Then you'd have to jump in the water to see the fish just like the fish has to jump out of the water to see you. That's why the best thing to do is just whack a trout as fast as you can and not think about it. He doesn't think about it so why should you? You should just put your line in the water and know you're pretty lucky you're not a fish.

The train set was perfect, but the best present was my dad coming over and everybody being together. I couldn't wait.

*

My dad got to my mom's place around four o'clock. It was pretty exciting seeing him pull up. I saw him from my bedroom window where I was waiting. I was hoping everything would go okay. As soon as my dad walked in, Mom and Dad said hi to each other. They didn't smile but they didn't yell either. It was pretty good.

My dad gave me a new pair of blue and white Jofa hockey gloves and gave my sister a pair of gold earrings and my brother a Chicago Black Hawks hockey shirt just like they wear in the NHL. It was number twenty-one. That's Stan Mikita's number. Me and my brother were wearing ties and my older sister was wearing a purple dress.

At dinner around the table my older brother started talking about how bad Dave Schultz of the Philadelphia Flyers beat up Dale Rolfe of the Detroit Red Wings. We saw it on TV the week before. It was on the American station on Sunday morning. Right in front of the Detroit goal. They grabbed each other but Dale Rolfe was too slow and before you knew it Dave Schultz was punching him in the face so hard Dale Rolfe's head kept pounding back just like when you open a Pez container, except his face was bleeding. He must've got hit about two hundred and twelve times and the crowd was fifteen thousand Tasmanian Devils wearing Philadelphia Flyer shirts and screaming like Yosemite Sam.

My dad said, "Well, that's the end of Rolfe's career." I don't know if that's true but he shouldn't fight any more, that's for sure. I looked over at my mom and my sister and I could see they were pretty bored talking about hockey. My sister was worse. She had a scowl on her face. My mom didn't have anything on her face. Still, it was going pretty good. I thought I better try and change the subject. I started talking about my goalie friend who I hit in the balls and how his nose was bleeding and how his dad was going to beat him with a strap. My dad said that wasn't right. A man should go to prison for that.

Then my brother said to my dad, "You've smacked me before."

My dad said, "Come on."

"You have."

My dad got that look and said, "I've never smacked you."

"Yes, you have."

"I'd like to smack you."

"You have smacked me."

My dad said, "If I smacked you, you'd know I smacked you."

My brother said, "I know you have."

I was really wishing my brother would shut up. I think my dad might have spanked us but I don't think he's ever smacked us before. A spanking is scary but a smack'll knock you right into the third row.

My dad said, "You don't even know what a smack is."

My brother rolled his eyes.

About then my dad went crazy. "I'll f---ing smack you!" he yelled. He jumped across the table like he was Pete Rose sliding for home plate. My brother jumped about forty feet in the air. That's when everybody screamed. Turkey and stuffing went flying and Brussels sprouts rolled all the way out of the kitchen and down the stairs. Rex went after them, eating them as he found them. My brother jumped up and took off but my dad got one hand on his shirt and tried to drag him back. We all jumped on my dad on the table to stop him. Then we were all on the floor and crying and still on top of my dad, who was looking even more like Old Yeller. My brother lost his shirt but he got loose. He sprinted out of the house like Speedy Gonzales. Just a tie around his neck. You could even see the smoke behind him. I'm not kidding. All I remember is, we were crying and screaming and Rex was barking and the front door was slamming.

After that my mom and dad had about seven screams and then my dad took off in his car back to Rossland without even saying goodbye. Me and Rex took my brother's

Chicago Black Hawks sweater and went out looking for him. We found him in the garage, still wearing his tie but no shirt. He looked pretty cold. I gave him the sweater. He didn't say thanks but he put it on right away. Then we started taking shots without even saying anything. I was the goalie and he was the forward. I stopped most of the shots, too, until my brother slapped one as hard as he could that I didn't even see. Right in the top corner. I was just glad I was wearing a mask. My brother threw his stick into the snowbank and said, "When I get my licence I'm outta here, man. Sayonara." He took off walking down the street with his hands shoved in his pockets. I watched him go until I couldn't even read the twenty-one on his sweater.

The only one who was happy was Rex. He got the turkey and a couple of Brussels sprouts.

That was pretty much Christmas.

*

The Penticton Christmas Hockey Tournament started on Boxing Day. My dad didn't want to pick me up and my mom was working so the best player's dad had to come and pick me up in his Cadillac that smells like cigarettes, and drive me to meet the team bus. He looked where my rink was and asked what that mess of dirty plastic was doing in the yard. I told him I didn't know. I knew all right. The plastic won't hold anything. It looks perfect by the time I go to bed. The next morning? Plastic and mud. I didn't say a word. I just sat in his car wishing he wasn't smoking and that I had a rink I could skate around on by myself.

The team took the bus to Penticton and the whole way we had to listen to the Toronto Maple Leafs against the Montreal Canadiens on the radio and I hated Ken Dryden more than Hitler. Nine to two! I've never heard of anything like that. Why even have a goalie? Nine to two! If Montreal ever loses 9-2 again I'm going to jump in the Columbia River. I kept thinking to myself, Eat the fish, Bunny! Eat the fish! Then Toronto would score again.

The best player thought it was the funniest thing in the whole world. He hates Montreal. He calls them a bunch of frogs. That's the thing about the Montreal Canadiens. You either love them or you hate them so much you wish their bus would crash. The best player said, Let's quiz each other. I said okay. He said, "When was the last time the Montreal Canadiens lost 9-2?" Everybody laughed. Ha-ha.

Nobody even stops to think how Cournoyer might be feeling. I told the best player I'd eat my jockstrap if the Canadiens ever lost 9-2 again. After that, I just sat by myself and stared out at the road. I wondered about Hobey. When you're dead are you happy or just nothing? Sometimes I pretend I could disappear into the darkness. I think about the Columbia River. If you look over the bridge at night it's all black but you can see the swirls of water spinning by. You can't believe what's in that water. There are fish called sturgeons in there that are twelve feet long. I'd love to swim with a fish twelve feet long. I'd just grab onto the fins and take off.

One time I rode my bike down to where Beaver Creek runs into the Columbia River. I took my Lucky Louie with me. That's a green and silver plastic painted fish with a big hook that's made for catching the big one. I caught a big one all right. It was a sucker and it weighed about twenty pounds. It had a big gut and it was green and white and had this round mouth like a vacuum cleaner. Its gut was moving. I'm not kidding. Maybe it got like that from eating all the pollution where Cominco dumps in the zinc. I got too scared to touch it. I was so scared I cut its mouth off where the hook had him. It fell back in the water and swam away. There I was with my Lucky Louie and a pair of sucker lips hooked on like false teeth. Later when I learned that suckers eat with their lips—that's how they suck—I couldn't sleep. I was too busy hoping he was okay.

*

It's pretty good when you've got a hockey jacket and you're playing on one of the best teams in the tournament. The whole team walks into the arena with jackets on and you hear some of the other players say, "That's the team." People watching us walk in can't even tell that the rest of the team hates me. Hockey jackets cover all those things up.

We played two games the first day. We trounced Rutland 9-2. That felt pretty good. It made up for the Montreal Canadiens game. I got two goals and the best player got three goals.

My dad showed up at the game that night. Almost all the parents were there for the tournament. When it was 4-2 for us, our big boy assistant captain skated from about forty miles away and crosschecked one of their players right into the net for no reason. About four people went in with them. Their player didn't get up for about five minutes. That's what I mean about those big boys. You just never know what they're going to do. That's what they call a dumb penalty.

Big trouble for the team, right?

Don't worry about it. Me and the best player had to kill

the penalty. We *both* scored short-handed. After that, it was game over. Six-three, final score. My dad said I played great. He said I had guts. If we won the next two games we'd be in the finals. Penticton was coming the other way and everybody was talking about that game. Coach said, "I don't want to hear about Penticton! We've got two games today!" But we kept talking about Penticton. Even during the game against Salmon Arm we talked about Penticton. The Penticton team was sitting in the crowd with their blue jackets and caps watching us, so we couldn't help but think about them. It didn't matter that much because Salmon Arm had one of those teams like Rossland or Grand Forks or Beaver Valley. We trounced them. But Coach was right. Thinking about Penticton almost cost us the semi-finals against Kelowna. That's what happens. If you don't concentrate, next thing you know you're sitting in the stands with a hot chocolate burning your tongue, wishing you were in the finals.

We were losing 3-1 when me and the best player both scored in the last three minutes to tie the game up. I made it 3-2 on a perfect wrist shot from right in front of the net. Then before the tying goal I fell into the boards exactly like Paul Henderson did against the Russians. I got up just as the best player batted the puck towards the net. I was right there to shoot home the rebound just like Paul Henderson. I would have, too, but the best player's shot went right through the goalie's legs and that was it. No rebound. It was all tied up. Our team went crazy. Everybody jumped off the bench and mobbed the best player.

Then came overtime.

Big chance in the first minute. I deked the defenceman

and then the goalie but I missed the corner of the net by a couple of inches, not even. Everybody would've gone crazy. A minute later the best player went end to end through the whole Kelowna team and popped it in the corner. We all jumped off the bench and jumped on the best player. The best player's dad was standing on the bench next to Coach. I looked back out of the pile of players and I saw him. He had an eensy smile on his face and looked pretty proud that the best player was his son.

I missed the net by about two inches.

*

In Canada we have a thing every year called Minor Hockey Night. That's a special night when the whole town comes out to watch the players play. I scored my first-ever goal on Minor Hockey Night. I was five and I was playing mighty mites. I don't even know how I scored. I probably just pushed the puck into the net with kids lying all over the ice. That's what kids do in mighty mites. When I scored that goal I raised my hands in the air and started skating like I'd won the Stanley Cup. I skated as fast as I could all the way around the rink, twice, with my hands in the air, and then fell over. The crowd was cheering and that's all I remember.

The final game of the tournament against Penticton had a crowd even bigger than on Minor Hockey Night. It was packed. More than anything I wanted to play my best game ever but my legs just wouldn't work. I don't know why. It was like I had one of those Arby's roast-beef-sandwich bums. My dad was getting so mad in the crowd that the referee warned Coach that if he didn't stop yelling he'd get a bench-minor penalty. Coach yelled back at the referee, "That's bullshit!" Then Coach leaned over the glass and said, "Come on, Doc, keep it down." My dad did keep it down until I got a penalty for charging. It was a terrible call. Even my dad's girlfriend couldn't get him to calm down. My dad went crazy and yelled out, "You f---ing homer referee!" and "You're teaching the kids to f---ing lie!" That one got him the penalty. He has to be the first parent in history to get a penalty from the stands. So there I was in the penalty box with my dad. Not that he was in the penalty box with me, but I had to serve my two minutes and his two minutes. Penticton scored twice and we were losing 4-3 with time running out. The best player had all three goals. We were losing the biggest game of my life because of me! We needed a goal more than anything. I wanted to score more than anything!

With thirty-four seconds left Coach put me and the best player out there. I felt so bad about those penalties and how my legs wouldn't move that I went crazy trying to score. After the face-off I got the puck on the boards and took a shot from a bad angle that went right through everybody, through the crease and skinned the goal post. I was almost the hero.

That's when the best player took off after the puck. I was trying to figure out the best place to go. I ducked behind the net just as he took the puck out of the corner and deked one of their defencemen. If he slipped me a pass I'd cut out in front and stuff it in. If he shot I'd be there for the rebound.

Their other winger went after the best player. The best player deked him. Then their other defenceman got nervous, made a big mistake. He took off after our best player, too. I couldn't believe it! That left me wide open. I scooted around from behind the net, screaming, "Hey! Hey!" Their goalie didn't even see me. Right away the best player spotted me and slipped a pass through their defenceman's legs, past their goalie, coming right to me, right on my stick with a wide open net.

That's when I started to lose my balance. I don't know how. It was like somebody tripped me but there was nobody there. All I know is I was falling backwards just as the puck was coming towards me. I swiped at it as I fell. All I got was air. The puck flew on by and into the corner of the rink.

No!

I got up and skated after it as fast as I could but the buzzer went and the game was over.

On the bench after the game I sat there like Tony Esposito after he blew the Stanley Cup. I knew exactly how he felt. Even now I can still see that big open net. I can see the puck like I'm right there.

When they announced the tournament all-star team, the best player was picked as the best centre in the tournament. His dad was pretty proud, I could tell. If they had a second all-star team, like in the NHL, I think I would've been picked, just like Cournoyer. That would have been good too. In the lobby after we'd changed, I heard some guy with no hair talking about the best player. I don't know who it was—maybe a Penticton parent or an NHL scout. "That kid got all three goals. If he had a team around him he'd be unstoppable." That was about all he said. I'll never forget it. Maybe that man who was talking didn't see the four games before this one. I got six goals! But nobody remembers the games before the big game.

My dad didn't say much. I guess getting the penalty himself that cost us the game didn't leave him much to say. The parents on the team already hate us and this was about as helpful as throwing their Christmas turkey on the carpet. Having a young girlfriend makes it worse. Some of the players say things about her body. Mostly the hairy players. They say she's got big tits.

I say to them, "So what? What's that got to do with hockey?"

I didn't go home on the bus. I went back with my dad and his girlfriend. I sat in the back. It was a blizzard all the way home. My dad's girlfriend drove with her learner's licence while my dad slept in the passenger seat with his sheepskin jacket undone and his mouth hanging open. She was pretty nervous all hunched up over the steering wheel. We went about two miles an hour and couldn't see anything for all the snow.

I like it when everything's all white like that. Or black. When I was a kid I used to make these forts with sleeping bags. My sister made them, too, but mine were the best. You'd make 'em so no light could get in. Then you'd bring a flashlight in with you. Inside I'd read my books or draw goalies. Man, I must have been as small as Rex back then. If you can build a fort and get away for a while, I'd say that's about the best thing you can do when things aren't going so good. No matter where I go now, though, all I see is that wide-open net.

*

Even though it was still the Christmas holidays, the Trail Smoke Eater Peewee Reps only had one practice over the next few days. I worked harder than Bobby Clarke. I worked so hard I almost threw up. I told my dad I'm not eating another jelly donut until we win the B.C. Championships.

On the ice Coach said he didn't care about the game against Penticton. It was only a tournament and we showed we could just as easily beat them. The B.C.s are what really matter. And first we have to win the Kootenays. He said he was the boss, too, and that we had to play by his system. I never understand systems. Two forwards back, one up, no pinching. What does that mean? I can barely understand the drills in the practice. I just don't listen very well. At home my dad says I'm a non-learner and a non-listener. At practice I just move to the back of the line and hope I catch on. The coach said we have a few problems. A few too many prima donnas. A few coasters. A few ballerinas who aren't willing to pay the price. He said it's his way or the highway. He didn't mention any names. Then he said some of the parents are butting in too much. He didn't have to mention those names.

My dad is loud and all, but everybody's his pal when someone gets injured and he goes out on the ice. Everybody's glad there's a doctor around when that happens. There are a lot of injuries, too. Once my dad pulled a tongue right out of my winger's throat. A winger he said had no talent. It doesn't matter to my dad. He saves them all, talent or not. He just reached in and pulled out that tongue like an eel. Our big boy? My dad calls him Hollywood. Every game he gets injured. Two guys carried him off the ice against Kelowna. His leg was just dangling behind him like a puppet leg. Everybody slaps their stick on the ice and the crowd claps when he gets up. That's what you do to let a player know you're glad he's not paralysed. With the big boy our crowd doesn't even clap any more. He said his knee was broke. He said he heard something snap just like a hockey stick. He didn't even have a bruise. He played the next shift and knocked a guy right over the boards. After the game my dad said the only thing that might have snapped was his brain stem.

Against Rutland the big boy got injured again. He said he couldn't feel his feet so nobody moved him. Six of us carried him off on a stretcher like he was on the news in Vietnam. He played the third period and shot a slapshot over the boards. It cut the timekeeper for seven stitches.

Against Penticton, Coach told the big boy to stand in front of the net on the power play. The big boy went there and got tripped by their goalie. Down he went, backwards on his helmet. My dad says he hasn't seen eyes flutter like that since Snow White.

The big boy's dad got pretty mad when my dad said, "Fortunately he landed on his head."

The big boy's dad said, "What do you mean?"

My dad said, "Well, if it'd been his ass we'd have to check for brain damage."

I don't know why my dad says those things. He just gets pissed off and says what he feels. He gets right to his feelings. He gave the big boy smelling salts and the big boy jumped up and skated right to the other team's bench and sat down. I was on the ice and I had the "A" on my shirt so I had to go tell the big boy he was sitting with the wrong team. I could've called him an idiot but I shouldn't talk. Only one idiot missed the open net.

*

Staying at my dad's over the holidays I got my three hours of ice time a day. I practised with the Rossland Junior Warriors, I played with a couple of older house teams in Rossland and I skated on the outdoor rink at my dad's friend's farm. I went to public skating and I even got to go on the ice at the Rossland arena by myself at five a.m. one morning. Me and the junior coach's kid skated around passing pucks and shooting them against the boards. Pucks sound perfect booming against the boards when everything is quiet and you can skate free. I was getting in my three hours like Bobby Orr said you have to. My dad said I was looking pretty good. He thinks I'm heads up. He says I'm the best stick-handler and the best face-off man on the team. He says the rest'll come—size, skating. My brother says I'll never make pro but my dad said I could. He said I could do anything I want.

My dad kept saying he was getting sick and tired of picking me up in Montrose for hockey. He kept asking why I hadn't told my mom I wanted to live with him. I was thinking about my mom and how much easier it would be for her if my dad didn't have to pick me up every weekend. No yelling. All the hassle from hockey would be gone and maybe everybody would be happier.

*

Even lying in the dark at my dad's house I can see the Yvan Cournoyer poster. You can see how fast he is just by looking at it. Right behind him is Tim Horton of the Toronto Maple Leafs. The other guy is Jean Béliveau. You can see Cournoyer's hair blowing. You don't get that look by standing still.

I was lying on the mattress on the floor. I had two quilts,

a sleeping bag and all my clothes on just to keep warm. I still couldn't sleep. I kept thinking about that open net. I started thinking about Hobey, too. I could picture his face and I felt bad that I didn't like him much. Once a person is dead you wish things were different.

Sometimes I think about crazy things. Once I was in the hospital because I had a hernia. That's when you have one big ball and they want to make it smaller. I can't remember how big it was. It didn't hurt and I didn't care that it was bigger, but they just had to make both balls the same. I don't know why. One big, one small, was fine by me. Look at Yvan Cournoyer. He's five foot seven. Dryden is six foot four. You don't get rid of Dryden and go looking for a goalie who's five foot seven to make the team photo look better. With balls you do.

I remember going to sleep before the operation. One hundred, ninety-nine, ninety...so long! My mom and dad were both waiting when I woke up. That was in the old days before they split up. I remember my eyes rolling around like that swirling water in the Columbia River. I threw up right on my mom's hand. She didn't care. It takes a pretty good mom to not care about that. I remember those black stitches holding the cut together. It looked like a train track. If I moved, it hurt like a stick in the gut. You'd be surprised how much it moves down there when you try to walk. I couldn't walk for a long time. Now my balls are almost the same size. The weird thing is that the scar to change the size of my balls isn't even on my balls. They cut me from my hip joint right to my dink.

It's numb if I touch that scar. It would take a lot of time but with enough scars and enough operations, you probably wouldn't feel anything. When Rejean Houle skated on Pat Stapleton's face, right across his mouth, Stapleton got seventy stitches. Seventy stitches! That would look more like a train station! Man, that must have hurt. Stitches inside and out. I bet he can't feel anything from his neck up.

Then there's Hobey. Who knows what he feels?

*

For the rest of the Christmas holidays my dad was all over the place. One minute we were drinking milkshakes and he was singing along to Gordon Lightfoot, the next minute he was screaming at me in the basement when we were cutting plywood and the table saw jammed. My dad yells at himself the same way. Sometimes when I'm upstairs I hear him yell, "You f---in' clown! Idiot, use your goddamn head!" I don't know if it helps him.

All I knew was that the holiday was over and me and him were in trouble after what happened on Christmas Day. I shouldn't have talked about hockey. I knew I needed a new plan to make things start to look right again. I knew I wanted to win the B.C.s, that was for sure. I knew I could take the yelling, too, but I didn't know how much my mom could take. I didn't even hear from her over the holidays. I felt as cold as a Popsicle. Like I'd sat on the bench for ninety-two years.

That night my dad drove me to the Cominco Arena in Trail. That's where I was getting picked up by my mom to end the holidays with my dad.

I knew I was supposed to tell her.

Driving down the hill from Rossland, I couldn't even think.

When we got there I could see my mom's boyfriend's car

in the parking lot under the streetlight. Mom was sitting in the seat next to him. Dad dropped me off and waited in his car. I walked to my mom's boyfriend's car about two miles an hour. I couldn't even look up. It was dark out except for the streetlight, just like when Hobey went out on his gold bike. I thought, If I could get injured, everybody would stop yelling. Nobody yelled when they made my ball smaller or when I broke my arm or when I fell out of that chairlift. When you get injured everybody remembers how much they care about each other.

When I got to my mom's boyfriend's car I could see my sister and my brother sitting in the back seat. I stood by my mom's window with my head down. My mom rolled down the window and asked me what I was doing. I didn't look up. I felt like I did in Spokane just before I threw up, except worse.

I said, "I want to live with Dad."

"You what?"

"I want to live with Dad." I don't even know if any words came out.

About then my memory gets like a Fudgesicle when the sun comes out. Everybody went crazy and I kept backing up until I was standing in the doorway at the Cominco Arena, where I go in every Saturday morning to play hockey. There were no lights on now, though. There was no game, either. Everything was black and I wished I was a June bug. They just fly away like they've really got somewhere to go. You can hear their wings like an engine. But it wasn't June. It was January and freezing out. My mom and dad started yelling but I wasn't looking at them. I couldn't look at anyone.

Next thing I knew, I was in the back seat of the car squished beside my brother and my sister. They weren't talking to me either.

My mom was so mad. She put her hand in the window from outside and pointed at my sister.

"Where do you want to live?"

My sister said, "With you."

My mom said to my brother, "Where do you want to live?"

He said, "With you."

Then she asked me.

I don't remember if I answered.

The ride back to my mom's house was about as quiet as a ride can be. We went over the bridge and up the hill and up the cut-off and we were home. I just kept my head down and waited for the next bomb to come. Like it or not, there'll be one. I know there'll be a bomb every Friday when my dad picks me up. I know there will be a few more bombs on the weekend but I can't say when. Other than that, you just have to keep your head down, because some bombs you know about and some bombs you don't.

Nobody said anything when we got home. Everybody just got out of the car and went into the house and went wherever they had to go. I was sort of watching with my head down. I went to my room and sat on my bed with the door open. I sat there and waited but I didn't hear anything. Everything was quiet outside, but in my head I felt like one of those crazy bats had got caught up and was as scared as I was. I sat there on my bed, waiting. I just wanted someone to come and say something, even if it wasn't nice.

Finally, I heard some footsteps coming towards the door.

I looked up and there was my mom's boyfriend. We were just staring at each other. He wasn't my first choice but I was glad someone was in the room with me.

"You're a yellow bastard" was all he said.

After that the room was empty again. Even the crazy bat had left.

*

If there is a time to ruin everybody's lives, I'd say the Christmas holidays is the best. At least everybody has new presents and a chance to get organized. Imagine doing it on a school night, or in the morning when everybody runs around like hamsters.

Now I was leaving. My mom was pretty nice about it. She helped me pack up my clothes and my hockey cards. She told me to make sure I eat breakfast and to come back whenever I want and to call whenever I want. My mom told me everything would be okay. She seemed pretty sad, even though she was smiling. I think she was smiling because she knew the yelling would stop and plus she wouldn't have to deal with hockey or the notes the teacher sends home from school with me. I wished my mom played street hockey. If she did we could take shots on each other and forget about everything.

Outside and waiting for my dad to pick me up, I sat on the steps and stared at the rink. Some rink. It was a mess of plastic and a few puddles.

Rex came and sat next to me. He leaned right up against me. He didn't ask any questions. He just knew. We both sat there for a while looking around. A cat walked by and Rex didn't even move. That's how much better he is than the counsellor. Next thing my dad drove up the cut-off. I said goodbye to Rex. He gave me a kiss on the cheek and then I got in my dad's car. I didn't slink down in the seat like when I got kidnapped. I didn't do anything. I just stared straight ahead. I didn't look to see if my mom was standing in the window. I'd seen that before. When me and my dad and my brother left for the first time after they split up. We were moving to Vancouver. We had one of those Jeep trucks. I remember the sky being bright blue like it was made out of china. My dad was driving and my brother was sitting on the other side of me and he had Rex on the floor between his legs. I was sitting between them but I had turned all the way around and I was holding the back of the seat. I was staring out the back window of the Jeep and my sister was standing in the doorway of our house with my mom. She was holding my mom's hand in the doorway as me and my brother and my dad drove away. They waved and I waved and I watched them until we turned the corner. I remember crying for about two hours.

I didn't cry this time. There was no point. I didn't look back at the window or at the door. I didn't look at the rink either. I didn't even say hi to my dad.

I just stared straight ahead.

SECOND PERIOD

The thing about being the new kid in class is that every-body stares at you like you've got a big booger in your nose. Like you're a Martian. Then the teacher tells the class to say hello to the new kid. They say it but they don't mean it. So you just sit there with a bunch of people staring at you.

I had underwear that made people do that. When I was little we drove down in a camper to the Grand Canyon and the United States of America with another family who all had crew cuts. My mom didn't come. Just me and my brother and my sister and my dad and this other family. From scratching, I got two pretty big, brown skid stains on a pair of bright orange gonch. I stuffed them down the side of the mattress in the top bunk in the camper. I didn't know what else to do.

My brother found my gonch and laughed his head off and passed them all around to everyone and then stuck them on my head. After that, somebody snatched them off my head, put a rock in them, and started swinging them around like Hercules on the cartoon. When we crossed the border back into Canada they threw my gonch out the back door of the camper while we were driving. The rock was still in them so they really flew. The kid who threw it yelled, "Go home, Yankees!" It was pretty neat the way he did that.

That's about how you feel being a new kid in class. Like they're passing around your gonch with a pair of skids.

A few kids in the class smiled at me. Two. Maybe three. Kids from when we all lived in Rossland way back. They weren't so bad. They knew me. They'd seen me when everything was normal. The girls were pretty good, too. Girls are always pretty good. I like 'em. I like their hair and all that. I knew a few more kids—boys—from hockey. They weren't bad either. Mostly, though, I played hockey against the older grade. That was the grade who really hated me. They hated me and my dad. That's what happens when parents split up and the whole town knows. Some of my parents' friends don't even talk to them any more. Or they talk to one of them but not the other one.

*

I didn't know my new friend was a Negro until we were playing box ball outside and someone called him that. Box ball is where you knock that red rubber ball around these four boxes. I stopped and looked at my friend when I heard he was a Negro and I got a frozen red rubber ball flat in the face. It makes your whole face go numb. After that your eyes water until you've got two waterfalls coming out. Next thing I knew, when I could see again, my Negro friend and the guy that threw the ball at me were fighting in the snowbank. Negro or not, it's a pretty good friend who'll fight some older guy for you.

My Negro friend has an Afro but he's not very dark— like tea with milk in it. After the fight he had snow all stuck in his Afro. He got whacked pretty good and his nose had a little trickle of blood coming out of it but he was still smiling. I thought about Dryden and how he let his friends down. That's when I threw that red rubber ball as hard as I could right back at the guy who beat up my Negro friend.

I got him in the head. Everybody laughed. Man, he came after me. I ran for a bit and then I got beat up too.

My Negro friend's parents don't live together either, so he understands. We're about the only two. He lives with his dad and his older brother and his dad's girlfriend and her kids. They're as white as I am. That I noticed.

Once you notice one thing you notice a lot more things. They live in a place in Rossland called Happy Valley. I went there on Tuesday after school and we took shots with his older brother right in his house—right in the front room! I didn't think anybody else did that. They have an old piano that we used as a goal. Every time you let one in and the ball hit the piano, you could hear a little bit of music come out. His place wasn't as messy as my dad's basement but it was messy. The front room was linoleum so it was perfect for street hockey or boxing or whatever.

My friend's older brother is a lot bigger and a lot darker. When we box he thinks he's Joe Frazier. His arms are pretty long and when we first started boxing he put one glove on my face and held me away. I couldn't reach him. With his other hand he whacked me about twelve hundred and thirty times and kept saying, "I'm Smokin' Joe! Say my name! I'm Smokin' Joe," every time he hit me. I knew if I didn't do something I'd end up looking like Joe Bugner after twelve rounds with Muhammad Ali. So I spun around like Serge Savard doing a Savardian Spinorama, and before he could react I yelled, "I'm Muhammad Ali!" and corked him right in the gut. He doubled over and then he went crazy. I grabbed on and kept yelling, "Tie! Tie!" while he punched me in the back of the head. My friend shot one of those orange plastic street-hockey balls at his older brother and whacked him right in the back of the leg. When he screamed he stopped punching and grabbed the back of his leg. He had a pretty big welt and then he pounded his brother, who was laughing the whole time, and then we took shots again. Me against my friend's older brother. My friend was in goal. He's a good goalie. After that I walked home and I was so tired I drank about seven milkshakes.

*

As soon as I moved in with my dad he signed me up for hockey in Rossland. They said I couldn't play there because it was too late in the season. After that they said I couldn't play in both Rossland and Trail. My dad yelled and now I'm playing in Trail and Rossland. The competition is crummy in Rossland but it's all about ice time.

Everybody in Trail thinks that even though the Trail Peewee Reps lost to Penticton in the finals of the Christmas tournament, we still have a pretty good chance of winning the B.C. Championships. We do have a chance. We heard Penticton beat North Shore Winter Club. That's one of the Vancouver teams with all the stocked players. If Penticton can beat North Shore Winter Club and we almost beat Penticton, why can't we win the B.C. Championships? We would have beat them if I hadn't missed the wide-open net. That's the only difference between us. I'm going to be so ready when I play them again. We'll win the West Kootenays. Then the Kootenays. After that I'll get my chance at Penticton.

My dad wants me to start weight-lifting. He bought me a couple of dumbbells and a bar with ten-pound weights on either side. They're made out of blue plastic and they're filled up with cement. I've got a chart on my wall with the exercises: squats, curls, bench press. The only thing I hate more than weight-lifting is going to public skating in my hockey equipment. I asked my dad why I had to weight-lift. He said because I had a pigeon chest. I didn't ask what that meant but I told my dad that Bobby Hull never lifted a weight in his life and he's got arms like Popeye.

"He lifted bales of hay," my dad said. "All you ever lift are jelly donuts."

That was good enough for me.

I'm going to lift weights, get my three hours of ice time in, work as hard as Bobby Clarke at all these practices and then score the winning goal against Penticton in the B.C. Championships. I don't even care if my teeth get knocked out or I get a big cut like Pat Stapleton. I'll never quit.

My dad says a great goal scorer sometimes has to take a hit to make the play. I'd do that. I'd get hit by a diesel to make the play.

*

My dad's young girlfriend's dog Ted is one of those bull terriers like Bill Sykes' dog in Oliver. She even has a red scarf around her neck. Man, did my dad get mad at her when she chewed up my new Jofa hockey gloves. He was chasing her all over the house in the nude until Ted tried to jump out of the front room where the plastic wall is. The plastic came down with her and she almost suffocated inside it when she landed in the snow all rolled up like a big plastic cigar. Her legs kept pumping until she finally got out and took off down the road, my dad's girlfriend right behind her. Me and my dad put the plastic back up while my dad yelled at me for leaving my gloves on the kitchen floor. My dad says

I don't respect anything. I haven't seen my dad's girlfriend or the dog since.

My dad's young girlfriend is okay but I figure that if my mom and dad don't yell at each other for a couple of months, they'll start to think about getting back together. They'll forget about what happened at Christmas. They'll forget about what I did, too. I just have to keep them apart for a little while and keep thinking about hockey when I'm playing hockey.

At practice, Coach said we have to play for the name on the front of our shirts, not the name on our backs. I told him we didn't have our names on the backs. Not one person laughed. For that I had to skate lines. He kept yelling, "Come on, funny boy, skate!" Blueline, back. Red line, back. Far blueline, back until you can't keep your tongue inside your mouth. I didn't mind. I shouldn't have said anything. The best player should say those things. I missed the open net against Penticton and now I'm trying to be funny. That's not funny. That's stupid.

Nobody laughs at my jokes on this team. I don't know why. Maybe you have to like the person to laugh. I hope it hasn't got anything to do with my tuque. I never crack jokes barenaked, anyway. I don't even like being barenaked. My dad loves it. My dad was completely nude when he made raspberry roll-ups and stuck them in the oven. He worked on the front room. No clothes. Sanding a bookcase. No clothes. I don't remember him like that when we lived in Vancouver. He took some therapy and now he's always naked. Just like a statue that walks around. He doesn't even put on clothes when my friends come over. You might get cocoa and toast with blueberry jam in bed in the morning, but if you do, no clothes. I don't mean gonch, either. Maybe slippers. Maybe his sheepskin jacket. It doesn't matter that the house is freezing cold. No clothes. It doesn't bother me but I think it would make my friends nervous. It's probably good that I don't have any friends. I have one friend other than my Negro friend in Rossland. He's got a family that goes to church and doesn't swear. I think his parents tell him to be my friend because once my dad delivered one of their babies in a snowstorm. In the morning he comes by to get me on the way to school. I wait outside. I don't care if it's a blizzard. What choice do I have? My dad is upstairs in the kitchen with no clothes on.

My religious friend has a sister in the next grade up. I saw her yesterday after school when I was walking home. My face felt all blotchy, like I had poison ivy. I walked with her until I had to turn off to my house. She asked me why the living room had no wall. All I said was "No." Dumbest answer in the world. She's as pretty as any girl I've ever seen.

*

Hard work pays off. I scored a goal against Castlegar like I've never scored. I got a pass from the best player, scooted around the defenceman and shot the puck harder than I ever have. It went right into the top corner and the goalie didn't even move. We won 10-3. The next night we didn't play as well but we won 5-2 and I got two more goals.

The team is so serious. Coach told us we might never have another chance like this. The best player's dad cut up oranges for us in between periods. That's what they do in pro. We got a sugar pill and a salt pill, too. Gets all the stuff back you sweat out. You feel pretty good after taking those things. Like you've got rockets on your legs. They told us not to drink too much water, either. It makes your legs get waterlogged.

On the way home we drove by Blueberry Corner. It was dark and blizzardy like the night I saw the gold bike and the diesel lights and my dad found Hobey all munched. I couldn't look. I pretended I was asleep until I saw an Esso gas station reflected in the window and I knew we were almost in Trail.

My dad said I played pretty well but I stand around too much. He said I need to keep my legs moving all the time. To always be on the fly. That's what they call it when you're moving at full speed. If you can do everything on the fly you can pretty much do what you want. You shouldn't even slow down when you stick-handle. The only time you should slow down is when you change on the fly. That's when you go to the bench so your teammate can go on. If you don't slow down you'll just fly over the boards and your skates might cut Coach or anyone else who's in the way. Just before the boards you should slow down, yell out your position so the next person knows to jump on, and then climb over. But in the game, keep up full speed. Stick-handle like that. Pass like that. Forecheck. Backcheck. Bobby Orr never slows down. He gets the puck and goes faster and faster until he flies. That's how he scored the Stanley Cup winning goal before I watched hockey. Before Dryden, even. I saw it on highlights. He scored on St. Louis and then flew about thirty feet. I think that's how he hurt his knee. You fly thirty feet, you're going to hurt something when you land.

*

I was surprised when my mom called. I jumped when the

phone rang. I used to jump when my dad called. Even now I'm living with him I still jump. That doesn't make any sense at all.

At first when I was on the phone I didn't know what to say. It was the first time I'd talked to her since I'd gone and caused all that pain. After I moved here I just tried not to think about it. I didn't think about anything. On the first weekend I didn't go back and visit, either, because I had games both days. My mom said she'd called a few times but we were never home. I said we were playing hockey a lot. She asked me how school was going.

I said, "Fine."

"Have you made some friends?"

"Yeah. Two. It's pretty good." That's when I felt sad. "One's a Negro and one's from a religious family." I didn't mention his sister.

My mom said that was good.

I said my Negro friend and me get along well because his parents aren't together either.

"How's your father?" she asked.

She didn't say it like she wanted to say I was like him or anything. She said it like a real question. Like she liked him. Like she was really interested. I knew this time apart would be good for them. I knew if I could just stop the yelling and my dad could make my mom laugh, it might just work out.

I said, "Dad's good."

Then we didn't say anything for a few seconds.

She said, "How's hockey?"

That's what she said. I couldn't believe it.

I said I'd been playing a lot. I didn't tell her I'd been weight-lifting. My mom doesn't like that stuff. After a while you can pretty much tell what my mom likes. I asked her how the rink was. She said she'd left it there so I could work on it if I came home on the weekends. She said she got some more plastic for it but the weather seems to be getting even warmer. She said she went outside one night to put some water down. The next day, she said, it was all gone and she knew how I felt. I felt sad there for a minute and I said, "Well, thanks for trying."

I asked her how Rex was. My mom said he was pretty good. She said kids come and get him to play street hockey but he doesn't stay very long. My mom asked me if I was coming to visit next weekend. I said I wanted to but I had hockey on both days. She said she missed me. She said everybody missed me. That's when I heard my dad walk in. I said I had to go. I didn't want my dad to pick up the phone.

It wasn't time yet.

*

I don't let my religious friend into the house. Some people you let into the house and some people you don't. I think I'd let him in if I didn't like his sister so much. She's about the only time I don't think about hockey. I don't think about anything when I see her and I can't even talk right. Like those pictures of Archie when he's with Veronica and he gets those hearts around his head. Now I understand everything in that cartoon. They both have dark hair too.

My Negro friend has slept over a couple of times. I was nervous about it. I told him my dad walks around with no clothes on and my friend laughed his head off. The next morning he was in his sleeping bag in my room and I was on my mattress and my dad came in with cocoa and toast and no clothes just like I said he would. My friend didn't even notice. He just said, "Man, hot chocolate in bed!" It's pretty good when he stays over. I know that if my religious friend stayed over, he'd tell his family about seeing my dad's dink and the sawdust in the blueberry jam and the swearing and that would be it. His sister wouldn't even talk to me. I wouldn't blame her, either.

My Negro friend was at my house one day after school when my dad was yelling at me. My dad was screaming his head off and saying I don't respect anything because I dropped a spoon into the blender while it was going. Bent the blades. My dad said I don't help out and I'm a useless, non-learning, non-listening little shit.

When my dad finished screaming he went outside. I looked at my friend and he grinned and said, "Let's have another milkshake and then go take shots." He didn't even care. He doesn't care about the mess. He doesn't care about my dad not wearing clothes. I don't have to worry about anything with my Negro friend. His brother can beat him up. I can beat him up. But he's not afraid. Before you know it he's digging his head out of a snowbank and his Afro is all full of snow. He might even have a bleeding nose or a fat lip but he's still smiling.

He's like that in school, too. If he gets something wrong he'll turn around after the teacher says he's an idiot and make a goofy face at me. We had to do a report on someone famous from history who overcame hardship. I did Yvan Cournoyer. It was called YVAN: HOW HE KEPT TRYING EVEN THOUGH DRYDEN DID WHAT HE DID. That lasted about two seconds. All I'd said was Cournoyer's height and his weight and where he played junior. He was a junior star, I said. If you're not a star in junior, you can forget about making pro. That's all I said when the teacher sent me back to my desk.

At least I had a report. My Negro friend didn't even have a report.

The teacher said, "Do you have a report?"

He stood up and stared straight ahead. "No, sir."

"Sit down."

"Yes, sir."

He's funny like that. He pretends he's in the army. We were supposed to write a poem for school but he didn't do that either. I wrote one on January 20th after Montreal was trounced 8-0 by Boston. It was a good poem.

Ken Dryden played for Montreal
They call Montreal the Habs
Ken Dryden quit Montreal
Now the Stanley Cup is up for grabs
Some of you might find this funny
But you can't win with a goalie named Bunny.

The teacher hated it. He knows less about hockey than my mom. He said I had to write another poem.

When I told my dad what happened, he said he'd write one for me. Actually, he wrote a limerick. That's what he called it. That's the thing about my dad. He can really make you laugh. When he makes fun of the big boy's injuries, me and my Negro friend laugh our heads off, and my friend doesn't even know the big boy.

We were taking shots in my room and my dad walked in and gave us the piece of paper. It was about my teacher. It said:

A teacher whose name was McCammon
Had a thumb the size of a cannon.
He stuck it, they say,
Up his arse all day,
That teacher whose name was McCammon.

We laughed our heads off. My dad said we should put it on the teacher's desk before school starts. No way was I going to do that, and I said so. That was the last I heard of it until Monday morning when my Negro friend whispered to me, "Hey."

I looked up and my teacher was standing at his desk reading a piece of paper.

My friend had a grin as wide as a banana.

I said, "What?"

"Your dad's poem," he whispered.

I looked at the teacher just as the teacher looked at me. That fruit bat was flying in my throat again.

The teacher didn't read it out. He just held it up and said, "Who wrote this?"

The whole class was quiet. I was going to take the blame but I didn't. I had nothing to do with it and I couldn't fink on my friend.

My teacher said, "I can see it's in the handwriting of a doctor."

I don't know how he could tell but that's exactly what he said. It was like magic.

My teacher said, "Let's see. There are two doctors' kids in this class. And I know Dr. Ganzinetti wouldn't write this poem."

I don't know how he knew that either. How could he

know what that other doctor would write? Maybe that doctor writes poems. Maybe he doesn't. Either way, I was done for, but I wasn't going to say anything. Why should I? I didn't do it.

My teacher looked right at me and said, "And it's not even a *good* poem."

I said, "It's a limerick."

Dumbest thing I could've said.

*

After a month in Rossland I was going to go and see my mom for the weekend and tell her my dad had stopped yelling but it turned out my mom is having therapy too. She wanted to see me but she said she thought I had hockey all weekend so she arranged a Get Salt weekend. That's where a whole bunch of hippie people come over and sit on chairs and touch each others' faces and talk about their feelings for two days. So I'm not going over to my mom's to tell her my dad's not yelling any more and that we have a good supper with vegetables every night and that his girlfriend is almost never here. Instead, my sister is coming over for the weekend and she'll tell my mom the truth about everything. That's how fast a good plan can go bad.

My dad and me picked up my sister at her high school, where she's in grade eight. Her arms were crossed and she seemed kind of embarrassed getting in the car. It was pretty good to see her. She had a purple choker on and her jeans were so wide they covered her boots right to the tip. We went to Dixie Lee Chicken for dinner in Trail. I asked my sister if she noticed anything about me.

"Like what?"

"Anything." I was wondering if I was looking more

muscle-bound since I started weight-lifting. Some people get muscle-bound in just seven days. I've seen the pictures. I'd been doing it for a month and didn't know if there was any difference at all. I flexed my muscles inside my hockey jacket.

She said, "Your hair is longer than David Cassidy's." That was true. I always had long hair but now it was a month longer. My mom would have trimmed it by now. My mom cuts hair one way. Straight across the bangs so you look like Prince Valiant. I used to cry every time. I'd get her to cut it on Friday after school and then eat lots of food and pull on it in my room on the weekend and hope it'd grow back to normal by Monday for school. It never did. That's how dumb you are when you're a kid.

My dad asked my older sister some questions about this therapy my mom was doing. My sister didn't know much about it.

Then my dad asked some questions about my mom and my mom's boyfriend. My sister didn't seem too comfortable. She'd just pick at the chicken skin while he asked her stuff. I pretended I wasn't listening but I was. I pretended I was drinking my strawberry milkshake and looking around. My dad wanted to know how much my mom's boyfriend had been around. My sister said she didn't know.

"What do you mean, you don't know?" my dad said. I could tell he was getting mad. He gets mad and says none of us have any guts. I could see he was about to say that but he didn't.

My sister said, "Sometimes. I don't know."

I didn't have any way to know but I'd guess that means he'd been there a lot. The amount he hated me, and with me gone? I'd say he's there all the time, in her room with his boxer shorts.

"How's my rink?" I asked.

"What rink?" my sister said.

"In the back yard."

"We threw it out."

I stared.

"It was blowing everywhere," she said. "We had to."

"But I was making a rink."

"It was a big mess."

"Does Mom know?"

"Of course she knows. It took about five years to get all the nails out of the ground."

After Dixie Lee we went to my hockey practice. My sister was going to go to the library while I practised but it was closed so she sat in the stands with a frown on her face. My dad was talking to some parent. After the hockey practice we went to the sporting goods store and my dad bought my sister some Adidas runners. The white ones with the blue stripes. That helped a bit.

When we got home my sister didn't seem too happy with the mess in the house. Plus the place was colder than the fridge. The plastic wall had blown down again and there was a little snow on the front-room carpet. My dad got my sister to brush it off while me and him tacked it back up. My sister didn't smile at all. She looked at the ground mostly.

My dad's girlfriend and her dog Ted came by and met my sister for the first time. My sister didn't say anything but I don't think she could believe how young my dad's girlfriend was. I just hoped she wouldn't say anything to

Mom. My dad's girlfriend was nice to my sister, though. She said she thought her choker was cool. That's what I should've said to my sister. I thought it but I didn't say anything.

Then she showed my sister her headband and her bracelet. It was made out of real Indian beads from the Grand Canyon. That's when Ted the dog took one of my sister's Adidas runners out of the shoebox and took off with her quick little legs moving faster than Cournoyer. My dad took off after her, screaming like crazy. Ted ran through the front room with my dad right behind her. In the end she had nowhere else to go so she jumped right into the plastic wall and brought it all down again. It was exactly the same as last time except this time my dad had clothes on. Ted got all caught up in the plastic, yelped like when a dog gets hit by a car but not dead, and then took off. My dad got the shoe back. He was swearing his head off. "Take that f---ing dog out of here!" Then he looked at me and said, "And your hockey gloves better not be on the f---ing kitchen floor!"

The girlfriend said, "You're a f---ing prick! He's just a kid and leave my dog alone!"

My dad's girlfriend and her dog Ted went home. She was carrying Ted and calling my dad an asshole. My sister sat in my room with her arms crossed. She got her shoe back with a couple of chews in it. My dad and I put the plastic up again. That was Friday night. All I could do was try to tell my sister that it was all the dog's fault. Anybody would've got mad.

Saturday morning wasn't much better. My dad came into the room with no clothes on and gave us toast and cocoa. My sister was so embarrassed.

I told her, "Don't mention that to Mom. That's the first time he's ever done that."

My sister still hadn't smiled since she arrived at the house. She smiled when she got the runners but that was it and now one had some chews in it. She didn't eat her breakfast, either. It just sat there until the cocoa had a layer of skin like custard. It sat there until I got home after my hockey game and, by accident, kicked it all over the floor.

When we were sitting there with our breakfast my sister told me my dad and me lived like pigs. I didn't know what to say so I snorted just like a pig. That was the only time she laughed. Then we all went to my hockey game. On the drive down she sat there with her arms still crossed while my dad told me to make sure I finished my checks.

The big boy got injured again. Nobody saw what happened but he was rolling around on the ice behind our goalie. Somebody thought he yelled, "My sandwich!" That would be ridiculous. All I know is, nobody moved to help, not even his own parents. My dad just sat there too. Then the big boy started to roll so much I got worried. He reminded me of a trout that gets away on the beach after you've caught it. When that happens they flop like crazy, like they're having a nightmare about never being in the water again. The big boy rolled for a while and then he stopped rolling. When the fish does that it means he's dead. Then I saw the big boy's head move. He looked around like he was shot in the leg with a bazooka—like his leg was just hanging by gristle. Then he stopped and looked around some more and finally he just got up. He put his head down and skated to the bench as fast as he could. He was pretty mad. He slammed his stick against the boards and sat down. That was the end of the injury. He must be a fast healer. All the parents were laughing.

My sister didn't even make it for jelly donuts afterwards. She phoned my mom from a pay phone. My older brother with his new licence came down in my mom's car and picked her up. That's what my dad told me. I knew it was back to square one again. My sister would report to my mom just like a spy. Right then I decided I'd eat twenty-five jelly donuts even though I'd said I wouldn't. It didn't matter. My dad drove right past the bakery and home.

*

Nothing makes things worse than therapy. My dad went away for therapy. He took off for a while after the divorce and went down to Los Angeles. That's where the Kings play. They stuck my dad in a little room so he could scream. With this therapy you remember everything that ever happened to you, even being born. No wonder they scream. I saw a picture of a baby being born. Everything was scrunched up and he was covered with that white stuff you put on when you pull a muscle.

My dad went down to Los Angeles to get to his feelings. They stuck him in a little room and said, "Start screaming. Get to your feelings. We'll see you in a week." I guess it worked. Now my dad gets to his feelings anywhere. Big rooms, small rooms, bathrooms, arenas. If he has a feeling, he gets to it and you know about it. Most of his feelings are pretty loud, too.

Sometimes I think my dad is trying to get to his feelings but his feelings find a way to get to him first. Sometimes when he's getting to his feelings about me or about how I play hockey, I cry. Most of the time I don't cry. But some-

times I'm so tired that a little tear comes out. Sometimes
when one comes, that's it. You can tell you're in trouble
once one comes out. I think it loosens up the hole like
grease on a bike chain. Like springing a leak.

That's what happened this Saturday morning. We won
but my dad said I played like I didn't f---ing care. But I do
care. It's Dryden who doesn't care. I've been caring more
than I ever cared. I've been practising and running and
weight-lifting. I just couldn't get going. My legs had the big
bum problem. My dad says if you don't care you might as
well play f---ing softball. Softball! He kept yelling and I was
crying and he said, "What are you crying about? What are
you f---ing crying about?"

I said I didn't know and that's when he told me to get to
the feeling.

He said, "You're not crying about hockey. There's no
reason to cry about hockey! Get to the f---ing feeling!"

I didn't know what he was talking about but he kept
yelling it. "What are you crying about? Get to the feeling!
Get to the f---ing feeling!"

I kept saying, "Hockey! Hockey!"

"No, you're not! Get to the f---ing feeling! The feeling
behind the f---ing feeling!"

I looked so far ahead, way past Rossland, way past the
Columbia River and the black water, way past Hobey's
eyes, so far that everything went quiet. I started to think
about that counsellor who smelled like cigarettes and all
the dumb questions he asked me. Therapy makes people
dumber than they were before the therapy. That's what I
see. Get to the feeling? What feeling? I just want you to
shut up! I just want to put up a big plastic wall in this car

between us. I just want to go into my room and make up statistics. That's how I'm feeling!

I kept thinking about two weekends ago, when my mom had all those people at her house for therapy. All weekend. They should go play street hockey! Instead they all sit in a stinky room asking dumb questions. By Sunday they must be asking the dumbest questions in the whole world. I can't even think about how dumb those questions are. Somebody should ask them why they're asking such dumb questions. Man, would he get yelled at. That's what would happen if someone asked a smart question. At therapy, asking a smart question is the last thing they want you to do.

*

You feel the pressure when nobody believes in you except your dad. My dad knows I can make pro. That's why he buys me CCM Super Tack skates and the best equipment in the world. That's why he gets mad, too. He tells everyone how great I am and then I let him down.

I don't mean to. I shouldn't let him down because it's just me and him and nobody else believes. But then some games I think about other things like French words. My dad's yelling at everybody and telling them how f---ing great I am and I'm skating around thinking about *le troisième étoile* and *le gardien du but*. That's not right. I bet Cournoyer never thinks about English words when he's breaking out of his own end. I think about French words and my dad has to stand up for me all on his own. That's what makes him mad. I understand that now.

It's the same with me and Dryden. I told everybody how great the Montreal Canadiens are. Better than the Russians. Better than Bobby Orr's Boston Bruins. Better than

Philadelphia's goon-heads. I say, If the Montreal Canadiens don't win I'll eat my jockstrap.

What happens? Dryden quits. That's why I get so mad this year. My dad feels the pressure and so do I because he knows what I can do and nobody else does. My brother doesn't even think I'll make pro. That's what he said. Man, will he be surprised when I'm playing in the Montreal Forum and he can't get tickets for the game. I'll leave a note for him at the ticket place. He'll open up the envelope thinking it's tickets. It'll say: "Enjoy the game...on TV." Ha-ha. That's what I'll do.

Maybe I'll get him a ticket. Probably I will. You can't stay mad forever.

My dad told me that Coach was watching me at practice when we were scrimmaging. When I had the puck Coach leaned over the boards and said to my dad, "Now there's a kid who'll play in the Western Hockey League." The Western Hockey League is the junior league where all the young kids play and lose their teeth before they go pro. It's called major junior. It's all hockey. You ride on a bus across the prairies every night and the crowds go crazy when you skate onto the ice. No school. Just hockey. Everybody knows hockey facts and that's all they talk about. Coach said I'll be in that league.

It's pretty good when my dad and Coach get along. Coach didn't say I'd make pro but he said I'd play major junior. My dad likes to hear somebody who thinks that. Last year he was always telling his farmer friend with the crew-cutted kids how good I was. My dad's farmer friend was getting sick of hearing it. They'd be sitting at the kitchen table and the farmer's wife would be smoking a cig-

arette with the ash waiting to jump off and the kids would
be coming in and out and all dirty from milking cows and
shovelling cow pies. My dad would be talking about how
good I was and I'd feel pretty embarrassed. I'd pretend I
didn't hear or I'd go watch cartoons or even watch fishing
or, when they had a rink, I'd go out on the rink. That's
what I really loved. Skating at night with the sky above me
as black as a puck with sparkles on it.

Finally last winter the farmer drove down to the
Cominco Arena to see me play against Cranbrook. I scored
four goals. One was a backhand that dribbled through
about forty-seven people. The other was a deflection like
Cournoyer and two were garbage goals like Phil Esposito
gets. But they were still goals so who cares? I remember
that farmer saying afterwards, "Doc, he really is good.
Tough, too." I'd never heard anyone say that before.
Except my dad. My dad didn't say anything to me but I
could tell he was pretty proud because most of the time he's
all on his own when he talks about me, because nobody
believes in me or likes me. It gets tiring for my dad trying
to make people understand that I can make pro. So when
Coach said I'd make major junior, it felt pretty good. My
dad got quieter, like the best player's dad. He didn't have to
fight for me for a while. That's when I figured out why my
dad yells. He's standing up for me. Everybody else wants to
see me fail. Parents don't even talk to me. They want to
laugh at me and they want to laugh at my dad. They think
he's bad because he swears. They want to say I'm a nobody
and he's a nobody.

That's why I have to stop thinking about French words.
My dad believes in me. Coach does a little. That's why he

made me assistant captain. The farmer friend does too. Maybe the best player's dad. But that's all. My dad will not let me down. Ever. My dad's dad died when he was four. You can't make pro if your dad dies when you're four. Dryden doesn't know what it's like. That's why I lift weights. That's why I'm working as hard as Bobby Clarke. That's why I have to score the winning goal against Penticton in the B.C.s. I just gotta.

*

If you have a piece of hockey stick about a foot long, a piece of rope and a two-and-one-half-pound weight, you can make your arms look like Popeye. You tie the rope from the stick and the weight from the rope. Then you hold the stick in front of you and roll up the weight with your fingers. Roll, roll, roll. It makes your forearms bulgy. You can snap the puck way better when you do that for a couple of weeks. Snap it right past the Penticton goalie.

I've been shooting about two hundred and twelve thousand pucks a day at my dad's bed. Sometimes they miss and hit the wall. The last shot yesterday made the whole wall collapse. All the gyproc turned to white dirt. I could barely breathe in the dust. Lucky there was another wall behind it or we'd have two walls missing. My dad wasn't too mad but I had to take a day off school to help him put up another wall.

My dad can fix anything. After the new wall was built, we put a big sheet of plywood above the bed to make sure it doesn't happen again. Dad let me draw a goalie on the board with a Jiffy marker. I ran out of room with the shoulders and head. The rest was life-size but no head. I didn't mind not having the head and shoulders on there. I only know how to draw Dryden's head anyway. Even at school now I've been drawing goalies without heads. I drew the Montreal emblem on the shirt but I left out the number. You can't tell who it is. It could be Bunny Larocque or Frank Fred or Michel Plasse. Or even one of those old goalies like Jacques Plante. Now he was a good one. He got hit in the face with a puck back in the days when goalies didn't wear masks. He had two broken cheekbones, four broken noses and a cracked noodle. He still didn't quit. That's what Jacques Plante was like.

Andy Bathgate hit Jacques in the schnozz with a backhand in 1959. Seven stitches right under his nose.

Jacques said, "Enough's enough. I ain't going back between the pipes without a mask." I bet he said it in French.

That's the thing about backhands. You never know where they're going. They're like knuckleballs in baseball. Toe Blake was Jacques's coach. He was against using the mask. The coach is against the mask. Figures. Lucky Jacques won that game 3-1 when he wore the mask or goalies still wouldn't be wearing masks.

I woke up pretty frightened the other night from another dream about Hobey. He stares at me with those black eyes. That's the whole dream. I was lying there thinking about that dream when I heard this rumble sound. Louder. Louder. Moaning. I thought for a minute it might be Hobey coming back from the dead. Next thing I heard the yelling getting louder.

"Oh godgeezuzgod! Come on! Oh god! Mmmm! Come on!"

It was my dad's girlfriend. It had to be.

The next sound was strangled. I've heard it before. Frankenstein strangled his bride on Creature Feature. It was exactly the same. I didn't know what to do. She was yelling, "Ohgodogodogohgod-comon-aah!" Somebody was jumping on the mattress, too. I couldn't even hear my dad. That's why I didn't think he was there. When he's mad, he yells like crazy. If he was so mad that he was strangling somebody, like his young girlfriend or my mom's boyfriend, he'd probably yell so loud you could hear him in China. But I couldn't hear anything. Maybe he was on call and went out and someone else snuck in.

But what if he was strangling her?

I couldn't turn him in to the cops. We'd have to pack up the car and head for the hills and live in a cave until we were so old nobody could recognize us. So much for pro.

I got even more scared when everything went quiet. At least when someone's moaning because they're getting strangled it means they haven't been strangled all the way.

No yelling. No pounding.

Nothing.

Then a little noise. Moaning.

I knew one thing. Somebody was still alive.

Before I did anything I put on my longjohns and my runners in case I had to sprint out of the house to look for the police. Then I grabbed my Sherwood hockey stick and I tiptoed out of my room and leaned my ear up against my dad's door. That crazy fruit bat was right back flying around in my throat. I was ready to burn out of there. I knocked.

"Son? Is that you?" It was my dad's voice. Happy. Like they were drinking milkshakes in there.

121

I said, "Hey."

He said, "You okay?"

"Yes. Are you okay?"

"Yes, we're fine."

"Both of you?"

That's when my dad's girlfriend finally spoke. "Yeah, I'm fine too."

"I heard some noises," I said.

My dad said, "We're okay."

"I heard screaming."

"We were moving furniture," she said. "I hurt my finger."

"I was going to call the cops," I said.

My dad laughed. "Don't call the cops."

"I heard some screaming."

"My finger," she said again.

"Oh, yeah."

"You wanna come in?" my dad said. That's when I saw the light go on underneath the door.

I pushed open the door. They were lying in bed. Smiling. Not even a chair was moved. I said so, too.

My dad said they liked the furniture where it was so they moved it back. Then he asked me if I was planning to play some hockey because I had the hockey stick in my hand.

I said, "How's your finger?"

My dad's girlfriend said, "I jammed it a little."

"I'll say," my dad said. They laughed.

Then I pointed to the corner and yelled really fast, "I see a rat!"

They both turned to the corner right away. Both necks were working.

My dad said, "What are you doing yelling shit like that?"

"It's gone," I said.

"Jesus Christ." That's what my dad said.

Then we all looked at each other for a few seconds until my dad said, "Go back to bed, you're being stupid."

I went back to bed, but I kept my stick with me. I lay there staring at my poster of Cournoyer until I fell asleep.

*

You can't believe how great it feels to score. That's the thing. I try to tell my mom but she doesn't understand. She doesn't know one thing about hockey.

Think of something you like. Anything. Scoring is better than that. Better than blueberry milkshakes. Better than Bugs Bunny. Better than Johnny Quest. Better than missing school. Better than catching trout. Better than finding bones. It doesn't matter what you think of.

Even closing your eyes and thinking about scoring is pretty good. Scoring at the Montreal Forum. Scoring in street hockey. Even scoring in practice, if the goalie is trying. I can just lie there and think about it.

If my mom could do that, I know she'd be happier. That's why Gordie Howe keeps playing. He's playing with his sons in the WHA. It's a bum league but it's better than no league at all.

Big goals are better than anything. A goal when your team really needs a goal? The best feeling in the whole world. Goals with one minute left to win the game. That's what Paul Henderson did. Thirty-four seconds. They made a painting about it. Or a goal that ties the game. That's what Cournoyer did against Russia just before Paul

Henderson scored. Cournoyer got a backhand past Tretiak. Team Canada went crazy. Or a goal to finish off a team. Goals to give you a two-goal lead, even a three-goal lead. Or a goal to give you a hat trick. Goals with ten seconds left in a period. Goals when you're short-handed. Power-play goals. Goals right after the other team scores. Goals to put your team back in the game. Slapshot goals. Deke goals. First goals. Garbage goals. Deflections. Rebounds. Playoff goals! Overtime!

Overtime. Oh, man. Overtime. I've never scored in overtime, but I saw it once. This year at the tournament over Christmas. The best player scored. We went crazy. We all jumped off the bench and piled on top of him. His dad was so proud, I could see that. I looked back from the bottom of the pile and I could see the best player's dad standing on the team bench shaking hands with Coach. After that I saw the best player's dad's eensy smile. That's all it was. He knew his kid was the best player.

That's what an overtime goal does. It makes you know everything for sure. Scoring makes you forget about everything, too. Maybe only for a second but probably for a few minutes. You forget about the yelling. You forget about school. As soon as the puck goes over the goal line you go crazy. It makes you so happy you throw your arms up in the air and jump around. You can't help it. If you get hit right after you score you don't even feel it. A goal makes you hug people you don't even like.

That's why I keep working so hard. That's why I wish that outdoor rink would've worked. All the best scorers grew up playing on an outdoor rink. That's how you get your three hours a day. Cournoyer. Bobby Hull. Gordie

Howe. Rocket Richard. Bobby Orr. All of them. You lift bushels of hay and skate on a river. That's the best way to get Superman muscles and your three hours a day. If you can't do that, you have to wear your equipment for public skating and lift weights. It's worth it, though. Scoring goals is worth everything.

The weights are helping. My dad said so. Me and my dad helped my dad's girlfriend move some of her stuff to my dad's house. My dad's back was hurting and he said I was a big help. That was good to hear because me and my dad aren't exactly pro movers. One time when we moved in Rossland my dad was in such a rush we didn't even wash the dirty dishes. We just packed 'em up. My dad wrote DIRTY DISHES right on the box. My mom would've swallowed her head.

My dad's girlfriend lives in South Slocan, which is about an hour away from Rossland. When we were packing her stuff my dad said I was getting as strong as a bull. I thought about that bull who fights Bugs Bunny at a bullfight. The bull swallowed a rifle and it went right back into his tail and started shooting out his horns. When the bull figured out what he could do, you should have seen the look he gave the camera. Man, was it funny. He started chasing Bugs all over the stadium, shooting at him until the rifle in his tail ran out of bullets. So the bull stopped and swallowed a whole box of bullets. The next shot he fired? *Kaboom!* Blew himself up. You should've seen the look on that bull's face. Hilarious. Bugs Bunny said, "What a gullabull! What a nin-cow-poop."

We lifted my dad's girlfriend's couch and her bookcase and her kitchen table and her chest of drawers from her house in Slocan. It went pretty good and my dad was really happy about this moving trailer we got out of the newspaper for fifty bucks. It was a good size and it was made out of chipboard and two-by-fours. It was hooked onto his car with the chains and everything. The taillights worked. We filled it up and took off.

I was sitting next to my dad in the car when he looked back in the mirror. You should've seen his face. We'd only been driving about two minutes. My dad said, "Oh, f---!" like he was in slo-mo replay. I looked back and I could see that big trailer had broken off from our car and was spinning away just like a hubcap but about nine hundred and twelve times bigger. We were driving over a bridge at the time and the trailer crashed into the railing and furniture flew all over the bridge. Except for a lamp. That went over the railing and into the Slocan River. Once we got out, you could see the lampshade going down the river for quite a while. The bridge looked like a front room with pavement instead of carpet and no walls. Everything was smashed and scratched and broken.

Some people were coming around and sitting on the chairs. My dad was so mad he threw one of the bookcase shelves into the river. A hippie-guy was there with long hair and a beard—the kind that always has food in it, especially jam or mayonnaise. He said, "That's littering, mister."

My dad said, "F--- off or I'll throw you in the river."

That was as far as we got with that move.

*

I couldn't believe it when I heard Tim Horton died. I was waiting for the sports scores. Bill Good, Jr., came on and said, "Buffalo Sabre veteran defenceman Tim Horton died early this morning."

He crashed his car and that was it.

After all those hockey hits with no helmet. All those teeth gone. Three broken legs. A broken jaw. Blood coming out of his ear. All those years against Gordie Howe's elbows. For what? Tim Horton gets the third star in a game against Toronto, his old team. His new team, Buffalo, loses the game 4-2. Tim takes off in his sports car after the game. Maybe he was mad because they lost. Like me when I throw my skates down the stairs. Next thing, he's dead. Just like Hobey. Goodbye, electricity.

Tim Horton was the guy who took over for Bashing Bill Barilko way back in the fifties. Bashing Bill scored the winning goal in the Stanley Cup finals in overtime for the Toronto Maple Leafs against the Montreal Canadiens. The winning goal in overtime! His dad must've gone insane! That summer Bill went fishing. They took a floatplane into the lake. The floatplane crashed. Goodbye Bashing Bill. They didn't find his body until 1962. Now Tim Horton is dead. I wouldn't want to be the defenceman who takes his place in Buffalo.

I saw his car on the news. It looked like tinfoil. He was going over a hundred miles an hour when he flew off the road. Bill Good, Jr., on the TV sports said it was an Italian sports car but I couldn't tell where that car was from. All I could think about was Hobey riding his gold Mustang bike. Now Tim Horton. They said he might have fallen asleep. When you fall asleep like that anything can happen. When me and my dad and my brother lived in Vancouver, my dad got his car washed at one of those big carwashes with the big sprays and the big brushes that make all that noise while you sit inside your car. You have to close your windows and your car gets pushed through while you sit there. My dad must have been tired because during the carwash he fell sound asleep. My dad always falls asleep the same way. His head falls back and his mouth opens like a cave. The carwash kept pushing his car through and he still didn't wake up. The big brushes rolled his car right out of the carwash. The kid who was filling up other cars with gas saw my dad in his car with his mouth wide open. I don't know what he must have thought. Maybe he thought my dad was dead. The kid ran after my dad but it was too late. The car rolled right out of the carwash and down onto the main road. It didn't stop until another car zooming along the highway smashed into it. Imagine that. One second you're in a carwash, next thing you're in your car and it's clean but it's all smashed up. That's how fast everything can change.

Like the year I came back from Vancouver and my bone collection was gone. My mom threw it out. They say they'll leave your room the same but they never do. Fossils two hundred million years old and my bone collection is gone in six months. The room looked the same but it wasn't. I sat on the bed for an hour. I checked my hockey cards in the bottom drawer. They were still there. Everything was quiet. Rex came in and sat next to me and then it felt more like it used to feel.

But that's how fast everything can change.

Now Tim Horton.

At least he won four Stanley Cups.

*

I was playing street hockey last weekend down by my religious friend's house. I knocked on his door and his religious sister answered. My mouth went frozen like I'd got hit in the face by a red rubber ball.

Her teeth are like snow. Her hair is as black as hockey tape. Her eyes swirl like when I mix up a chocolate sundae.

I was standing there with my hockey stick.

She said, "Do you ever iron your pants?"

I said, "Street hockey."

That was my answer. I looked down at my beige corduroys. I'd left them in the dryer for about three days. They looked like a wrinkled lunch bag. The thighs were all worn out smooth and the hems were so high I could see my ankles.

My religious friend's sister kept looking at me and I knew my runners had holes. I should have been wearing boots. I should have worn something nicer but I never thought about it.

So I stood there in my wrinkly corduroys, looking at her, and next thing I knew I had my pants off and she was ironing them for me. I didn't feel too uncomfortable. I had gonch on and socks and a shirt. Plus there were statues of God hanging everywhere. I saw one in the front room and one in the kitchen. Just hanging, dressed about like me except his chest was bare and his head was bowed. He was so skinny I doubt he ever lifted a weight. I think he had what my dad calls a pigeon chest. I didn't know it was God until I asked her.

"He died for us," she said.

I said, "Did the Nazis do it?"

"No, he died on the cross. They hammered his hands

129

and feet onto that cross and then left him there because of the bad things we all do."

I looked at God on the wall there for a minute. The house was so quiet.

I looked back at my religious friend's sister. I couldn't imagine what bad thing she'd ever done. I asked her if she knew if Tim Horton died for us too. She'd never heard of him. I said he played for the Buffalo Sabres. She said she didn't think he'd died for us. I asked her if God played hockey. She said God can do anything.

I stood beside her while she ironed my pants. She was a little bit taller than me and her blouse was as white as the Montreal Canadiens home sweaters—white and shiny and lacy at the collar all around her perfect neck. I told her I used to iron stuff but then I quit. I showed her the ironing scar on my left arm. It's still a red triangle. I was ironing a shirt last year in the morning before school. I started thinking about Cournoyer and I ironed right onto my other arm. That blister oozed for about two weeks. That was the last time I ironed anything.

My pants were perfect when she finished. Warm, too.

I came home from street hockey after only a couple of hours because I had a hockey practice in Trail. From the path of my dad's house I could hear Gordon Lightfoot singing through the plastic. I know all the Gordon Lightfoot songs. My favourite is The Pony Man. It's about this guy who has a pony and we all go off looking for apple pie. I like Early Morning Rain, too. That's the song that was playing. Gord says you can't jump a jet plane like you can a freight train. That's the truth.

I broke off a huge icicle with my street-hockey stick and

then I went inside. I walked upstairs like I always do.

My dad had the little electric heater plugged in in the front room so he didn't even hear me. It's the same one I use when I watch cartoons on Saturday morning. The sun was coming through the plastic covering. Outside everywhere was bright blue and bright white.

My dad didn't see me come in. He was sitting in his big chair, slumped like he does when he sleeps, but he wasn't sleeping. His hand was hanging over the side of the chair and he had a cigar in his hand. He was naked except for his sheepskin jacket. His cigar was just hanging there, burned out. Those Old Port red wine-tipped cigars. He used to let me chew on the tips when I was little.

I could see he wasn't moving. His brown and grey hair was all everywhere. He was wearing a purple shirt and sheepskin jacket and no pants and he was covered in sawdust and he was staring straight ahead, but all slouched in the chair like if a carrot was a potato.

I peeked my head around a little farther and I could see my dad's eyes were open and all red. Red like when you really cry and you're not faking.

"Dad?"

My dad jumped up.

"Are you okay?"

He took his pants off the chair. "Yeah, of course."

"Are we going to practice?"

"Yeah, yeah. Come on."

He walked right by me and put his pants on and we went to practice.

*

Everybody plays the recorder in music class except me and

one girl. She plays the guitar. I don't play anything. The recorder is a bad instrument. We had a dog before Rex. It ate a pair of my mom's nylons. The nylons were in the garbage with a bunch of gravy. It was garbage day and Nugget couldn't help himself. Not with all that gravy. Man, when that nylon was coming out his bum! That's what a recorder sounds like. Not like that nylon coming out. A nylon doesn't make any noise when it comes out. It makes a little noise, maybe like a garter snake in the grass. I mean the noise that Nugget made. Moaning. A recorder is like that but higher. Like if a dog was a cat.

That's not the worst, though. My friend in Montrose, they had a yappy little black dog named Snoopy that everybody hated. It was always tied up and yappin'. I don't know why, but one day Snoopy ate a Neil Diamond eight-track cassette. The whole neighbourhood was there on their front lawn watching Snoopy. You couldn't help but feel sorry for him. All they could do was grab one end of the tape and keep pulling. Everybody was laughing. It went for about twenty miles and no music. The dog just lay there moaning. He didn't yap once.

That's the thing about dogs. They never think about what they're eating. They don't have a clue about nutrition. Rex at least is picky with his food. He wouldn't eat a pair of nylons. He doesn't even like dry dog biscuits. Rex loves milkshakes but we hardly ever made milkshakes at my mom's. I gave him a sip of one once, right out of the glass. He had a purple moustache over his black nose. He loved it.

Music class is good because it lets me think. I put my recorder up to my mouth and move my fingers like little spider fingers while the whole class plays Hot Cross Buns. I think about scoring the goal against Penticton or bad things like missing that goal against Penticton. I think about Dryden or my mom. Sometimes I just see that wide-open net. I think about how sometimes I think about French words when I'm playing hockey while my dad is in the stands, all by himself, yelling at everyone about how good I am.

With the recorder I make sure I don't blow out my mouth. Once I sneezed and tooted really loud. The music teacher looked at me and I thought he'd remember I was in the class. He didn't.

I used to be afraid in music class. What if my music teacher asks me to play? I don't know how to play.

I don't have to worry. Every week my music teacher calls out names to play the recorder. Every kid in the class, one by one. My music teacher has never called my name. I know why, too. All the kids have their name on that piece of paper on the music teacher's desk. Alphabetical order. A to Z. It's like a hockey team roster. It's done with a purple stencil. The secretary types on the first copy and it prints all the names on the sheets below it. New kids like me come in the middle of the year and they're supposed to print our names under the typed names. My music teacher forgot to print my name at the bottom. He must have. He's gone through the whole class about forty-seven times and never called my name. So I just move my fingers and blow out my nose. Who cares? If the recorder was never invented it wouldn't make any difference. No one would ever think something is missing. Imagine the Roadrunner playing the recorder! After a hard shift Yvan skates to the bench all sweaty, reaches into his hockey pants, pulls out a recorder and plays Hot Cross Buns. His teammates would punch his face in and I'd help 'em. Or they'd shave him. I don't know why, but that's what they do on the junior team. They hockey-tape the rookies to a table with no clothes on and shave all the hair off their bodies and rub hot muscle stuff on their balls and their dinks and then they roll the table out on the rink and leave the rookie taped there all bald and barenaked and covered in hot muscle stuff. I don't know why they do that but they do. I heard the junior guys talking about it and I saw the two bald rookies. That's about the only time I'd be glad I have a tuque.

*

You can taste pressure. You can taste playoffs. That's what Coach says. I can't taste them. I try but it's not like lemon and sugar on a pancake. That you can taste. But the play-offs do make you a little bit cold. Not so cold that you feel cold but cold enough that you shake a tiny bit. Hot, too. Not hot enough that you sweat. Hot enough that you tingle. It's all you think about. That goal—and winning. That feeling is perfect. When you're sitting in the dressing room at the end of the second period and you're tied with the other team, all you want to do is push your legs as fast as a train and yell, "Give me that puck!"

We played a game against Creston. They're terrible. We clobbered them 11-3. Every period we got a slice of orange. Sugar tablets, too. That's how serious everybody is. Preparation for the Kootenay Championships. That's what Coach said.

We had individual meetings where Coach talked to everyone on the team on their own to tell us what he expected of us. I saw the big boy come out of the room. I bet Coach said, "Come on, big boy, stop faking injuries." I bet that hurt the big boy. But the big boy came out smiling so Coach must've said some good stuff too. I could see the same thing when the best player came out. He was walking tall and smiling. I bet Coach said, "You're the offensive weapon. You gotta put the puck in the net." I bet the best player said, "I can do it, Coach. You can count on me." You can, too. Coach would've nodded his head and said, "I know I can." The best player is always ready to go. He doesn't lift weights but he's got muscles in his legs, that's for sure.

I felt pretty nervous when I sat down in the dressing room by myself with Coach just before practice. Excited nervous. I knew how badly Coach wanted to win and I was pretty sure he knew how badly I wanted to win. I knew he might have a few complaints but I also knew he believed in me. Not like I was the best player, but he believed. So I sat down with my Trail Smoke Eater Peewee Rep jacket on and I felt all fired up. Come on, Coach, let me have it.

Coach said he expected me to pay more attention in our own team's end. Pick up the centreman on their team and make sure he doesn't get a shot on goal. Make sure you're always ready to pick up his stick. Get between him and the puck. Coach told me he expected me to hit more. Finish the check. Every check, every time. Take the man. If their guy has the puck, make him pay after he passes. Don't float around like a duck waiting for that breakaway pass. This isn't road hockey. That's what Coach said. Be serious. Be ready. One chance. And stop making those fancy-dancy drop passes. You're not a Russian. You're a Canadian. Play like one. Come back deep into your own end and help out. Don't hog the puck in their end. Pass the puck, but don't pass the puck across the rink in your own end. That's what Coach said.

Coach didn't mention me scoring big goals. I thought he would mention something about big goals. Or the power play. Or how me and the best player are a scoring threat even when the team is short-handed. I thought he'd mention how my shot is a weapon. I've been pushing so many weights I thought he'd see how much better my shot was and how the team was counting on me to score the big goal. He didn't say anything about that. He said I have to play better in our end of the rink.

But what else, Coach?

That was it.

I think since I missed that open net in Penticton, Coach has given up on me. It doesn't matter. Coach'll see. Coach'll remember and go, "Oh, yeah."

Everybody will.

*

My mom was really missing me. That's what she said on the phone. She was hoping she could see me on my birthday. I was turning eleven on Saturday. My dad doesn't even think about birthdays. Me neither, really, unless I really want some present. My mom asked if I was playing hockey on the weekend. Of course I was playing hockey on the weekend! My mom didn't even know the playoffs were coming up.

I missed her too. Over the phone it sounded so quiet at her house. Here my dad was downstairs with no clothes on using the table saw and sawdust was everywhere and the plastic wall was flapping and he was yelling at himself. My mom wanted to see if I could come up to Montrose to spend some time there. I said I had a hockey game Saturday evening. My mom said she could pick me up on Friday and drop me off at the Cominco Arena on Saturday afternoon. I said okay.

I didn't want my mom and dad to get together yet so I got a ride down to Trail on Friday after school with one of the teachers who lived in Trail but taught up in Rossland. I figured my mom and dad needed to wait until after the hockey season to get together. That way there would have been more than two months to forget about Christmas and forget about yelling. I forget yelling in about twelve hours so two months should be plenty for my mom. My dad's girlfriend didn't seem to be hanging around too much since me and my dad left all her furniture on the bridge. I didn't know what was going on with my mom's boyfriend. Truth is, as long as he wasn't around I didn't want to know.

If my dad isn't yelling at my mom, she's got to miss him. If she misses me, she's got to miss him. She says I'm just like him.

*

My mom picked me up at Dixie Lee Chicken in Trail. She just finished work at the clinic and she was pretty happy to see me. She was pretty much the same, too. I was glad the therapy didn't change her too much. She had all her clothes on and she was like normal.

We didn't talk much in the car. It was hard to say stuff. I told her it was good up in Rossland and Dad's a lot quieter. He doesn't yell too much any more—except sometimes at that crazy dog, like when the dog ate those runners.

That's what I said. It was sort of a lie but a good one. Mom was surprised. Everybody's going to be surprised after hockey season when we all get back together and there's no more yelling.

A bad lie is more like when I sent away to New York, New York for that spy-scope. It cost $1.49. The back of the comic said it was no larger than a fountain pen and you could see everything a block away. Excellent for sports, counter-spying, baseball, hikers. All lies. I might as well have been looking through corn on the cob for all I could see.

Same thing for the snowstorm tablets. Five packages for a dollar. They don't make indoor miniature snowstorms like they promised. They make just enough mess to get your dad chasing you around the house like you're Ted the dog and your mom yelling, "He ruined the carpet! What next?"

Those are bad lies. This lie about my dad was to remind my mom how much better it was when we all lived in the same house. That's gotta be a good lie.

I asked my mom about her boyfriend. His sons are still at the house but he's spending quite a bit of time at his own house. I asked her why. My mom said it's for the best. I knew what she meant. Push him away slowly. Then kick the kids out.

It was pretty good to see Rex. I almost felt like crying when he started licking my face. He jumped up on me about four hundred times. My mom said she had to pick up my sister from school. She asked if I wanted to come. I said I'd stay with Rex.

My mom drove off and me and Rex went out to the

front yard to take a look at what was left of the rink. Not much. It looked pretty sad just sitting there. Just dead. The plastic was gone. You couldn't tell I'd been out trying to make a rink all winter except the grass was worse than usual. The snow didn't look too good either. Just bits of snow here and there. Dirty like little islands in a mud sea.

I don't know what Rex was thinking. He just walked straight out past everything and onto the highway. That's what he did. He wasn't chasing a car or anything. He just walked onto the road. Right where cars come zooming up the cut-off about two hundred miles an hour. Rex just walked out and boom. He didn't even see it. I looked up but it was too late. Rex went flying and that was it. That's a terrible sound. It's like the sound of nothing.

I ran out and grabbed him. I tried to pick him up. I grabbed his collar. It still jingled but Rex didn't do anything. I said, "Come on, Rex! Come on, boy!" He didn't move at all. That was the end of Rex.

I got so mad at that driver. He stopped and tried to tell me he was sorry but I went crazy. My mom drove up with my sister and they tried to stop me from yelling but I was screaming at that guy. My sister started crying. My mom started crying. Everybody was crying. Rex was just lying there. I tried to get Rex to lift up his head but it didn't do anything. I don't remember what happened after that.

Me and my mom and my sister had to pick up my brother at the Hudson's Bay Company in Trail that evening. That's where my brother works after school. Rex was my brother's dog. We met my brother in the parking lot because he didn't like us coming in the store.

My mom told him right there in the parking lot. It was

dark out and cold and they were standing beneath the streetlight. We were right there behind her.

Man, did he cry. We were all crying again. All four of us standing in the parking lot crying.

My brother has had some bad luck with dogs. The dog before Rex was called Nugget. He was sort of brown with a hot-stove temper like Old Yeller after he got the rabies. Nugget bit the grocery delivery boy in the calf. The grocery boy dropped all the groceries—milk, jam, pickles. We had to put Nugget down because it wasn't the first time and you didn't know if it would be the last. It's not like hockey where you can keep getting penalties. When you're a dog you only get a couple of bites. After that, goodbye.

I remember my dad picking up Nugget to take him away and I remember going into my brother's bedroom downstairs. My dad brought back another dog. His name was Brandy and he was all different colours. I remember my brother sitting on his bed crying with his hand on his new dog Brandy.

With a dog you have to give it an operation if you don't want it to have any babies. You have to put it to sleep and fix something inside like with my balls and then wake it up. You send it to a vet. That's what my brother wants to be. I want to play in the NHL and he wants to be a vet.

My dad and his doctor friend figured, "Why send the dog to the vet?" They were doctors so they had all the chemicals you need to put Brandy to sleep and do the operation.

That was the last time we saw Brandy. They put Brandy to sleep all right. Brandy's still sleeping.

Next thing I know, I'm downstairs again peeking into

my brother's bedroom and he's crying again. This time he's got Rex right beside him. Rex was a black dog and he'd already had the operation. My brother was crying because of Nugget and Brandy. Rex knew how my brother felt. He was like Einstein that way. No stupid therapy questions. He'd shove up beside you until you felt good enough to go out and play street hockey. If you cheered up then he'd cheer up. But if you didn't, he'd wait until you did.

Everybody loved Rex. Even after I moved to my dad's this year, kids would come around and ask if Rex would come out and play street hockey. Rex would play for a few minutes, but when he saw I wasn't there he'd go home. The kids would yell, "Hey! Rex! Come back!" but he wouldn't even turn around. That's the kind of dog Rex was.

The best dog of all.

I'm going to win the B.C. Championships for Rex.

And my mom and dad, too.

And everybody.

*

We had a little birthday party at my mom's on Saturday morning. My sister and brother were there too. We had waffles and an angel-food cake with strawberry icing and the Montreal Canadiens emblem on the cake and eleven candles. Twelve candles next year will be perfect. Cournoyer's number. There were a few presents: hockey magazines and hockey books and a sweater and some model paint I could use on my train set. Everyone was pretty sad with no Rex.

That night I had a hockey game and I played. Not playing won't bring him back. Best thing you can do is score a goal for him. I didn't play too well at first. I scored two goals in the third period but I didn't concentrate. I kept thinking about Rex getting hit. So fast. Just like Hobey.

I bet Hobey didn't see the bomb coming either. I read about a bomb like that in the war. A soldier would stick his head out of the foxhole to see what was happening. Goodbye head. Just like that.

We would've buried Rex on a hill behind the house but the pound guy took him away. I guess my mom didn't know what to do with him so they picked him up by his four legs and threw him in the back of the pound truck like when Gordie Howe used to toss bags of cement.

I don't know what they did with Hobey and Tim Horton. Maybe a truck came by and got them too. It was the same, though, with dying. They got hit so hard it knocked the electricity out of them. I've seen that with a robin. Sometimes they land on a wire by a telephone pole. Then *zap*. Down they go. Dead. If it's not too bad, but bad enough, the electricity drains out of you slowly. That's what happened to the silver God on that little wooden cross at my religious friend's house. That's what my religious friend's sister said. They tacked him to a cross and swore at him and starved him until he died. God didn't die fast like Tim Horton. His electricity dripped away slowly until he was dead. Like a battery. For some reason, though, God had rechargeables. Three days later he got up and flew away. That's what my religious friend's sister told me.

I phoned my mom every day for four days—I gave Rex an extra day because he was a dog—to see if he had showed up at the door. My mom said he wouldn't show up. She said it's very sad but he's dead. I said God showed up. She said that was different.

I asked my dad why God came back to life after three days.

My dad said, "Because humans are stupid enough to believe anything."

I think he's right. People hope dead people will show up but when do they? I used to believe it with Rex but he didn't show up. If Tim Horton ever plays again I'll eat my hockey socks. My dad told me that when he was eight his mom told him his grandpa had died. My dad didn't want to believe it so he took off and went to all the old spots where him and his grandpa used to play in England—the train station, outside the pub, down to the river. My dad didn't find his grandpa. Of course he didn't. When you're eight you think you might find someone after they're unplugged. When you're eleven, you know better.

That's why I have to forget about Rex.

*

The team practised four times this week to get ready for the round-robin West Kootenay playoffs. Monday, Tuesday, Wednesday, Thursday. Just like the pros. I played in Rossland too. Twice with the juniors and once public skating. I lifted weights. I practised my snap shot every day after school. Picturing the goal—boom, scores!

I can't sleep. That's my problem. Playoffs make your blood all bouncy. But if you don't sleep you'll get sick. I thought I was getting the flu. I felt sick Friday morning but I didn't throw up. I had the runs. Just once. Twice if you count the first time that wasn't quite the runs yet. My dad let me stay home in the afternoon to think about the game.

I'd been thinking about the playoffs all week. Coach told us we might never get this chance again. Coach said winners never quit, quitters never win. Coach said we have to rise to the occasion. Coach said we're playing for the emblem on the front of our shirts, not the names on the back. I didn't say our names aren't on the back this time because they are. The best player's mom sewed our names on the back just like the pros. Coach said the Trail Peewee Reps would see what they're made of this weekend. Coach told us Trail is a city with hockey pride. Coach said Trail is the last Canadian team to win the world championships. I knew that from the Bobby Kromm summer hockey school that I go to every summer. Bobby Kromm was the coach of that Trail team. I've seen Bobby Kromm flex his muscles. His biceps look like tennis balls. That's why I keep rolling up that weight for my forearms.

Coach said Bobby Hull was in peewee once. So was Gordie Howe and Bobby Orr and Rocket Richard.

Coach didn't have to say anything else.

*

We found out on Friday when we got to the Castlegar arena that the Nelson Peewee Reps had nipped the Castlegar Peewee Reps 10-9 in an overtime thriller on Thursday night. Nelson was a better team so that wasn't surprising. Close game, though. Sometimes you never know.

I was so pumped up before the game against Castlegar. Like when you shake a can of Orange Crush before you drink it. I closed my eyes and tried to get Rex's electricity into me. I think it came, too. I got a goal in the second period but the game wasn't going as easily as we had hoped. Our goalie played like Bunny Larocque. Finally we got the lead with five minutes to go in the third period. I got an assist on that goal. I did one of my fancy-dancy drop passes that Coach told me not to do. The best player didn't even stop the pass. He just shot it right into the corner.

I hit the goal post a few seconds later. That would have been a two-goal lead. With two minutes to go in the game our goalie went out of his crease to get the puck and he tripped just like Phil Esposito when he was introduced to the Russians and he skated out from the blueline and fell over. That's what happened to our goalie except the game was on! The Castlegar player had a wide-open net. That was that. He just skated out from behind the net and shot it in. We couldn't believe it. The game was tied with one minute and forty-two seconds to play. Tied, against Castlegar! One of their players—their big boy, with a brain like a big boy (no brain)—skated up to our goalie and started laughing his head off. The referee gave him a penalty for unsportsmanlike conduct. Their big boy went crazy and threw his stick. The referee gave him a ten-minute misconduct. What a break for us.

Coach sent out the power play and I went to jump over the boards when I felt his hand pull me back. I looked at him. He didn't say anything but I wasn't on the power play. I could see my dad in the crowd. Oh, man, I thought. Don't get too mad. I was mad too! One minute to go!

The best player took the face-off at centre ice. He pushed the puck through their centreman's legs and took off like Cournoyer. Their defenceman pushed him into the corner and then a couple of other players went in after the puck. The best player got the puck and passed it back to our defenceman. The puck bounced right over his stick and

Castlegar's speediest player got a breakaway. You should have seen him. Little legs but they were moving like Ted the dog's and his hockey pants were too big and his helmet kept falling over his eyes and he kept pushing it up with one hand and with the other hand on his stick he pushed the puck ahead. He had his head down the whole time.

I was yelling to our goalie, "Poke-check him! Poke-check him!" Our best player took off after him but he was so far behind he couldn't catch up. One on one on our goalie. Come on, poke-check! Poke-check! The speediest player deked to his backhand but the puck rolled off his stick and slipped right into the far corner of the net while the speedy little guy wiped out and fell into the boards. Castlegar scored short-handed!

We were the best team! How could this be happening?

Our big boy rammed that little guy into the boards so hard after the goal I couldn't believe it. The little guy was so excited he got up like he hadn't even felt it and threw his gloves into the air and the whole Castlegar team jumped off the bench and piled on top of him. All season we'd clobbered Castlegar and now with twenty-two seconds left we were going to lose.

My dad was in the crowd, spinning around just like the Tasmanian Devil. "Nice f---ing power play!" That's what he yelled. He was so mad at Coach. I thought, "Don't come down to the bench." I buried my head in my shoulder pads.

Coach put me out with twenty-two seconds left. My dad yelled, "It's about f---ing time!" I thought, this is no time to be mad. Tie the game up! I thought about Rex and I thought about Cournoyer. I thought about Bill Mosienko of the Chicago Black Hawks. About fifty years ago he scored three goals in twenty-one seconds. We had twenty-two seconds and we only needed one goal.

I was going to take the face-off at centre ice. We didn't have a power play any more because our big boy got a penalty for charging when he flattened their speedy player. We pulled the goalie so we had the extra attacker. I talked to the best player before the face-off. We made a plan. I said I'd shoot the puck forward as hard as I could. The best player would take off after the puck. I'd skate as hard as I could to the front of the net. The best player would throw the puck on my stick and I would have my stick right on the ice. Boom. Tie game. That was the plan.

I bent over at centre ice for the face-off. I dug my skates in and I was ready. The referee bent his knees and dropped the puck. I swiped at it to knock it forward. The best player took off like a cannonball. The puck hit the ice and bounced right over my stick. I swiped again but their centreman whacked it all the way down the ice into our end. By the time our defenceman got to the puck to pass it back up it was too late.

We'd lost to Castlegar.

Coach was on the bench and my dad was up in the stands and they had a few words. I pretended I didn't hear and went straight to the dressing room. In the dressing room Coach told me he didn't put me on at the end because I get so carried away trying to score I forget about defence. I didn't say anything. Coach told us that all good teams face our situation. Tomorrow against Nelson we have to come out ready, he said. We have to win and we have to score eleven goals. Eleven goals! Against Nelson. And then we'd play Nelson again in the finals if they scored more than four goals. If we scored eleven goals and Nelson scored less than four goals, then we'd play Castlegar in the finals. If we scored less than eleven goals, we're out and we can forget about everything. That's how confusing a round robin gets when every team has one win and one loss. Coach said it didn't matter a donkey's ass who we played. We needed a win and we needed eleven goals. That was it.

Coach left the dressing room and slammed the door. There was yelling outside the door for a few seconds. I knew who it was. I pretended I didn't hear it. My dad yelled, "If you've got a problem with me, don't take it out on my f---ing kid!"

Coach said, "For Christ's sake, Doc, would you back off?"

One kid in the dressing room said, "I wish that guy would just shut up."

I knew who he was talking about. I didn't look up from undoing my skates. I said, "Let's just think about Nelson."

*

I watched cartoons Saturday morning. It was five-thirty and still dark out and I was watching a show called Davey and Goliath. The worst thing about watching cartoons in my dad's front room is you have to wrap yourself in a quilt because of the draft that comes through the plastic wall. I wear a full-faced tuque, too. That way only my eyes get cold, and the end of my nose. I turn on an electric heater and let it blow. It's warmer in the middle of the day and even warmer if you get the kitchen woodstove going. Until then, you better wear a tuque.

Davey and Goliath is the first cartoon that comes on TV on Saturday morning. There's this dog with this deep voice called Goliath. His owner is a boy called Davey who always wants to do something really dumb and Goliath says, "Davey, is that the right thing to do?" They're made out of Plasticine. I'd like to squish 'em like an accordion. I can't wait until it's over and Bugs Bunny comes on.

Sometimes I wake up so early on Saturday mornings I have to watch the national anthem with all these horses and Mounties, or sometimes with a bunch of kids who wear red and white clothes and look like the Canadian flag from far away. If I wake up really early I have to watch these coloured lines on the TV. Colours with one black square along the bottom.

Goliath made me think of Rex and I cried. Just sitting there I cried. Stupid Goliath lives and perfect Rex is gone. If I stop doing something I see Rex walking onto the road again. That's why I keep doing something. He was so happy to see me, licking my face. I was happy to see him, too. Super-happy. If only I wasn't looking at that stinking rink. That was the problem.

I phoned my mom after Davey and Goliath to see if Rex had been back but I woke up her boyfriend. That didn't go over so well. My mom took the phone from him and she was nice. She said he hadn't come back. I told her we lost to Castlegar last night and we have to score eleven goals against Nelson to stay alive. She sounded like she wanted to be interested. I could tell she wasn't. My mom wouldn't know eleven goals from a pair of touchdowns. She still calls baseball rounders, which is what they call it in England. But she's not in England any more even if she wishes she was. That was pretty much the conversation.

I watched Bugs Bunny and it was the one where that

bum finds the dancing frog and he thinks he's going to be a millionaire. The frog kicks up his legs like a chorus dancer and he wears a top hat and he sings Hello My Baby, Hello My Honey. But when that frog is put in front of an audience he just sits there and goes ribbit. Like Guy Lafleur since junior. They thought he was going to be as good as Big Jean Béliveau. He only got twenty-eight goals last year and he's doing worse this year. The bum who carries the frog around goes crazy because he's seen what that frog can do but the frog never comes through when an audience is watching. The guy stops shaving. He stops washing. He wants something so bad but he can't get it.

That's when my dad woke up. He walked into the front room barenaked. He sat down in his big chair but before I knew it he had his sheepskin jacket on and a pair of slippers. Nothing on his dink. At least my dink has a tuque. Plus I wear underwear, longjohns and pants. His dink is right out there facing the winter.

We watched a couple more cartoons and we had a pretty good laugh. Bugs had to stop a Martian with sneakers from blowing up the earth with his Illudium Pew-36 Explosive Space Modulator. Bugs said, "Say, listen, Doc, why are you going to blow up the earth?" That Martian had the funniest voice in the world. He said, "Because it's blocking my view of Venus." Did we laugh. If my mom could just see us sitting there laughing, man, she'd want to be here too.

It's pretty good when you watch TV with my dad. If my dad is watching golf on TV or reading about psychology, you can pretty much do what you want around the house. I can practise my shot or draw or read Tintin books or hockey magazines. But if my dad is working around the house, that's when you better be working too. If he cleans up the kitchen and you didn't help, you're in for a rough day. Don't be watching Gilligan's Island while he works downstairs, that's for sure. He'll yank the plug right out of the wall.

*

Coach played me and the best player about forty minutes of the game against Nelson. My dad yelled out, "Now you're coaching to f---ing win!" Nelson tried to play defensive but we were like worker ants when you spill jam on the counter. We scored three goals in the first ten minutes and Nelson acted like the ice had broken through and their whole team was drowning. At the end of the first period it was 5-1 and we knew we had a chance. Coach even pulled our goalie at 4-1—in the first period! He kept yelling, "Goals! Goals!" You can't imagine how fun it is playing for goals. I scored with twelve seconds left in the period. Perfect pass from the best player. Right across the crease. I pushed it in before their goalie could even move. After I scored the team went crazy. We knew! It's so perfect when you know you can.

Some of the Castlegar team came in to watch the game. We could see them in their blue and white hockey jackets. You should've seen their faces as we started popping in the goals like we were playing street hockey. At the beginning of the second period our big boy skated about forty feet across the ice to hit the fastest player on the Nelson team. The Nelson player stepped out of the way just in time. Our big boy went into the boards and down he went. I thought he might go through the boards like Bugs Bunny. He didn't.

The boards won. The big boy didn't get up. Being playoffs, my dad came down onto the ice. Big boy was lying there on his back.

He looked up and said, "Everything's blurry!" My dad lifted his head and the big boy said, "I can't feel my feet, Doc!" My dad twisted his ankle and the big boy said, "Ow. That smarts."

My dad said, "Well, which is it? Eyes or feet?" In the end we had to get the stretcher.

It was both.

That meant one thing. When the big boy came back, he'd be mad as a bulldog. We kept playing without him. Coach wouldn't let me and the best player off the ice. We bombed their goalie just like the Nazis did to England when my dad was a kid. Pucks were hitting the twine, too. My assist was just like Cournoyer. I was zooming down the right wing when their defenceman turned to hit me. I stopped on a dime. He went flying. I left him five cents' change and passed the puck to the littlest guy on our team. Hard worker but no skills and no strength. It was his first shift. He shot without thinking and that puck flew all over the place like a butterfly. Handcuffed the goalie and went right past him. I felt pretty good for the little guy. When he plays on my line I hate it normally because he's no good. I felt different today.

By the end of the second period it was 8-4. Three more goals and we were in the finals.

Sure enough, in the dressing room at the end of the period the big boy was getting ready to come back. His back wasn't broken after all. He didn't eat a slice of orange. He ate the whole orange without even peeling it. He bit into it like a peach. We all laughed but he wasn't fooling. "Those bastards!" That's what he yelled. You could see the smoke coming out of his ears. In the first minute of the third period our big boy ploughed right through their defence and let go with a slapshot that their goalie didn't even see. Nobody saw it. I'm surprised it didn't burn a hole in the net. Nine-four with nineteen minutes to go.

It wasn't even close. Coach pulled the goalie again to give us an extra attacker. Nelson scored two goals into our empty net but we scored three with ten minutes still to go. You should have seen the Castlegar guys up in the crowd with their blue jackets. They couldn't believe it. Like me when Dryden quit. Crying buckets of salt water. Too bad. That's what I say. We won 13-7. I got three goals and the best player got five. Five goals! Even Yvan Cournoyer doesn't score five goals. Rocket Richard did once. All five. Montreal beat the Toronto Make Believes 5-1 and Rocket Richard got all five goals and all three stars. Imagine the Rocket's dad that night.

I was pretty happy with three goals. I wanted to think about the B.C. Championships but Coach said we still have to play Nelson again tomorrow. Don't forget what happened our first game against Castlegar, he said. I hadn't. I hadn't forgot about the power play Coach didn't put me out on against Castlegar, either. That's the thing about a coach. When you've got a coach they can do whatever they want and you're stuck. All you can do is sit there. Even if it's the dumbest move in the world.

*

The next day we blitzed Nelson 7-2.

The Trail Peewee Reps were the West Kootenay champions. We were expected to win from the beginning so it was a huge relief.

I'm just glad we clobbered them in the final.

Next stop, the Kootenay finals. It'll probably be Cranbrook.

The team didn't practise Wednesday after school. I ate dinner and then went out to play street hockey with my religious friend. When I got to his house they were still eating so I stood in the foyer waiting. It was pretty dark in that foyer. Not bad dark—sort of shady and brown like a forest. Everything was wood. The floor. The staircase. The walls. Winter coats with their hoods and their furry collars were hanging up everywhere. Some still wet and musty and thick. Boots and mittens were on the rubber mat. The end of the daylight was shining through four little panes on the big wood door and right onto my religious friend's sister's blouse that was hanging over the railing and was a perfect colour like purple tulips poking through the winter snow. The arms were hanging over on one side of the railing and the rest of the shirt was hanging down the other side.

I didn't even think. My gloves and stick fell out of my hands and I reached forward and sniffed it like you might sniff Yorkshire pudding when it comes out of the oven. It smelled perfect, like an angel would smell. You smell that and you want to marry it. I sniffed it just like Rex would have done. That's what I am. Part dog.

I touched the blouse, too. Like if you were petting a rabbit. It was like a velvet painting only no paint. I felt all funny but good. Like when you score a goal you forget everything bad.

Right then my religious friend's mom yelled from the kitchen, "Are you sure you don't want some dinner?"

I jumped so high I could have won the high-jump gold medal at the Olympics. "No, no, thanks," I said.

My religious friend's dad said, "Come on, son, come on in and have some sauerkraut. Put hair on your chest."

Even though I have no hair I said, "No, thank you. My boots take about eleven years to take off and about twenty-seven years to tie up again."

I heard them laugh. I picked up my gloves and my hockey stick as fast as I could.

"I know why he won't come in," said the angel smell with the angel voice even sweeter than Danny Gallivan. My heart started bouncing like a basketball but super-fast—like when Curly the bald guy from the Harlem Globetrotters does that dribbling really close to the ground. "You forgot to iron your pants again, didn't you?" she said.

My face got that poison ivy feeling and my mouth smiled about as wide as a Frisbee. They couldn't see me but they all laughed. My religious friend's sister wasn't being mean. The way she said it was perfect. That's when I noticed God hanging on that little wooden cross on the wall. The light made his silver body all shiny just like the blades on my CCM Super Tacks.

After a while I sat down on the stairs in the foyer. It was quiet like in the morning when you wake up and the sun hasn't come up yet. I could hear the sounds of everybody eating and mumbling and laughing. I watched the snow melt off my Arctic boots. I looked at God and I thought about everything.

Just sitting there in the quiet I looked around. I could have stayed there forever.

*

155

I was walking home from school with my Negro friend on Friday when my brother drove by in his car. It's a blue Datsun 510. Same colour as the Pittsburgh Penguin shirts except no penguin.

My brother said, "You wanna ride?"

It was freezing out. I said, "Man, you bet!"

When we got in the car I asked my brother about Rex. He didn't even answer me. He said, "Check this out." My brother has an eight-track cassette tape player right in his car. You just push that little box into the machine and it plays music. He said it was in stereo. That's twelve times better than when it's not. He had a song on called Smokin' in the Boys' Room. My brother doesn't even smoke but it was good. The guy singing says, "Sittin' in the classroom thinkin' it's a drag, listenin' to the teacher well it just ain't my bag."

My Negro friend said, "Man, that's the truth."

I wished I would've said that. It was perfect. Sitting in the classroom is a drag. You don't want to go to school in the morning and you can't wait to go home in the after-noon.

We had to do an essay about Rudolf Hess. He was that guy who took off on Hitler the Nazi and crashed in a plane like Bashing Bill Barilko. Rudolf Hess lived, though. He crashed in Scotland right near where my teacher grew up. Scotland is right near England where I was born.

Our teacher said we had to decide if Rudolf Hess was a traitor or not. Then we had to write about another traitor from history like Benedict Arnold. I wrote about Ken Dryden. Our teacher was pretty mad. I said Ken Dryden was a big traitor who didn't care about anyone.

Our teacher said, "Sit down!"

I said, "He just quit hockey. For no reason!"

The teacher said, "Sit down!"

I said, "They lost to the Atlanta Flames!" Before I could even mention the part about Bunny Larocque's rickets I was sitting down at my desk.

My teacher doesn't know anything about hockey.

We had to write a report on what we want to be when we're older. I told him I wanted to play pro. He told me that I have to think of something else. I said, "No. I'm going to play pro in the NHL." He got so mad. He said he was sick of hearing about hockey. Then he lied and said lacrosse is Canada's national sport.

Driving with my brother, we turned a corner and the door flew open and me and my Negro friend almost flew out.

My brother said, "Oh, yeah, that door is f---ed."

We hung on a little tighter after that. My brother didn't have any winter tires so we slid all the way down to Happy Valley where my friend's house is. We were happy all right, happy to get there.

When my brother dropped us off he made us both pay him a nickel for gas. He said, "Sorry, man, gas shortage. Pay up."

I didn't have any money with me so my friend went inside and got a dime. My brother's right about gas. This show sometimes comes on in the middle of cartoons called In the News. It's a couple of minutes long like a commercial. They show this world spinning and the music goes, di-di-di-di-di-di-di....this is: In the News. Like that. They showed a million Arabs on the news screaming and yelling and burning an American flag. Those people scare me like Nazis. They showed pictures of the gas shortage in the United States of America, too. Cars lined up for about three hundred miles at a gas station. People were getting out of their cars and saying, "This is crazy."

I couldn't believe it. I thought you could get anything you wanted in the United States of America. Maybe you still can but now you have to line up for it.

*

The Cranbrook Peewee Reps had to come into our arena for the Kootenay Championships. It was best two out of three. Friday night, Saturday afternoon and Sunday if necessary. I bet the Cranbrook team was shaking after they heard about how we clobbered Nelson in those two games.

On Friday night I scored two goals in the first period but we were losing 5-4 when the third period started. In the dressing room before the third period Coach took an orange right out of the best player's dad's hand, just as he was going to cut it up for us to eat, and threw it against the wall as hard as he could. It splattered everywhere. He yelled, "Follow the system! Two men in, one back. That's how we forecheck!"

I hear Coach say that but I never remember on the ice. If I have a chance to go after the puck, two men in and one back doesn't mean anything to me. I think, Goal! After that Coach sits me on the bench for a shift but I still don't remember. Against Cranbrook I even followed their defenceman behind the net once. He took off the other way and that was it. I said to myself, Dumb move. You should never follow someone behind the net unless you know you can catch him. You go one way, he goes the other. Before you know it you're backchecking. My dad yelled, "Dumb move! Get your head in the f---ing game!" Two minutes later I did one of my fancy-dancy drop passes that went past everyone and their fastest player got a breakaway. That was the goal that made it 5-4 for them. Coach said, "I said no more goddamn drop passes! Play like a Canadian!" Coach didn't complain at all when I gave that perfect fancy-dancy drop pass to the best player and he scored against Castlegar. That's the thing about fancy-dancy stuff. If it works, everybody's your friend.

Coach hardly played me at all in the third period. Our big boy got injured again. He skated after one of their players who was behind their own goal. Our big boy was going straight down the middle of the ice. When he got close to the net at about two hundred miles an hour you could tell he hadn't decided which way to go yet. At the last minute he changed his mind. As he cut across the net his skates went one way and his body the other. He caught the goal post. Flew about twenty feet, like Bobby Orr when he scored the Stanley Cup winner in overtime, only our big boy flew right into the backboards. He didn't move at all. He just lay there like Dracula in his coffin.

My dad came out on the ice in his boots and his sheepskin jacket and gave him some smelling salts.

Suddenly our big boy yelled, "I'm going to throw up!"

My dad said, "You're fine."

Big boy threw up. I didn't know anybody could eat that much. All over the front of the Smoke Eater emblem on his shirt and onto the ice. Nibs, spaghetti, macaroni, corn, hot dogs. I wanted to say, "Coach, are we still playing for what's on the front of our shirts?" I didn't say it. Two

159

things you never do during a game is joke or smile. You can smile if you score, but not for very long. You score. You hug your teammates. You smile. You look up at the clock to see what the score is. Then you frown again and spit. You can spit as much as you want. But don't crack jokes, especially if you're losing.

The throw-up took about ten minutes to scrape off the ice. It froze pretty fast. Right after that our best player scored to tie up the game. He went through the whole team like Gilbert Perreault. Head fakes and fake slapshots.

Two minutes later I assisted on a goal on a two-on-one. I passed to the best player right through the defenceman's legs. The best player deked the goalie but he went too far. He didn't care. He went all the way around the net and jammed it in the other side. That was with three minutes to play.

Cranbrook pulled their goalie in the last minute. I didn't get on the ice for that. Coach said, "I'd put you out there but who knows? You'd probably do one of those Russian back passes." I should've taken the face-off at least. The best player took it in our end and lost it clean. They got a clear shot and it hit the goal post. The goal post! The puck bounced right to the best player and he shot it all the way down the ice for an empty-netter. Three goals to win the game. Man, was his dad proud. We all jumped up on the bench and we were happy but I was a little mad. I looked back at Coach and he looked at me. He grinned. It was a funny grin. Crooked. With his eyes, too. I knew what he was thinking. "That's the last time I don't put you out when it matters. It almost cost us a second time." Both me and Coach knew I should've taken that face-off. My dad knew, too. I looked up and his arms were crossed. His girl-friend couldn't even uncross them. He was shaking his head. "You're f---ing lucky! You almost f---ing blew it again!" All the other parents were clapping.

We were one game from the B.C. Championships. One game closer to a second chance.

*

We won. We beat Cranbrook 4-2. I should be happier but I played about as good as Bunny Larocque. My dad told me I play good one night and I'm a piece of shit the next. Once when I was sort of coasting in the middle of the game my dad yelled out, "Keep your f---ing legs in motion!" Right away I pictured Fred Flintstone when he's about to run. He pumps those tree-trunk legs of his so fast you can't even see them but he's still not moving. Then *boom*! He's gone.

I wasn't watching the puck when I thought that and I got another backhander in the face. This time in the chin. Two stitches and no points in the second game. All this great equipment and I couldn't get one point in the biggest game of the season. I couldn't stop thinking about my religious friend's sister and Fred Flintstone and Dryden and how that big clock hangs over the arena. I don't know how they got it up there or how they fix it when a light burns out. Big wires hold it up but I don't stand under it too much any-way.

My dad knew I was dreaming. Just like my teacher knew my dad wrote that note about his thumb. "Get your head in the game!" That's what my dad kept yelling. He was yelling at the referee, too. "Where's your seeing-eye dog! You're teaching the kids to lie!" He yelled at Coach too, and all the other players. He got in a shouting match with a couple of parents when he called one of the kids chicken shit. He was pacing all over the place.

That was it. We won. The Trail Smoke Eater Peewee Reps were the Kootenay champions.

Bring on the B.C.s.

*

Peter Puck got cancelled right in the middle of the hockey game on Hockey Night in Canada. Peter Puck is a cartoon puck with skates and a face and in between periods he tells the viewers about icing and off-side. Everybody in Canada except English women already know that stuff. Peter Puck drawings are so dumb. All the players look like blockheads and they never give them real uniforms. Blue-and-white and red-and-white shirts and socks. That's it. Peter Puck tells us about some playoff guy in NHL history and the team isn't even wearing the real colours of the uniform he played in. Sometimes Peter Puck tells us what it's like to be a puck and get whacked around with a stick at a hundred miles an hour. He says how much it hurts to get whacked like that. That's how dumb this cartoon is. Everybody knows it's way harder on the sticks. Who's ever seen a puck break? Sticks go flying all the time.

Peter Puck got stopped for the news. A report about the President of the United States that says he's a pretty rotten guy.

"F---ing crook" is what my dad said. But the President said he wasn't a crook.

The news said a bunch of guys were in trouble for covering up a bunch of stuff about a watergate. I don't even know what a watergate is but there's a lot of people in trouble about it.

I said, "What's a watergate?"

My dad said, "That's when we get to see what a bunch of crooks our politicians are. I knew Nixon was a crook the minute he went to China."

I don't know what was going on with China, but I heard the word lawyer about ten times. I looked for Ken Dryden but there was no sign of him. I thought maybe he'd be wearing his Montreal Canadiens shirt.

I said, "Dad, what's a lawyer?"

My dad said, "A guy who takes all your money and then says you're free to go."

"Go where?"

"Never trust a lawyer," my dad said.

I don't. They're traitors.

"And keep your f---ing stick on the ice," he said. "You could have had three goals against Cranbrook."

I was still thinking about Dryden.

"You've got everything it takes to be the best," my dad said.

I didn't say anything.

"What the hell do you think about out there?"

I didn't say Fred Flintstone or my religious friend's sister. I said, "Dad, how come God's silver?"

"What are you talking about? Watch the game. Watch Lemaire. Watch how he always keeps his legs moving."

"Does God make people quieter, Dad?"

"No," my dad said. "Stupider."

The news had ended by then and the game was back on. I could barely watch it as time ran out at the Montreal Forum. My dad was downstairs yelling at himself and I felt sick. The Montreal crowd looked like those fish you catch and then hang on a stick. They were staring. They couldn't believe that Montreal was losing again. They couldn't believe Dryden didn't care. They booed, too. Montreal lost 3-2 to the California Golden Seals! The California Golden Seals wear white skates like Karen Magnussen. California is the worst team in history. Montreal has given up without Dryden. The whole team is yelling at each other. I'm serious. The Big M Frank Mahovlich hates the coach. He might even jump to the WHA, he hates him so much.

In the second-period intermission the announcer said the Montreal Canadiens have a Russian coming to their training camp next year! I asked my dad what his name was and my dad said, "Ivan Yourpantsaroff." He thought that was pretty funny. It's about as funny as wearing a sheepskin jacket and no pants in the house. I can't even have my religious friends over! I don't find that funny. A Russian left-winger. He'll probably be best friends with my mom's boyfriend. Just because of Ken Dryden. Montreal does not need a left-winger! Montreal has tons of left-wingers. They need a goalie. Dryden quits hockey and now the Russians are coming.

Since Ken Dryden quit the Montreal Canadiens? Rex is dead. Hobey is dead. The rink won't freeze. I missed the open net.

I yelled out, "F---er!" after the game ended. Just like that. I was talking about Dryden.

From downstairs my dad told me to take it easy.

If I could only keep my head in the game everyone would stop yelling. That's the answer. My dad says I'm the best player when I do that.

I'll do that at the B.C. Championships. I gotta.

After dinner I went down to my religious friend's house and we got a game of street hockey going. As soon as we picked teams I yelled out, "We're the Montreal Canadiens and I'm Yvan Cournoyer!"

My Negro friend said, "Who cares? They stink!"

Ha ha ha ha ha ha ha.

I said, "Take that back or I'm taking my net home."

He said, "If you're Montreal then we're the California Golden Seals!" Ha ha ha ha ha ha. Then everybody laughed. I felt like that fish when he gets that hook in his jaw. My friend was only poking fun, but I went crazy. We got in a fistfight and before I knew it everybody was on top of me, hitting me and kicking me. Everybody piled on and got in that punch they've been dying to get in forever. Just like the Philadelphia Flyers and I was Dale Rolfe. I ended up with a pretty sore face because I was at the bottom of the pile, face down and pushed into the icy road. My nose was bleeding. Everybody was laughing until I got up and they saw my face. My chin was bleeding again where the stitches were. I looked like Jerry Quarry when they stopped his fight with Muhammad Ali after three rounds and his face looked like a pepperoni pizza. There was blood on my Montreal Canadiens shirt, which you could barely see because my shirt was red. My Negro friend didn't laugh when he saw my face. He said, "Maybe they'll do better in the playoffs."

I didn't say anything. I couldn't think.

"I was just joking," he said. "I think they'll do great in the playoffs. Serious." He held out his hand to shake.

I didn't shake. I said, "Everybody jumped on me! Bunch of f---ers!"

The game started without me. I went inside my religious friend's house. Only my religious friend's sister was home. She took care of me just like a real nurse. Like an angel, if an angel could be a nurse. I sat on the toilet seat in their bathroom and she wiped the scab on my chin and cheek with a warm cloth. It hurt but, man, it was good too.

I found out a few more things about God. I found out his name is Jesus Christ. I'd never thought about what Jesus Christ meant. My dad yelled it enough. It turns out it's not a swear word, it's God's name. I asked her why people yell his name so mad. They're not churchgoing people, she said. I asked her if God had a family. She said he has a father in Heaven and we're all his children. I knew she got that wrong. Otherwise my last name would be Christ. I asked her who God Dammit was. She said I shouldn't say that and she closed the bathroom door and we were in there all alone. I thought maybe God Dammit was Jesus Christ's grandfather. I told her my dad yells Jesus Christ about forty-seven times a day. She said she knew that but her parents said that it wasn't up to them to judge and that they should be nice to me.

She said, "It's wrong to use the Good Lord's name in vain."

"Who's the Good Lord?"

"God," she said. "He's our saviour. He made the world."

"And he gets ticked if you yell his name?"

"He can ignore you or kill you or whatever he wants to do," she said. "You never know."

That's when I figured it out. That's when I got scared. "And who's God Dammit again?"

No answer. She didn't like to talk about God Dammit. She said, "We shouldn't talk about this any more."

We didn't have to. I knew more than I wanted to know. I knew what Tim Horton yelled just before he crashed. I knew who tripped me in Penticton, too.

Just before I went back outside, I asked my religious friend's sister where God got the energy to live again after he died—maybe I could give some of that to Rex or use it when I get a breakaway and need more speed.

My religious friend's sister looked at me strange, like Rex used to when I'd blow on his nose and he'd tilt his head to the side. She said, "If you want all these questions answered, you should come to church with us tomorrow. That's where you find out about God."

*

I couldn't sleep at all on Sunday morning. My head was spinning all over the place and it was freezing in the house and still pitch-black outside. I pulled my pants over my long underwear and my full-faced tuque over my head so all that showed was my eyes. I put on my hockey jacket too, and snuck into the front room without even using the light. I knew exactly where the little heater was. I knew where the TV was too, off by heart. I love clicking on the TV. Especially in the dark. It flashes on like Frankenstein's brain when he gets that jolt of electricity from his doctor. It's just like you woke the TV up. Then it opens its big mouth and shows you everything good that you ever wanted to see or know.

Even though it was Sunday, I was hoping I could find Johnny Quest and Hadji or even Davey and his Plasticine dog Goliath. Anything would have been good.

But as soon as I pressed the button this guy flashed on the screen and he was jumping up and down and waving his fist in the air. And when the sound came on the man had an accent like baseball players from the United States of America. But he wasn't a baseball player. He was one of those preacher church guys my dad always makes fun of. I make fun of them, too, but this guy was serious. He would start rumbling all low. "He died for you, Sinner!" That's what he'd whisper. "Do you believe, Sinner? Do you? Sinner? Sinner?" Then crazy like my dad when Ted the dog took off with my hockey gloves. *Do you truly believe, Sinner, in the power of the Good Lord Jesus Christ?"*

Right in front of him was this shrivelled-up old guy. About four thousand years old. His face was like a piece of bark if a piece of bark had a big red nose. He was shaking and crying and his legs were dangling behind him. He was being held up by these two guys in nice suits who were bigger than Bobby Hull. The old guy threw his hands in the air and started yelling, "I believe! Lord, how I believe!"

The preacher church guy's eyes went as wide as peppermint Life Savers and as scary as Charles Manson's, who cut up all those people in California. His mouth was frothing like Old Yeller's. He yelled even louder. "With the power invested in me through the Lord Jesus Christ I command the Devil to leave your legs! *Sinner, I pronounce you saved and capable of walking again!"*

That's when the preacher man punched the old guy right in the head. I couldn't believe it. If it wasn't for the two Bobby Hull guys who caught him, he would've flown right off the stage and broken his neck. I'm serious. I thought he might be dead anyway. But as soon as they caught the old guy and lifted him up, he started shaking his head and shaking his hands. Then he started dancing like he scored a touchdown. "I can walk! I can walk! It's a miracle! I believe! Lord how I believe!"

It was a miracle. The guy hadn't walked in thirty years. That's what he said. Not since he was gunned down in the war against the Communists who hate God's guts.

Then deaf people and blind people came up. And cancer people. People with back problems and people in wheel-chairs and people with lung problems.

All whacked—*bam*—right in the noodle.

All fell over. All picked up. All cured.

Then the preacher guy who fixed them all thanks to Jesus looked right at the camera. He looked mean but he wasn't. Then he looked like he had to take a crap but he didn't. He started crying. I almost started too. He said that if we wanted to we could just put our hands on the TV set with all our hearts and get whatever we wanted. Just close your eyes. He said, "Feel the power of the Good Lord going right through you."

I didn't even think. I put my hands on the TV. Right away I could feel the electricity cracking and tingling. I never knew that was God's love. No one ever told me. I closed my eyes and I prayed about winning the B.C. Championships and my mom and dad getting back togeth-er and Bunny Larocque getting his bow legs fixed.

Then he said you could get even more if you dialled the number on the screen. Man, did I dial. Long distance to Austin, Texas. I asked for everything. Montreal winning the cup and Rex coming back from the dead and my mom and dad having a baby and a homemade rink freezing over and dinosaur bones all over the back yard and even being able to sit in the foyer at my religious friend's sister's house forever and sniff her perfect neck without being crazy!

The man on the phone said, "Slow down, pardner." He sounded just like that big rooster Foghorn Leghorn. I told him, too. Man, did we laugh. He was super-nice. He said if I sent twenty dollars I could get even more. I said I only had ten dollars. That's what I got from my grandma in England for Christmas. I stuck it right in my Everything You've Always Wanted to Know about Hockey book. Right next to the photo of Lord Stanley of Preston. He's the guy who gave Canada the Stanley Cup. Best present in the world. The man on the phone said ten dollars would be fine. I told him I once sent $1.49 to New York, New York for a secret spy-scope and you couldn't even see through it. He said Jesus is worth a billion spy-scopes. He said Jesus sees everything. He gave me the address. All I have to do is send the money right away and believe in Jesus.

I can't wait.

My dad woke up a while later and went downstairs to work on my sister's bookcase. He wants it to be for her birthday.

I knew I had to go to church more than anything. That's why I practised my wrist shot for an hour. When he came up for a cup of tea I showed him how I could hit any spot at the edge of his bed. It didn't matter where I put that pillow. I'd say, "Watch this, Dad." *Bam.* I hit it. We were talking about the B.C. Championships and keeping my stick on the ice and taking a check to make a play. After about twenty hits on the pillow I asked my dad if I could go to church. He was pretty surprised.

"I've got some God questions," I said.

"God questions? What kind of God questions?"

I just looked at him. He didn't really want to know.

He shook his head and sawdust flew everywhere. "You can go if you want," he said, "but it's a load of f---ing crap."

I thought, Crap? Tell that to the old guy who's walking for the first time in thirty years.

*

I wore my best clothes. I wore my furry snowboots and my ironed corduroys and a checkered shirt and a brown and orange tie with a sweater over it and my hockey jacket buttoned up. My dad wouldn't tie my tie. He was sanding smooth my sister's bookcase and he was covered in sawdust. He said Jesus likes slobs better anyway.

My religious friend couldn't believe it when I showed up at his door with my hair combed and no hockey stick.

His sister was there too. She smelled perfect, like Lemon Pledge.

At the church I sat right next to her like she was my linemate. I was going to be on the outside of the bench but I jumped in front of my religious friend at the last second. He looked at me like I was crazy.

I said, "Just in case I have questions. I can ask your sister."

He said, "I have a question. What the heck are you doing here?"

You should have seen the windows in that place. They were about forty-seven different colours. There were white candles, too. At the back of the church they had a gold Jesus but it was life-size, even bigger, tacked up on a gold cross all skinny and shiny like a million melted skate blades. You could see how sad he was. I guess so. Hanging there all tacked up. I'd love a big one of those in my room. I'd stick it right next to my Cournoyer poster.

Then the church guy started talking.

I was surprised to find out my folks are evil sinners. That's what the man in the church said about divorced people. When he said it my religious friend's mom looked at me and smiled like she felt sorry for me. I whispered, "Don't worry about it, they're not divorced yet."

The man in the church said divorce is an evil sin and do whatever you can to stop it from happening. You should, too. My mom told me what happened to Henry the Eighth after he got divorced. He packed on four hundred pounds. They had to lift him around with a crane. I don't think my dad has put on any weight yet.

The man in the church asked if anybody here was having troubles in their marriage. Hands went up like they were in slo-mo. I put mine up, too. I couldn't believe it. I counted eleven hands before they went down.

It got worse.

The man in the church said the end is near. I'm not surprised. I've been feeling that for a long time. The end of what, I wondered. This sinful world, he said, for those who will not change their ways. Well, I'm changing my ways. Next year I'll have a rink and skate *four* hours a day. Everything, he said, will be no more. He was serious. He had the bushiest eyebrows I've ever seen. Like rolled-up chicken wire. He said the end is near and the gas shortage proves it. All the signs are here, he said. Like those starving Negro kids on TV. And wars like on TV. I wanted to yell

out, "And missing the open net!" but I didn't. I didn't find
out who God Dammit was, either, but I was learning a lot.
Just like my religious friend's sister said I would. I learned
my folks should get back together right away. I learned that
the Good Lord and Jesus were the same people. Good Lord
was his nickname, like Roadrunner is Cournoyer's nickname. And then the man asked us if we were doing the best
we can. That's what he said. He said he'd asked himself
that a thousand times. He'd stare in the mirror as hard as
he could and say, "Are you truly doing the Will of the Good
Lord?"

When I heard that my head almost went crazy.

The will of the Good Lord! The *Good Lord* Stanley! The
Good Lord Stanley of Preston! The guy who gave us the
Stanley Cup!

He's God.

It's mental how many things you can figure out if you
just think about it.

No wonder I missed the open net!

I turned to my religious friend's sister. She didn't look
like she'd noticed a thing. I looked at her mom too. Same
thing. Nothing. Then I looked way past the man at the
church and stared at the poor, skinny gold Jesus up on that
cross. It was definitely the Good Lord Stanley when he was
younger.

It makes sense, too.

See, way back, the Good Lord gave the Stanley Cup to
Canada and then went back to England because his brother had the flu. I've read that. The part they leave out is the
Good Lord getting the flu from his brother. That's probably when he started to lose the weight. That's when they

173

took his clothes and tacked him up on that cross, probably because he liked hockey more than soccer. English people hate people who like hockey. Not just my mom. All English people. They barely even know what hockey is. They don't even call it hockey. They call it *ice* hockey.

And those buggers left the Good Lord on the cross there because he knew that hockey is the best sport in the world. They didn't want to know that. And of course he died up there. Who wouldn't? No food. No clothes. But ha ha, three days later who got recharged and flew up to Heaven? Now he's coaching up there, waiting to come back and coach us down here.

On the drive home from church I asked my religious friend's family a few questions, but I was super-careful. They knew the guy on the cross had a brother and that he died and went to Heaven. But when I asked if his name was Stanley, they all had a good laugh, ha ha. Truth is, they didn't have a clue.

I could barely talk after that. When they dropped me off I jumped out of the car and ran up the stairs into my dad's place as fast as I could. I had to tell him right away. The problem was, he was watching golf on TV. You can't talk to my dad about anything when he's watching golf.

I said, "Dad, why don't you believe in the Good Lord?"

He said, "Wha...?" He was so busy with the golf he didn't even bother putting the letter T on the end of the word.

It was about as cold as an arena in the front room and the plastic was flapping. My dad had no clothes on except for his sheepskin jacket. He was watching the golf and dipping his cookies in his tea. He didn't even look over.

I said, "Dad, why don't you believe in the Good Lord?"

He said, "Because there is no Good Lord." Then he stuffed that cookie in his mouth.

For the first time I started to get mad. "Think about why Dryden quit, Dad."

That's when he looked over. "Jesus Christ! What are you on about?"

"Dad, you say Jesus Christ way too much." That's what I said back—super-fast and pipsqueaky like Oliver when he asked Mr. Bumble for more food.

My dad looked at me like he couldn't believe what I was saying. That's when the crowd on the TV yelled. He looked back at the TV. "I missed the putt. I missed the f---ing putt!"

I'm talking about God and he's worried about golf! He's gone nuts without my mom. Just like Henry the Eighth did.

"Dad, I've seen photos. The Good Lord is as real as Cournoyer."

"You've seen photos of God?" he said.

"And he's not smiling," I said back.

My dad grinned. "Those aren't photos. Those are old paintings."

"*Photos*, Dad. Black and white. He has a grey moustache and a beard and he's going bald."

My dad laughed his head off. "Well, I hope he gets a better toupee than Bobby Hull."

I said, "If there's no Good Lord, how do you explain his family back in England?"

My dad thought that was hilarious.

He was doing just what the man at church said the evil ones would do. That's what they did to Noah. They laughed at him. But they weren't laughing when they were treading water and the Ark floated by with all their pets on board.

I looked straight at my dad. He was just about to put a dunked cookie in his mouth. He stopped and it broke off and fell into his tea.

He said, "Yes, my son?" He thought that was hilarious too, and he laughed even more. I was pretty scared for him.

"Dad, think about what I'm saying."

My dad tried to stop laughing but he couldn't.

That's when I pictured the Good Lord Stanley way up there shaking his head, looking as sad as he did when he was tacked up on that cross. I felt sad, too. I said, "I can't make you believe, Dad, but we at least have to figure out a way to stop this divorce or I'll never make pro."

That stopped him laughing.

Stopped him cold.

*

My teacher was madder than Yosemite Sam when he got the note saying I had to miss two days of school for hockey. He phoned my dad and that was the last I heard about it. I guess they don't play sports in Scotland. Who cares what my teacher thinks? The only thing he's ever wanted to teach me is how I can't make pro. He's never come to one game and he thinks he knows. Only my dad believes in me. Problem is, he swears so much God'll probably cut off my legs in a car accident and throw me in the Columbia River. With God around, you make one mistake, or your dad says the wrong thing—*boom*. Car crash. Bike crash. Miss the open net. So long. That's why I felt pretty good once I'd sent that ten bucks to Texas.

The team practised Monday, Tuesday and Wednesday.

One time in the practice I was skating as hard as I could for a pass but I couldn't reach it. The puck was too far ahead. It was a crummy pass. Coach yelled, "Jesus Christ! Get your goddamn ass in gear!" I stopped right where I was, right at centre ice, and looked straight up.

Coach yelled, "What the hell are you doing? Why the hell are you staring at the goddamn clock!"

I wasn't staring at the clock. I was looking up at God. That's where my religious friend's sister said God was.

I said, "Stanley, that Jesus Christ was not my fault." It wasn't. I was moving my legs as fast as Ted the dog.

Coach said, "God dammit. Get down and give me twenty."

He meant push-ups. I didn't mind. I got away with eighteen.

I figured something else out, too. If you want to be a great pro you have to drop out of school. Sooner the better. Gordie Howe quit school. So did Bobby Hull. Cournoyer dropped out of school too. They all had an outdoor rink and they all dropped out of school. The only one who didn't was Ken Dryden. He went all the way to college like my dad.

But Dryden's a traitor.

And a quitter.

I asked my dad if I could drop out of school to concentrate on hockey. He said, "At least wait until you finish grade six." So I've got a few more months of school left and that's it. Then I can concentrate on hockey full-time. I'm already a good reader. That's all you need to know to play pro. You don't need the Ancient Greece stuff. What does Gordie Howe know about Ancient Greece? You need a few

French words to play for the Montreal Canadiens. *Salut.*
Troisième étoile. Gardien du but. You have to be able to
read menus so you can order the pre-game meal when
you're in Pittsburgh or Los Angeles. You have to be able to
understand what it means when there's eight minutes and
twelve seconds left in the game. I know that. I know how
to work out goals-against averages. That's it. In the winters
I'll play hockey. In the summers I'll work for my dad's
farmer friend and bale hay and get arms like Bobby Hull.

Rink, school, family and the Good Lord Stanley. That's
all that matters now.

The Trail Peewee Reps were on their way to the B.C. Championships.

This was my chance to make up for the open net against Penticton and everything else. I was happy to be forgetting about the Montreal Canadiens for a while, too. In their last three games they'd lost 3-2 to the California Golden Seals, 6-nothing to Philadelphia and 9-2—*again*—to the New York Rangers. I'm just glad the best player doesn't remember I said I'd eat my jockstrap if they ever lost 9-2 again. I don't plan to remind him, either. If he remembers, I'll have to eat it. Stitch by stitch would be the only way.

The B.C. Championships are in Vancouver, which is the biggest city around. It's about ten hours away from Trail and they even have McDonald's there.

Riding down on the team bus, I found out the best player's family is Catholic . They go to church every few weeks. In between hockey questions, I asked him what church was like.

"Boring," he said.

The best player didn't know a thing about Jesus Christ. He knew more about the Montreal Maroons and nobody knows anything about the Montreal Maroons. The Montreal Maroons stopped being a team about twelve million years ago. The best player thought that Jesus Christ was sort of God and that he got a lot of presents as a baby and that's why we have Christmas. I asked him if he knew if God Dammit was Jesus Christ's father or grandfather. He said, "I'm a hockey player. How many shut-outs did Terry Sawchuck get?"

"You've asked me that before. A hundred and three."

"Okay, okay," he said. "How'd he die?"

I looked at him. "Everybody dies."

He looked at me.

"This bus could crash," I said. "If it crashes, forget about wagging your tail again."

He grinned. "You don't know how Sawchuck died, do you?"

"As if. Terry Sawchuck got in a fight with Ron Stewart in his back yard and fell on a barbecue."

The best player couldn't believe it. He shook his head and said, "I guess he was cooked after that, eh?"

Man, that was funny. Not for Terry Sawchuck. I said, "I bet I know what Sawchuck yelled just before he landed on that barbecue."

"Pass the ketchup," the best player said.

We laughed again, but I know what Terry Sawchuck really said. Same thing Tim Horton said just before he crashed his car.

I can't even say the words but the initials are J.C.

We looked back at the rest of the players on the bus and shook our heads. Like always, they were laughing and talking about stuff that didn't matter.

Me and the best player looked at each other. I said, really quiet and serious, "Hey, you think we can win?"

"The B.C.s?" he said.

I looked right at him.

"I think we can. Why can't we?" he said.

I didn't say anything.

I think we can, too.

*

Almost all the parents came down to the B.C. Championships. My dad was there with his young girlfriend. They mostly hung around on their own. Me and my dad had a bit of a fight. I asked him if he had to say J. C. so much.

He said, "What are you talking about?"

"J.C.," I said. "You say it too much. That's probably why Tim Horton died."

"What the hell are you talking about?"

"Dad, I already told you this. You say Jesus Christ too much."

My dad stared at me. He blinked. "I'm forty-five years old," he said. "Did you know that?"

I nodded.

"I'm your father. Did you know that?"

I nodded.

"I pay for your food. I pay for your skates. I pay for everything. Did you know that?"

"Yeah."

"Good. Now shut up. Jesus Christ."

He didn't know how dangerous that was. I said, "Well, if you say it, could you only say it when the puck is around centre ice?"

He looked at me like I was crazy. That's what happens when you talk about God. People think you're crazy.

"Dad, who's God Dammit?"

My dad turned to his young girlfriend. "And you wonder why I yell."

There was a big ceremony before our first game on

181

Friday against Fort St. John. All the players got introduced
and had to skate out from the blueline to centre ice and
then back again. They played the national anthem on a
record player but at the very end it started to skip. It's supposed to end *stand on God for thee*, but it just said *stand
on God, stand on God, stand on God* about forty-two
times until some guy lifted the needle. I didn't know if that
was a good sign or a bad one.

Fort St. John were the Northern B.C. champions. That's
all we knew. We knew we were ready, too. Coach went
with two lines and we came out like a pack of Cournoyers.
It was the best game our team ever played and the best
game I ever played. We won 11-2. I scored four goals. They
picked a Most Valuable Player for the game. Guess what?
Me. I couldn't believe it. Nobody had ever said I deserved
anything except my dad. Most of the time he said I
deserved a kick in the ass. When I got the MVP given to me
at centre ice I looked up at my dad. He was standing in the
crowd but by himself, next to his young girlfriend.

That's when I figured it out.

My dad had the same face he always has. The same broken cheek like a sea when there's a big storm and the waves
are crashing. The same sheepskin jacket. The same long
brown hair with grey streaks like Charlie Rich.

But there was one thing different.

My dad had an eensy smile on his face. I knew I had seen
that smile before but I didn't know where. Then I remembered. It was the same eensy smile the best player's dad got
when the best player scored in overtime. When the best
player won the tournament first all-star centre. When the
best player scored a goal. Or even when he didn't. That's

when I figured it out. If I was the best player I don't think my dad would yell at my mom any more. If I was the best player he'd never say Jesus Christ again.

That's when I figured out another thing about all the best players: Gordie Howe. Bobby Hull. Yvan Cournoyer. Even our best player.

Their folks stay married no matter what.

That's when I knew my mom and dad had to be together.

I knew what I had to do, too.

*

There were five guys in each hotel room. In my room we had the big boy, the best player, the back-up goalie, one of the shrimpy wingers with no skill and me. We talked about the game and about playing the Vancouver Island champions in the morning. The goalie was showing off the jack-knife he'd shoplifted from the Army and Navy store. It had about forty-two blades. It even had scissors and a magnifying glass and a spoon and fork. The handle looked like it was made from wood but it was plastic. He's the best shoplifter on the team. I never shoplift. Once I took a packet of miniature Chiclets—the purple and yellow ones. My mom saw me chewing like a cow in the car. She said, Where'd you get the gum? I said, from in the store.

"Did you pay for it?"

"No."

She made me take them back all chewed. That was the last time I ever stole anything.

Me and the best player quizzed each other with a couple of questions. The whole time I had my MVP medallion around my neck. The medal was gold and it said MVP on it. The bit around my neck was red, white and blue.

A couple of the guys snuck out to the pop machine and got cans of pop. They got some ice, too. I don't know what for. It was there in the ice machine so it was pretty cool to just take it. The big boy stubbed his toe on the pop machine. We heard him yell all the way down the hallway. The goalie was with the big boy and he had to drag the big boy back over his shoulder. The big boy fell on the floor. He was moaning. He thought he broke his toe. It wasn't even bleeding. We all started laughing. He said, "F--- you!" and stood up and went into the bathroom and slammed the door. That's when Coach came in and said, "Biggest game of your lives tomorrow, gang. Lights out."

After he left, we talked for a while but pretty soon everything went quiet except for the little winger with no skill. He coughed every two and a half seconds. I was on a cot and I just lay there thinking about the game. That's when I started to feel something coming up. It was that crazy bat. He was back and flying around my throat. I got all sweaty and pretty soon I was in the bathroom throwing up. I don't think anybody heard me. Everything came up, though. The Big Mac. A small fries. My throat was sandpaper. Lying in the cot I felt cold and then hot.

I kept picturing the Columbia River. It's so big and black you can't believe it. I pictured Hobey and his eyes were swirling like the Columbia River just before that diesel hit him.

I threw up again. Strawberry milkshake. Apple pie. That was it. After that it was yellow. I just lay there in my gonch on my back on the bathroom floor, wondering why I was throwing up yellow stuff. I couldn't even move. Then more yellow stuff. I got goose bumps so I pulled a towel down and put it over me. That's how they found me in the morning.

At the arena at the North Shore Winter Club my dad checked me out. I was getting dressed for the game against Victoria. My nose was plugged but I was ready to go. The best player's dad gave me an extra slice of orange. He didn't say anything. He just winked. Salt tablet and sugar tablet. No water. Coach was giving us a speech about how we hadn't won anything yet. It's not who wins the first game that matters, he said, it's who wins the last game. He said, Two in and one back, two in and one back. Finish your checks. One of their players makes a pass, hit him to let him know you appreciate his good work. No dumb penalties! We're not playing for the name on the back of our shirts, we're...that's when coach waited. We all yelled, "We're playing for what's on the front of our shirts!"

"Who are we?"

"Smoke Eaters!"

"Who are we?"

"Smoke Eaters!"

"Who are we?"

"Smoke Eaters!"

Coach put his fist in the air and yelled, "We are the Trail Smoke Eater Peewee Reps! Now get out there and beat the shit out of those guys!" We all cheered and started walking out of the dressing room. We had this chant. It goes like this: "I don't know but it's been said, Victoria's balls are made of lead! I don't know but I've been told, Trail's balls are made of gold!"

That's when I started thinking about my balls and the

operation I'd had and the big smelter in Trail called Cominco. It's a zinc plant. And lead. No gold.

On the first shift of the game I got cross checked with the stick right in the chin. Knocked me flying. I think it even knocked me out. I guess I was still feeling sick, too, because the whole first period all I could think about was Cominco and those chants. I made up a whole bunch of chants: "I don't know but I think, Trail's balls are made of zinc!" I thought that would have been better. One made me laugh. "Almost everybody's dad works on the hill, and when we win they'll work there still!" That's what they say when your dad works at Cominco. He works on the hill.

I didn't stop thinking about those chants until my dad reached over the bench and grabbed me by the shoulder pads. I jumped about forty feet. I didn't even see him come down from the stands. He grabbed my Smoke Eater shirt with both hands. "Get your head in the f---ing game!" Spit was spraying everywhere like the Tasmanian Devil.

Coach said, "Do I need this? To hell I need this!"

My dad yelled, "All the way to Vancouver! Jesus Christ!"

"Doc, I'm coachin' here!" That's what Coach said.

My dad let go and I fell back down on the bench. My dad was right, though. Not only that, *that* Jesus Christ he said was my fault even though I didn't say it. I didn't say it but I caused it. That's why it's so hard to keep track. I apologized for it right there. That's what my religious friend's sister calls confession.

When I looked up at the clock I didn't even know what the score was. I found out. It was 3-1 for Victoria. I was so mad at myself. Biggest game of the year, all I'd been waiting for, and I wasn't even there. I felt sick, too. But this was the B.C. Championships! Come on!

Next thing I knew, we were in the dressing room after the first period and Coach was yelling at me for throwing away the puck on the third goal. I didn't even remember the goal.

After that I tried everything but my legs just wouldn't move. The crowd was going crazy and I wanted to get injured. If I could get injured and carried off on a stretcher everyone would clap and I'd have an excuse.

That's when the big boy got injured. He was skating down the boards about two hundred miles an hour. At the same time the door gate on the boards to the Victoria bench was open. Our big boy got checked by their almost-as-big big boy. Our big boy flew in through their door and *wham-mo*, right into the inside of the boards that never move, with their big boy on top of him.

As soon as you hit the boards or the bench you can say good-night. Their big boy got up and skated away. He got cushioned by our big boy. We couldn't even see our big boy. He was down and out on the ground in the Victoria bench.

The big boy's parents were pretty scared in the crowd. They got in a fight with my dad because my dad wouldn't go down to check the big boy out. My dad stood there with his arms crossed in his sheepskin jacket.

My dad said, "He's a faker. You raised a f---ing faker. Just get the stretcher and get him off the ice. If we get the stretcher now he's good for a goal in the third period." I think my dad was mad at me mostly.

The big boy's dad yelled, "Bastarday!" He sounded like Colonel Klink when he yells, "Hogan!" He's even bald like Klink.

You could hear it all over the rink. Then the big boy's dad ran down the bleachers to see if his son was okay. That's when he tripped. He went down way worse than his son—like if you chuck a big speckled trout down a river-bank. It flops, then nothing.

My dad uncrossed his arms right away for that fall, and ran down as fast as he could to help the big boy's dad. We were all looking over the boards at him. He was groaning pretty good. As soon as my dad got there he said, "Broken collarbone." It was.

From lying on the ground the big boy's dad said, "Check my son. Check my son!" The big boy's dad's wife was screaming like an owl that really wants to talk. All the play-ers were looking up in the crowd.

"Check my son!" the big boy's dad screamed again. My dad ran down to check the big boy. He took one look and shook his head. The big boy's mom screamed again. She thought he was dead. My dad said, "Jesus Christ. Get the stretcher." We thought he was dead too.

The big boy and his dad both had broken collarbones. Gone for the tournament. Maybe longer. With the big boy a broken collarbone could mean his career is over. Faker or not, we'd miss him. Coach calls him the X factor. We'd lost the X factor.

We were losing 5-3 at the end of the second period. Our best player had two goals. My dad kept yelling at me, "You're stinking the joint out!" That's embarrassing. Coach told us to go out there and win this one for the big boy. After what happened, I knew I was going to do every-thing I could to win. I still couldn't do much. My legs had no gas. Thank God for the best player. He made it 5-4.

Then he made it 5-5. I know everybody in the crowd was saying, "If that kid had a team around him...." I was trying but I just couldn't do it.

With one minute and twenty seconds to go in the game I was on the bench. That's when Coach looked at me. I looked at him. He said, "I've made a couple of mistakes. I'm going with you this time."

I said, "Okay, Coach."

Coach didn't exactly say that. He thought it. All he really said was, "Don't screw up."

The whole season was on the line!

I skated out thinking about Paul Henderson scoring that goal against Russia to make it 6-5 for Canada with thirty-four seconds to go. I thought about Cournoyer scoring the winning goal in last year's Stanley Cup final and all the trouble he's having this year. That's when I figured out how important this was. I stopped right there and looked up into the crowd. I looked up to where my dad was standing but I didn't look right at him. The crowd was staring back.

I yelled, "Please! Nobody rooting for the Trail Peewee Reps yell Jesus Christ!" That's what I yelled as loud as I could.

I took the face-off in our end and I won it clean. Our defenceman got the puck and he took off. I thought I better stay back to play defence—to cover for the defenceman. Coach would be proud of me. Our defenceman went all the way down the ice and into the corner where he always goes because he goes so fast he passes the goal before he can shoot. I followed up and then hung back at the blueline while we buzzed around their net. One of their players got control of the puck and backhanded it out over everybody's head. I skated back to get it. I was what they call last man back. That's when you're the only player left between your own goalie and everyone else. I picked up the puck at our blueline. I was looking for the best player to pass him the puck but he wasn't open. One of their players came checking me. I did a Savardian Spinorama to get away. Only thing was, my blades didn't dig into the ice. It was like I was wearing my boots on the ice. I started to slip and then down I went. The puck scooted away. Before I knew it the guy who was checking me had a breakaway and I was on the ice. I remember yelling, "No!" as I reached out with my stick.

It was too late. If he scored, the whole world would hate me. He was going down on the goalie. That was it. Him and the goalie. No!

Next thing, our best player caught up to him about seven hundred miles an hour and lifted his stick. The guy couldn't believe it. Like when you miss an open net. Our best player took the puck and spun back around. He looked to pass to me but faked it and kept on going. Through one player, then another player, then another. He splits the defence! The best player is cutting in towards the net! He's in the clear! Going right in on goal! The puck wobbles! He shoots! He scores! The goalie slumps to the ice! Trail has won! Trail has won! The crowd goes crazy! The team goes crazy!

I head for the bottom of the pile-up and hope nobody ever gets up because I don't want to go back to the bench and look at Coach. Everybody's screaming and jumping. Then they try to get up and get back to the game but I hold a few of them down and keep screaming. A couple get away. Finally I'm the only one still on the ice.

I looked up and everybody was gone. I went back to the bench.

Coach looked at me. I said, "My skates...." Like that. Coach turned away. He saw the best player, who was still getting congratulated by the team. Coach grinned about as long as a highway. "Helluva goal, kid." That's what Coach said. The best player's dad had that eensy smile on his face. He said, "Helluva goal, son." It was a hell of five goals. In one game. Like the Rocket.

I looked up at the crowd. My dad wasn't even there. He was gone. He couldn't stand it. I would've left, too, only if I went outside it would ruin my skates. Plus I'd still be with me, and that's the last thing I wanted.

*

Later on, Coach said no more McDonald's for the team. He said we're 2 and 0 and we need a real hockey meal with nutrition. I didn't care. I never wanted to eat at McDonald's again. That's what happens when you throw up a Big Mac, french fries, apple pie and a milkshake. After that you hate the Hamburglar and all the rest of them. You can't help it.

We went to the best player's aunt's house in Vancouver. They pushed three tables together and cooked a real hockey meal for the whole team. Coach said that was how they did it in training camp in Detroit. An NHL training camp! Coach said he sat next to Terrible Ted Lindsay and passed him the butter twice.

We all got a thick steak, two scoops of mashed potatoes, corn niblets and a glass of milk. No water. Coach says it makes you sweat too much and you get dehibernated.

Coach said steak and potatoes is what Gordie Howe used to eat.

I said, "Coach, I'm not sure I can eat anything."

"Eat your steak, son. It'll make you better."

The best player's aunt poured some more gravy on my potatoes. Coach said Cesare Maniago might drop by later to give us a pep talk. Cesare Maniago! He played for the Montreal Canadiens once. If you can believe it, one of the players on our team didn't know who Cesare Maniago was. An NHL goalie who grew up in Trail and the kid didn't know who he was. Boom Boom Geoffrion scored his fiftieth goal against Cesare Maniago! Bobby Hull scored his fifty-first goal to break the all-time scoring record against Cesare Maniago!

No wonder that kid's on the third line.

Coach said we have to come out hitting to make up for losing the big boy. Coach said that's how to play the game. That's what the Philadelphia Flyers are doing and they're about top of the NHL. If it's good enough for the NHL, it's gotta be good enough for peewee rep. Coach said if we beat the North Shore Winter Club, we'll be playing the winner between Burnaby Winter Club and Penticton tomorrow for the whole B.C. Championships. That would be the Pee Wee Stanley Cup.

After that Coach made us all drink a second glass of milk. He said Bobby Hull drank milk in between periods and we should too. The best player said he'd heard that Gump Worsley—he was an old-timer who played goal for Montreal—he used to have a cup of coffee and a cigarette before and after every game so he wouldn't mind a smoke himself, if Coach had one handy. Everybody laughed. Even

Coach. Laughed their heads off. That's what happens when you score five goals in one game. You can say what you want.

All I knew is that the biggest game in the world was a few hours away and my stomach felt like I'd swallowed one of those bats again and he was flying around in there with a bunch of milk and corn and potatoes and steak.

*

I knew Bobby Baun with a broken leg had scored in over-time to get the Toronto Maple Leafs one game closer to the Stanley Cup. I knew Rocket Richard was knocked out and had a big cut over his eye with blood pouring down when he scored on Sugar Jim Henry to give Montreal the Stanley Cup. I'd seen the picture of them shaking hands after the game. I knew Jacques Laperrière played the whole 1971 playoffs with a broken arm, too.

This was different. This was the flu. No hockey player had ever done anything great while they had the flu. Look at Bad Joe Hall. He had the flu and he tried to play. What happened? Dead. I'm not kidding. That's why they can-celled the playoffs in 1919. It says so in the book. Playoffs cancelled due to Spanish influenza. Bad Joe Hall dead as Hobey.

Bobby Baun got a needle to freeze the pain in his leg. If you tried to freeze the flu you'd have to freeze everything. Even your brain. Then you'd play like the big boy. I laughed when I thought of that. Just to myself, sitting there in the dressing room feeling sick.

The three glasses of milk and the steak didn't seem to be helping. Every time I tried to tighten my laces my head felt like it was filled with SOS pads.

The best player's dad cut me a slice of orange in the

dressing room and patted me on the arm. "We need you tonight," he said. He gave me an extra salt pill and a sugar pill too. I wanted a glass of water but they all said, "Oh, no. Water makes you waterlogged and your legs won't move." That's what they said. The best player's dad said, "Just suck on that orange."

Coach was yelling about pride and honour and something about his fingers. That's when I looked up. Coach said he finished the game with the tips of two fingers bit off. He held up his hand and said that's what hockey's all about.

North Shore Winter Club was the best team from Vancouver. A stocked team. That's what my dad said. He was back in the crowd but his girlfriend was gone. Coach said North Shore Winter Club were a bunch of rich kids. None of their dads work on the hill. Bunch of doctors, he said. When he realized what he'd said he looked at me. Doctors who wear suits, he said.

North Shore Winter Club had brand-new, bright red uniforms and red tape around their socks and three big boys. Three! We didn't even have one big boy any more.

As soon as the game started, North Shore Winter Club came out hitting. I got corked in the first minute. I got a sucker pass from one of my shrimpy wingers. That's when you get a slow pass from behind. So slow you have to look back. Then *wham!* Their defenceman gives you a one-way ticket to China.

I should've gone straight to the bench but I was hit so hard I was thinking about as much as Oscar Bonavena when Muhammad Ali knocked him out in the fifteenth round and his legs turned into Jell-O.

But guess what? Thirty seconds later it was 1-0 on my rebound goal. The best player's shot bounced off the goalie's pad. I was held back by one of their big defencemen but at the last second I dived past him and poked the puck in. On the bench Coach whacked me on the back and said, "What'd I tell you about that steak?" Whatever he told me about it, I puked it up like beef stew in the dressing-room bathroom at the end of the first period. It was 2-2 at that time. My legs were like licorice.

Coach peeked in and said, "Kid, maybe you shouldn't play."

I looked up from the toilet with my diarrhea and said, "Coach, this is the B.C. Championships!"

I wasn't faking when I said that, either. It's one thing to not want to play. But for someone to tell you you shouldn't play when you know you can? Like Bobby Baun. If everybody thought he should play and then he scored? So what? But they thought he should be in the hospital and he still scored! That's the thing. I thought about all those guys in the trenches in the war. Imagine if they didn't play. We'd have Nazis everywhere. I thought about Tim Horton and Hobey and Rex and Bad Joe Hall. Unplugged before you know it. They couldn't play if they wanted to. I thought about my dad and that eensy smile on his face.

I said, "Coach, I gotta play!"

By the end of the second period it was 5-3 for us and I had two goals and an assist. The best player had a goal and three assists. Even our little wingers with no skill were hitting. One of them got only one shift in the second period. On that shift he tried to cork their big boy. Bounced right off like a bird on a window but it got us going even more.

When he got back on the bench he sat down and yelled, "Come on Smoke Eaters!" He was pretty proud of trying. I felt proud for him. I looked over and said, "Hey, good shift. Serious." I felt bad about all the times me and my dad hated him for being on my line.

Coach was going mental in the dressing room. "One more period!" he kept yelling. "One more period!"

"Who are we?"

"Smoke Eaters!"

"Who are we?"

"Smoke Eaters!"

"Who are we?"

"Smoke Eaters!"

The North Shore Winter Club scored in the first minute of the third period and we all groaned. That little winger with no skill sitting on the end of the bench getting only one shift said, "Come on, Smokies, don't get down."

One shift in the whole game and he's yelling like that. I said, "You heard him, guys. Here we go, Smoke Eaters!"

Our best player scored a minute later on a breakaway and we all jumped up.

Twenty-two seconds after that, North Shore scored again. We all sat down like salad in my dad's fridge. We bought it once but we didn't know what to do with it. We stuck it where the butter was supposed to go and it just hung over the edge. It's still there. We could've made a salad like my mom does but we didn't have any tomatoes. We just left it there and ate a lot of pancakes and tons of milkshakes.

After that North Shore goal our goalie played like Ken Dryden against Chicago in game one of the finals in 1971. Dryden had fifty-eight shots and only two went in.

Our two lines were deader than Rex. The North Shore Winter Club kept sticking out their third line, their fourth line. North Shore peppered nineteen shots on our goal in the third period. My legs felt like I'd been unplugged. There was eight seconds to go in the game and there was a face-off in our end. We were still up by a goal. Eight seconds from the B.C. finals. I was on the bench with my arms leaning on the boards and my head down. I felt worse than Bad Joe Hall. North Shore Winter Club had pulled their goalie for an extra attacker. Their crowd was going crazy. It was the biggest face-off ever in the history of me.

The best player said, "Coach, what do you want me to do?"

Coach tapped me on the shoulder.

I looked back. Coach said, "Take the face-off."

"Me?"

"Yeah, you. Get out there."

I took it, all right.

Won it clean.

One game to go.

*

That night I saw Rex in a nightmare. All his skin was turned inside out and when I tried to pet him he yelped and my hand stuck to him. I woke up and I still felt sick and I was all sweaty. It reminded me of a robin I found one time with a little lung sticking out of it. I think a cat got to it. It was still moving and the lung would go in and out. I tried to feed it munched worms but it died.

Next to me the winger with no skill was coughing and everybody else was asleep. I lay there for a second and thought about my religious friend's sister. She has the kind of face you just want to touch with your face. I'd like to sniff around her neck and her clothes. I don't know why. I bet it would smell perfect, that's all. I've been feeling like that since Rex died. I'm wondering if some of his electricity was whacked out of him so hard it went in my ear or something. I was right there. I touched him right after, too. It probably jammed into my ear. That's probably why I want to sniff so much.

I got up and pulled on my corduroys and my shirt and my hockey jacket and my shoes and snuck out of the hotel room. I took the elevator to the lobby. I phoned my mom collect from a pay phone. I didn't know it was two in the morning.

"Where are you?" she asked me.

"I'm in the lobby of the hotel we're staying at," I said. "I woke up and I thought I should give you a call."

"Oh," she said. "Of course. Are you okay?"

"I just was thinking...was wondering if Rex had come by," I said. "If maybe he'd got plugged in."

My mom said I sounded terrible.

I told her I had the Spanish flu like Bad Joe Hall. "We're playing for the B.C. Championships tomorrow against Penticton."

"I know," my mom said. She sounded excited for someone who thinks icing is something you spread on a birthday cake. That's something Foghorn Leghorn would say. "I heard it on the radio," she said. "They said you scored two goals."

"Did they mention the steak I puked after the first period?"

Mom laughed.

I asked her if she was alone. She was. Maybe that was

why she laughed. Maybe she was home waiting, knowing the end of the season was here and if we could win and stop the yelling....

Or maybe it was just funny about the puke. You can't tell with parents. Why they get mad. Why they get happy.

"Maybe we can come over next weekend, after we win," I said.

"Even if you don't win," she said.

I didn't say anything.

She said, "Of course you can."

I said, "Mom, when I make pro I can just fly back whenever I want. That's the thing about pro. In between games."

"That would be wonderful," she said. "Are you sure you're okay? You sound very sick."

"Bobby Baun had a broken leg," I said.

My mom didn't say anything. I don't think she even knew who Bobby Baun was. I asked her not to say Jesus Christ tomorrow. She said she wouldn't. She hardly ever does anyway. She said she missed me and couldn't wait to see me and give me a big hug.

"Wait until I get over the flu," I said.

"Just make sure you only eat chicken noodle soup," she said. "And drink lots of water. Keep drinking water."

Water.

That's the thing about my mom and hockey. She tries hard but she just doesn't know anything about hockey food. If I told Coach all the different vegetables we eat, he'd probably kick me off the team.

I said, "Mom, do you know what happens when legs get waterlogged?"

She didn't.

"Mom, I don't mean this in any crummy way, but you'll never be a hockey player."

Then we laughed and I told her Dad had been pretty good lately, hardly yelled at all. I couldn't remember the last time I heard him yell. She seemed interested. I was just about to ask her if she thought her and Dad would ever get back together. I didn't, though. I didn't have to. I knew what would happen if we could just win tomorrow. I said, "Dad still loves you, Mom. Don't kid yourself."

She said that was because they had kids together.

I said, "Well, maybe you should have another one." That was all I said. It just came out.

It was a perfect idea.

*

Turns out I locked myself out of the room so the best player had to let me back in. He asked where I had been. I said I thought I'd walked into the bathroom but I went outside by mistake.

Lying down on my cot I got to thinking about how big the game against Penticton was. How I'd die to score the big goal. If I could score that goal everything would change. I thought about the Pocket Rocket. That's Rocket Richard's little brother. All his life he was never as good as the Rocket. Way after the Rocket retired, what did little Henri do? He scored in overtime in the sixth game of the Stanley Cup finals to beat the Detroit Red Wings for the Stanley Cup. He pushed the puck in with his glove but the referee didn't notice. The Red Wings went crazy but it didn't make any difference. The goal counted. After that everything went right. In 1971 he scored the tying goal and the winning goal against Chicago in the seventh game to win the Stanley Cup. In the end the Pocket Rocket won eleven Stanley Cups. More than anyone ever.

If I could score tomorrow with my hand and get away with it? In a second. My skate. My nose. My ear. I'd put the puck in my gonch and throw it in the net if it'd mean I'd score the winning goal. Once you become a winner it becomes a habit. You just have to become one first. That's the last thing I thought before I fell asleep.

*

"You gotta believe." That's what Coach said at the end of the second period. It was still 0-0. I'd never played in a game that was 0-0 at the end of the second period before. I'd seen it in the pros but not here. This game was the closest I'd ever been to the pros. It was for the B.C. Championships.

I was trying but my legs were like licorice. I was working hard. I was thinking defence. I didn't have the speed to do offence so I hit everything that moved. I hit and hit and hit. I won face-offs. I backchecked. I forechecked.

The thing is, I was dizzy. I was killing penalties and on the power play but I was spinning around like a fly after you pull off one of its wings.

Penticton scored in the third period.

I wasn't even watching. My head was hanging like a dead man. I was so tired. Come on, Rex. That's what I was saying. Hoping to get some of his electricity. I heard the noise and I looked up. One to nothing for Penticton.

Coach was yelling, "That was goddamn Russian interference! What is this? Basketball?"

All our parents were going crazy, not just my dad. My dad was leading the way, though. He was yelling at the ref,

"Here's fifty bucks! Go buy a seeing-eye dog! You're teaching the kids to f---ing lie!"

I had a breakaway with about ten minutes to go but their defenceman caught up to me like I was waiting to get a parking ticket. I had no juice. Thank God I hadn't drunk any water or I'd be skating backwards. My dad yelled, "Move your f---ing legs!" I was. It just wasn't helping. So I kept forechecking and hitting and taking face-offs and hoping we could somehow get a goal.

We weren't getting many chances. Even the best player was mad. They had some pipsqueak shadow who was following him all over the ice. The best player said, "If I took a crap he'd probably follow me to the can and wipe my ass." It was pretty funny but I was too tired to laugh. The best player didn't laugh either. We were just sitting on the bench waiting for the next shift.

That shift we got a break. The puck bounced past one of their defencemen, and me and the best player burst out two on one. I was skating my hardest to keep up and trying to decide what to do. Go to the net or drop back. Their other defenceman kept backing up between us. Our best player took it over the blueline. I was right there with him when I decided to burst for the net full blast. The best player wound up for a slapshot! Fake! He slipped the pass right across to me. I let the shot go first time. Off the goal post...in! All tied up!

Our whole team jumped off the bench and on top of me. They were patting me and going, "Yeah! yeah!" We skated off the ice and I knew we had a chance. I knew we were going to win.

But before we'd even looked up from the bench, their

best player took the face-off, pushed it through our centre-man's legs, dashed around our defenceman and let a wobbler go. Somehow it trickled through our goalie's legs. He couldn't believe it. We couldn't believe it. Our goalie just sat on his knees with his head down. Eleven seconds after we'd tied up the game.

The Penticton team all jumped off the bench and mobbed their best player. We had to go out and tell our goalie it was okay.

Two-one, Penticton. Four minutes to go.

Me and the best player looked at each other and said, "Come on." My legs were in Kalamazoo. Come on, I kept yelling at myself. Come on! The crowd was screaming.

We couldn't get anywhere on that shift. Back on the bench the best player said to me, "We tie this thing up, guaranteed I'll score in overtime." I dream about those kinds of things. The best player says them.

Coach was yelling and the parents were yelling at the referee. Coach kept calling him Helen Keller. Penticton was holding and sticking, as usual. Every time I looked up another minute had ticked away. We barely got any pressure on them. Penticton didn't have any on us, either. Sloppy hockey. Everything around centre ice. Hitting and hooking.

The whistle blew. There was one minute and thirty seconds left to play in the whole season if we didn't score. Coach tapped me and the best player on the shoulder and said, "Get out there and pop one." We hopped over the bench and I thought about all the great players who scored feeling like a dog with a nylon half hanging out of its bum. Bobby Baun. The Rocket. That's all I could think of.

I took the face-off in our end. I won it like Jean Béliveau. Our defenceman had it and he skated around the net. He passed it up to our best player, who had slipped away from his pipsqueak shadow. I circled and took off too. Our best player took it over the centre line and shot the puck into the corner. I screamed and took off with my legs moving like Cournoyer. The Penticton defenceman got there a second before me. *Pow.* I creamed him into the boards. I stole the puck. I was still screaming. I was going like crazy behind the net. Their centreman was checking me. *Pow.* I pushed him away. Another player came and I was looking for someone to get open. I threw it back to our defenceman and headed for the net. He let a slapshot go but it was twenty-seven miles wide.

Now they had the puck. This could end the season! Their big boy tried to throw it down the ice. I dove in front of it like Don Awrey and blocked it. That saved us! Gave us one more chance. The crowd was screaming. My heart was screaming. I was screaming. "Aaaaah!" That's what you yell when you're scared but sick of being scared at the same time. That was me. This was my chance! Like the Pocket Rocket.

Thirty seconds to go.

The puck bounced into the corner and our best player took off after it. He got it and swooped around one player and cut for the net. I was spinning and fighting away from their defenceman and still screaming like Geronimo. I couldn't stop. The best player jammed the puck at the side of the net but their goalie kicked it out. The puck got knocked behind the net. Our goalie headed to our bench for an extra attacker. Their defenceman couldn't clear the puck.

Twenty seconds to go.

I was fighting and fighting along the backboards for the puck. The referee should have blown the whistle but he didn't. Come on! Come on! The puck squeezed loose.

Ten seconds to go.

The crowd begins their chant. Nine! Eight! I bounce the puck off the backboards with a fancy-dancy back pass to the best player. The checker is all over me. But with my pass he makes a big mistake. He leaves me and goes after the best player. I spin away and swerve towards the front of the net, my blades chopping away from any defenders. My scream changes to, "Hey! Hey! Hey!"

The best player has the puck. He spots me through the traffic.

Six! Five!

I'm wide open. The net is wide open on my side. Everybody's forgotten about me in the panic, even the goalie. "Hey! Hey! Hey!" Three players go towards the best player. "Hey!"

Four! Three!

The best player sees me. He slips to his left looking for an angle to get me the puck. "Hey! Hey!" Wide open net. Nobody yelling Jesus Christ. Nobody thinking about French words. Just the net. And me. "Hey! Hey! Hey!" And the pass. Two! One! "Hey! Hey—!"

The pass was perfect.

*

Not everybody on the team cried. I cried. I cried because we lost. I cried because everybody hates me. I cried because I missed the open net. I didn't miss the open net. I missed the puck altogether. I cried when we shook hands with the

Penticton team. You don't really shake hands. You slap their hands and say, "Good game," but you don't really mean it. I just looked away and said, "Good game." I knew what they were thinking. They were all staring at me.

The one thing about great goal scorers is, they never wave for the puck with their stick in the air. That's like swinging your bat at a baseball an hour after the game is over. Great goal scorers put their stick on the ice, keep it there and yell, "Hey! Hey! Hey!"

When the puck comes?

Boom.

The twine snaps back. The red light goes on. The team goes crazy.

That's what a great goal scorer does.

When their goalie said, "Hey, thanks for being a loser," I went mental, just like J.P. Parise did against the Russians when he swung his stick at the referee. I jumped on their goalie and started swinging. The other players jumped in too. But everybody jumped in on their side against me. My own players even hit me. Kicked me. Everybody hated me. I just hid my fingers and held on as everybody beat on me. Somewhere in there I got whacked in the nose with the goalie's blocker. My nose was bleeding on my shirt when the coaches pulled us all apart.

I never told anybody what the goalie said. Coach yanked me off the ice. He dragged me right across the ice like you do with your dog when it craps in the neighbour's yard. By my collar. He dragged me right into the dressing room and pushed me down on the seat. He called it the worst sportsmanship he'd ever seen. Seeing as Coach had two fingers bitten off in a fight and his favourite team was the

Philadelphia Flyers, I was looking pretty bad. Then Coach took off.

After a while I stopped crying and just sat there with blood on my nose, staring at my Super Tack skates that my dad bought me.

All that money. All the times he yelled for me, hoping I could be the best player. All the times he said, "Keep your f---ing stick on the ice."

I could hear the announcements from the dressing room. "Congratulations to the champions of British Columbia and the future leaders of tomorrow: Penticton!" The crowd cheered, muffled through the door.

I wondered where my dad was. He probably went home. I wouldn't be surprised if he left a note for the coach that said, "Tell him to go back and live with his mother."

I heard the announcer announcing the MVP for the tournament. It was our best player. Man, to win that when your team loses! That's what Roger Crozier did when he was a goalie with Detroit. So did Glenn Hall with St. Louis. But a centreman?

They named the all-star team, too. I could hear the names through the door, like when your brother ties you up in a sleeping bag. I was thinking, "Come on! Come on! One thing!" Our best player got that too. The centreman position, that is. I played left wing a lot. Maybe I'd get left-wing all-star.

Maybe not.

I wished they had a prize for missing the biggest wide-open net. The announcer wouldn't even have to call my name. Everybody would just look at me and start punching.

That's when I heard another scream. "Don't ever f---ing touch my kid again!" That's what I heard. "You ever drag my kid like that again and I'll—!" That was the last word. It was my dad. For sure. Then there were more screams from other people. I jumped up and ran towards the door. It opened just as I got there and knocked me flying backwards and onto my bum. My dad was standing in the door in his sheepskin jacket. He had a good old red welt over his eye. I was sitting on the ground staring back. He looked about as crazy as the Tasmanian Devil when the Tasmanian Devil doesn't know what to do.

My face was filled up with that poison-ivy feeling.

My dad said, "You worked your goddamn guts out."

He picked me up right there and threw me over his shoulder like Gordie Howe used to do with bags of cement. He carried me past everyone, skates and all. Even past Coach, who had a pretty good welt over his eye, too. He carried me up the stairs and out of the arena and into the parking lot.

It was still light out. My dad's girlfriend opened the back door of the car and my dad put me in the back seat. His girlfriend got in the passenger seat. With one swoop of his big arm, my dad cleared the snow off the front window. He got in the car and we took off.

"F--- 'em," was all he said. He handed me his hankie for my bleeding nose and said, "Just wipe, don't blow." We drove for a few minutes and didn't say anything else, just the motor of the car and the traffic.

I sat in the back in my hockey equipment. Even my skates and helmet were still on. My dad's girlfriend took what was left of a pack of Life Savers out of her purse. She popped a cherry one in her mouth. Just like that. Right then she looked back at me and my bleeding nose.

I was looking at her, too.

She seemed surprised. "Oh, sorry," she said, "that was the last one."

And that was the B.C. Championships.

*

I made the headlines.

The Trail *Daily Times* said:

POST GAME BRAWL MARS CHAMPIONSHIP

The little line beneath the headline said: *Trail Youth Wins MVP.* The best player's dad wrote the article. The paper said I missed a wide-open net with two seconds to play off a perfect set-up. It said I waited until the handshake to sucker-punch the Penticton goalie. I didn't tell anyone about what the goalie said. Nobody asked, either. They were more than happy to hate me.

I was thinking about how everybody says, "Play like the Philadelphia Flyers! Finish your damn checks!" The Flyers bite and kick and stick and have names like Mad Dog Kelly and Moose Dupont. Their captain, Bobby Clarke, with no front teeth, broke Kharlamov's ankle with his hockey stick just like a Nazi would.

Why was that fine with everybody?

In 1955, Rocket Richard beat up a referee. When the Rocket got suspended for it, the people in Montreal were so mad they rioted like Arabs on TV, burning the American flag. They named a riot after him! The Richard Riot. Like he did the best thing in the world. They didn't call it the

Poor Sport Riot. Cars were flipped over like Dinky toys. Windows were smashed like bottles in Mickey Redmond's basement.

Why was that okay?

I crack a goalie on the noodle and get a blocker right in the schnozz and everybody hates me. What's the difference?

Think about it, Einstein.

Even the kids in Rossland heard about it. They all called me poor sport. They think I'm like this because my parents aren't together. The only one who didn't care was my Negro friend. He said, "Hey, you want to go shoplifting in Trail on the weekend?" I didn't because I don't. Plus everyone there would be watching me. There's that poor sport. The one with the crazy father? Yeah, that's the one. Oh, now he's shoplifting. I'm not surprised. Me neither.

I said, "Don't you know what happened?"

"Yeah. You missed the open net and jumped the goalie shaking hands. It could happen to anyone."

He was wrong there.

With the news in the paper, I couldn't stop my mom from knowing what happened. Everything was doomed. My sister would be embarrassed and hate me and hate my dad. My brother would say, "Told you, loser." To my mom I could've sort of lied and said we lost and it was a rough game and that Dad doesn't yell any more. Now she knows Dad walloped Coach and Coach walloped Dad. Actually it was the other way around but they probably blame my dad for that too. I got carried out like a duffel bag over my dad's shoulder, with blood all over my face. My mom's probably thinking I'm spiteful and just like my f---ing father. She'll hate my dad. And hockey. Maybe even me.

Her boyfriend will, that's for sure, and she'll listen to him.

Two months of not yelling at each other down the crapper.

Jesus Christ.

God Dammit.

Not even Benedict Dryden can ruin the Stanley Cup play-offs. They're too perfect and they're named after God and they're all that matters. I told everybody who called me a loser for missing that open net that I'd jump in the Columbia River and freeze to death if Montreal didn't win the Stanley Cup. I didn't have to worry. Not with the Good Lord Stanley looking over the whole thing. That's what I said at school before the first game of Montreal's best-of-seven quarter-final series against the New York Rangers. I said Montreal will win in four straight games. Maybe five, if the Rangers get horse shoes and steal one at home. The fact is, the Rangers haven't won a Stanley Cup in thirty-four years and Montreal's won seventeen. They're the best team in history.

I couldn't wait for Hockey Night in Canada to start. I'd had the TV on since I got home from school at three o'clock. Two hours. Finally, there it was.

In colour.

The theme song blaring. Dick Irvin the announcer saying, "Live from the Montreal Forum...."

I was sitting on the floor right in front of the TV, with my milkshake and my Montreal Canadiens tuque. My heart was bouncing like a Super Ball. I started yelling, "Come on! Come on!"

My dad was sitting in his chair. He was wearing pants for a change. He said, "Take it easy."

The cameras zoomed in on all the guys warming up:

212

Cournoyer! Jacques Lemaire, the Pocket Rocket, Guy Lapointe, Pierre Bouchard, Shutt, Lafleur, Chuck Lefley, Larry Robinson, the Mahovlich brothers, even Bunny Larocque. They were so ready!

My dad said, "Breathe!"

The phone rang during the national anthem. I jumped about twenty feet. It was my mom—and the first time I'd talked to her since missing the open net against Penticton. She said with the game on she knew she'd catch me at home. I told her it was my fault Dad got mad at Coach. I told her what the goalie said while shaking hands, too, calling me a loser and all. I told her I missed the open net and lost the game for everybody, but I still couldn't help but jump him when he called me that.

My mom said, "Well, I hope you at least got one good punch in." I couldn't believe she said that! I said I did—and for a second I thought that even an English woman could start thinking right if she lived in Canada long enough. I was wrong. My mom said that goalie only called me a loser because he didn't feel very good about himself inside.

Inside what? I could've yanked that phone right out of the wall!

Doesn't feel good about himself? They're the B.C. champions! As if he doesn't feel good about himself! She doesn't understand anything about Canada! When I got mad—and of course I was mad!—she told me she thinks I should see that counsellor again.

"Oh, you mean the nail-biter who knows less than Rex!" That's what I said.

Then I heard Danny Gallivan doing the play-by-play. I told my mom I had to go because the game was on and I had to watch Montreal win. She asked if I could come up for the weekend. I said I could but I had to go.

Three periods later, Montreal won, all right.

Montreal 1, New York 4.

My face felt like poison ivy when the game was over—even worse when the Hockey Night in Canada theme song came on. I thought my eyes might blow up. I pictured Cournoyer sitting in his stall, all sweaty and wondering what he could do. What could he do? You can't do anything when everybody lets you down! I was cursing at Dryden and swinging my hockey stick about missing the open net and swearing at the Good Lord Stanley. If I hadn't done that I would have bawled my brains out like a two-year-old.

That's when my dad came upstairs, covered in sawdust and with his black eye where Coach whacked him and his sore hand where he whacked Coach back. My dad clicked off the TV, told me to settle down and gave me the truth about the Good Lord Stanley.

He isn't God.

I've been kidding myself. That's what my dad said.

As soon as he told me that, I went into his bedroom and started shooting pucks against his bed even though I was crying like a two-year-old. Wrist shots. Then snap shots. *Bam. Bam. Bam.* I could hit any spot I wanted but all I could see in my head was that wide-open net.

He's not Jesus or the Good Lord, either.

That's when I started taking slapshots. *Bam! Bam! Bam!* All that mesh. The goal net is six feet by four feet. If you piled up pucks you could fit over a thousand of them in there—one thousand one hundred and fifty-two to be exact. I'd worked out the math at school. I couldn't fit one in!

It turns out Lord Stanley is just some joker from England who had tons of money and lived in Canada for a while. He was nothing special. He was never tacked up on a cross. He never came back to life. He probably did get the flu now and then when he was alive. That's because everybody gets the flu sometimes. But now he's dead and he's not coming back. As dead as Hobey and Tim Horton and Rex and everybody else who's dead.

*

I didn't care what all the idiot kids in my class said at school the next day when we were playing box ball. My Negro friend stuck up for me. He was the only one. He threw a ball at one kid and beaned him right in the head. Then that kid's older brother came to beat up my Negro friend. He called my friend a shithead nigger and put him in a headlock. All I could see was my friend's Afro sticking out like the older guy had a curly beard. I could hear my Negro friend laughing, too, all muffled. He always laughs, even when his nose is bleeding or his brother is beating the crap out of him or the teacher is yelling at him. I knew it was now or never, just like for the Pocket Rocket, so I jumped on that older kid from behind. Together we threw him in the snowbank, which was pretty small and covered in dirt on account of the spring thaw. We pushed his face down in it and then took off. That's the only way to do it when they're older than you are. Two on one and then run. We'll probably get our heads punched in but it was worth it. In class after lunch, before the teacher showed up, I told everybody else I was only joking about the Good Lord

Stanley and they were too dumb to figure out a good joke.

Yeah, my Negro friend said, a big joke. Then he laughed his head off.

That night who was laughing his head off at the two biggest jokes of all, Dryden and the New York Rangers?

Me and Cournoyer.

Who broke the one-all tie with two minutes left in the second period?

Cournoyer.

Who made it 3-1 in the third period on a breakaway going about a thousand miles an hour?

Cournoyer!

Who scored his third straight goal two minutes later? Three goals in a row. A natural hat trick!

You should have heard Gallivan doing the play-by-play. You could hear his eyes bulge out. He was losing his voice, he got so excited. I was jumping around like Daffy Duck and my dad thought I was crazy. Final score: Montreal 4, New York 1. The series was all tied up.

That night I got to thinking about what if my mom and dad did have another baby. They could. Why couldn't they? All you have to do is get together and screw until you're blue. That's what my Negro friend's older brother said. I'm not sure what that means but my parents have done it three times already so they must know. After that it only takes nine months to cook a baby. About one NHL hockey season if you make the playoffs and go to the Stanley Cup finals.

It's hard to believe, but all people look like babies when they first start out. Before that they look like white tadpoles. Then they look like pink martians. Then after about nine months of treading water they come out looking pretty much normal except for the fat head.

That's what I was thinking about. That's why I couldn't sleep. Plus my dad's ex-young girlfriend was sleeping over in his room. I couldn't believe it. I like her and all. I said that already. But she's been traded. That's all there is to it. I was going to go knock on their door and tell her to pack up and get out, but I knew my dad would blow his top.

Instead I snuck out of bed and went into the kitchen and made myself a milkshake. Vanilla, strawberry and chocolate ice cream, then milk and three spoonfuls of strawberry jam. I mixed all the stuff by hand so I wouldn't wake anybody. It took a while to froth it up but it was worth it. At the end there was so much jam on the bottom I had to add more milk and more ice cream and make another half one.

It's a strange place to be, crammed up there inside your mom with no directions at all. That's what I was thinking while I was drinking. You've got no light and no pants and no alarm clock and no hockey practices and no TV and no school. You don't know anything. You just float around until you're perfectly cooked. Then when you come out everybody's screaming and crying and mad and bleeding. I saw photos of that in one of my dad's books. Moms lie in bed with their dresses pulled up and they sweat more than Bobby Orr. They even hurt more than when he broke his knee. You should see the faces everybody makes. That's why it's so hard being a family. It starts off hard and you haven't even done anything yet.

I think most things are hard. Making pro is harder than anything. Even making junior is hard, especially by fourteen. And imagine dying! All that electricity sucked out of your ears and mouth and nose and then it's just like it was before you were here: no hockey, no anything. Even scoring on an open net is hard. I didn't think it was but it is.

I'd say pretty much everything is hard. That's what a baby must feel when he first pops his head out. Everybody crying and screaming and bleeding. He must just think, "Too hard." Why else would he start bawling? That's why the first thing I'll tell the little raisin is, don't worry about it. You saved the family and you didn't even know it. You came in the nick of time.

And there's good stuff, too. That's what I'll tell the little tadpole. I'll tell him what it's like to score in the third period and tie up the B.C. Championships. That's the most perfect thing in the world. Just wait and see. That's what I'll say. Just keep trying.

That won't stop him crying but it'll still be good if he knows it.

I finished my milkshake and wrapped myself up in a blanket from my bedroom and lay down on the kitchen floor by the woodstove. Orange was glowing through the crack where the door is and you stick the wood in. I was wearing my long underwear and my wool socks and my Montreal Canadiens sweater and my Montreal Canadiens tuque. I was all wrapped up like a butterfly. Only my head stuck out and the heat on my face was perfect. I closed my eyes and my nose and cheeks were all warm. That's about what it must feel like being a baby up there. That was the last thing I thought about. That and the three goals Cournoyer scored.

I laughed when I thought of that. Right out loud.

That's a perfect way to fall asleep.

*

On Saturday night at my mom's place, Montreal won again and Cournoyer got two more goals! Five goals in two games. Even Bunny Larocque was playing like he'd eaten the fish I sent. I bet Dryden was at home pulling out his hair. He should be about as bald as a bowling ball by the time Montreal wins the Cup.

After the game was over and the announcer said it was brought to us by Ford and Esso, the Hockey Night in Canada theme song came on. That song is twice as good as O Canada. It should be the national anthem. I just lay back on the floor and closed my eyes and listened to it with a grin the size of a banana touching both ears. The song was playing and I was going over all the goals from the game. Then it faded away until there was no noise at all. Nothing. Totally quiet. Just my head filled up with a million things to remember from the game.

Best song in the world.

Especially during the playoffs, which is the best time in the world.

You get a game on TV every day, sometimes every second day. My mom goes crazy. "Turn that racket down!" She hates the commentators. She said she hates hockey and is so sick of hearing about it. I told her what I thought of that—best sport in the world!—and she asked me why I'm so angry all the time. What could I say? I was happy! Montreal won. Cournoyer got five goals in two games. I was totally happy until she started telling me how rotten hockey was. She doesn't have a clue. Why am I so angry? I said, "I guess I'm just like my father." When I said that it made her laugh. Just like my dad I can make her laugh. I

219

told her about Dryden and how he'd ruined everything. She didn't understand a word. She said she didn't blame him one bit for quitting hockey. She was still laughing when she said that. I didn't find that funny at all.

I said, "You just concentrate on making babies." That's what I said. She didn't know what I was talking about. She asked me why I was so angry again. Forget it. I might as well talk to the Zamboni. I learned one thing. Never talk about hockey to an English woman. You can try, but it's like counting on Dryden.

*

On Sunday afternoon me and my mom had sausages and potatoes for lunch. She calls it bangers and mash. She has strange names for everything. She says mall like pal but with an M. She says yogurt like dog-urt except with a Y. When she says aluminum you might as well run for the hills. It makes no sense at all. But everything was going fine. My dad was coming to pick me up and I'd go home with him to watch the game. Fourth game of the series. Biggest game so far. If Montreal wins, the series is pretty much over except for the New York fans crying like babies. If New York wins, I'll start biting my nails like that counsellor. That's what I was thinking about when I told my mom I was quitting school. She was taking the frying pan off the stove and putting it in the sink to do the dishes. She stopped moving.

"To concentrate on hockey," I said. "Dad said I could. He said I had to finish grade six but after that I could do whatever I want."

She asked me what I was talking about.

"Mom, don't you understand how hard it is to make

pro?" That's when my sister came home. She was wearing her Guide outfit and her blue hat and her Adidas runners that Dad bought her. "You have to play junior by fourteen or you can forget it," I said.

My mom said, "What do you mean, your father said you could quit school?"

My sister said, "I wish they'd both move to Timbuktu."

I said, "Every hockey legend quits school. I missed two open nets. The sooner I quit the better."

Right then my dad walked in. He never knocks. He just walked in in his sheepskin jacket and his hockey-puck eye.

My sister barely looked up.

Before he could say anything my mom said, "What are you doing telling him he can quit school to play hockey?"

My dad said, "What the hell are you talking about?"

"To concentrate on hockey, Dad. You told me to finish grade six and then I could quit like Gordie Howe."

My dad looked at my mom and then at me. "What the hell is going on?"

My brother walked in with his purple pants and his suede moccasins and hair even longer than mine.

That's when the bomb blew up. I didn't even hear it ticking. My mom and dad were yelling at each other and my dad said all of us kids were chicken shit and my mom said my dad was an animal.

My sister stood there yelling with her hands over her ears. "Move to Timbuktu! Move to Timbuktu!"

My brother said, "Sayonara, man," and took off.

My dad asked my mom where her f---ing boyfriend was.

My mom told my dad to get out.

My dad said, "Probably off f---ing somebody else's

wife!" That's when the sausages flew from the counter all over the floor, rolling everywhere. The mashed potatoes ended up on the wall and slid down like a giant potato raindrop. Rex would've had a feast. I was standing right in between my mom and dad. I didn't know what to say. Another fight and I never know what to do! Ever since Dryden quit!

My mom yelled, "You're traumatizing the children!" I think that means hurting our eardrums.

My sister was still yelling, "Move to Timbuktu!" with her hands over her ears.

I didn't even get to grab my hockey magazines or my drawings. My dad grabbed me by the collar like Coach did after I punched the Penticton goalie. The door slammed and we were gone.

In the car my dad looked like Old Yeller when he got the rabies. He peeled out and gravel went everywhere. He didn't turn left to go down the cut-off back to Rossland, either. He turned right towards Fruitvale.

The only person who lives in Fruitvale that my dad knows is my mom's boyfriend.

I didn't look at my dad but I knew what he was thinking. The chains from the winter tires were on the back seat. For a second I thought about what a person could do to another person with one of those if he was so mad he couldn't help himself.

I said, "Dad, I don't want you to go to jail."

My dad drove for another minute and then pulled the car to the side of the road. He was staring out his driver's-side window. I don't know what he was staring at. The muscle in his jaw was twitching and he was gripping the steering wheel so hard his knuckles were red and white like the Canadian flag.

"Sorry, Dad. I thought you said I could quit school."

My dad did a U-turn and we drove back to Rossland.

We were going home to watch the game.

We did. Montreal lost 6-4.

*

When the Rangers tied up the fifth game of the series with sixteen seconds left in the third period, I wanted to smash that TV with my bare fists.

Bunny Larocque lay on the ice like he was dead. I wished he was. The puck had dribbled over him like a mouse running all over your body. Then boom, onto the ice, and the Ranger player smacked it home.

Everybody at my dad's house was going nuts: my dad's farmer friend and two of his sons, my brother, my dad, my dad's young ex-girlfriend. They poked me and laughed at me when the Rangers scored. "Is he gonna cry? Is he gonna cry?" That's what they kept saying.

My brother and the farmer's sons started chanting, "Don't you know? It ain't funny, you just can't win with a goalie named Bunny!" about twenty times.

My dad told them to leave me alone. I didn't care. There was no way I was going to cry. Dryden can die before I cry.

During the intermission before overtime I moved closer to the TV and closed my eyes and kept drinking my milkshake.

One of the farmer's sons said, "What's he doin'?"

My brother said, "He's crazy. Leave him alone."

"Why are his eyes closed?"

"Just leave him alone," my brother said. "My dad said to leave him alone."

"Is he praying? It looks like he's praying."

I should have been praying! But I wasn't. I was thinking about Dryden and how he used to stand in front of that net leaning on his goalie stick. How big and calm he was, just daring people to come down on him and try to score. He'd stop 'em, too. Every time. All the saves. Kazillions of great saves. How he was there when it mattered, when you needed him.

This time it mattered more than anything, and he was in Toronto playing rec hockey.

And at the Montreal Forum it was down to overtime with a goalie named Bunny.

My brother and the rest of them were swearing and saying Jesus Christ about twenty-eight times, and then laughing their heads off.

"You'll see." That's what I said back to everybody who was bugging me.

I saw, all right.

Ron Harris scored in overtime.

Not Steve Shutt. Not Cournoyer. Not the Pocket Rocket.

Does anybody even know who Ron Harris is?

The Rangers do. They went crazy. The whole team jumped off the bench and jumped on him like my teammates would have jumped on me if I'd popped it in the open net against Penticton.

There it was on the TV screen:

NEW YORK RANGERS 3
MONTREAL CANADIENS 2
OT Final
Rangers lead series 3-2

My dad tapped me on the shoulder and said, "Don't worry, buddy, the series isn't over yet."

*

The next day at school I didn't talk at all. How could I? I just wandered around in my head, even at recess and at lunch. I was so mad at Dryden I couldn't open my hands. I knew what my dad had said about the Good Lord Stanley. I said a little prayer anyway, to Jesus and God. I mentioned Stanley too. Just quickly. Just in case. That's what I was doing with my eyes closed when my teacher asked me a question about something. That's why I didn't hear him until he whacked his pointer on his desk as hard as he could.

"Sorry to wake you up, Gordie Howe, but I was asking you a question!" That's what he said with that stupid English accent from Scotland.

I said I wasn't sleeping, I was praying.

The whole class laughed because they don't think about anything. All they do is talk about things that don't matter.

I thought my teacher's head was going to blow off. "Well, hockey player, you'd better bloody well pray you pass the school year!" That's what he yelled.

I didn't say a word.

"Did you hear what I said?" Everybody in the school heard what he said.

"I don't pray for school," I said.

"Oh, is that right? And why's that?"

"It doesn't matter why," I said.

The teacher's face turned red and veins popped up on his bald head like rivers on a map. He put his pointer two inches from my face. "You tell me why you don't pray for school, hockey player, or it's straight to the principal's office for you!"

I said it. "Because God doesn't give a crap about school."

*

I was still fuming when the principal sat me in a chair in front of his desk. The first thing he told me was, it's good to think about God but long division is important too. I told him I knew how to work out goals-against averages and that sixty-eight percent of pro hockey players are missing at least one tooth. That means sixty-eight people for every hundred. That's very interesting, he said. He had no idea it was that many. I asked the principal if there was any way I could drop out of school because it just wasn't working out for me any more around here. He got pretty mad. He said I was insolent. I said Bobby Clarke takes that for his diabetes. He didn't know what to say when I said that. He said it was pretty important I finish school. Look at your dad. He's a doctor. That took a lot of school.

I said I was going to be a pro hockey player and that takes no school. Look at Gordie Howe.

My principal smiled. "There was only one Gordie Howe."

"And he dropped out of school," I said. "Just like Bobby Orr and Bobby Hull and Yvan Cournoyer. Clear the Track for Eddie Shack can't even read."

My principal smiled a fakey. When an adult knows they're wrong but they want to act smart they do that. He said, "Dropping out of school won't make you a great hockey player. Hard work makes you a great hockey player."

226

"I know. I weight-lift, too. And I'm building a rink next year."

"Very few people make the NHL," he said. "It's good to have something to fall back on."

I said, "If I have to fall back on anything it'll be playing in the minors."

My principal said, "Lots of terrific hockey players finish school."

"Name one," I said back.

My principal stared straight at me. "Ken Dryden."

My body swelled up like poison ivy. I'm pretty sure I swore. F---ing and stuff. I can't remember. I might have gone crazy. I know I started swinging and yelling and clenching my fists and gritting my teeth. *"Look what he did to Cournoyer!"*

The principal jumped like a jack-rabbit. You should've seen the look on his face. Like Brad Park when Cournoyer's coming down full speed.

"F--- Dryden!" That's what I yelled.

The principal was trying to get me to calm down, standing in my way like a defenceman waiting to go one on one. His knees were bent. His eyes were on me.

All I knew was, I had to get out of that room and the principal was blocking my way. I threw all the papers from his desk onto the floor.

The principal reached out to grab me.

That's when I made my move. I knocked a photograph of his kids on the floor to decoy him, like how you try and get a defenceman to look at the puck when you're stick-handling. If a defenceman does that you've got him beat. So when my principal moved the way the picture fell, I faked to the right with my head and cut to the left like Gilbert Perreault. I was running as fast as Cournoyer.

"Ken Dryden can die in a plane crash!" That's what I yelled as I made my cut around the principal and headed for the door. I had him beat until the last second. That's when he forgot about the photograph and looked me square in the shoulders. I knew I was in trouble. I went for it anyway. Too late. He angled me off and grabbed me with both hands and then crunched me against the boards. *Boom!* I kept yelling, "Holding! Holding!" It was a penalty, hundred percent. But there I was, stuck in between him and the wall and the filing cabinet and no referee.

The principal was saying, "It's okay, it's okay."

I kept pushing and kicking and swinging and swearing but there was nothing I could do. I even tried a Savardian Spinorama but he had me in a bear hug just like Tim Horton used to grab Gordie Howe. I couldn't get away and I could barely breathe. My principal was all sweaty and smelled like the Old Port cigars my dad smoked. He just held me there and told me I didn't have to be like Ken Dryden.

If my principal hadn't said that, I would have quit school right there and gone all the way to Montreal. That's where you can play junior hockey and quit school and no one cares.

The principal held me like that and told me everything was going to be okay. That was it. After that I was okay.

*

I found out you can quit school legally once you've got your grade nine. That's what the principal told me. Legally means without the cops throwing you in jail. I know my dad's farmer friend's sons all quit after grade nine. By then I'll be fourteen and playing in Quebec for the Montreal Junior Canadiens just like the Roadrunner did.

Sitting there in the office below the picture of the Queen and waiting for my mom and dad to come and get me, I planned in my head my whole interview for Hockey Night in Canada. I'll be a rookie for Montreal. I'll be talking to either Dick Irvin or Dave Hodge. They're the commentators. First thing, I'll thank the Good Lord because all hockey legends do. Second thing, say hi to my folks back in Rossland where they live together. Third thing, say hi to all my brothers and sisters. Imagine if I had three or four more by then! Fourth thing, thank Cournoyer for letting me play on his line and have a stall right next to his in the dressing room. Fifth thing, remind all the kids who want to make pro to quit school first chance they get. They'll listen, too. People always listen to a legend.

My mom showed up at the principal's office first. Then my dad showed up. I figured a big fight. Not one yell. And when they came out of the principal's office nobody was mad at me, not even the principal. He asked me if I was okay. I said I was sorry about throwing his papers on the floor and getting so riled up. I said it's just that me and Dryden aren't exactly good friends. He said he didn't want to do that work, anyway, and we all laughed. He wanted to go home and watch the game on TV. I didn't even know he was a hockey fan. That was pretty good to find out.

It gets better.

When me and my mom and my dad were all outside, I hugged my mom. That's normal, right? Okay. But before I went off with my dad, my mom and dad hugged too. I'm

not kidding. Not a big hug. Not like when you score in overtime. But it was still a hug. I think my dad moved forward first. I'm not sure. I'd do anything to see it again in slo-mo. I'd never seen them hug before. Yeah, I'm pretty sure my dad moved first. My mom didn't head for the hills, though, and that's the truth. I can still picture it when I think about it. I think about it all the time.

Driving home, my dad said my mom thinks I should see that counsellor again. "The one who knows less than Rex and smells like old cigarettes?" I said.

My dad laughed. He said I should think about it, anyway. Then he asked me if I was okay.

I said, "Hey, you and Mom are getting along pretty good, huh?"

My dad didn't say anything but they were. They had to be. The Good Lord must've been working overtime.

I said, "Dad, next time you hug Mom you should try it with no clothes on."

You should've seen the look he gave me.

*

Me and my dad watched the sixth game of the series all by ourselves. That's the way I like it. Me and him watching the best sport in the world. Biggest game of the year. Montreal facing elimination.

I was sitting on the floor in front of the TV. The plastic was flapping. I had my Montreal tuque on. The milkshake was ready. The national anthem was playing. Cournoyer was moving his legs just standing there, rarin' to go. My dad was in his chair in his sheepskin jacket. He had an Old Port cigar in his mouth.

Come on, Montreal!

First period. *Boom.* One-nothing, Montreal.

Hello, seventh game.

Second period. *Boom.* Two-nothing, Montreal.

Good to meet ya, Stanley Cup.

That's when I got butt-ended right in the gut. The Rangers scored two goals forty-six seconds apart in the second period.

All tied up. *Bunny!*

My dad said, "Take it easy. Lots of time left."

Third period. After a thousand saves by the Ranger goalie, the Rangers scored with less than nine minutes to go.

Three-two Rangers. I couldn't believe it was really happening, but it was. Like watching Rex die except a million times slower.

Come on! Come on! That's what I was yelling.

You should've seen the look on Cournoyer's face. Like he could die. Like he'd given up.

And there was still eight minutes to play!

Seven minutes to play.

Six-five-four-three-two.

Come on!

The whistle blew. Less than two minutes to go. I was punching my fist into the carpet. Me and my dad sat there staring at this commercial about the Big Fig Newton. "They should've put him in net!" That's what I was yelling.

My dad said, "Take it easy. It's not over yet."

My nose was running like crazy. My eyes were full of water.

The game was back on. Montreal pulled Bunny for an extra attacker. Come on! Come on!

New York scored on the empty net.

I was paralysed.

New York scored again.

Five-two.

There was nothing Cournoyer could do. Or the commentators. Or Bunny. Or me. It was over.

The crowd was chanting, "Ed-die! Ed-die!" for the Ranger goalie. Then they counted down the seconds. Ten, nine, all the way to zero. The siren went off.

It really was over.

Montreal was dead.

My hands were clenched. The colours on the TV blended together like a milkshake. My dad touched me on the shoulder as he walked by and said, "Hey, don't worry about it. There's always next year."

Next year!

He went downstairs to finish my sister's bookcase. Another coat of varnish.

I didn't take one breath until the last notes of that stupid theme song came on. I hate those high notes!

I grabbed my pucks from my hockey bag—three brand-new pucks with the Montreal Canadiens emblem painted on them. I lined them up as fast as I could on the front-room carpet. Fifteen feet in front of the TV. Point-blank. I put on my old hockey gloves. I grabbed my Sherwood hockey stick. I took one look at the commentators and wound up as hard as I could.

"*Whoooa!*"

That's what my dad yelled.

He must've just been coming back from downstairs when he spotted me. I was at the tiptop of my wind-up. Just like if I was posing for a photograph. I wasn't smiling, though. I was swearing my head off.

I turned my head to where my dad was, standing there with his hands out and his balls out and his eyes bulging like jumbo jawbreakers.

"Don't shoot!" That's what he said.

That's when I figured out what I was doing.

"I mean it," he said. "Drop the stick."

My dad knew how much I practised my shot. He knew I could blow that TV to smithereens.

My dad was looking right at me. "Put the stick...down."

My arms started to shake. Like I didn't know what they'd do. My face was all trembly. My teeth were gritted like when a hand turns into a fist.

My dad pointed. "Now don't you shoot," he said. He looked like he might go for me.

I pushed my wind-up even higher.

My dad didn't move. He glanced at the colour TV, then back at me. Our eyes glued together.

I stared. That's what I did. I just stared at him.

That's when my dad took a step towards me.

My arms tightened even more. The blade of my Sherwood clunked on the ceiling.

My dad stopped in his tracks.

My stick started to knock on the ceiling. I couldn't stop it.

Knock-knock-knock-knock-knock.

My dad looked up at the ceiling where my stick was knocking, then back at me. "It's going to be okay," he said. "Now give me the goddamn stick."

I don't remember the next second. I remember bits of it.

I pictured Dryden's mask like the Devil—that's what it's like with those ribs on his cheeks—staring straight at me. I pictured Cournoyer when he'd given up with eight minutes left. His face was sadder than Jesus hanging on that cross. I pictured my mom and dad hugging, too. My dad made the first move but my mom was right there. And Rex just before the car, then *boom*, right afterwards, lying there, his electricity spinning everywhere.

After that all I know is, my dad made a run for me, I saw him coming and I let a slapshot go.

It was perfect.

Dead centre.

The TV blew up.

You should've heard the noise. Seriously. Like a bomb went off inside the Hockey Night in Canada control room. Glass and smoke and electricity were spitting out like a dog with the rabies. Like the Richard Riot outside the Montreal Forum when the Rocket got suspended was right inside the TV.

My second shot was perfect too, except the wind-up clipped my dad in the chops just before he got to me.

I still got it away, though. That's because I've been working on a quick release.

Just like Espo. Knocked the TV right over.

The third shot went wide into the plastic wall, but that was because I was getting tackled just as I let it go. I took a hit to make the play.

That takes guts.

Just like Bobby Clarke.

Me and my dad both went flying.

When he was lying on top of me I don't think he could

believe how much my shot had improved.

I remember wishing that TV could've been the open net against Penticton. If I'd scored on that open net, the whole team would've jumped off the bench and piled on top of me and squished my face into the ice. It would've been just like my dad on top of me now, squishing my face into the carpet.

*

Me and my dad sat on the front-room floor for quite a while. The TV kept smoking. Everything was quiet. Even the plastic had stopped flapping. I think I might kill my son if he did what I did. Just kill him. My dad didn't say a word. I didn't say anything either. I just looked down at the carpet. The Hockey Night in Canada theme song was going over and over in my head, and everything else I'd ever known was racing around in there, too, like a whole bunch of crazy bats. My dad's lip was puffy and there was blood. He ignored it like he was Bobby Baun. He stood up, put on his work boots and unplugged the TV. Barenaked except for those boots and his sheepskin jacket, he started sweeping up the broken glass. He vacuumed, too. I put on my sneakers and started helping him pick up the pieces. All I was wearing was my baggy long underwear and my Montreal Canadiens shirt and my Montreal Canadiens tuque.

Not one word was said.

*

I didn't go to school the next day. My dad told me to stay home. I don't know why. We didn't talk at all. My dad normally talks and talks but not the day after I blew up the TV. He worked downstairs on my sister's bookcase for her birthday. I read the Hockey News and practised my shot for a while.

We took the smashed TV to the dump but we didn't talk about it. We didn't talk about anything. We took a whole bunch of other garbage, too—four big bags of sawdust and the gyproc from when I smashed the wall from all those slapshots.

Driving the dirt roads on the way there, my dad looked out the front window of the truck and I looked out the side window. The sky was all blue. The roads were clear except for little islands of ice and loose gravel. I don't know why, but I could hear cracking everywhere. Trees cracking. Snow cracking. Streams of silvery water cracking and running down the road and going wherever they wanted. Even the ground was cracking—like when a cat stretches from the tip of its tail to its head. Like old, dead dinosaurs were waking up and they were going to lift the ground right up.

On three we tossed that TV as far as we could. It flew pretty good with the insides already gutted. It smashed pretty good, too. We watched it for a while, all busted up on top of the garbage pile.

On the drive home my dad stopped in to check on some patients at the hospital. I waited in the truck for about fifteen minutes. I wondered if we were ever going to talk again. When he came back, he threw me a bag of rubber gloves that are pretty fun to blow up and some plaster of Paris stuff, too. You just add water to the plaster of Paris and start wrapping it around your arm or on your face. It makes perfect casts and great goalie masks. You can paint 'em, too.

I didn't know why, but we drove right past our house

and right past my school. I didn't know where we were going. Turns out to the Rossland arena.

There were no cars around but the door to get in opened when my dad pushed it. Inside it was dark and quiet. We snuck up the stairs and every footstep bounced away like a goal from so long ago you can barely remember it.

My dad sat me in the bleachers. All the lights except a couple were out and all the ice was gone. It was nothing but cement.

Just sitting there in the darkness, I pictured a hockey game right away. Everything. The crowd. The bright lights. The sound of the ice and the skates cutting away on it. The sound of the boards and the pucks and the grunts and the hits and the yells and the leather and the wood and the rubber and metal all spinning around. I could smell the hot chocolate and the frozen rubber floor mats. I could picture the skates walking out to start the game and the colours of the uniforms and winter jackets and the scoreboard all lit up and the clock ticking away. I could hear the buzzer and the announcer and I could feel that perfect feeling I get every time I step on the ice. It feels like the biggest day of your life and the last chance you'll ever get, all at the same time.

My dad sat on the back of the bleacher in front of me. I could barely see his face in the darkness but I could see it enough. His eyes and his broken nose and his browny-grey hair all tousled. He said, "I got some news for you."

I didn't say anything.

He said, "I know you want me and your mother to get back together. Well, it's not going to happen so you have to stop hoping for it and you have to forget about it."

The colours from the hockey game in my head had faded away.

"I love your mother very much and I want you to be good to your mother."

I stared but I didn't say anything.

"Now listen, because this is the way it is. I'm having another kid but not with your mother. My girlfriend and I are having a kid. I haven't told anybody else yet but she's pregnant. We're going to have the kid at home. Natural childbirth. You can be there if you want. Do you understand?"

The crazy bat was back flying around.

My dad closed his eyes for a second and breathed out. He looked at me like he expected me to cry. "You okay?"

I could see my mom and dad hugging right in my head. It didn't mean anything! My nails were digging into my palms. I nodded.

"By the way," my dad said, "I just heard on the news that Ken is coming back to play for the Canadiens next year."

*

When we got to Montrose, I felt like a statue on the outside. Inside I didn't know what I was feeling. Me and my dad carried in the birthday bookcase for my sister. We bought a bucket of Dixie Lee chicken and a tub of ice cream and pop, too. I knew the bomb was going to go off. I didn't know when but I knew once my dad told them, that would be it. Game over.

My sister was wearing a purple dress and she was hanging up the phone. She had a purple hat on, too. We put the bookcase down right there in the kitchen. It was all yellow and shiny pine, like if you poured honey on a rink.

"Happy birthday, darlin'." That's what my dad said.

My sister loved it like crazy as soon as she saw it. I knew she would. She even uncrossed her arms and started rubbing it.

But she couldn't hear the ticking.

I stood there with my head down. My brother had his Black Hawks shirt on. He was sitting at the table reading a comic. My dad threw him a pop. He caught it and said, "Hey, sniveller, Dryden is coming back next year with Montreal so you can stop your bawlin'."

I looked up with my eyes but kept my head down. "I know."

Tick-tick-tick-tick-tick.

I didn't look at my mom. She must've looked at me, though. She said, "What's going on?" like she knew something was wrong.

My eyes were open but I closed my head.

That's when my dad said he had something to tell everybody.

TICK-TICK-TICK-TICK-TICK.

He told them what he told me. That he was having a baby with his really young girlfriend.

My sister just stood there.

My brother looked back down at his comic.

My mom said, "You're *what*?"

"What I said," my dad said.

"You're forty-five years old! She could be your bloody daughter!"

My dad said, "F--- off."

My sister ran into her room with her face in her hands, screaming, "I'm so embarrassed!"

239

My brother said, "Sayonara, amigos." He was out the door.

As soon as it slammed, my mom and dad started yelling. I watched back and forth for about eight seconds. Then I walked outside.

Rex was right there waiting for me. His electricity, anyway. Come on, boy. That's what I said. His collar and his tag jingled together when he jumped up on me. You forget how perfect that sound is.

I looked up. The sun was just about to say so long. Good thing I had my hockey jacket on. The crest said *Trail Peewee Reps. Kootenay Champions 73-74.*

It had been a pretty good year when you think about.

We sure thumped Cranbrook. We lost to Castlegar and then came back. All those goals against Nelson. We beat North Shore Winter Club with all the rich kids and three big boys! I might have missed two open nets but I was still the second-best player on the team. I had to be. Assistant captain. Second-most goals. Second-most assists. Think about it, Egghead.

I stuck my hands in my pockets and me and Rex walked across the lawn where I'd tried to make the rink. The grass was mud and I was leaving footprints the size of Big Foot. You could see exactly where I'd laid the boards to hold the plastic down. Man, those nights were cold. I must have poured about twelve thousand and twenty gallons of water on that ground. It's a miracle the whole house didn't float away. Next year I'll just get my dad to buy me one big chunk of plastic and do the damn thing right.

Walking down the alleyway I could still hear my mom and dad yelling, but only if I stopped walking. It was so far away it sounded more like noisy wind.

I looked out at the road to where Rex got hit. I said, See ya, Rex. I had to. I didn't want him to cross that highway again. What kind of friend would that make me? So Rex flew off and I kept walking.

That's when I pictured my dad doing that funny dance he does. Sometimes just wearing a sheepskin jacket and nothing else. You'd have to see it to believe it. It's the funniest thing you'll ever see.

When I got to the edge of the mountain bank, I'd gone as far as I could go. Looking out, I could see everything. Twenty miles away a pack of tiny black-and-white cows that never move. Just like a train set. Roads and fences and caves way off in the mountains. The Columbia River floating away, spinning and bending and turning like a highway as black as Hobey's eyes just before the diesel came. You never see them, but below the surface of the river twelve-foot sturgeons are swimming everywhere. That river goes all the way to the United States of America. I bet the sturgeons are even bigger down there. Bigger bums, anyway. I laughed when I thought that.

I stood there for a long time. The wind was cold on my cheeks and my nose but I liked it. The sun was gone except for the orange nightlight it leaves behind until the moon shows up.

I could still hear an eensy bit of yelling but you wouldn't know it was yelling if you hadn't just walked away from it.

The only thing left to do was go and play street hockey. I knew I should. How else would I improve my stick-handling for next year? I knew there'd be a game going on down the road, too. There's always a game—especially during the playoffs. The streetlights would be coming on. In my head I could even hear the sound of the sticks on the road and see that net with the holes in it.

The thing was, I didn't want to play street hockey.

I sat on the ground and stared out at the black mountains and thought about all those old dinosaur bones waiting to be dug up. There must be a million of 'em. I thought about that little tadpole, too. I wondered if he was looking forward to sticking his head out. When he did I'd have my pep talk ready.

I thought about my mom and dad. And the sun going down. And Yvan Cournoyer's grin with a tooth missing when he heard the news about Ken.

I was glad Ken was coming back. It had been a pretty long year without him.

I didn't know what else to do. I was too tired to think any more so I just sat there at the edge of the mountain and closed my eyes.

Sometimes if you want to you can just sit there for a while. That's what I did. I sat there for a while.

I wasn't quitting.

I was just taking a little time off.

GAME OVER

A Family
Place

Praise for *A Family Place*

"Leila Philip's view of her family's land is, in part, sweeping and romantic, a panoramic view much like the luminous paintings of the Hudson River School, yet nothing in her detailed narrative of this cherished place dwarfs the lives of those who have lived here. They live again in her telling. Philip grafts history, natural history and autobiography into a stunning performance, as tempting as the Golden Delicious apples that grace the trees of her orchard."
        —Maureen Howard, author of *Big as Life*

"In this eloquent memoir, Leila Philip deftly braids elegance and struggle, memory and loss, past and present, place and time. With wit and insight, she probes the intricate ties of landscape and history, finding in her family farm deep reserves of meaning and mystery."
        —Alan Taylor, author of the Pulitzer Prize–winning
        William Cooper's Town

"Leila Philip understands better than anyone just how complex our ties to the land are. In deliberating over mysteries of her family's history and questioning her own dreams and responsibilities toward the family orchards, she has created a rich and textured world for a reader to inhabit. *A Family Place* is full of intelligence, gracefully written, and guided by a devoted heart."
        —Jane Brox, author of *Five Thousand Days Like This One*

"Like the house at its center, Leila Philip's *A Family Place* is elegant but also generous, full of feeling but never sentimental; more than once its subtle moral shadings reminded me of Forster's *Howards End*. Larger in scope than a memoir but more intimate than mere history, Philip's genealogical ledger expands with each new chapter, reflecting and readjusting American notions of family, land, lineage, service, and country."
        —Dale Peck, author of *Martin and John*

A FAMILY PLACE

A Hudson Valley Farm,
Three Centuries,
Five Wars,
One Family

~~Leila Philip~~

excelsior editions

AN IMPRINT OF STATE UNIVERSITY OF NEW YORK PRESS

page i: An 1858 map of Claverack,
courtesy of the Columbia County Historical Society

Galleries of family portraits follow pages 57 and 114

cover photographs by Laurie Searl, 2009, used by permission

Published by
State University of New York Press, Albany

© Leila Philip, 2001

All rights reserved

Printed in the United States of America

For information, contact State University of New York Press, Albany, NY
www.sunypress.edu

Production, Laurie Searl
Marketing, Fran Keneston

LIBRARY OF CONGRESS CATALOGING-IN-PUBLICATION DATA

Philip, Leila.
A family place : a Hudson Valley farm, three centuries, five wars, one family /
Leila Philip.
p. cm.
"Excelsior editions."
Originally published: New York : Viking, 2001.
ISBN 978-1-4384-2760-7 (pbk. : alk. paper)
1. Columbia County (N.Y.)—Description and travel. 2. Columbia County
(N.Y.)—History. 3. Hudson River Valley (N.Y. and N.J.)—Description and
travel. 4. Hudson River Valley (N.Y. and N.J.)—History. 5. Country life—
New York (State)—Columbia County. 6. Philip, Leila. 7. Phillips family.
8. Columbia County (N.Y.)—Biography. 9. Fruit growers—New York
(State)—Columbia County—Biography. 10. Orchards—New York (State)—
Columbia County. I. Title.
F127.C8P47 2009
974.7'39—dc22   2008055624

10 9 8 7 6 5 4 3 2 1

IN MEMORY OF

John Van Ness Philip Jr.
(1922–1992)

This edition is for
MY MOTHER
Julia Willis Philip

Sheet from the ship's log of Admiral Van Ness that hung in the library

Contents

On May 27, 1649, the Mohican Aepjen, or chief, Keesieway began to exchange his lands in Columbia County—what would become thousands of acres of verdant rolling hills, winding creeks and sheltered inlets that led onto a shimmering tidal river—to the Van Rensselaers for a payment of ten fathoms of cloth, ten kettles, ten axes, ten adzes, ten swords, ten necklaces of strung beads, ten knives and one firelock gun.

In the Beginning

BEFORE ME STOOD TALAVERA, but all around was darkness. Light was spewing out from so many of the tall windows that the house could have been a ship sailing the night sea. But instead of feeling cheered by what I saw, I felt frozen. Talavera, that grand vessel of the past, how much of it was illusion, a house of cards, precarious, hostage to the slightest breeze?

Even now I could shut my eyes and see each room as it had been. On the uppermost floor in the west room sat the mahogany cradle that had rocked generations. My sister and I had found it a perfect place to nurse the baby rabbits that we sometimes found abandoned in the fields after the mower had gone by. Determined to save them from the dogs and the cats, we wrapped them in old sweaters and nursed them with tiny droppers of milk, feeding them every two hours. The rabbit kits never lived more than a few days, but we would always try, stroking their impossibly small ears and frail, quivering bodies with a finger until they fell still, asleep in our palms.

In that same room was the strange armadillo basket, a Victorian horror made from an armadillo shell, the nose wired to the long tail to form a handle. Boredom was never possible on rainy days at Talavera. It was an adventure merely to open the huge old doors and wander through these rooms. Each was filled with strange old things to finger and collect or just to stare at from a wary distance. Downstairs the curio cabinets were stocked with prehistoric and Mohican arrowheads collected each season in the upturned plow furrows. I loved to look at them and at the shelves of relics from an ancestor's travels. Medals, bits of stone, a tiny shoe with a message written on the sole, a stone lantern, a piece of Roman tile, the broken edge of an old relief, a square of embroidered fabric, a pile of coins, a strange torpedo-shaped Civil War bullet: so many things that each time you looked you could find something new.

My family saved everything, a habit that would make my search possible when it came to digging up the past. I loved the funny silver and porcelain thimbles, the faded, falling-apart packets of needles and thread and blanket binding, the old quill pens and nibs and the glass inkwells that I painstakingly strove to use when I was twelve, blotching ink all over the white pages of my leather-bound journal. The books were old; the wastebaskets were old; the drapes were old; even the bottles of alcohol and Pepto-Bismol in the medicine closet were from a time long before I was born. Once I went looking for a Band-Aid and pried open the rusting metal box only to find that the Band-Aids inside had withered. I dumped out a dozen yellow strips that crackled and broke to the touch like dried cicada shells.

જી

Talavera was not just a house and not just the past. It was not just my father's dream, and it was not just my aged rival. Somehow Talavera had absorbed my own childhood, becoming me. Once I walked out of the house, across the lawns and onto the farm's land, time would conflate, and I was not just the age I was then but all the ages I had ever been. I was five years old and climbing on, then falling off our Shetland pony. I was nine years old and riding my first new bicycle, down the big hill faster and faster until my wheel caught in a rut and I came to a stop, smack against the boxes of a beehive. I was twelve years old and proudly backing up a tractor and trailer. Then sixteen and racing my horse, faster and faster without a saddle or a bridle, across the meadow.

I walked slowly back up to the house and crossed the north porch. All around me the tall Corinthian columns spired up, echoing the tripartite structure of the house with its north and south wings and its central pavilion, designed to appear as if a temple lost within a grove. I reached out to open the door. Beneath my fingers the brass door handle felt solid, reassuringly smooth and cool. But as soon as I began to turn the knob, I felt myself grow weak. The knob turned and turned, but the door would not open. Broken, the inside mechanism separated from the catch. A simple matter, but at that moment my insides split into panic. I couldn't get in, I couldn't get away.

I thought back to the psalm that my mother and I had chosen for my father's funeral: "You sweep us away like a dream; we fade away suddenly like the grass." Then, as if on cue, the knob on the front door caught and turned. I pushed the door forward and walked in, listening to my footsteps echo in the now-darkening house.

One

My father is trying to teach me how to prune a tree. "Here," he says, holding the center section of a young tree in one hand and angling the clippers toward it with the other. "See these two terminals growing close together. That won't do. They are competing. One has to go."

His large hands hold the clippers easily, almost carelessly as he bends his tall frame over the young tree. I watch his fingers squeeze over the orange grips. The blades snap. A long, slender branch slides down the length of the tree. "You have to find the leader, make a decision, then cut.

"There, now we'll just top the one we've left a bit." He bends the tip of the tree's new leader toward me and fingers the silver, bullet-shaped buds. "You always want to cut just above a bud." His clippers snap again. This time the length of tree falls onto his boot. He bends down and grabs it, then flings it over his shoulder. The cut wood lands with a thud in the broken winter grasses, startling the dog.

"These trees got away from us last year," he says, still holding the clippers up as a pointer. "Look at all this side growth—"

My father interrupts himself to begin pushing down some of the side branches, or scaffold limbs, so that instead of angling up around the trunk of the tree, they jut out from the center of the tree at right angles. He studies the tree for a moment; then his clippers begin again, snapping a limb off here, another one there, twisting around the soft new growth, to cut the wood clean and close to the trunk. Each time he makes a cut, my father flicks his wrist so that the newly cut wood twists away from him, rustling down into the tree. Sometimes branches fall against his chest, but he just brushes them away without looking down. He has a vision for this tree: the strong limbs studded with red apples, the entire tree a green spreading focus to produce good fruit. No excess limbs to cut the light, a leader rising straight and tall.

I rub my gloved hands together in an effort to keep them warm and continue watching. My father's clippers flash silver in the cold winter air. Only when several more branches lie at the base of the tree does he step back to look. So much of the bushy side growth is gone that the tree looks awkward, shorn. The limbs and trunk are dotted with white marks where the soft underwood has been exposed. For really deep cuts on the older trees, my father will coat the surface with tar and turpentine to prevent disease, but for clipper cuts on a young tree like this, he will count on the tree's vigor to heal over the wounds. A leader now rises; evenly spaced side branches push out on all four quadrants.

"That's enough for now," says my father. "Next year we can work straightening out some of those side limbs, but I don't want to cut off any more fruit buds since this is its first bearing year."

While I pull the branches away, piling them in the center of the row so that they can be scooped up by the brush picker, my father pulls his gloves off and adjusts the wire guard around the tree's base. Then he pulls a handful of mouse bait from a coffee can and scatters it around the tree. "If we can just keep the mice and deer off of them, these trees should be okay."

ONE

I look down the rows of young Empires that now line the slope of the meadow as it cuts down from the garden.

"Here"—my father hands me the clippers—"you try the next one." He walks back to the tractor with its wooden pruning tower and pulls out a saw.

I move down the row to a short tree, dense with limbs. I see only one central branch shooting up, no competition to clean out of the way. But the central terminal seems crooked and stunted. Sometimes my father looks at trees like this and decides to get rid of the weak leader and restart the tree. He cuts the old leader back and chooses one of the lower branches to be the tree's new leader. Should I do that, letting one of the lower branches, already beginning to spire up, become the tree's new center? I decide to go with that idea but then can't decide which lower limb to choose as the new leader. The branches are all about the same size, all vigorous. I try pushing down the side branches, as I have watched my father do, to get a handle on which scaffold limbs should stay, but that only confuses me more. I want so much to get this right. I know it will please my father. When he heads out for the orchards, he is always glad when I come along.

But there are too many branches, each one twisting this way, that way. I tell myself I will just have to begin, start cutting somewhere. I bring my clippers up against a limb, pushing them close to the trunk to make a clean cut as my father has shown me, but just as I am about to squeeze the handle, I am overcome with fear. What if I make the wrong cut? I back up and study the tree again, but even then I can't decide where to begin. I try a new tactic. I push myself into the center of the small tree so that I can look at the branches from that angle. But now I am simply wedged into the chaos of branches.

When I push my way back out of the tree, a branch snaps in my face. The sudden sting makes me only more determined to begin cutting in somewhere. I raise my clippers, but it is no use. I am stumped again. All the bottom branches

3

look identical. What if the one I choose to be a leader becomes stunted? Then I will have cut away the tree's other possibilities and chosen the wrong one.

My father, busy cutting a split limb off a nearby tree, doesn't seem to notice that I am just standing there, clippers poised. Everything seems to depend upon a kind of confidence I don't feel. Knowing how to prune a tree, like knowing how to handle a horse, is important here. I am already a competent rider. I will learn how to prune an apple tree. Tomorrow.

I push myself back into the center of the small tree and resume cutting the sucker growth off limbs. I know it is not real pruning, those cuts that determine the fate of a tree, just cleanup work. I snip quickly and decisively at the forest of suckers, thin, upright terminals that shoot up from each limb almost parallel to the leader. I hate the sense of defeat that I feel, but I will not admit to my father that I have no idea how to prune a tree. He makes it look so easy, like something I should already know.

Suddenly the dog leaps up and runs across the meadow and onto the frost-heaved expanse of back lawn, chasing a rabbit. His feet clatter through the large heart-shaped catalpa leaves. I look up for a moment at the borders of old shade trees that ring the huge yellow house. Lined with snow and ice, their unpruned shapes etch a mysterious calligraphy across the blank winter sky.

CHAPTER TWO

The Count

I am standing at the edge of the world. All around me young apple trees spread down and out in obedient lines. But if I look across the meadow below, past the pond, past the road leading up the far slope to the enormous house, shouldering in among tall white pines, and past that too, the mountains begin, their smooth blue flanks crowding the sky. I have arrived just in time. Waves of yellow light are spreading over the land, so much orange today that the clouds begin to throb, the dark outline of the Catskills looming closer, pushing back the foothills that rise up and down in green waves to the river, five miles away.

The sky shudders, suddenly gone neon, psychedelic, blazing with color. It won't be long now before that final diving down and the drawn-out afterglow, that famous Hudson Valley light that drove landscape painters wild. Soon the trees around me are glowing too, absolved somehow of all responsibility to bloom and produce, to grow tall, not to falter. I watch the gray bark turn purple in the softening rose-colored light. Their limbs, still leafed out and loaded with red fruit, shimmer. The brisk October air is musty with rent pollen and the slightly burned smell of falling leaves. I take a deep breath. I will never grow tired of this drama, just as I will never not love this land. I whistle for Danny, my father's dog, and walk back to the silver truck to finish the closing-up chores.

My family has owned this land since 1732, but that is only European time. For generations before the arrival of Henry Hudson and then my own family, Mohican Indians lived here, hunting and fishing along Claverack Creek and farming in a small way. That is, until 1649, when the Mohican chief Keesieway began to exchange his lands in Columbia County to the Van Rensselaers for the pathetic payment of ten fathoms of cloth, ten kettles, ten axes, ten adzes, ten swords, ten necklaces of strung beads, ten knives and one firelock gun.

Soon after that historic land deal, Admiral Adrian Van Ness set sail with a broomstick tied to his mast, indicating his intent to sweep the English from the seas. Back in Amsterdam, he might well have known Kiliaen Van Rensselaer, who, having recently acquired 850,000 acres of Hudson Valley land, had begun to establish Rensselaerswyck Manor and himself as the first lord or patroon. In the library of the large house on the hill hangs a framed sheet from the log of one of Admiral Van Ness's seventeenth-century voyages. Growing up, I had no idea what the strange faded sheet of almost illegible Dutch writing was or why it was hanging by the library closet where we always kept the green cashbox of harvest money. My father's middle name was Van Ness, as his father's had been, and his great-uncle's had been. Before that, Van Ness had been the surname of men whose names were listed on the deed for this land.

For years my family has grown apples and pears here, running a commercial fruit orchard named Philip Orchards. We sell the entire crop to customers who come to "pick your own." Now that my father is sick, my sister, my three brothers and I are taking turns managing the orchards on weekends throughout the ten weeks of harvest. I don't have time

6

to linger because it is time for me to begin the orchard check, driving through the various orchards to see how many last-minute customers are still picking and to look over the remaining fruit so that my father can plan where to send customers the next day. By the end of October, or by the first frost, whichever comes first, we need to sell eight thousand bushels of fruit.

I had parked the truck on the main farm road so that any remaining customers could see it if they were on their way out. Most of our pickers have picked here for years and would know to stop and find me in order to pay for their fruit. Still, I walk quickly now, cutting along the top of the ridge so that I can look over the whips of Harrow Sweets, planted in an effort to reenergize flagging pear sales. Harrows are a new breed of pear that should ripen later than the sweet, juicy Bartlett, which always comes on too early in September for the Pick Your Own crowds. I see that over the summer the infant trees have pushed up two and three feet of new terminal growth, just as they should. My father will be pleased. But when I look closely at the young side limbs, I see that they are growing too close to the slender trunk, the angle of these new scaffold branches more like forty-five degrees instead of the strong right angle desired. Unless side limbs emerge from the trunk at the proper angle, once loaded with fruit, they will snap. The trees need shaping, the still-pliant growth pushed away from the leader with toothpicks or small props of wood or pulled down to the correct angle by weighting the limbs with stones tied on with string. Normally my father would have done this by now, for in a few weeks the plant tissue will be too stiff. Given a few days, I could do the work too, but I don't have the time, and neither does my mother. It would just agitate my father to mention the wayward trees to him. I head down the slope so that I can scan the Empires. A perfect set here, the apples large and low to the ground for easy picking.

Soon I am in the M-Nines, a block of semidwarf Red Delicious trees. My family called this sorry-looking section of trees the M-Nines after the name of their rootstock, and they were something of a family joke. Back in the 1970s, my father's idea had been to replace the large old orchard trees planted by my grandfather with semidwarf stock that produced significantly more bushels per acre. Basically, his strategy worked, for within eight years the orchards were producing as much as they had once done on twice the acreage. But the M-Nines were an exception. The tentative rootstock didn't like the rocky feel of our hill, and the root base spread out far too slowly for the ambitious apple cultivars that had been grafted on to them. The trees began to produce magnificent purple-red apples, but just as they reached maturity, they began to topple. Still, my father would not give up on the trees. Instead of cutting them down, he'd be out on the hillside, endlessly staking leaders, wiring and pruning limbs in an attempt to keep them upright. When I came home from boarding school at Christmas and Easter, we'd head out and work on the M-Nines together.

8

I grab a leaf from one of the trees and pull it off with a flick of my wrist. Crazy old fools. They are like aging family pets, naughty, untrainable, but impossible to get rid of. Still, as I pass the trees now, I see several good bushels of large red fruit peeking out from the leaves. The caravan of Chinese families that drives up from Queens every fall and heads straight for these trees will not be disappointed when they get here tomorrow.

The truck starts easily, and I turn right onto the farm road, heading away from the mountains and the house so that I can make a quick loop of the back orchards. I haven't gone twenty feet, however, before I come across a yellow sign with orchard directions lying facedown in the grass. I stop the truck, grab the heavy steel mallet and, holding the sign with one hand and the huge hammer in the other, gently tap the sign back in. I had painted many of these signs myself the summer after I graduated from high school, and now many need replacing. The wood splinters a little when I step back to give the sign a final whack, but it stands firm.

Back in the truck and I'm on my way. No customers and no deer. I am moving along in good time. Danny runs alongside me, and I rev the engine, racing up the hill so that he has to run full tilt in order to beat me to the next ridge. There, at the hedgerow, I slow down to pass into the next orchards, and scan the trees on my right. They all are Mutsu apples, most of them planted on my eighteenth birthday. Now they produce some of our fastest-selling and most lucrative fruit. Almost every tree I see is picked clean. I drive on, following the road down now into a mature orchard bordered on all sides by plantings of oaks and maples and conifer trees. Just before the next hedgerow I pass an enormous hemlock that my mother had always called the wild bee tree because wild bees nested in its top. The trunk was so wide I could not get my arms around half of it, and trillium grew beneath its draping limbs.

Soon I am in the backlands, where long lines of trees spread to the woods and the old railroad bed where the Hudson & Boston line had once passed through. Stone walls bound this orchard on all sides, although the woods have crept up over them so that the only use we ever put them to was to head our horses over them as we rode, way too fast, through the trails my father and uncle had cut through the woods.

The truck bounces easily along the soft orchard grass, and I can't help speeding up a little, remembering how my horse, snorting in the spring air, would always take off the minute we came bounding out of the woods and his feet touched this springy orchard turf and how I would let him. In the center of this back orchard rises a twisted oak tree, which, like the hemlock, has a trunk far too wide to stretch one's arms around. I park the truck on a level area near the tree and head out to walk the back rows by foot. During my childhood one of the last vestiges of my grandfather's many farm improvements had stood here: a corncrib, which by then was empty, the weathered gray boards slanting like an enormous dilapidated rib cage.

I walk down long rows of ten- and fifteen-foot trees,

thirty- and forty-year-old McIntosh, Red Delicious and
Cortland trees that my father considered too productive to
replace with semidwarf stock. On either side of me the tall
trees here are acrobats, strong limbs arching up and over,
down and out. They are beautiful, like huge silver spiders,
and a short history of pruning shows in their arched and
jointed limbs. When they were young, the trees were open-
center pruned according to the thinking of the day so that
they rose in perfect storybook apple tree shape, the top of
each tree a green globe of leaves. But one year, after he attended a pruning workshop at the Geneva Agricultural Experimental Station, my father had decided to top the trees,
bringing the fruit down low for Pick Your Own. That winter
he spent days in the orchard with a chain saw and several
men cutting off the upper limbs so that the trees were forced
to spread down, letting light into the center to color the fruit.

Most of the trees look pretty well picked over to me, with
only scattered pockets of fruit in the upper limbs. I make a
mental note to tell my father to have some ladders set out
here tomorrow, and I whistle for Danny. Soon a white and
brown blur appears. Delirious with the scent of deer and
other animals, he races back to me, pretending that he can't
stop and must crash into my legs. This time I let him jump in
the cab with me, and we ride back together, each of us sticking our head out our side window to get a better view. I
drive to the opposite end of the orchard and exit there,
crossing the hedgerow by a small wooded pond that had a
pump in it to fill the spray rig when I was growing up. Because the water was used to fill the spray rig and the sprays
were added to the tank there, we weren't allowed to swim in
the back pond. But the bank was gradual enough and firm
enough for our horses to walk in without slipping, so we
would often ignore our parents' warning and take our horses
swimming there.

As we drive by, a duck flashes up, and I have to lunge for
Danny's collar to keep him from leaping out the window of
the moving truck. In a few minutes we are heading up again,

over the hill, through the hedgerow and back to where we started. A huge white pine tree towers over the road here, and I stop for a moment under its swaying limbs to look across the meadow at the house pond. In the settled light, the water shimmers, a bronze gray disk framed with willows. Danny and I study the smooth surface.

The pond is a place where things happen. When the ice breaks in spring, the open water provides a rest stop for blue herons, migrating geese and wild ducks. Flocks of red-winged blackbirds love to perch in the swaying willow limbs, where they squabble. By late summer the edges blaze yellow and red with jewel and fireweed. All winter wild turkeys would leave their tracks across its surface. It is a spring-fed pond, dug thirteen feet deep, and was designed by my uncle as an engineering project when he was still in graduate school. It was our childhood swimming hole, but these days only a muskrat family and at least one large snapping turtle swim in its murky water.

Nobody there today. I put the truck back in gear and let the wheels pick up speed as we roll down the long hill, around the meadow, then another hill and back to the house and barns. As I pull into the barnyard, I catch up to a green minivan, the last customer of the day. Once the van stops, two children leap out and run across the barnyard, then down the hill, chasing each other, falling and laughing through the bright leaves. A man gets out next. I hear the kitchen door slam.

"Got it, Mom," I shout toward the house, and walk over to add up their tally. It doesn't take me long to take their pair of crisp twenty-dollar bills and hand back change, but the man doesn't seem in any hurry to leave.

"How old are these barns?" he asks, looking toward the three barns, built at right angles to one another, forming a large open barnyard.

"About the same age as the house, I think," I answer. "The house is almost two hundred years." It occurs to me that I don't really know when the barns were built or by whom. It will be a long time before I discover that kerf marks in the timbers indicate that they were milled before 1820. Or that the triangular martin holes cut into the south side of the loft indicate an early Dutch barn-building practice. We both look at the barns for a moment.

"Still run by your family, right?" asks the man.

"Yes," I say without hesitation.

"Good. Keep it that way."

"We're trying," I answer with a laugh, which he echoes.

Then he adds, "You know, I do a little building. I like to work with wood. Those barns"—he nods toward the complex—"they're old, that's really something."

As if on cue, a lemony band of fading sun moves down through the trees to strike the siding along one barn. It is as if this last glance of sun has found the long-forgotten colors in the graying barns, and for a moment they don't look so weathered, the long boards so old they seem ready to slide off. Even the black lines of strap hinges, forged sometime before the Civil War, look blacker, more definite where they secure doors and windows.

The man calls his children, and when they pile into the van, he turns the key and they zoom off. I stuff the twenty-dollar bills into the blue vinyl bank bag and quickly pull the zipper. Long stripes of shadow have begun to pull away from the resting ladders like peels of fruit. I hurry toward the packinghouse and pull the enormous doors shut.

In the open shed area of the farm office, I stop to pull out a tarp to throw over the apples, although we no longer have animals we have to worry about getting into the fruit. Jostled by the thick canvas, an apple rolls out of the box and stops at my feet. An Ida Red, *Pyrus malus,* as large as a small grapefruit. A good half pound. I recognize it as one of the Ida Reds we had picked in early September to show in the fair. It had been left behind because it had a slight bump on the bottom. Fair entries must have size, color and perfect conformation. I had picked the fruit with my mother and Willi, the man who now does all the tractor work—spraying and mowing, plowing and disking—for the farm. My father, unable to walk far, watched from the truck, bending over to choose from among the apples we brought in. When looking over a pile of apples, my father had an eye for choosing a winning plate, the set of six that complemented one another, making the whole group glow. On the tree, however, it was my mother who could spot the winners.

I brush the dust off the smooth surface. There on the bottom is the small bump, like a callus, the touch of scab that roughened the surface and disqualified the apple. Back in March, when the blossoms were setting, warm, wet days had sent scab spores migrating across the orchards. Spraying was not possible until petal fall because the sprays that could kill the scab would also kill the blossoms. Scab that overwintered in the fallen leaves had a heyday, setting out with each warm wind, infecting and blighting entire orchards, while farmers waited, helpless until the rain stopped so that they could get their rigs through the orchards and apply a spray. We had been lucky and were saved from the epidemic that had hit most Columbia County growers. Our orchards had been clean the year before, so few inocula were present in the dead leaves wintering over under the snow. This scab had probably blown up from the abandoned orchard that now bordered ours to the south among an emerging housing development.

Generally, winds here come from the west and don't blow too much inoculum up from the South Place. Still, a spore inoculum must have penetrated this apple's blossom, pushing its way inside the sepal of the flower and moving down through the fruit bud. Perhaps it came on the feet of a pollinating bee. By May the spray rig had made its rounds, shooting out fungicides to kill the scab, but where spores had landed on this tiny, yet-to-emerge apple, the fungus had blemished the skin.

No one knows exactly how flowering happens, that mystery by which some plant cells are chosen and instructed to develop as flowers rather than as stems, leaves or wood, al-

13

though botanists have identified a hypothetical plant hormone that they call florigen. I am not consumed by the desire to know more about the mystery by which vegetative cells change to those with what botanists call floral initiation, but I am deeply envious of the synchrony that whispers to each cell, "Get ready, expand, flower." On St. Patrick's Day I had walked out to check block thirteen. That orchard, planted on a west-facing slope, was a warm pocket, and sure enough, the tiny, bullet-shaped fruit buds on the Ida Reds had cracked, revealing layers of leaf and blossom still covered with a silver fuzz. The swollen buds were just opening. One week later pussy willows had sent up their own silver points, the back pond was yellow with marsh marigolds and the apple blossoms were in full silver tip, green tip and then tight cluster.

In late April the bloom began in earnest. The orchards were dizzy with bees, and along the sides and in the woods, the ground was feathered white with wind anemones and bloodroot. To walk in the orchards was to believe that there could never be a winter. Thick green grass was overtaking the brown stalks of winter grass. Birds were delirious. I put my ear to the cool ground and heard it buzz.

I stood on the top of the ridge and let the soft wind travel my face. When my father turned seventy that April, we had the first of our apple blossom parties, a large picnic in the orchards with dozens of friends. To celebrate his birthday, my family gave my father Danny, an English springer spaniel, like the kind his father had kept for hunting. My father and his brother had spent summer evenings chasing spaniels across the lawns in order to kennel them in their runs by the smokehouse. He was delighted with the wriggling pup. My father was recovering from his mysterious collapse the previous summer. None of us knew yet that his body was struggling to breathe with only 30 percent of his lungs still functioning, the rest damaged by years of smoking and by the tanks of Guthion, Lannate, Alar, Captan and Manzate that he himself had sprayed on the orchards to save money during those years

14

when the farm, recently divided, could not yet afford to hire a professional spray applicator to apply the pesticides. Unwilling to believe that the sprays were really that lethal, my father didn't take seriously the need for protective clothing.

Within two weeks of the orchard picnic, the silver apple buds were green pearls. By June they had blown up to the size of golf balls, still green but showing the promise of size and beautiful shape. Weeks of rain and heat through July swelled the fruit to fantastic size. By mid-August, while we battled mite infestations, my father worried that if the days of perfect August sun that followed were interrupted by any more rain, the fruit cells would expand too quickly, resulting in mushy fruit. Just in time the August haze lifted, and September days were clear and, most important, cool. As soon as the temperatures dropped, the leaves responded, producing ethylene, which signals the fruit to ripen. Each night along the branches where clusters of apples hung, starches turned to sugars, pectic compounds changed shape and flavor esters were produced. Then a farmer's dream. Snappy nights the first week of September that put a stop to chlorophyll formation so that the shy pigments—anthocyanin, carotene and xanthophyll—were revealed and the apples turned pink and rosy, mauve and scarlet, russet, burgundy, tawny and, like the apple now in my hand, the parrot colors of bright yellow and fire engine red.

15

I have a sudden impulse to bite the apple in my hand, crunch down into those vibrant colors. But I have already eaten so many apples since breakfast that I have lost count. I throw the apple into the box with the others and secure the tarp over its top.

Out of habit I glance at the house, where by now my father is certainly waiting. Talavera, William W. Van Ness's old mansion, glows between the trees. I have a lot to tell my father about how the day has gone in the orchards. We need four more good weekends for the farm to break even. As late as 1935 more than four hundred orchards existed in Columbia County. Today fewer than forty remain. The price of apples is just too low to keep up with the costs of spray and fertilizer, labor and taxes on this increasingly valuable land.

I grab the bank bag and the basket of tallies and turn to look west for a moment, out and down the farm drive. The light, chimeric now, flattens the blue mountains until they seem mere cutouts pasted against the darkening sky. Reassured by these harvest colors, by the rosy orange light, by the boxes of red, red fruit, by the barns standing the way they always have and by the money bag, now fat with bills, I stop worrying about the farm's ongoing struggle to pay its bills. What a good day we have had in the orchards, each row cascading with the sight of bright red fruit. I feel the way I did when I was fifteen and had just come back from riding, sweaty and tired but completely at ease. Talavera, that familiar place, that resting stop, always the same, always there. A place where dream and reality never collide because there is no distinction. Like the shadows, stretched confidently out into the barnyard, striping the cooling dirt, I know where I am when I am here. I am home.

16

By the time I head up to the house, my calves ache from the constant walking, and my arms circling the basket of tally slips and receipts feel tired too, but I don't care. I think about my next job, the day's count. As I get closer to the house, however, I see that my father has been waiting for me on the back porch. Is that really my father? His bent figure could be a hunched silhouette in an Edward Hopper painting. The face is half hidden, chiseled with blue shadows. But even without looking, I can tell you every detail of how he sits there, his large hands clutched around his drink, the knuckles chapped and scraped from work. His face, gaunt, worried, brightening when someone appears, but otherwise still. There he sits on the porch, staring out over the view he loves. If I follow his gaze, my eyes take in the sloping lawn, the meadow punctuated by the round pond with its willows, the rise of the hill, the parklike hedgerows and plantings and the lines of hearty young dwarf apple trees, but what is the landscape that my father sees? After fifty years of running the orchards, does he think of the land in fruit-growing terms? *Leaf color bad on the plums by the pond, remember to add nitrogen this winter. The top row of young Delicious, outperforming the others, plant more there. A bad frost pocket on the dip where we put the young Macouns.*

Or does my father feel something less direct, less tangible or considered, his own father's heavy touch upon the land, an expectation, an obligation? Does the sight of the round pond in the meadow that my uncle designed cut my father with sadness, as he thinks of that happier time before his brother became ill? Is it the soft reach of my grandmother's voice he hears there, her poems every holiday, the parties, her blue dresses? Petunias and asters cascading from crystal vases placed throughout the house? Tall orange gladiolus under the banjo clock in the hall? The knowledge that wherever they lived or traveled, they would return to Talavera, their home? Perhaps it is nothing coherent, articulated or even thought. No specific memory or memories at all, but that complicated sense of belonging to a landscape, of knowing the press of light on the hills as surely as one knows one's own palm. I will never know exactly what holds my father to this place so strongly, but I will always wonder.

The October evening has already grown cold, and my father should be wearing a sweater over his blue flannel shirt. But he will not think to check if he needs one before he sits down, his evening drink in hand, and once seated at the round picnic table on the back porch, his long legs scrunched up under the bench, he will not want to get up and go back inside. Neither will he call into the kitchen and ask my mother, who is busy making dinner, to get a sweater for him. I have never known if my father did not mind discomfort or if he grew up so attended to that waiting patiently to be served has become a habit that he has never outgrown. But perhaps my father is so glad to have completed his day of mandatory resting and to be enjoying his end-of-the-day ritual that he does not mind the chill already making its way up his back.

As I get closer to the house, I see my father more clearly, and anxiety rises through me. How thin and frail his shoulders look under his blue flannel shirt. His thick hair, tousled as usual, is more gray than I remember. And his face, with its long family cheekbones, square jaw and prominent nose— the old patroon's face is thin. My perpetually tanned good-looking father is old. Out of habit I begin to rush. I clutch the basket with receipts and the money bag a little tighter. It must have been a record day.

Ahead of me, Danny bounds across the lawn and charges up the back porch stairs. Without hesitating, he rushes to the kitchen door and claws at the screen door enthusiastically until it opens enough for him to squeeze his body through. The door bangs after him. I can hear my mother, busy stirring dinner, greet him. I do not follow but ascend the steps, two at a time, and walk over to where my father sits at the table outside the door to the office.

"Hi, Dad." Immediately I fall into my childhood role as my father's eager helper. "Empires are picked clean except for a row by the M-Nines, and there's not much Red Delicious left in the far back. I'd say we had a good day."

Although I have been reporting on the progress of the harvest since morning, my father nods and looks pleased. His eyes, a deep smoky blue, hold no worry. How I love it when his eyes look that way, clear and satisfied. He takes a sip from his drink.

"I'll do the count," I say, putting the bank bag down on the table and pulling up a bench.

"Why don't you take a break? We can do that later," my father says. His voice is quiet. I look at him and smile. My father could bark out orders one minute as if he were still a U.S. Marine, then surprise me with his gentleness.

"All right," I say, and sit. We are silent the way we often are, sharing a kind of intimacy that is not about the exchange of information. As usual, my father does not ask me about myself, and only the extremity of his illness makes it seem okay for me to inquire about him. It has always been like this, and what makes this moment feel close and not cold or distant, I couldn't say exactly, but I know it has something to do with the way we both love the place around us yet feel the heavy weight of its past as well.

"How are you feeling, Dad?" I finally ask.

"Not bad, it's just the breathing." My father shakes his head slightly and clucks as if observing bad weather, not the state of his failing lungs. "I've got to get some breathing lessons. Then I think I can beat this thing."

"What about seeing a specialist?" I ask, hopeful. "There must be an emphysema institute somewhere; they probably have new treatments—" Midsentence I stop myself, realizing that I am talking faster and faster. That my father is not really listening. That I am falling into my other role of wanting to fix everything.

"Yes, that's a good idea," my father says vaguely, but I can tell that he is saying the words only to make me feel better. I promise myself to make some phone calls when I return to Cambridge.

Yet perhaps my father's quiet this evening is of a different order. He has even less to say than usual. For a while I accompany him, the chill of the evening swirling around us, the soft chirr of insects and the busy calling of birds filling the gaps where words might be. It seems as if we sit there forever and for no time at all. Then I notice that the sunset has faded to a whisper of light. It is late.

"Dad, I better start the count," I say, louder than I intend. "I've got a long drive ahead."

My father nods. "Sure, let's get started." He looks down. It's an ambivalent gesture. I know that he is disappointed.

The screen door bangs as Danny leaps out onto the porch, bounds over to my father and pushes his head into my father's lap.

"Hi, Danny boy." My father's large hands stroke the springer's head in generous fumbling gestures, and the dog

19

wriggles in pleasure. I hear the tenderness in my father's voice as he speaks to the dog, and I forget about my life in Cambridge. I am ten years old again.

"Lift," shouts my father, and I do. I am sitting on the wheel guard of the old Case tractor, one hand holding on to the metal seat where my father sits, the other grasping the rope that operates the lift mechanism on the hay rake. Sun presses through my T-shirt and my perfectly worn blue jeans. A stalk of hay is caught in the toe of my favorite blue Keds with the hole above the toe. We come to the end of the row and this time, right on cue, I yank the rope so that the hay rake lifts with a screech of metal and a tawny hump of straw falls out. My father turns the tractor and we start back across the meadow. My left arm has begun to ache with the effort of hanging on to the back of the metal tractor seat while the tractor bumps along, but I don't care. My ears fill with the powerful grind of the engine on each turn, and I love the smells of sweat and oil and exhaust as much as I love the hot sun beating down, turning everything golden. I am working with my father and that is all I will ever need.

"I guess I'll get some tea first," I say, and go into the kitchen. When I come back out with a steaming mug of tea for me and a plate of cheese and crackers for my father, I see that he has already begun to list figures on the page and has completed a rough count of the money that I'd brought up from the barn over the course of the day.

"Dad," I say, putting the tea and crackers on the table, then sitting down, "I've been thinking. Next spring I want to come stay for a couple of weeks and paint the barns. I can take some time off if I really work hard now."

"That would be great," he says simply, and takes a piece of cheese.

"I think June," I say, and in that moment I am only thinking about how good it would feel to run a brush over the beat-up old boards, leaving them a dark russet red.

My father balances another piece of cheese on a cracker, then puts the whole thing awkwardly into his mouth. He

20

does not disturb my daydream, even though he knows what I know. My idea is absurd. Painting the barns would take far more than two weeks even if I did devote that much time to working here. I am the one who finally changes the subject.

"What was the rough count?"

"Up from last year, I'm sure," my father says, and I immediately understand the buoyancy in his voice. Earning more on the harvest than the previous year is always our goal, and this year we have made it. I am thrilled. I look at my father and know that I am grinning.

"Let's do the count here," I say.

My father answers without hesitation, "Okay."

I go inside to get the other bundles of today's cash from the green box in the closet where they have been stashed. We will each count the total amount of cash brought up from the barn, then compare our figures. It is a long process that begins by sorting, then counting the number of bills in each denomination so that they are ready for the bank deposit bag. We will each do this to avoid mistakes.

Usually my father would have never permitted us to do the count there on the porch, where a late customer, driving up to the back porch, could see the money. "Don't get sloppy," he might have said. But things are different today.

This has been a better harvest. For the past two years a frost in May, then rains during the fall have killed Pick Your Own sales, so that the farm didn't meet expenses even with my parents working without wages as usual. But this year has been miraculously rain free. Days like today with its warm wind and constant sun inspired people from Westchester and Manhattan, Queens and Long Island to drive north. Many of our customers have come to pick at our farm since the sixties, when my parents first had the idea of having people come in to pick as an alternative to packing out wholesale with Jamaican picking crews. Many have come for two generations or more. Just as many speak English with heavy Italian, German and Polish accents or come from places like Korea, the Philippines, Thailand and Vietnam.

21

Over the years we have come to know which groups prefer what apples and pears, and these preferences tend not to vary. Asian pickers want sweet apples like Red and Yellow Delicious and Mutsu. These are given as gifts, eaten as dessert fruits and prized for appearance and size. Italian pickers, many of whom have families that emigrated to the Hudson Valley in the late nineteenth century to work in the iron mills, seek a good pie apple like a Cortland and most of all want Bosc and Seckel pears.

Beautiful Bosc pears with only a touch of psylla fly damage had delighted the Italian customers this year. "You still got Boscos?" I had been asked all day, and when I led them to the rows of tall trees still loaded with brown fruit, they hurried out of their cars to set to work.

Periodically I had driven up to the house to give my father reports on how the day was progressing:

"The only good Cortlands left in number eleven are too high to get without ladders. I think it's time to move to the dogleg or orchard sixteen."

"The Filipinos are spread out on their usual spot at the top of thirteen. Danny's been there all morning filching food from the picnic. This year they're roasting meat!"

"The pickers just can't keep out of the Mutsu, so I've taken the new boy out and posted him there as orchard patrol."

"A group of Italian women want to pick watercress from the irrigation ditch. Said you told them they could last year. I couldn't think of why they shouldn't, so I said yes. They're down there now."

But today my father had been only mildly interested in such news. That alone should have told me everything, but I was too rushed to notice. I hadn't stayed inside with him long. I told myself that I was on orchard duty, that he wanted me busy on the farm the way he would have been, on the move all day. But now I realize that this is only half the truth. I couldn't stand to see my father the way he was, head back in a chair, feet up, resting. I rushed back out to join the crowds of cheerful pickers, reveling in the glorious October weather and the rows of trees studded with fruit.

All day customers had asked me about my father. "Best apples in years," they'd say, "but where is that man who we usually see? Where is the tall man? Where is your father?" I had mumbled that he was resting, then changed the subject.

By afternoon I was encountering the usual problems. So many cars had parked in one spot that a traffic jam had ensued. A bunch of nine-year-olds were throwing apples. The ladders I had just placed in block eleven for people to reach the pears had dropped in the grass. At three o'clock the bus from a Baptist church in Queens arrived right on schedule but then promptly drove to the exact spot where they got stuck last year and had to be pulled out by a tractor.

But all in all, as if in response to the gorgeous weather and the fine fruit, customers had been better behaved than usual. When I made early evening rounds, I found that the picnic crowds had carefully cleaned up their garbage. No hastily flung diapers had to be fished out from under trees. The ladders that I had reset in the afternoon were leaning neatly against the trees, and I found no piles of fruit dumped by an overzealous picker who then decided not to pay.

On my way back I had stopped to look at the McIntosh whips and had encountered a strange and wonderful sight: a blue minivan parked by the ridge with its doors open. Inside sat four saffron-robed Thai monks busily eating apples; their driver, a man dressed in black, waved from where he was still picking under a tree. The monks waved when I drove by and kept on eating and chatting, their saffron robes glowing as they sat hunched in the back of the minivan. I knew not to try to talk to these monks, although I wanted to know where they were from. In Thailand I once brushed the robe of a monk by accident on a crowded Bangkok street. He immediately prostrated himself. By touching him, even accidentally, I made him unclean because I was a woman. The thought of some of our Red Delicious piled high on the altar of a gilded Thai Buddha seemed like another fine omen.

23

Most notable this year perhaps was that my three brothers, my sister and I were working together without our usual bickering. Were we sobered by our father's collapse or responding to the great optimism of this harvest? Whatever the case, he was different too. When each weekend one of us stepped in to run the Pick Your Own operation, he was uncritical of our efforts, staying out of the way and letting us do the job. In previous harvests his silver truck would have been heard zooming through the orchard rows. All day he would have been on the move, looking and fretting, moving ladders, talking to pickers, fussing over the placement of signs, annoying all of us with constant commands. Back at the house, the weather radio would have been on full volume, blaring out hourly reports of weather in the Hudson Valley. But this year my father has only turned the weather radio on each evening to listen for frost warnings. His silver pickup sat idly by the back door.

This time, when I step out onto the back porch, my arms are full of money, packets of bills held by a rubber band. I drop the bundles on the table in front of my father, and some of them bounce slightly, as the rubber bands hit the hard wooden surface. My father reaches over and pulls the band off one bundle, then begins to sort the bills. I pull the dollars out from the blue bag. The change spills on the table.

"Put the bag count in first," my father reminds me.

I nod and count out thirty dollars of ones, fives and coins and put that back in the bank bag so that it is ready for making change for customers tomorrow. Now I begin to sort through the remaining pile of money. Quarters, dimes and nickels get stacked into rows. Then I begin to lay the bills out on the table, one pile for each denomination. My father takes a stack and makes his own piles. He lays each bill down carefully, each one facing the same way, right side up. Soon he comes across a piece of paper with initials and an amount written on it and squints at it, then scowls.

"I can't read this damn thing," he says, and hands the paper to me.

I take it and read an IOU for forty dollars signed by my mother.

"I wish people wouldn't do that," my father says grumpily. "We have to keep the house expenses separate."

"Mom just didn't have time," I say quickly, hoping to head off my parents' age-old fight over two different styles of bookkeeping.

"That's no excuse," he says.

In a way he is right, but as usual he is also forgetting about all the demands on my mother, most notably the fact that he is now disabled. I knew that she had hurried off to get groceries while I was there because she does not want to leave my father alone.

We resume sorting. When the table is covered with faded green faces—Washington, Hamilton, Lincoln, Jefferson—we begin the count. My father leans over and grasps the pile of twenties, then shakes it slightly like a cook weighing a piece of meat.

"Eighteen hundred," he says, then puts the pile down.

I look at him and smile. I know this game. I pick up the stack and weigh it in my own hands; then I also guess at the total of the twenty-dollar bills there.

"Seventeen hundred and eighty." I put the bills down. "Hey, Mom," I shout into the kitchen, "can you come here?"

"What?" she calls back.

"The count," I say, speaking shorthand.

My mother appears with her "I'm busy" look on her face, but she doesn't hesitate to come over to where we sit.

"Here," I say, handing her the stack, "take a guess."

My father is grinning, wide and boyish.

My mother shakes the wad and purses her lips. "Exactly nineteen hundred," she says, squinting, "and just watch, I'll be right."

The phone rings and my mother disappears. My father and I begin to count our piles of bills. When I was ten, eleven, twelve, even thirteen, this ritual of the harvest seemed magic. We couldn't really be poor with so much money piling up. All day the money poured in as if from nowhere. And the harvest with its endless bounty lasted weeks. I eagerly helped at the barns, hurrying up to the line of waiting cars, counting bags of fruit, identifying varieties, answering questions. Then came the hard task of writing up receipts, counting up numbers while customers stared, scrutinizing my addition. I tolerated their glances. I rarely made mistakes, and I knew that in a moment they would hand me a twenty or a fifty and then I'd get to run to the small table and make change, dipping my fingers into the bowls of change and grabbing a fistful of ones that I would dispense slowly into the hands of the waiting adults. By the end of the afternoon my throat would be burning dry from the dust swirling up from car tires, but I felt elated. I would push the money from apple sales into the pockets of my blue jeans until they bulged so high the cloth tightened around my legs, making it hard to walk.

When we gathered in the library in the evening, emptying our pockets was the start of the count. What heaven to pull out handfuls of the hot, crushed bills and to do it confidently, carelessly so that they fell to the floor, scattering like leaves. Sometimes when the bills were scooped up and carefully unfolded, a hundred-dollar bill was revealed. I would finger it in amazement. Enough money back then to buy the ten-speed I was saving up for, but it never occurred to me to take any of this money for myself. So many bills soft and loose under my touch, and I wanted oh so many things. But harvest money was not like the quarters I filched from under the table where my father emptied his pockets at night, always spilling a little change onto the floor. Harvest money, like everything else at Talavera, was of this world but not of it too. The past sanctified everything. I also knew, without knowing anything about that history and without anyone's saying so, that this past meant everything. Harvest money was farm money; it was sacred.

After the count, done by the fire in the library, it would

be time to call the dogs and drive the money bag to Hudson to drop it in the night deposit chute at the bank. I usually volunteered to go along as a lookout, just in case of robbers. "Get the six-shooter," my cousin would shout if he was there, and insist on getting out the six-chambered pistol that my father had carried in World War II from where it was locked in the gun closet. The dogs jumped in the car, grinning and drooling. The drive to Hudson and the night deposit chute took only ten minutes, and in that sleepy part of town meeting a mugger was about as likely as stumbling upon a great horned owl, but I'd be getting ready for my dash to the bank deposit chute, one hand on the car door handle, the other clutching the locked canvas bag. Under the glare of the high-intensity streetlamps, the silver door marked "Hudson City Savings" glistened dangerously.

While the driver waited, I'd sprint as fast as I could to the box, jam in the key, turn the lock, pull open the heavy metal door, then push the bag in and slam the chute closed. Only when I heard the bag's satisfying thump at the bottom of the chute did I breathe a sigh of relief. Then I'd climb back in the car, pat the dogs and begin trying to convince whoever was driving, either my father or one of my brothers, to stop at Dunkin' Donuts on the way home.

Time was nothing then, unlike today, when the counting has begun to feel like yet another chore I have to finish before I can leave. Before I realize it, I am thinking about my long drive back to Cambridge and the pile of work waiting on my desk when I get there. I have counted my stacks twice, and I am still waiting for my father to finish counting his stack of ones and fives. Methodically he sorts the bills with his large hands, but periodically one or two bills fall off the table and float to the floor. I lean over and pick them up, but my father is so busy squinting in order to see the numbers he is writing down that he doesn't notice. How tired and cold I now feel.

I tell my father that I am going in to get a sweater. When I come back out, I bring one for him as well.

"Thanks, Lele," my father says, using my pet name as he takes the sweater. He pulls the sweater over his head and continues counting, but not before I hear it: the hoarse rasp of his breath caused by the small exertion of putting on his sweater. Seventy percent of my father's lungs are filled with fluid. He is slowly drowning. Is there really nothing anyone can do?

My father has gone back to his counting without bothering to arrange his shirt, and it sticks out in an uncomfortable-looking bunch at the neck. He looks tired then and weathered like the boards of those falling-apart barns. Once again I feel overwhelmed: the young trees that need training; the signs to be fixed; the barns nude of paint; my father, who can hardly breathe. Why can't he at least fix his collar?

"Dad, your collar," I say, and even though I try, I can't keep the frustration from my voice.

"Oh, thanks," he says absently.

Finally, he is done with his count, and we compare figures. I read off mine first. "I get one thousand eight hundred and sixty in twenties—hey, Mom's the winner. What about you?"

"I get—" my father squints down at his writing and studies it. Suddenly he pushes the paper toward me. "I can't read these numbers."

"I can," I say quickly, and lean over the paper. My father's handwriting, always long and slanted with decisive angular strokes, has become faltering. At first I can't read the numbers either; the sevens look like ones and the fives could be eights. I rapidly study the lines until I can make out a series of figures that match mine.

"You got one thousand eight hundred and sixty as well. Looks like Mom's the winner," I say quickly. My father chuckles.

I compare the figures from our separate counts. The total for the day comes to $2,955. When I flip back the pages of the black-bound farm journal, it appears that we have made at least twice what we did last year.

"A record day," I say, closing the book.

"Could be," my father says, and begins to arrange the piles of bills into stacks for the bank deposit, "but I don't think so. Mutsus came on a week early this year. You can't go just by the calendar."

"Still, it's good, isn't it?"

"Very good." Then my father adds, "Thanks for all your help today."

His words catch me off guard, and I say only a mumbled "You bet." Still, I am pleased and surprised by his remark. Then my father begins to cough, and again everything in me cracks. He doesn't cough long or hard, not nearly as deeply as when he smoked and his hacking cough would echo through the house. But even this shallow clearing of his throat is enough to leave him panting for breath. And it is as if I too were drowning, in frustration and grief and fear. They rise up and engulf any feeling of sympathy that I might have for my father. I am mad at him for fifty years of smoking, for never seeing a specialist, for ending up sick. Under the table my fingers clench and I tell him that I had better get myself ready to leave. All I want right then is just to get in my car and drive away.

⁂

What would we do differently if like Cassandra, we could see the future? I do not know it, but this evening will be the last time that I see my father alive. In two weeks he will call me at the number where I am staying in Brooklyn to say that he just wanted to make sure we were on for meeting the next day. Such a call was unusual for my father, and putting down the phone, I will be pleased, thinking that finally my formal, old-world Dutch father was reaching out to me instead of the other way around. And he was finally going to see a lung specialist. I was planning to meet my mother and him in Manhattan the next day after his appointment. We talked about the prognosis. My father's voice was thin; mine was eager and hopeful.

29

"Dad, I'm really glad you're coming down. There's a whole emphysema institute now doing research, new ideas about treatment—"

"Well, I hope so. I have to lick this thing."

"You will. Maybe it will take some time, but you will."

"We probably won't be done until after lunch."

"Okay, I'll be here, just call when you're free . . . Dad?"

"Hmm?"

"I'm really glad that you're coming down."

"Yes, well, see you tomorrow then."

"Yes, see you tomorrow."

We will never meet. A half hour after he puts down the phone, while my mother is helping him get ready to leave, my father will lean down to reach for his boots and his heart will constrict, once, maybe twice, and then stop. My mother will hear him fall and rush back into the bathroom with his socks. By the time the rescue team races upstairs, they only confirm what my mother already knows. My father is dead.

✵

Only. That moment with its crushing awareness has not yet come. I am still back in time's sweet web, sitting with my father while the sunset fades, while birds and a light whisper of a wind signal the coming of night. Leaves are dropping from the trees, each one glazed with sun. But I see only the aftermath: bright swatches of color on the lawn. These will be the last moments that I share with my father. How I wish I could say that I am cherishing him, but I am not. I am worried about a bunched collar, some dropped dollar bills, irritated by his handwriting, which I cannot read. I wait impatiently for him to finish sorting the bills. I feel pursued by the silent yellow house looming up around us, by the hopelessly old barns and especially by the relentless work of the harvest. I am not conscious of history, or if I am, it is simply that escalator back to a better time, back then, when the family was rich and the farm prosperous.

Claverack, 1732

In 1732, Willem Van Ness (1711–1790), the son of a well-to-do farming and merchant family from Halve Maen just north of Albany, married the daughter of an equally well-established Dutch family some forty miles south, in Claverack. Willem was the great-grandson of a brewer named Cornelius Van Ness, who acquired fame in New Netherlands for feuding with the sheriff. This feud took a new turn when Cornelius's wife knocked the sheriff off his horse with a broom. The family packed their belongings and the already parched sheets of paper recording Admiral Van Ness's sea voyages and moved to a location somewhat south of Beverywyck, or Albany. Willem Van Ness inherited his ancestor's travel account and his great-grandfather's intolerance for authority.

The young woman whom Willem moved south to marry was Gertrude Hogeboom. She was born into a landed family in Claverack, meaning that they were definitely not tenants, those at the bottom of the economic spectrum of the manor system in the Hudson Valley. But they did not have lordship privileges either. Interestingly, Willem Van Ness and his bride did not set up their household on Hogeboom land. Instead, they began to clear a 294-acre reach of land along the Old Post Road, not far from the Mohican hunting camp of Pot Koke on Claverack Creek.

Traditionally understood to be the southernmost tip of Rensselaerswyck Manor, although in eighteenth-century New York, property borders could shift depending upon who employed the mapmaker, this land may have been initially leased by Willem. By 1790, however, his will clearly passed ownership of the land down to his son William. *"Mack ik aen my soon Willem Van Ness en syn erfgename en assins al myne stad . . ."* read the faded will, written in Hudson Valley Dutch, which went on to delegate one plow to his son Peter but the house and land, barns, tools and other livestock to the eldest son, William, who was responsible for caring for his mother.

When I finally found the old will, I studied it carefully, looking, among other things, for any mention of slaves. It was the practice of early Dutch farmers in New York to hire laborers to help clear land and work their farms. Many owned slaves. By 1714 the Claverack census listed a population of 216, 19 of whom were black slaves. I suspected that descendants from Van Ness slaves still lived in the area, for I knew of several black families just north in Kinderhook who had the surname Van Ness. But I found no slaves listed in Willem's will at that time, a fact that, for the moment anyway, filled me with relief.

Farmers like Willem were motivated by the demand for wheat and potatoes coming from New York City. Wheat from the Van Ness farm may have also found its way onto Livingston Manor trading ships bound for the West Indies. These ships, loaded with wheat flour and grain, among other stuffs, traded such products for more exotic items, including slaves. Willem Van Ness could well have made an increasing profit each year. He soon built what for that time was a large Dutch-style farmhouse and raised a barn complex nearby.

This early founding date of 1732 for the Van Ness farm

was significant, for most of the valley at the time was divided up into huge manorial estates, an Old World model of tenant and manor lord rather than the ideal of the yeoman, or independent farmer. Rensselaerswyck Manor was largely disbanded by then in the Claverack area, but just to the south of Claverack Creek began Livingston Manor, a holding of almost one million acres. Livingston tenants generally worked hundred-acre parcels and paid rent in schepels of wheat. Robert Livingston, the first manor lord, calculated that by the late 1700s the average tenant farm was producing an income of eleven to fourteen pounds or twenty-eight to thirty dollars. A take of ten bushels of wheat per acre was considered good.

Tenants and manor lords lived at the opposite ends of an economic spectrum. While a typical tenant farmer would have eaten dinner in a farmhouse that probably had a dirt floor, the Livingstons dined on seven-course meals, attended by the many servants who also lived with the family in their Hudson River mansion.

As a landed farmer, however, Willem Van Ness inhabited the middle ground and was thus well suited to act as something of a go-between, as he did. This was the practice among the landed Dutch families of Claverack, such as the Hogebooms, the Van Nesses and the Van Alens. In the role of landed farmer Willem and later his son William collected rents, advanced the claims of the Livingstons for new lands and, at times of tenant unrest, directed militia forces. It was an affiliation that enabled Van Ness sons to receive gentlemen's educations. Unlike tenants, whose burden of high rents prevented upward movement, Van Ness sons could raise their fortunes. They inhabited the beginnings of America's middle class, a place of opportunity but also of instability and risk. By virtue of hard work, the right marriage and individual talent, they could attain wealth and status. But unlike the sons of manor lords, who had the land to pin their status on come what may, Van Ness sons could also fail.

Talavera, the grand house on the northern end of the

33

farm, was built in a moment of Van Ness family fortune. By 1807 Willem's grandson William W. Van Ness had risen to considerable acclaim as a lawyer and was appointed judge of the State Supreme Court. Not surprisingly, he decided to build a house that would reflect his passionate belief in the ideals of the new Republic and his social and economic rise. That house was Talavera, a Federal-style mansion whose ornate columns and grand public spaces incorporated diverse and ambitious elements of classical architecture. At Talavera one can see the ideas of Benjamin Latrobe and other leading architects of the day, put together in a personal, at times idiosyncratic way, probably by William W. Van Ness himself. He did not engage a professional architect to plan his house, and the elegant and exotic arrangement of rooms that some scholars attribute to French influences deviates considerably from the Federal-style patterns that would have been typical of that time.

It is not possible to date Talavera or the barns exactly for a fire in the Hudson City Courthouse in 1909 burned most of the early property transfer records and Van Ness ledgers that might have detailed payments for bricks, nails, wood and carpenters' fees also did not survive. The house may have taken as many as five years to complete, for Judge Van Ness first mentioned moving into his new house in a letter to his friend and fellow Federalist Colonel Solomon Van Rensselaer, dated November 23, 1812.

Colonel Van Rensselaer had just returned from the War of 1812, during which he was wounded in the attack on Queenston. William W. wrote from Kingston, where he was presiding over the court.

Dear Sir,
In a paper which I have just seen while holding court in this place, I have with heartfelt satisfaction read the above, your safe arrival at your own house. . . . As soon as I have moved into my new house and can leave home, which will be in about a fortnight, I shall

go to Albany, to tell you in person how much I re-
joice that you are still in the land of the living, and in
the bosom of your family.

    With unabated affection and friendship,

    Yours &c.

    W. W. Van Ness

By the winter of 1812 then, Judge William W. Van Ness
was settled in his stylish new house, which, through the setting out of grounds and the building of a long, curving
drive, signaled the establishment of a country seat in the English tradition. What had begun as a Dutch farm took on a
villa overlay that also signaled a way in which William W. was
choosing to separate from his roots, by then the much-
maligned Dutch tradition of the valley, and to identify with
the rising English establishment. He named his new establishment Talavera, after the Battle of Talavera de la Reina in
Spain, Napoleon's first land defeat. With this exotic name for
his new residence, William W. further established his allegiance to British culture. Now that he was a venerated judge,
no doubt he also chose the name to help correct his earlier,
youthful exuberance in initially supporting the ideals of the
French Revolution.

In keeping with the villa tradition, Talavera was sited on
the top of a hill overlooking a panorama, the Catskill Mountains to the west and the Berkshire foothills to the east. Gardens, initially of Italianate design, were laid down as a series
of terraces that marked a clear separation between the house
grounds and the agricultural lands. Yet these farmlands continued to be farmed. From 1812 on Talavera became a *villa
rustico,* a self-sustaining agricultural estate.

With the building of Talavera, then, Judge William W.
Van Ness signaled not only his desire to live in a house that
reflected the ideals of the new Republic through its very architecture but also, in concrete ways, his family's rise from
landed farmer to landed elite. Not long after the building of
Talavera, his daughter Analiza married Henry Livingston,

the younger son of a manor lord, John Livingston of Oak Hill, and the couple moved into Talavera.

Henry and Analiza Livingston had so many children that soon several more rooms were added to the house. Emma, Herman, Catherine, Henry, William Van Ness, Ancram, Anna and Cornelia were born at Talavera and spent their early childhood there. In a noted portrait by Charles Inman, all eight children are depicted "on the piazza of their father's house," with the Catskills looming up through the trees, a stylized version of the view from Talavera.

Henry Livingston died young, leaving Analiza a widow at Talavera. When she remarried, one year later, ownership of Talavera and much of her husband's Livingston lands in the Ancram area passed on to her son Herman, only eleven years old at the time. Mystery surrounds what happened next. Analiza, the children and her new husband lived at Talavera for several years, but when they moved, they dropped out of the family record.

When Analiza's father died some years earlier, his lands had been split into north and south parcels. The north farm, which Analiza and Henry Livingston had taken over, became known from that point on as the homestead, since it contained Talavera and grounds, while the southern section, on which the original Van Ness farmhouse still stood, was called the South Place. Analiza's aunt had taken over ownership of the South Place after her father's death, but not long after Analiza's remarriage, her aunt's name was on the deed for Talavera as well.

For the next thirty years the family clearly endeavored to keep Judge William W. Van Ness's grand house and the surrounding Van Ness lands in the family. Ownership was transferred back and forth between cousins many times. In 1847 the north and south sections were reunited by Abraham Pierce, a cousin on the Livingston side, and run as one large farm for more than ten years. But by 1855 it had been split into north and south farms again with different branches of the family living on each place. Perhaps even then maintaining the exotic house was more than most family members could afford. Then another cousin, this time on the Philip side, appeared on the scene. He left his rising career in the navy and moved north from Annapolis to throw himself into restoring Judge William W.'s fine house and to seek his fortune by running the farm.

In my father's papers I found notes that my father had made about a letter written by his great-uncle Lieutenant John Van Ness Philip to his mother, Catherine Douw. The letter was dated 1855. According to my father's penciled notes, Lieutenant John Van. Ness, then teaching in the newly founded U.S. Naval Academy, had proudly announced: "I can no longer serve my nation through teaching. I am returning home to buy *that* farm." That farm was Talavera, his mother's family homestead, the vast columned house, landscaped grounds and 120-acres plus my father envisioned keeping together by running Philip Orchards.

After

After my father's funeral, my mother, my three older brothers, my older sister and I met in the sitting room to decide what to do. We didn't usually gather in that room of the house, a sunny place just to the right of the formal south entrance. We usually gathered in the library, sprawling over the arms of the worn armchairs, one of us sitting in my father's straight-backed chair at the octagonal writing table, one of us pushing aside the dog beds to make room by the fire.

The sitting room was in good repair, for just a few years earlier my parents had replastered the walls and painted them a rich sunflower yellow. The armchair and Georgian sofa had been recently recovered in burnt umber velvet. Perhaps we knew intuitively that we needed the distance, the formality of this room to begin to work out a way forward, a way that didn't include our father. We also needed more chairs, for gathered together we filled the room.

I took a place on the footstool, as if following an instinctive role as the youngest to seek low ground. I didn't mind: My back was to the fire, and that way I didn't have to look at the portrait of Leila Whitney Stott, my grandmother's mother.

Leila Whitney was only nine years old when the artist sat her down and began to sketch her plump rosy cheeks, still smooth and open with childhood. In the picture she is smiling in a charming, delicate way that changes from child to young woman depending on the angle from which you gaze. It is a bewitching, impish, ambiguous, almost Mona Lisa smile. Her clothes only increase the effect. She is dressed to perfection in a gray coat with an elegant fur ruff. Pearl drop earrings hang from her small ears.

But that day I took no pleasure in looking at one of my namesakes. Instead, the fact of her being on the wall above left me feeling even more scruffy and uncomposed. My then-long hair was pulled back in a hasty, half-tangled pony-tail, and the cuffs of my pants were wet and muddy from my mad rush to get to the meeting in time. That morning I had walked out along the farm road, east toward the back or-chards, then on through the woods. Brush had grown up over our childhood riding trails, but I pushed through until I came to the sudden rise and the long, elevated roadway, the abandoned railroad tracks. There I walked along the even road, soothed by the rhythm of my feet, by the tawny browns and reds of late fall, by the foggy November air.

Now, back inside Talavera, my shoulders to the fire, I wished I were still walking along that road. Everything in the house seemed to oppress me just by the fact of its being there. So much stuff. So much old stuff, and all of it needing tend-ing. Even Leila Whitney, behind her beautiful smile seemed to have joined the other portraits in judging us from her place on the wall, her very elegance bearing witness to our fallen present. My father, the oldest son, my grandfather's namesake, had struggled to keep Talavera from being sold out of the family. He had succeeded, but I was sure that the effort had been a large part of what had killed him. Now he was dead, and we were supposed to carry on. The question was how.

My father had believed that the farm could be made to

support Talavera, and for many years his plan had worked. But the national trend of small-farm bankruptcy had arrived in the Hudson Valley. All around us fruit growers were buckling under high taxes, the cost of labor and the bottomed-out price of fruit. To keep Talavera now, we would have to find a way to support the farm, not the other way around. Anyone looking from the outside would have probably advised us to sell the house and land and salvage what we could. But I knew that wasn't going to happen. I wrapped my arms around my knees, hugging them as I waited for the meeting to begin.

My eldest brother, named after my father and my grandfather and my great-great-uncle and my great-great-great-uncle, passed out copies of my father's will. I accepted one, although it would be weeks before I could make myself read it.

At the funeral it seemed that my three brothers had ascended to take on highly sanctioned, if invisible, roles as the sons of a dead father. When the time came, each had stepped forward confidently and read the eulogy he had written. Each of them memorialized my father in a different way, but each described him in clear, loving terms as a patriot, as a business pioneer and a farmer, as an uncompromising individual. Their eulogies had placed them as the sons of a successful, landed father. Since we were reading in order, I stepped forward last. But when I looked out over the crowded church, at the gleaming polished red wood of my father's casket, flooded with yellow flowers, words seemed impossible. For minutes that seemed like hours, I stood there, rocking wildly in an uncharted sphere. Then I took a breath and read a short poem in which I described my father trying to teach me how to prune a tree. When we left the church, my eldest brother had made the sign of the cross and, in his honoring of the Presbyterian tradition, bent over and kissed his father's coffin.

Historically the transfer of an ancestral place in an established landowning family like mine, in keeping with the English tradition that it followed, would have had nothing to do with me or my sister. Perhaps we still felt that even though we inherited equal shares of Talavera. At the meeting my eldest brother, who, as the coexecutor of my father's will and as a lawyer, had drafted our trust agreement, did most of the talking. My sister and I were quiet.

I was trying to listen, but at first I couldn't hear a word. Moments from the previous week, surreal, disorganized, came flooding back. The day after the funeral, my eldest brother, my mother and I had driven my father's ashes down to Washington, D.C., where the family gathered again in the Oak Hill Cemetery to place them in the Van Ness family mausoleum there.

For most of the way, I had sat in the backseat next to the little brass box with my father's ashes inside. It was unbelievably odd to be sitting there amid tree wire and loose tree tags, things that only recently my father had tossed into the back. If I reached my hand out, I could touch the blue velvet bag that held the brass box engraved with my father's initials, JVNP. When we stopped for coffee in Maryland, I was worried because the doors to the car didn't lock properly and I thought someone might try to steal the box, thinking it was gold. Besides, it didn't seem right to leave my father alone. For a moment I considered taking the box with me into Roy Rogers, but then I lost my nerve. Once someone was dead, how did you know anymore what was the right thing to do? In the end I stayed in the car and let my mother and brother bring me a cup of coffee for my turn at the wheel.

When I brought my attention back to the meeting, my brother was saying words like *trust, lifetime, our mother, legal transfer.* Unanimously and with little discussion, my three brothers, my sister and I agreed to form a land trust to keep the house and the farm together for as long as my mother lived and for three years thereafter. After raising five children, working in an office in Manhattan, helping my father found his business newsletter, then participating on the farm each weekend, my mother was retiring to the relative leisure of only running the farm. "I've always wanted chickens," she joked, showing us through her humor the fine steel from which she was cast. "Now I'll be able to get some."

Soon our meeting was over, all of us supportive, together, intact. But for me, that meeting only confirmed my confusion. In many ways, what we just agreed to made no sense. None of us had the kind of income needed to maintain a Federal-style mansion or to subsidize a farm. How would we ever manage? Even if the larger economic picture for farming in the valley improved and the farm had a chance at solvency, we had a more important challenge. Could we learn to cease our sibling spats long enough to own and operate a business jointly? Like most brothers and sisters, we could provoke one another so that even the clank of a glass in the dishwasher could hit a nerve, starting an argument.

Yet we had not discussed the words *sell, divide, withdraw* with any seriousness or conviction. Such conversation was taboo. We could rail at Talavera or despair over what could seem like a vain pretense of heritage, but we could not sell the place and feel that we had done the right thing.

"Five years," my mother said simply. "Let me see if I can make it work in that time."

ЯР

The night after the meeting, I walked out along the drive and looked back at Talavera. For a moment I felt a thrill as I looked up at the enormous house, at the tall white pines spiring up on all sides. All that I did not yet know about Talavera only heightened its mystery. Gaston Bachelard says that we spend our lives trying to dream our way back to the house that was our childhood home, but what if this house still exists, still encompasses your family, what then?

In many ways the meeting had made me realize all that I loved about my family. Perhaps, although we didn't have a plan or money in the bank, our instinct of keeping together, of staying put would carry us through. But I was worried. I was pretty sure that my mother was the first woman in the history of the family to manage the larger farm, and I was proud of her. But could she live at Talavera alone and avoid the despairing loneliness that I had seen come over my father?

I was filled with unsettling questions. All this was supposed to be worth it because of the past. That was our inheritance: this history, our sense of place, Talavera and all its glamour. Certainly Judge William W. Van Ness, who had built the house, had been both eminent and rich. But that was so long ago. What of the family since then? What of the family aunts, women like my great-aunt Bessie, who had fled Talavera? What of us? If we were poor when we appeared rich, couldn't this grand elusive past be bankrupt as well? I hated thinking such things, as if I were betraying my father even to ask such questions. But it was worse not to. We were at a crossroads: Either commit to saving Talavera or accept its loss. The fact that our dilemma stemmed from great privilege only made it feel worse.

CHAPTER FIVE

Yesterday's Harvest

I had come up with a plan. Maybe I couldn't change the dismal economics of small farms in the Hudson Valley. Maybe I could not prevent the strange paralysis that came over my brothers and sister and me when we tried to think about Talavera's future. But I could find out about Talavera's past, that elusive force driving us forward. My plan was this: I was going to dig out all the old papers from the house and barns, pull these clues out and study them. Yesterday's Harvest. I wanted to find out exactly who had lived at Talavera and when and what their lives had been like there. I wanted to find out if the farm had ever been profitable, and if so, when and how. I wanted to uncover Talavera's secrets.

I told myself that I was sick of being bullied by a past I didn't even know. But really I was scared, scared that like my father, I would get sucked into a way of living that revolved so much around Talavera that it lost touch with the larger world. If I looked, I could see signs of this in my own generation, in me. We all were a little too comfortable with Talavera's state of disrepair, that slippery state of mild neglect and denial. Success in the outer world involved a strange sense of betrayal.

I knew the myths. That my family had lived here as if forever in splendor and elegance. That the orchards, with their
yearly renewal, were as resilient and holy as thousand-year-old
olive trees. That if we cared for the land, we would be caring
for ourselves. What I didn't know was how much of this remembered past coincided with historical reality. If I could understand what Talavera had been, then maybe I could find a
way to Talavera's future, and maybe I could set myself free.

My mother had left for a week of much-needed vacation
in Vermont, and I was at Talavera house- and farm-sitting.
On a previous visit I had mapped out the location of trunks
and boxes and closets full of papers: the scrapbooks and files,
the boxes of letters and rows of farm journals, the piles of
unsorted papers that filled places like the library closet where
each harvest we kept the farm's cash. I was going to read
through these things and map out Talavera's history. I would
begin with the library closets. On my yellow pad I could see
the words *Library closet, left side—top shelf.* But that had been
three days ago. I still had not opened the closet doors.

45

Instead I cleaned the kitchen, weeded the flower beds and
washed the dogs, who had rolled on a dead woodchuck. A
thick, humid heat spread over the land, over me. Each
evening I walked out into the cooling rows of trees with the
dogs. Animals that we did not usually see appeared like
omens at unexpected moments. Along the leafy tunnel of
the railroad bed, we came upon a snapping turtle so large
that at first I thought it was an abandoned tire that someone
had flung onto the road. The next morning a red fox came
sauntering up to the edge of the back lawn, then drifted, red
smoke, back into the woods.

When it grew too hot to be outside, I walked the cool
interior of the house, around and around as if circling a man-
dala. Library, kitchen, dining room, parlor, hallway, sitting
room, boot room and up the curving stairway. Nursery, blue
room, hallways, then the third-floor landing, the east room,
the west room and down through the north wing and back
to the library. Talavera was a game of Clue. Mr. Mustard in

the ballroom with the revolver. Mrs. Peacock in the library with the candlestick. Up in the cavernous west room, I looked out through the windows at the massive columns of the porte cochere, then turned to notice a rope of cobweb draping from the corners like the dirty ends of Miss Haversham's gown. I opened the doors of the dark armoire and dug my hands into the thicket of men's coats: scarlet riding jackets for fox hunting, black-tie jackets and tails, cummerbunds, silk-lined dress pants, then a row of my father's floppy tweeds. It was just like my family to have a closetful of dead people's clothes and no room to put our own.

Soon I simply began to trace my steps from room to room, feeling my way like a blind person, the pads of my fingers touching the chipped places in doors and windows, the broken ends of furniture, the delicate patterns of wear on the arms of brocade chairs and sofa covers, the brittle husks of lampshades. Another cup of coffee. Another loop around the house. I had become a kind of rapt pilgrim, only I wasn't arriving anywhere. I began to shrink from the outside world. I stopped going to the village in the morning to pick up the mail. When the UPS truck arrived with a package, I ran upstairs. Willi arrived one windless evening to apply the first of the apple mite sprays, preventing me from taking the dogs into the orchards for twenty-four hours, so I piled them into the truck and headed for the local cemetery. There, while the hot evening dwindled down, the dogs leaped and played in the oval stone-lined pond while I walked among the gravestones. Only three days alone at Talavera, and already I was more comfortable with the dead than the living.

I found myself calling a local stable to make an appointment for a riding lesson. I hadn't ridden in years. Only when I had finally completed the long process of sorting and reading through my family's long and complicated history at Talavera would I see how in desperation I was invoking a historic family passion, horses.

"Okay, canter right," shouted the instructor. I pressed with my outside leg, the usual signal, but the pony just began a be-grudging trot, then, when I kept signaling, trotted even faster. I was being jerked so roughly I could feel sharp spears of pain along my spine. I was not riding; I was being bounced around the ring like a sack of meal. If the pony had chosen to fling her head down, the kind of trick our old Shetland would have tried, she could have sent me sailing. I pulled her back to a walk, took a deep breath and tried again. Once again, I sig-naled, but the pony ignored me. She was bored. Stop. Start. The riding instructor said nothing, but I could tell she was not impressed. Neither was the pony. Her walk was sloppy; she stiffened when I signaled with the outside leg. We were at an impasse. Could it be that I had really forgotten how to ride? The thought was so mortifying that I stopped the pony for a moment and re-collected my reins, eyes blinking.

Peter, his mane flying, his eyes wild with de-light, is galloping hard across the meadow. I am on his back, crouched down, bareback, the pres-sure of my legs urging him on. We reach the end of the meadow, and when he feels the touch of my hand across his neck, he turns right, heads up the final hill, legs still moving at that thundering pace. I bend down like a jockey until my face is almost level with his mane. He smells sweet and salty, sweat beginning to dampen his copper hide. I will never fall because he will never let me. He is Pegasus, one wing dipping as he turns, racing through the clouds.

47

This time, when I moved the pony out, I did so with a more determined pressure from my calves. Her walk picked up a little, and I increased the pressure in my legs but held her back when she tried to trot. She woke up a little. I pressed my calves even more firmly and still held her back by checking her with the reins. Her head began to lift; she began to feel frustrated, to want to move. I kept this up, pushing her forward, holding her back until I was sure that she knew what was coming. At the next corner I made sure that I was sitting back, then signaled her to canter. This time I focused everything I had on the gesture. I imagined my calf pressing into her side. I looked only at the point in the ring at which I was headed. I insisted through the position of my body that she follow my command. But it was still not enough. She started to canter, then broke into a trot. She was all pony, sizing me up, figuring out what she could ignore.

I didn't hesitate. Little flares of anger shot through my brain. I remembered this contest of wills. *Canter, canter.* I could think of nothing else. I sat back and imagined her front leg, reaching out, finding the correct lead. *Canter, canter.* This time, when I pressed her with my legs, I did so hard, and this time she sensed my resolve. Miraculously, incredibly, it happened. She listened, decided to follow and threw her front leg out to find that even, rolling stride. I was overcompensating a bit, overeager, and she sensed that too and sped up, her canter becoming a gallop. I pulled her back, tried to relax my seat. My legs had all gone to hell. One foot had come entirely out of the stirrup. I couldn't get her moving and keep my hand steady and my legs in the proper position. Even now one circle of the ring, and my legs were on fire with the strain of trying to keep my balance.

But I didn't care. Everything now depended on whether I could control this animal, convincing her to follow my will. The pony was moving, smoothly now, her back relaxing into her stride, and for one more circle of the ring I was riding, that incredible sense of power, of communication with an animal more powerful than oneself. It was simple really. Once you resolve in your own mind where you are headed, a horse, even a willful pony, will go there too.

That night, when I shut my eyes to sleep, I could still feel the steady, pounding beat of the pony's hooves as she circled the ring. Each hoofbeat, the steady rising pulse of my own childhood.

"Want a ride back?"

"Sure."

"Hop on in front, here. You jump, I'll pull."

My cousin pulled her mare up and made her stand while I poured the water out of my sneakers and put them back on, preparing myself for the walk home. We had spent the morning swimming the horses in the back pond, all of us trying to stand on the back of my uncle's huge gelding, circus style, falling in the stinky pond. It was my sister's turn to ride our horse, and she had gone on ahead with the others. I looked up at my cousin with adoration. She was four years older than I was and an excellent rider. Her horse was a fast, hot-tempered mare that my cousin could convince to do almost anything. The mare stamped her feet impatiently but held still while I bent my legs and leaped up with all my might. My cousin caught the back of my shirt and helped guide me up in front of her. I twisted my fingers into the black mane to steady myself, and my cousin tightened her hold on the lead rope attached to the horse's halter. It was a point of honor to be able to ride without a saddle or bridle, what we called Indian style, on an excursion like this one. As soon as my cousin turned the mare toward the barn, she headed off in a smart walk.

We followed the grassy road through the orchard and began to climb the first of the hills that led up to the ridge and the hedgerow above the meadow. The horse's walk was rough. I could feel the sharp ridge of her withers under my seat, but it was much more fun to be riding home with my cousin than walking back on my own. Suddenly, at the first of the low hills, when we turned onto the dirt road, the mare threw up her head and gave a loud, anxious whinny. Within a few sec-

49

onds, from the other side of the hill, came an answering whinny. The next thing we knew, she was off, running as fast as she could to catch up to the other horses. We reached the crest of the hill in a blur of dust, both of us managing to stay on. But worse was yet to come. The big hill that she had just galloped up was about to lead down in a steep incline. We swept past the first hedgerow, past the huge white pine. My cousin was bent over me, pulling on the lead rope with all her might. Her efforts were to stop the horse, but her arms were forcing me down so that my head was level now with the horse's withers. All I could see was the road, hard-packed dirt and stones. Time stopped. I was past terror and into a strangely calm, prescient state. I found myself thinking only one thing: I am going to fall, and I am going to die.

Then miraculously, just beyond the hedgerow, I felt the horse swerve to the left and off onto a grassy orchard road. My sister and the others had not continued on to the barn without us. They were there on the left, waiting, the horses busily munching grass. By the time I slipped down to the grass, my legs were so wobbly that when they hit the ground my knees buckled. I looked down and opened my clenched hands. Bits of black horse hair were still sticking to my palms. My cousin and I looked at each and began to laugh.

When I fell asleep later that night, I dreamed that I was back in Japan and once again a potter's apprentice. But something was wrong. I sat at my wheel afraid to touch the clay. My teacher, Nagayoshi-san, came into the workshop, saw me sitting at the wheel frozen and handed me a piece of white Shinto paper like the kind found decorating shrines. He handed me a pair of scissors and walked out. I didn't know how it happened, but soon I was cutting the paper into the most amazing shapes. The paper fluttered in my hands. I cut and cut and felt nothing but joy.

ஊ

The next day I drove to the Columbia County Historical Society just north in Kinderhook, resolved to begin. The librarian there directed me to Franklin Ellis's 1878 volume on early Columbia County. When I turned to the sections on Claverack and Philmont, plates of men with names like John Van Ness Philip startled me with their physical resemblance to my own brothers. But there was no indication of who had lived at Talavera and when. Only one thing was clear: Whatever family myths existed were braided into a long and continuous involvement in actual events in early American history. Unraveling the strands was not going to be easy. On one hand, I felt relieved, even a bit proud to be flipping pages of description about these early men who seemed to have been eminent enough to have been included in an official history. On the other hand, it was depressing. If the past really had been grand and important, what had led to this great dive into the present, when nothing about my contemporary family seemed as grand or rich or entwined with history? I didn't learn until much later that at least as far as regional history was concerned, Ellis's book had been sold by subscription. Families that wanted biographies and plates included could purchase space. Sure enough, later I even found a letter written by my great-grandfather in 1878 to Everts and Ensign, Ellis's Philadelphia publishers in which my great-grandfather inquired about the price of including a short biography of his dead brother Lieutenant John Van Ness Philip.

I pushed the Ellis book away and looked over to catch the gaze of a slight, nervous-looking man who had been staring at me. He wanted to know what I was researching and, after I told him, explained that he was of Mohican ancestry, a descendant of the Rensselaer people. They had recently organized a protest of the building of a Wal-Mart on their

51

ancient burial ground near Saugerties. With his light brown hair and marble blue eyes, any connection he had to Mohican tribes was clearly thin, tenuous, so long ago. Couldn't one say that some gap in his present was making the past, that glamorous once upon a time glisten just a little too gold? Might the same be said about me?

As I began my next task, reading through the clipping files labeled "Philip" and "Van Ness," wasn't I also looking to the past to explain the present? However, so far what I was riffling through seemed too distant from my own experience to explain anything. There had been a Cornelius Van Ness who had been a brewer and merchant in Albany. His wife had knocked the sheriff off his horse with a broom. A Peter Van Ness who had built a mansion in Kinderhook named Lindenwald, which had been acquired by the eighth president of the United States, Martin Van Buren, then later had become a state park. Lists of other Van Nesses in the Red Hook and Rhinebeck regions. Then so many John and William Van Nesses followed in the genealogy that I became hopelessly confused. It was fun reading through the lists of seventeenth-century Dutch names—Martinus, Annetje, Catharina, Jacobus, Petrus, Hennik, Henrius, Hezkiah—but I felt no connection to them as early family.

I was about to close the file, weary of this litany of names and dates, when out of a sense of duty I turned over the last piece of paper in the file and uncovered a photograph. A man was standing on a tractor, an old Case that looked as if it belonged in a tractor museum, except that we still needed it on the farm. The man had one hand on the wheel, the other dropped by his side. His face, averted from the camera, looked shyly to one side. He gave a look both good-humored and embarrassed at being the subject of a picture. But his shoulders were full of pride. It was my father, heading out after a day at his desk to do what he loved most, mow the orchards. If the camera had looked down and to the left, it would have taken a picture of me as well, dressed in blue jeans and a T-shirt, looking on. The photographer for the newspaper had wanted very much to get a photograph of my father on the old Case. "What a shot," he kept saying. This had irritated my father, who refused to pose. But finally, when the interview was over, he had become so impatient that he told the man to get his camera out; he was going to start up the Case to head out mowing.

Looking at the black-and-white print above the story of Philip Orchards, I saw now what the photographer had been after. Dressed in his Brooks Brothers shirt and corduroy blazer, my father looked like a gentleman farmer. Only he was too familiar with the broken-down tractor, the khaki of his pants too stained with tractor grease and grass from pulling weeds out of jammed mower blades. He looked like what he was, a man who could make the transition from gentleman to farmer in the late twentieth century.

Clipped to that 1974 article about the orchards was another, smaller one, without a photo, that read: "John Van Ness Philip, Jr. Fruit Grower, Publisher, 70." My father's obituary, carefully clipped from the *New York Times*. Back at Talavera, my father hardly seemed dead. His boots still sat in the downstairs closet, as if waiting for him to pick them up and, as was his habit at five, to drop them with a bang on the kitchen floor. But someone at the historical society had clipped the obituary and added it to its Van Ness file. History was washing over me. According to the file that I had in my hands, my father had been the fourteenth generation of Van Nesses in New York. That made us the fifteenth generation. Fifteen generations: That was close to three hundred years. Could my family possibly have lived at Talavera that long?

❧

That night I took my yellow pad and sat at the octagonal desk in the library where my father had spent his days writing. According to family lore, it was the same desk where Washington Irving had once tutored an earlier generation. Outside, the cicadas began to moan, that great sea of yearning. Tonight I was determined to begin. Everyone dreams of finding that trunk of letters in the attic, to be able to flip back the lid of history and be in the presence of the past. Underneath the study of history, especially family history, must lie some primitive totemic need.

If this were Japan, we might believe in ancestor worship, the dead swirling around us, informing the present. We could give them a bit of sake, some salt and rice, even new clothes if we were in the mood, and ensure that they would not make trouble in the present. But here in the West we don't believe in ghosts. We believe in God or we believe in information, the truth as solace. I was no different. I too wanted to discover that one fact that could explain it all. Only paradoxically, now that the possibility was before me, not just the opening of one trunk, but an entire closet, then more closets, an entire basement, the lofts of barns, I felt dread. It was true the sheer amount of information was overwhelming, but I knew that was not the real problem. *What if I open the closet and find nothing? What if I find out what I do not want to know?*

Before I could lose my nerve, I reached out to grasp the Delft vase on the library mantel, dug my hand in and took hold of the smooth metal key for the library closet door. That familiar coolness in my palm, only this time I wasn't opening the closet to put the day's take of Pick Your Own money in the cashbox. Quickly I stepped in and pulled the frayed string that hung down from a lightbulb. I shut my eyes against the explosion of light. When I opened them, I looked out over stacks and piles and boxes of papers.

Each shelf was crammed: papers, records, books, things, all waiting. Behind a collection of glass soil sample tubes and the cashbox, I could just make out a row of hardbound journals. One peeling label read "Talavera Accounts 1911." Other books, with disintegrating leather bindings, were lined up along the shelf. I pulled one out and on the inside cover read the words *W. H. Henry Philip, Cash Accounts, 1855.* Relief flooded through me. How could I have feared there would be nothing? For a moment I simply stood there and looked in a state of shock and awe. It was as if I had just opened the door onto the brain of the house. Surely I would find in this mass of papers some of the answers that I sought.

After an hour I filled several sheets of my pad. My list began: "File Folders: Orchard Work Plans 1913–1916; Old Deeds and References Pre-1900; William H. Philip, executor of the Estate of Gaston P.; South Place; Stark Estate." Stark Estate? I blew dust off the old folder and opened it quickly. On the top was a newspaper clipping with the headline FEMINIST PIONEER. The file was about my mysterious aunt Bessie, whose paintings hung in several rooms throughout the house. According to the file, May 31, 1975, was the first Elizabeth Philip Stark Day in Jacksonville, Florida, established to recognize her work during World War I organizing the Cherokee Rose Girl Scout troop that patrolled Jacksonville's beaches on horseback in search of German spies. With great excitement I flipped through the file, but there was no time to read in detail. I noted the location of the file and placed it in a box for removal.

The archival principle of provenance states that before removing any materials from a site, one should note the location and condition of the papers being removed, the idea being that the way things are stored can tell as much as the items themselves about the people who put them away. In keeping with this idea, I carefully noted where I had found everything before I placed it in a box to be removed for later sorting.

Soon my list contained things I had not expected: "Spray records 1955–1960—6 files, 3 blue hair curlers, pennies, box of shotgun bullets, letter from President Roosevelt to grandfather, small can of chimney solvent, mouse skeleton, six loose bullets, soil sample kit." Hair curlers, chimney solvent, stray bullets, plastic tubes for rolling quarters, a stack of quarter- and dime-size paper rolls for coins, glass soil-sampling tubes, five pennies sticky and blue with spilled ink. What did such things tell me about my family other than that the closet reflected the confusion that I felt? On each shelf, there seemed to have been no attempt to distinguish what was of value from what wasn't. I had the impulse not to record these details, but to revise history as I went. Who would ever know? This is the nonfiction writer's greatest temptation, tinkering with the facts: "If it's not there, put it in . . . If it doesn't seem to fit, take it out." But I reminded myself that I was not here to make a story. I was here to find the story that waited. These details, however painful, would lead me to it.

I forced myself to write down these uncomfortable notes. From a file box containing notes on my grandfather's pure-bred hunting dogs, I extracted a signed invitation to the inauguration of President Roosevelt. Then I pulled out the mouse skeleton and marveled at the tiny, grasping paws. Digging in had become fun. I was Helen Mirren now, a detective hot after a lead with not a minute to waste.

Time stood still, until I realized that I was exhausted. Dust from the old papers crawled on the back of my neck as if tiny midges were dancing there. The idiotic dive-bombing of moths into the lampshade had become intolerable. I no longer felt like a detective. I felt more like Cinderella, cleaning up while everyone else was at the ball. As soon as my chair legs scraped against the floor, the dogs leaped to their feet. They rushed out ahead of me. We walked into a night swirling with heat, the rasping beat of cicada wings.

Psychoanalysis has revised Freud's evocative idea of the psychoanalyst's work as that of an archaeologist, pulling up sheaves and remnants of memory, then sleuthing through clues to reconstruct the past. Perhaps it is impossible to reconstruct or even remember a past faithfully or even truthfully. In that case, such clues can only partially explain the present. But one of Freud's greatest achievements was to show how both memory and dream stem from desire. Freud understood what literature has always known: that for the writer, each act of memory is an act of redemption, a transformation driven by want. Elizabeth Bishop's hard blue river of knowledge: our search for the truth. What is the analytic process anyway but that crude digging up of stones and pebbles, then the slow turning of a memory or a phrase over and over until it begins to gleam?

I had no choice but to try to make sense out of the mess of papers before me, those fragile tokens of lives that time had welded into totems. Although I was not on the analyst's couch here, I was in search of the story or stories that could set the record straight. I needed to know who these people were who had kept these files, those unsmiling faces on the walls, this place that always whispered, "This is who you are."

AERD VAN NES,
Luitenant-Admirael van Holland
en Westvriesland.

J. Houbraken Sculps.

1650

Lieutenant Admiral Aerd Van Ness
image dated 1650

Marcia Burnes, 1782–1832
image dated 1810

General John P. Van Ness, 1770–1846
copy of portrait painted by Gilbert Stuart, 1805

Catherine Douw, 1797–1866
newly married and now Mrs. Henry G. Philip
portrait by Ammi Phillips c. 1822

Colonel Henry G. Philip, 1824–1881
portrait by Ammi Phillips c. 1822

Catherine Douw (Mrs. Henry G. Philip), 1797–1866
when widowed and living at Talavera
painter and date unknown

Martinus Hoffman Philip, 1826–1888
son of Catherine Douw Philip and Henry G. Philip, the
brother who looked after Talavera during the Civil War
painter and date unknown

Lieutenant John Van Ness Philip, 1832–1862
son of Catherine Douw Philip and Henry G. Philip,
painted around 1855, when he began life at Talavera
painter and date unknown

Eliza Worthington Philip, 1842–1896
my great-great grandmother, the mistress of Talavera
as a young woman
painter and date unknown

Dr. Charles Worthington
Eliza Worthington's father who sometimes lived at Talavera
painter and date unknown

Mrs. Eliza Worthington
Eliza Worthington's mother who also spent time at Talavera
painter and date unknown

Talavera, 1969

My parents stand on the front porch dressed for a costume ball. My father wears my great-uncle's Rough Rider uniform: tan riding breeches, gorgeous brown leather boots, a khaki-colored shirt and a banged-up U.S. Cavalry hat. Seventy years earlier his uncle wore the same clothes to Cuba, then following Teddy's lead, charged up Kettle Hill. In his right hand my father grasps the Civil War sword of his great-uncle, after whom he and his father, my grandfather, were named. My mother wears something more contemporary, a flowing scarlet gown. Draped over her shoulders is a white silk shawl. Her hair is jet black; her lips are ruby red. Standing there, framed by the white pillars, each one rising twenty feet in the air, she could be Scarlett O'Hara. I am in awe of their transformation from parent to fairy tale.

My grandmother is settled into her room by the kitchen for the night, and her cook, Betty, is on

*call in case we have an emergency—only in case
of an emergency. She has drawn the line at preparing dinner for the grandchildren. All eight of us
are there: my three brothers, my sister, me and
our three cousins. We don't care. We hate it when
Betty cooks for us anyway. The kids have to eat
separately, in the kitchen. Every now and then we
hear the tinkle of the little bell that means my
grandmother is calling Betty to bring something to
the dining room table from the kitchen or to serve
the next dish. Betty hates that bell. She scowls
and wipes her hands on her frilled apron and
clomps out through the hall in her enormous shoes.
When she comes back, she expects to see that we
have finished the food that she scooped into our
bowls. When I complain that I don't like my
chicken and my peas and my mashed potatoes all
mixed up in a bowl like that, Betty says, "It's
just going to get mixed up in your stomach anyway, and aren't we a fussy little miss?" So when
Betty puts food in my bowl, I eat.*

*Betty thinks we are spoiled. When she was
growing up on the farm, her family never had
shoes, never had anything. They had so little to
eat that in the mornings, Betty explains, they ate
fried cow snot. I think Betty is marvelous. I usually wake up before anyone else and slip down to
the kitchen. While I sit on the stool, Betty cooks
bacon and tells me stories about when she was a
kid. One time her father got so mad at the bull,
which was making trouble, that he punched him in
the nose. Calmed that bull right down. No
doubt Betty's father had to be tough. Later I will
think about Betty's name, Scofield, and with a bit
of research, discover that in the early 1900s her
father bought their small farm in East Taghkanic.
It was hardscrabble land, too rocky for profit, land*

that in a previous generation had been farmed by a tenant of Livingston Manor: ten schepels of wheat as rent for eighty acres. Betty came to work as a fruit packer down in our barns when she was in her late twenties. Then word got out that Mrs. Philip was looking for someone to work in the big house. Betty went to work up there and stayed through most of my childhood.

But back to that evening, which I can see as vividly as if I were still there. Some memories are so painful it is hard to call them up; others come swooping down like barn swallows, winging circles in the air. My childhood memories of Talavera are like that, emblems of a time when life was not divided into categories of bad or good, moments to be regretted or moments to be grateful for. What happened was accepted and lived and believed in like the fried cow's snot, which of course I knew wasn't true, but which still made Betty my hero.

As soon as the wheels of our parents' cars crunch down the long, curving drive, we begin. First is croquet, which we love but which inevitably brings out the worst in us. When I skunk my cousin's ball into the tall grass, he calls me a bloody fool and begins to chase me with his mallet swinging. I think it is funny and dance away, flaunting my competence. I am winning, you see. Then I realize that he is seriously intending to brain me. I run to my older brother, just then taking aim at his own ball, which he is about to send through the final two wickets, finishing the game. My brother wants to hear that satisfying thunk of the ball against the wood. We are bugging him as usual. He grabs my cousin's arm and tells him to cool it, but my cousin, a whirling dervish by this point, hits him in the shin with his mallet and

*calls him a bloody fool too. So my brother grabs
him and gives him a wedgie he'll remember and
ceremoniously hangs him by the underwear from a
knot in a nearby pine tree.*

*I don't remember how long it takes my cousin's
underwear to stretch out enough so that he can get
his footing and wiggle free, or maybe my brother
takes pity on his shouts and lets him down. But
it doesn't matter because I am not fool enough to
stick around. I am long gone, down to the barn to
watch the funny bay colt that just this spring arrived. He is learning how to drink water, and
while I watch, he sticks his small, rubbery nose
into the water barrel, then snorts in surprise,
springing back, quick as a deer, flicking his black
flop of a tail. My parents named him Peter, after
Peter Van Ness, who built Lindenwald, and although he is to be a family horse, I have already
made him mine. When I watch his spindly legs
gather under him to run back to his mother, I
imagine us leaping over fences as high as those
that my father jumped when he was a boy my
age. Well, maybe we'll jump a little lower. In the
photographs in the library, my father is riding a
huge dark horse and leaping over solid wooden
fences, not over movable gymkhana poles. Wind
sweeps his hair back because he is not wearing a
riding cap. Such confidence, such risk. In the
room my sister and I share are the ribbons he won
in the horse show that day. Even at eight I know
that I can't quite live up to the past.*

*Soon it is time for dinner. When our parents go
out to one of their cocktail parties, we have
spaghetti if Betty relents and decides to cook. If
she doesn't, we make pancakes from the huge
bowl of batter that my mother has left in the re-
frigerator. We soak the pancakes in syrup. My*

61

cousin, no longer mad about the wedgie, has joined me in proposing a pancake-eating contest. I eat twelve and am sure that I am the winner, but then he stuffs two more in his mouth. "No fair, you have to swallow," I say. I know this trick. As soon as the count is done, he will go and spit them out off the back porch. But we don't get to resolve the matter because Betty appears in the kitchen, telling us that we are making too much noise, we will disturb our grandmother. We quiet down immediately and decide to play monster in the basement. We don't put the dishes away or clean up. I imagine that when my mother gets home, she will do that, hoping to fend off Betty's tirade of complaints.

Betty clumps back upstairs, and we troop down into the basement. One or the other of my older brothers is the designated monster. We turn out all the lights and hide. The chase begins. The monster comes roaring through the darkness. We race away from him, through the wine cellar, the fruit cellar, the old kitchen with the enormous iron pot, a real witch's kettle, still hanging on a hinge over the Dutch fireplace, through the laundry room and the furnace room. Someone is on a bicycle. My older cousin, who always has great ideas, has put on a pair of roller skates. I can hear the whir and skid of the wheels, ball bearings screeching as she races from room to room. Laughter, screams. In desperation for a new place to hide, one cousin and I push through the small opening into the coal bin. We scramble over the slippery sharp coal, safe. But being safe soon becomes boring. We crawl back out and join the fray. Then I am wearing the skates. I can remember their sudden speed where the floor abruptly tilts down by the old furnace, shooting me forward into the dark. The dogs are barking and chasing now too, biting our clothing in their excitement at joining the melee. It is a miracle that no one cracks his head or breaks any bones. Those on bicycles don't wear helmets—none of us even has a helmet then—and the floor is smooth concrete in the main areas, dirt in the wine and fruit cellars under the wings. Periodically we bang into pipes and insulation that release clouds of dust. Only when we're exhausted do we stop.

It is time to climb the steep steps up to Betty's room. I would have been too scared to do such a thing on my own, but my older cousin, the one with the great ideas, has told us that she knows Betty has a stash of candy in her room. Three of us troop up and knock at the door. We can hear the sound of the television and the recognizable rustle of a cellophane bag. To my surprise, Betty seems glad to see us. "You look like vagrants," she says, and this seems to please her. "Well, come on in." We do. "Wash your hands," she orders, and we do that as well. Then she lets us climb up on the bed. She continues watching the western, and soon we are too, staring at the small black-and-white television perched on her bureau and munching on Snickers bars while we follow the shoot-out.

Soon someone is shaking me awake. The movie is over. We head out to run through the fireflies, another evening ritual. The lawn is ablaze with flickers of green light, and we run through them, quickly beginning a game of king of the sundial, climbing up and pushing one another off the stone sundial in the center of the lawn.

We are filthy by the time my parents get home. None of us has worn shoes all evening. Even visiting the horses, I simply have hopped over the piles of wet horse manure, toes curling in the dust. Of course I'm not supposed to be walking down there barefoot among the rusty nails and piles of old machinery. I know the risk too. I have already cut myself on rusty nails and have had to have the gigantic tetanus booster more than once. But who is there to tell me no? That is one of the incredible joys of being at Talavera, the freedom that comes of life in a big family and the infinite number of places to explore. We get to do things that none of my friends ever do. It is, I think, part of why I have come to have this sense that somehow we are special.

When our parents return from their party, we know they will not make us take baths or scold us if we are not in bed. They sit on the wicker furniture on the south porch and talk in quiet voices. Maybe they have a few more drinks. I love going to sleep upstairs hearing the murmur of their conversation on the porch. It doesn't matter to me that they are probably smashed. They came of age in the forties and lived through a terrible war. What could go wrong now? Their pockets bulge with the slim outlines of Camel cigarettes, and each evening their glasses tinkle with ice, cocktail time. These are the good days. I snuggle myself down into the sheets, safe.

CHAPTER SEVEN

Wild Bees

Months, then a year before I could return to complete my excavation of family papers. When I arrived at Talavera on a hot July day, my mother was glad for company, for someone to share her worries about the fruit. The valley was in a drought, only six inches of accumulated rainfall when by then there should have been twenty-six. July was when the fruit produced all the fruit cells that it would make and the hot, sunny days gave the trees time to photosynthesize huge overloads of carbohydrates. Size should be fantastic—that is, if we had rain. At this point it could be an extraordinary season or a terrible one, depending on how much rain fell between now and August. The taste should be above normal as well. Apples are like grapes in that hot, sunny days help them develop an abundance of fruit zesters. The more fruit zesters, the more complex and rich the final taste. This is a matter of survival for apples and pears. The better they taste, the higher the likelihood that they will be consumed by animals that scatter their seeds, ensuring the next generation.

Like most farmers, my mother has seen too many summer

hailstorms and too many dry seasons to count on good weather until it has already come and gone. But something more than the weather was troubling her. The wild bees that lived in the old pine tree by the back porch were gone. Woodpeckers had pecked so many holes in the old tree that sections of the trunk resembled a colander, and the mostly hollowed-out core was perfect for bees. But this summer they had disappeared. My mother and I sat on the back porch and listened: silence. If the hive had been alive, the bees would have been coming and going from the dark hole. They would have buzzed for a moment at the entrance, the seven thousand facets of their lateral eyes taking in any relevant information necessary from bees that passed them by as they readied themselves to dive into their home. Careful to fold their four wings, they would have slipped into the darkness, that intricate city where thousands were working, tending the brood, cleaning or grooming their beautiful queen. She would have been busy as well, laying as many as three thousand eggs in one day. As long as the queen remained in the hive, they would never behave irrationally, robbing and engaging in other self-destructive acts. What had happened to the hive?

Starvation seemed unlikely, for we had had a mild winter. Even if they had run out of food, workers would have starved themselves in order to save their last bits of honey and pollen for the queen, hoping to save the unlaid eggs that she contained. On the coldest days they would have surrounded her like a living bee blanket, huddling their furry bodies together and fanning her endlessly in an effort to keep her warm. The brood, tucked into their hexagonal chambers, would have been similarly protected, surrounded by their nurses even when the hive was in a state of emergency. Something must have happened to kill the queen, and since it had not been a harsh winter, the probable cause was pesticides. We were careful not to thin the fruit with chemicals like Sevin, which kills bees. But they could easily have journeyed into a sprayed bed of clover somewhere else. Sometimes even a beehive, that place of architectural, political and economic perfection, cannot be saved from disaster. Their queen must have died. And if something had killed the wild bees, what was the state of my mother's predators? The ladybirds and lacewings and blackflies that she counted on for mite control?

After my father died, my mother attended Cornell fruit schools and took a spray applicator's course, then studied and passed the exam. She intensified my father's initial experiments with integrated pest management (IPM) strategies to replace traditional spray methods. IPM meant spraying for what pests you had, rather than what you thought might be there. The aim is to achieve biological control of marauding pests. It required checking the trees weekly, sometimes daily with a magnifying glass to identify what insects were there and at what thresholds. Then you could begin to consider how to use good bugs, or predators, to prey on those that harmed the fruit and trees. The risk was in missing an infestation and losing your crop. The old way was comforting. Each week Cornell sent out bulletins listing which insects were hatching at the Hudson Valley Experimental Station and which chemicals were recommended to kill them. You could follow those guidelines and know that your fruit was not going to get pocked and scarred or killed by infestations of mites and curculios, banded leaf rollers and the nasty psylla flies.

The problem is that those same chemicals wipe out any natural means of defense as well. They kill natural predators, such as ladybugs and blackflies. So once you got started that way, your orchards were hooked on a steady stream of chemical bathing. Breaking the cycle is not easy. It takes careful watching, and it takes guts. But my mother, with her appetite for risk, was an IPM natural. She could walk out into a block so infested with aphids the tips of the branches writhed green and shrug, saying, "I've seen worse. Give the ladybugs some time."

I helped my mother with the scouting whenever I could.

During the peak times we'd prowl the fruit trees two or three times a week, magnifying glasses in hand, looking for trees with a yellow pallor or curled leaves, those that were slightly off color. If a tree looked off—the leaf canopy thin or the usual green tinged with yellow—we collected leaves from four quadrants, turned them over, then began to scan, midrib to outer serrate edges, counting bugs and bug eggs of all shapes and sizes. Sometimes we'd just see their trails of frass, bug poop, and know they had been there. Or we saw the white stippling where leaf miners had been. Aphids are greedy and would leave whole sections of the leaf brown. We looked for good bugs too, the haphazard and finicky red-and-black spotted ladybugs and the busy black ants, which herd up colonies of aphids on certain leaf quadrants to use as food supplies for the colony. Once the aphid "corrals" were established, with guard ants posted to keep them there, or-derly lines of ant workers marched up to feed on them at regulated times.

But if something had wiped out our bees, chances were good that it was also affecting our predators. Aphids and mites could be having a heyday in the orchards. My mother and I decided to drive out to check. Sure enough, back in the far orchards, mites had begun to bronze the trees, espe-cially the blocks of Red Delicious, which they particularly loved. They were sucking the nutrients out of the leaves to such a degree that the trees had taken on a brownish tinge. The young pears were covered with aphids, so many piling up on the young terminals that I was worried, but my mother didn't want to spray. She pointed to the lower leaves, where an ant colony was already busy devouring the juicy aphids. The leaves on the young pears weren't curling yet. She would give the ants a week before she decided whether to spray. But the apples were a worry; we had better start a mite count.

We started in the block of young Red Delicious, a variety that must have sweeter foliage, for they are always hit with the worst concentrations of mites. Four leaves from each quadrant, north, south, east and west, meant sixteen leaves to collect per tree. Four or five trees from each block meant examining eighty leaves. By 11:00 A.M. the orchards were steaming with heat. We quickly bagged our leaves and drove them back to the house. For the next hour I sat on the back porch, counting red mites and bright orange eggs. My mother was edgy, another spray would cost seven hundred dollars. But that wasn't all: Having bronzed trees was a fruit grower's shame. She began to wonder what she had done; perhaps she'd miscalculated her predator population or put on the preventative spring oil spray too late. Worse yet, the bronzed leaves were a sign that some undetected soil deficiency had left the trees vulnerable to mite predation.

But we were in luck, at least for the time being. Despite the bronzed leaves in the back orchards, I counted only an average of four motile mites per leaf, one below the July threshold. My mother had a few more days to let the lacewings and ladybird beetles and syrphid fly larvae have a go. If the mite count was not down by Monday, however, she would have to spray. At this point in the cycle, mites could not only wither this year's fruit but also affect next year's crop as well. Already the trees had chosen which cells would develop into next year's fruit, and the tiny buds were there, growing alongside this year's crop. If the trees encountered too much stress in August, next year's fruit buds would not be strong enough to withstand the winter. Both drought and mites are August worries for the fruit grower.

69

⁂

By the end of the week twenty-five boxes of papers were stacked in the south hall, a huge cache of letters, diaries, journals and other farm and family papers. My husband and I would drive them back to the university where I taught so that I could begin to clean and sort and catalog them. Together with almost fifteen thousand items that had been removed from the house in 1973 and were now housed in the New-York Historical Society, they made up a collection of farm and family papers that stretched back to the early 1800s. Surely in that mass of information I would find answers to some of the questions I was seeking.

While we waited for my husband to arrive, my mother and I sat on the back porch, watching the evening light. All along the river, fog was descending, but here the light was still rosy. We wondered if the clear skies would hold through tomorrow. The weather radio announced rain. That morning my mother had driven down to the Germantown agricultural cooperative to buy Apollo, one of the weakest of the mite sprays. We had found a growing number of predator black mites and even some Ti pyri (*Typhlodromus pyri*), mite killers capable of consuming quantities of red mites a day, but even so, the mites were regenerating too fast. If she allowed the next generation to hatch out, she would risk losing complete control. Ironically, while at the co-op to conduct her depressing errand, my mother picked up some news that had cheered her considerably. Mites were out of control all across the valley, and Cornell was blaming the warm winter, which seemed to have allowed an unusually high number of eggs to overwinter and hatch out. It was not that my mother enjoyed other people's misfortune, but now she could stop worrying that her mite predicament was the result of her bad management.

We seemed to sit there for minutes, simply enjoying the breeze, while we waited for my husband's car to pull up. Then we heard it, that distinct high-pitched buzz. My mother and I both looked over to my right, where a bee zoomed along the porch rail, sighting us with its third cyclopean eye. A wandering bee out hunting pollen would never zoom so close and in such a bumbling, almost confused manner. Soon another bee flew by in an equally erratic pattern. It looked like a drunk, buzzing this way and that, coming toward us, then veering away.

It was my mother who pointed to the bee tree. A thick cloud of insect bodies was suspended over the hole, then began to funnel itself inside. Within minutes the bulk of the swarm was gone. Six or seven thousand bees were now sorting themselves out inside the trunk, workers heading one way, drones another. The queen, surrounded by her nurses, was settling down, safe in the darkness of the tree. Only the guard bees swirled this way and that across the entrance. We had just watched a swarm of wild bees descend into the old tree.

My mother was thrilled. After dinner, my husband and I told her some other good news. She had another grandchild on the way. My work on the project took on a new urgency. I no longer needed to resolve my quest for answers about Talavera just for myself. In seven months my son would be born. What did I want to pass on to his generation?

In the Hollow of His Hand

E ver since I uncovered my father's notes about an earlier John Van Ness Philip who wrote his mother to
announce that he was returning home to make
money through farming Talavera, I have been determined to
find the letter. The irony of his proclamation was simply too
great. Here was my own family, struggling to hang on to a
farm that by 1992 we needed to support, while in 1855 a
young man could consider building his fortune through it.

My mother had never seen the letter herself, so she could
only advise me to search through the Philip–Van Ness papers
at the New-York Historical Society, but she did think I
might be interested to know that she had found Lieutenant
John Van Ness's sword. Rather, the sword had found her. The
man who bought it recently from an antiques dealer had
contacted her, and they had begun an exchange. He had
come to see Talavera and to meet her. Now I was on the way
to Washington, D.C., to meet him.

When I arrived at the gleaming Reagan International
Airport, Ronald B. Moser was waiting for me at the gate. I
spotted him right away, a tall, lean man who was scanning the

crowd, looking for the woman from New York whom he had advised to locate him by means of his blue ball cap. Even dressed in civilian clothes and sporting a North Carolina ball cap, Mr. Moser looked like what he was: a retired U.S. Navy officer, once the commanding officer of the ocean surveillance ship USS *Alacrity* and the guided missile fast frigate, USS *Antrim*.

Mr. Moser greeted me warmly, and soon we were driving down Interstate 95 in his silver Jeep Cherokee, past the Pentagon, past Crystal City, where he sometimes worked while on the job as a senior analyst for EER Systems, a department of defense consulting firm. He drove the speed limit, south toward Virginia and his home in Woodbridge. Along the way we talked about one of his favorite subjects, the Civil War. Mr. Moser collected Civil War items, especially those used by the U.S. Navy. In March 1997 he saw a particularly beautiful U.S. naval officer's sword that a dealer purchased with him in mind. Mr. Moser was impressed by the sword, but not enough to pay the thirty-four hundred dollars that the dealer wanted for it.

One month later, at another gun show, he saw the sword again and this time knew that he had to have it. The sword was similar to a standard issue 1852 Ames naval officer's sword, one of which Mr. Moser already owned, but this one had an imported German blade from Solingen. Mr. Moser couldn't get over the quality of the blade and the fine condition of the brass detailing on the handle and quillon and the sword's sharkskin grip. But mostly he was impressed by the scabbard which bore the inscription "presented to Lt. John Van Ness Philip by his fellow townsmen of Claverack, Col. Co. NY May 20, 1861." This time he bought the sword, then began to wonder about the man whose sword he had come to possess, the man who happened to be my great-great-uncle.

"It's an absolute miracle that we are talking," Mr. Moser said when I first called him earlier in the year. "I had never even heard of Claverack. I just took a long shot one day. All

I had was the inscription on the scabbard and the sword. I called up the Claverack Town Hall and said that I had purchased the sword. I asked if they could give me any information on the family of J. Van Ness Philip. They said, 'Why don't you just call up Julia?' I said, 'What?' They said, 'Yeah, she lives there.' They gave me your mother's number. I had some trepidation. But I called your mom up and said, 'Do you know John Van Ness Philip?' and she said, 'Yes, I'm looking at a picture of him right now.' I tell you, I just about fell out of my chair."

My mother meant she was looking at a photograph of my father, but that was before Mr. Moser knew that three generations of men named John Van Ness Philip had come along since the owner of the sword that he now owned. Lieutenant John Van Ness Philip, my great-grandfather's brother, had signed up for the Union cause six days after the first shots of war had been fired at Fort Sumter. He was thirty-eight at the time and had retired from a career in the navy to return to Talavera and take up farming. Life at Talavera in the Arcadian vision of a gentleman farmer seemed to have been his life's dream, but he was no sooner settled in at Talavera, and the farm, revitalized by his interest and investment, had been transformed into Claverack's third largest dairy, than news of war traveled north.

John Van Ness reenlisted in the U.S. Navy and that night gave a rousing speech in the Hudson City Hall, where he called upon all able-bodied men to uphold the Union. The next day the *Hudson Daily Star* considered his talk the lead war news item. "The addresses were full of ardor for the cause of our country," proclaimed the paper, "the principal one being from our noble citizen J. Van Ness Philip, who though retired to the quiet pleasures of his farm and his home, like the illustrious Washington and Cincinnatus of old, leaves his plough at the call of his country and braves the hazards of the sea and the hostile foe, to sustain the honor of the old flag under which he has served for twenty years. All honor to such noble patriotism as this say we."

Quinctius Cincinnatus, that fifth-century B.C. Roman hero, was summoned from his fields to aid a trapped Roman army. In fifteen days he triumphed over the enemy and laid down his sword to return to his plowing. The comparison fascinated me. John Van Ness's decision also raised so many questions. Why would a man with a rising career in the navy have quit at age thirty-eight to take up agriculture? Why would the farm he chose to cultivate be Talavera?

I was more determined than ever to find that letter. Certainly it would offer clues to what I had come to see was a key moment in the history of the farm. John Van Ness's portrait had been hanging in the dining room at Talavera all along, but I had never taken much notice of it. The only thing I knew about him was that he was one of Catherine Douw's three sons. As soon as I could, I began searching through the files on John Van Ness Philip in the New-York Historical Society. Day after day I read through the files of parched letters, each a hieroglyph at first, then gradually a discernible, often highly ornate script. Lieutenant John Van Ness's formal prose seemed a foreign language to me. Only slowly, under the dim lights, did the swirl of letters become so familiar that I could discern words, sentences, a distinct writerly style. The story of his life began to unfold.

Influenced by his uncle General John P. Van Ness, who seemed to have taken a special interest in the nephew named after him, John Van Ness left home at the age of eighteen to seek his fortune as a midshipman. From the beginning he was in love with life on the sea. His early logs describe his sense of the romance of walking the decks at midnight watch and his horror at watching sailors flogged for insolence. Within ten years he witnessed the planting of the U.S. flag in California in 1846, then joined the USS *Mississippi* to sail to Constantinople to help free the Hungarian rebel Louis Kossuth in 1851. Once I saw his logs from his time aboard the *Mississippi*, I understood the inscription on the thick gilt-edged volumes of Archibald Alison's four-volume history of Europe, published in 1849, that I had found stored in the barns at Talavera.

He had signed the first volume "Midshipman JVNP, USS Mississippi." In all likelihood, it was these books that he read while crossing the ocean to Constantinople.

Soon after the historic rescue of Kossuth, John Van Ness developed an interest in life onshore. On August 8, 1852, he married Laura Johnson, the daughter of the wealthy John Johnson, the last chancellor of Baltimore. His ship, USS *Mississippi*, was soon to head out on another historic mission, this time sailing for Japan under Commodore Matthew Perry. In July 1853, she arrived in Uraga, the southern tip of Tokyo Bay, to begin persuading the Japanese that it was better to begin formal relations with the United States than to resist. On that day, two hundred years of self-imposed isolation ended and Japan was soon forced to open to the West.

John Van Ness did not mention any regret in having left the *Mississippi*, although he later purchased Commodore Perry's handsome volume about the mission to Japan. In letters to his mother he sent detailed and happy accounts of his new post, teaching mathematics to young recruits in the newly founded Naval Academy in Annapolis.

Letter after letter crackled under my fingers like dry leaves. Each slim, carefully bound ship log revealed more and more of John Van Ness's interest in travel as well as his intense love for his Columbia County home, a place he described with reverence as "the mansions of magic." But read as I might, through boxes and boxes of correspondence, I still could not find the key to his connection to Talavera, the letter in which he linked his fate with the land and the farm. I began to think that my father must have been mistaken. It would not be surprising. I was getting used to a disparity between family history and fact.

One afternoon, as I was about to leave for the day, I forced myself to look through one last folder labeled "Miscellaneous Correspondence 1850's." At first I didn't even realize that I had found the letter. Lieutenant John Van Ness began by talking about his delightful discovery of a pay bonus, but in his close, he made his legendary proclamation. I had found it! Of course, the wording was not exactly as my father had remembered it, but it was more interesting yet. The composed elegant writing explained John Van Ness's reasons for coming home, and they were decidedly financial. "Two horses and an *expensive* wife add a little to a fellow's expenses," he had written to his mother the previous year on March 11, 1854. Was he trying to convince her that farming was not a mistake? Was he bragging about his fancy wife, or complaining? One of the horses was his beloved Kossuth, named after Louis Kossuth, who, to judge from the copious notes about him in his ship's log from that time, had had a strong impact on John Van Ness.

I soon forgave him mentioning his pedigreed horses and his wife in the same line. Before I knew it, I became swept up in an unexpected soap opera of events at Talavera. Later, on April 1, 1856, he signed a deed with his cousin Stephen K. Hogeboom, purchasing Talavera from him for fifteen thousand dollars. His mother, then living on land she had inherited from her grandfather Peter Van Ness of Kinderhook, was delighted that her eldest son was returning home. "Lord bless you and keep you as in the hollow of his hand," she wrote back when he informed her that he intended to be the next master of Talavera.

Within months, she and John Van Ness's younger brother Martin Hoffman and his family were happily settled in at Talavera. Catherine Douw's slim red diary soon recorded the comings and goings of family members, sleigh rides and dinners and always, in keeping with her devout faith, how "the joys of each Sabbath with its exalted privileges has passed away."

Soon after, John and Laura Van Ness moved north to Talavera, taking along three black servants and a slave named Tom whom Laura had taken as part of her inheritance from her father earlier that year. "It would kill him to be sold away from us," John Van Ness wrote to his younger brother William Henry (my great-grandfather) about their decision to bring Tom north from Maryland with them. His tone was

77

apologetic. Whether this was because taking Tom was a poor business decision or because he was ashamed at having inherited a slave is not clear. "He will never leave us I am certain," added John Van Ness, "and then we will have a good servant. He can do almost anything and I am sure that he can earn his money in a short time." Presumably, since John Van Ness writes of money that he will pay Tom, he intended to free him by bringing him north. But the status of southern slaves in northern states was still unclear. The famous Dred Scott case of 1857 had decided that a slave, even if freed, could not claim U.S. citizenship. Moreover, African Americans had been emancipated in New York State by 1827, but slavery was not abolished in Maryland until the final months of the Civil War.

Once north, John Van Ness initiated a flurry of improvements. His letters from this time to William Henry, then starting his law career in Washington, D.C., mentioned the arrival of new china and glass, new carpets and the tidy sum of $125 for ornamental trees. From 1857 on, William Henry began visiting Talavera for lengthy stays each summer, foreshadowing his eventual purchase of the farm from Laura in 1869. Familiar with life on southern estates, Laura would have felt at home in the Palladian feel of Talavera's columned porches, the grand porte cochere and its long, curving approach.

Under Laura and John Van Ness's stewardship, the original gardens at Talavera—a series of terraces of simple Italianate design that led down from the south lawn of the house— were given the definition I grew up with. The entire garden was outlined and framed by plantings of ornamental trees and bushes. Lilacs were planted to establish walkways while a cedar lane soon bordered the garden to the east and a hawthorne hedge divided the whole into upper and lower sections. Varieties of trees were planted to create areas of light and dark in accordance with the ideals of the picturesque as espoused by the American landscape gardener Andrew Jackson Downing. When I walked the grounds at Talavera, I could see those efforts: white pine, hemlock, fir, spruce, maple, elm and that aristocrat of shade trees the American beech, a tree that 115 years later became my favorite climbing tree.

The basic concept of the picturesque—that one could shape the land so that it resembled a picture, particularly those pictures made by early landscape painters that evoked in the viewer poetic moods of nostalgia for purer, more bucolic pasts—was fascinating in itself. In the Hudson Valley, during John Van Ness Philip's time, what was especially interesting was the ways in which these ideas of the picturesque were extended to agriculture as they had been in England decades earlier.

At Talavera, as on other Hudson Valley estates, this aesthetic was not limited to the twenty-five acres surrounding the house. John Van Ness was equally concerned with the design of the farmland. Nothing summed this up better than the huge misshapen hemlock at the far edge of orchard thirteen, the tree that my mother called the wild bee tree because spring after spring it was filled with wild bees, bees she counted on to help pollinate the fruit.

Back in the mid-nineteenth century, when it was planted, the hemlock would have been expensive, a fancy imported breed fashionable at the time for its expressive, drooping limbs. Carolina hemlock reflected Downing's emphasis upon striking, irregular and spirited forms. A shade tree, planted for the utilitarian purpose of providing shade for horses, men and oxen doing fieldwork, would never have been planted at that location just up from a hedgerow. No, the tree's role on the farm was aesthetic; it served to punctuate the view, what in landscape gardening is called a visual marker, probably chosen for its deep forest looks, an emblem of the former wild state of a landscape now tamed.

Similarly, in 1857, the front meadows that began at the edge of the lawns, now kept open as fields of wild grass and wildflowers, were planted with hay. Within American ideas of the picturesque, beauty and agricultural function were to be integrated as they had been on British estates for decades.

Once you were aware of these ideas, you couldn't walk any-where at Talavera without seeing more and more vestiges of that romantic landscape: a spreading horse chestnut tree, stands of maples and hemlocks, sudden lines of larch trees, clusters of catalpa, the copse at the corner of the drive. Trees everywhere, spreading and lifting in the wind.

Not surprisingly, once I thought to look in the Talavera library for books on landscape gardening, I found an 1844 edition of Downing's *Treatise on the Theory and Practice of Landscape Gardening* sitting on a shelf crammed with the books on agriculture. Reading through the preface in the fragile, gold-leafed book, one and a half centuries after John Van Ness's time, I was struck by the connection between Downing's emphasis upon home and John Van Ness's return to Talavera.

Downing had most certainly been influenced by the Christian home movement that flourished in antebellum America. In his preface, he established the connection be-tween home and country: "The love of country is insepara-bly connected with the love of home. Whatever, therefore, leads man to assemble the comforts and elegancies of life around his habitation, tends to increase local attachments, and render domestic life more delightful; thus not only aug-menting his own enjoyment, but strengthening his patrio-tism, and making him a better citizen."

Such words must have had a profound resonance in my great-great-uncle, who had forged a career of military ser-vice, especially as they affirmed what on a personal level he wanted to do: to concentrate his wealth and his efforts on the cultivation of a rural life at Talavera. To beat his sword into a plowshare, retiring at the height of achievement like Cincin-natus. To serve his country by farming.

Of course John Van Ness also intended to serve himself. He was not being sarcastic when he said that he wanted to farm because he needed more money. Once settled in at Talavera, he would certainly appear to have joined the upper class of gentleman farmers in the Hudson Valley, although for him, the bottom line was different. The farm at Talavera needed to make money.

Luckily, in 1855, this was possible. Farming was still the major industry of the state, and several factors contributed to make it extremely profitable. One of these was population. Between 1820 and 1860 the population of New England and the Atlantic seaboard doubled. Columbia County went from thirty-five thousand people in 1790 to seventy-six thousand in 1850. As population rose, local areas as well as the nearby cities of New York and Boston needed poultry and eggs, and butter and milk. Hay and grain were in demand for the growing number of horses.

Meanwhile agriculture was being transformed by new machinery that increased production. Plows, harrows, planters, cultivators, reapers and threshers all were invented and perfected during the 1820s and 1830s, making them available for widespread use by 1850. Farmers could produce more and sell more. The era of scientific agriculture was well under way.

81

John Van Ness threw his efforts and modest inheritance into making improvements on the farm. The barns that we played in as children were built in quick succession, probably by a team of itinerant barn builders from the Berkshires, just to the east. Straight-timbered English-style barns, they signified a scientific departure from the low-roofed, heavily timbered Dutch barns that had been raised by John Van Ness's Dutch predecessors. A silo and hogpens completed the seven-building barn complex.

Within the next two years John Van Ness spent $321 on cattle, $82.50 on a pair of oxen and $100 on a pair of workhorses. He also splurged on another fancy horse, this time a fine gray mare for which he paid the exorbitant sum of $146.

Farm machinery included a hay press and a newfangled mowing machine, a new horse plow and saw and several hundred dollars' worth of tools. By 1865, when the next state agricultural census was taken, these improvements had raised the farm's value to twenty thousand dollars. John Van

Ness had invested a total of eleven hundred dollars in stock and one thousand dollars in tools and implements (a figure that presumably included the new barns). The farm was running 75 tons of hay and harvesting 500 bushels of winter rye and 150 bushels of potatoes. In addition, there were peas, beans, Indian corn, buckwheat and barley. One hundred apple trees produced cider, and some twenty hens were raised for eggs and meat. Four horses lived in the barns along with two working oxen, but the primary residents were twelve milk cows. Just down from them in newly built hogpens wallowed seven pigs.

Just nine years after John Van Ness had initiated improvements, Philip cows produced three thousand gallons of milk per year. A sizable hog operation, grown from the original seven pigs, produced two thousand pounds of pork. The farm had been transformed from a declining agricultural enterprise into the third-largest dairy in Claverack. In the process John Van Ness had transformed himself from Annapolis naval officer to Hudson Valley gentleman-farmer. Sort of.

The more I read letters between John Van Ness and his brothers, the more I realized that this transformation had not been easy. If there had been a glorious age of wealth and ease for my family, it had not been in 1855. John Van Ness had returned home to confront a considerable domestic problem. His youngest brother, Martin Hoffman, who had stayed at home to manage the Philip family's carpet mill in Philmont, had managed to run up ten thousand dollars' worth of debt, quite a remarkable sum, considering that the standard navy widow's pension for the time was thirty dollars a month.

At one point John Van Ness conjectured that his brother had not earned a dollar in over ten years. Why John Van Ness did not know of Hoffman's financial duress earlier is a story in itself. But it is one that perhaps even John Van Ness did not want to know about, for far from criticizing his brother, he threw himself into straightening out Hoffman's affairs.

The other brother, William Henry, was called on to help as well, but in every letter John Van Ness was surprisingly protective of Hoffman. According to family notes, their grandfather on their father's side, George P. Philip, had made a fortune building the first dam in Philmont, thus helping to found the town that took his name, Philip's mont. But a massive mill fire, then the bank crash of 1857 and what seems to have been Hoffman's screwball judgment had resulted in financial ruin. John Van Ness had used up his entire inheritance from Laura's father, and still there were debts to pay. William Henry began sending money north. I couldn't help wondering as I read: Would a family today, would my own family, come together so dramatically to take care of one of their own? Conditioned by life in the twentieth century, wouldn't we be more likely to let an irresponsible family member rely on governmental programs like unemployment and welfare or to take a Darwinian approach and let that person reap his own folly?

Something else was going on besides a nineteenth-century approach to family. For when John Van Ness wrote to William Henry in 1857, he expressed unveiled contempt for the carpet business and urged him not to criticize their younger brother. "My Dear Brother," the letter began, "I have just received your letter and I can only thank our father in heaven that your affairs are so that you can send us $8,000." He proceeded to write that Hoffman was a little better and had been to church, then added, "As to Hoffman's management, there is a screw loose somewhere. I will have a good talk with him after these matters are cleared up. But say nothing about it in your letters. Remember this poor fellow has not only sacrificed every dollar that he had, but spent the best years of his life in a business and a community which is horrible to contemplate." Clearly too close an affiliation with the scourge of industrialization was not considered gentlemanly.

John Van Ness went on to reassure his brother, writing, "I

have stopped all improvements and all fancy work. The only money I intend to expend now will be for the purpose of putting things in the ground. I am in for hard work and making money, and I think we can do it." The only luxury he admitted indulging in was a full-blooded Newfoundland pup, which he bought for the modest price of five dollars. He then added, "I believe that is all. Send the money by return mail by all means. Send it all to Hoffman in a letter to him. It makes no difference to me. His reputation is at stake. People even think I am immensely rich."

A year later John Van Ness was less patient with Hoffman's lack of progress. Usually the brothers took great pleasure in commenting on each other's "fast hosses." But when they were angry, they would insult the others' mounts. The first clue that John Van Ness was unhappy with his brother was the way he described Hoffman's horse as that "pitiful excuse for a horse." Then, in a letter dated March 11, 1859, he complained to William Henry that he was paying Hoffman's debts all over the county. "Don't say anything to Hoffman about striking off somewhere," he wrote peevishly. "He can't strike off. He must remain here. He has nothing to strike off with. It will kill ma to speak of it. No, our duty is here and here we must work and live."

Talavera, duty, work, live, debts, here. The words could have been written by my own father, also named John Van Ness. Had he known about his great-uncle's return home to take up responsibility for Talavera? If so, had his own decision to do the same been modeled on this past? I felt as if I were reading a novel and could recognize the themes: loyalty among brothers, a fierce, compelling desire to hang on to a family place, the need to settle inherited debts, the struggle to live up to the past, that glorious age of family wealth and achievement gone mythic. Only it wasn't South, it was North. I wasn't amazed by what had changed since 1855; I was dumbstruck by what seemed to have remained the same. Everything centered on Talavera. We were still this landed, aristocratic family. Sort of . . .

~%~

It took four years and all of John Van Ness's inheritance from his father-in-law, but he finally succeeded in bailing Hoffman out of debt and paying the mortgage on Talavera. The new barns were completed, and the dairy was in full operation. Talavera, renovated as John Van Ness's country seat, was perhaps even more resplendent than it had been when first built as the showpiece of John Van Ness's forebear Judge William W. Van Ness. John Van Ness threw himself into his new pursuit of agriculture. Engaging the interest of nine other county men, he founded the Columbia Agricultural and Horticultural Society and served two terms as president. The association was to organize Hudson's first agricultural fair, displaying imported cattle, agricultural innovations and a mammoth workhorse named Gentle Jim.

Throughout these years Talavera bustled with family. Catherine Douw's diary records her domestic joys of visits and visitations, dinner parties, luncheons, the flowers she planned for the garden and the births of Hoffman's three children. Each day she read the Bible, then selected passages from her thick but compact volume by Dr. Hook titled *Meditations for Everyday.*

By the close of 1860, however, her entries had begun to document the threat of war. Catherine Douw herself was not ignorant of the northern system of slaveowning that had existed in New York until 1827. As a baby and young child she had probably been reared, at least in part by a black slave woman named Sattin. Her grandfather Peter Van Ness had willed Sattin to her father in 1804, describing her as "the slave woman now in the possession of my son-in-law, Martinus Hoffman."

But when the war began, there was no question but that two of her sons would fight to uphold the Union. As soon as I opened the slim leather-bound volume and began to read, I could hear her voice, a mother speaking of the tension and drama of life in a country about to be torn by civil war.

JANUARY 30TH Van Ness and Hoffman have just left for Albany to attend a Democratic Convention—God save the Union.

MARCH 15 I have just had another letter from William Henry. Oh, if I could only see him. Lord bless him and keep him as in the hollow of thy hand and commence thy blessings to rest upon him.

MARCH 22 Our country is still in an unsettled state. I was in hopes that "Old Abe" would be able to heal our difficulties and bring peace to our unhappy land, but we are still in an unsettled state. There is no telling what will be the result of all this trouble

APRIL 7 This has been a delightful day. I do love a pleasant Sabbath

APRIL 18 The ground still covered in snow but not very cold. I have said nothing about the state of the country for it is a relief to me to get away from the newspapers and the sound of war. I feel so uneasy about my absent son William Henry down there in Washington among all the turmoil and excitement. Oh, that peace and quietness may be restored.

MAY 4 A bright pleasant day. I have been so anxious and excited of late that I have not felt like writing, our poor unhappy country

MAY 29 Tom just left with Van Ness's trunks and also his own. Hoffman has just taken him down to Hudson to put him on the Oregon, which goes down the river tonight.

JUNE 4 The RR Cuyler sails today and my dear Van Ness is gone. May the Lord keep him in the hollow of his hand.

Claverack was five hundred miles north of Richmond, but the war had reached Talavera. Within days John Van Ness was cruising the thousand-mile coast, pursuing Confederate ships that had broken the Union blockade of southern ports. Her younger son, William Henry, busy in

Washington, D.C., had already joined the Army of the Potomac and would serve as aide-de-camp to General William Buel Franklin. For the most part, John Van Ness's splendid sword remained in his stateroom along with his books on European history and the small dog that he had taken with him on board and named "Cuyler." But every evening, John Van Ness polished the long blade, then, in keeping with his mother's wishes, read a passage from his worn black Bible.

JP

By the time Mr. Moser and I arrived in his handsome Woodbridge home, it was clear to me that his great interest in the Van Ness sword had to do with Lieutenant John Van Ness and the way the sword connected the Civil War to Talavera, to the land there and to my family. As soon as we walked into the house, Mr. Moser led me directly into his study. He put his briefcase down and slipped behind his desk to lift down a long sword from its place on a bookshelf in the center of the room. While I watched, he turned the sword-point down and carefully drew it out of the scabbard. As soon as the sword was unsheathed, he handed it to me gently, the reverse side of the blade toward me so that when I reached out with my right hand, I could grab the hilt.

"Usually you get something and have no idea of whose it was," he said as I looked down the length of the gleaming blade, "but this sword had his name right on it. It's a very tremendous sword."

I grasped the handle, feeling the textured grip, and immediately my arm dipped. The weight surprised me. I decided to lay it on the desk while Mr. Moser began to point out details. "Look here," he said, pointing to the brass pommel. "You can see the thirteen stars, one for each state in the Union." He traced the naval pattern of oak leaves and acorns carved into the knucklebow, explaining that U.S. naval officers' swords always carried the motif of acorns to represent oak, the strongest wood for boatbuilding. As he talked, I fingered the brass dolphin heads carved into the quillon, com-

paring them with a similar dolphin head design decorating
the tip of the scabbard. The black leather scabbard had two
brass rings as well, for it was suspended by straps rather than
carried in a sleeve called a frog.

Mr. Moser bent his head to point out the faint but intricate designs etched into the blade. Where his finger reached,
I saw stars, floral sprays, a fouled anchor and a ribbon inscribed with the words *US Navy.* Any detail of the design
that he did not know, Mr. Moser looked up in a thick volume on American swords that he kept nearby.

I asked him if naval officers carried swords today. In answer, he lifted a short sword from its place on a rack nearby.
Again, his handling of the sword was precise, a practiced
movement full of respect. He pulled the sword out of the
scabbard to hand it to me. "You can see they've gotten
smaller," said Mr. Moser, "but the design is the same." As I
looked the sword over, I thought, *What purpose could a sword
serve in the age of Star Wars?* The sword is ceremonial, nostalgic, a symbol of continuity, and I was struck by the senti-
mentality and love of ritual that pervades this world I am in.

Abruptly, Mr. Moser turned and said he would be right
back. He left me in the room, saying something about giving
me a minute to look at Van Ness's sword as he went. He
walked out hurriedly, almost awkwardly. I realized that he
was leaving to give me time alone to hold and be with this
talisman of John Van Ness, an item that for him had great
meaning.

I picked the sword up and ran my finger along the tip or
false edge. With a start I realized that it was sharp. It was not
just a beautiful, ceremonial object but a weapon. And I was
struck by a thought so obvious I had never seen it before. I
come from a family of military men. General John P. Van
Ness, Lieutenant John Van Ness Philip, Colonel William
Henry Philip, Major John Van Ness Philip, Lieutenant John
Van Ness Philip, Jr. The names that I had come to know
from old photographs and letters fell one after the other like
dominoes. My great-great-great-uncle, my great-great-

uncle, my great-grandfather, my grandfather, then my own father, a marine in World War II: These men had all been in one way or another shaped by the military, and they had all forged relationships with Talavera, so much so that it suddenly seemed as if the history of my home were one of men and land and war. I could see how for a man like Mr. Moser, Talavera equaled a kind of American patriotism. It is my own generation, yes, we with our ripped blue jeans and tie-dyed shirts, my brothers with their once-shoulder-length hair, that had been the anomaly. What would Mr. Moser have thought of us if he had driven up to Talavera in the late sixties and come upon one of my brothers, love beads waving, as he concentrated on walking on high stilts through the columns of the porte cochere?

I put the sword back down on the table and looked around me at Mr. Moser's small study, crowded with books, photographs and awards that documented his own naval career and then the hundreds of items that made up his Civil War collection. Each bit of shelf not taken up by history books was full. I glanced over the lines of pistols, bridle bits, stirrups, powder kegs, photographs. Against one wall were racks of muskets and rifles; on another table rested a collection of swords and the mounted relic of a Civil War rifle that he had found in Gettysburg with his metal detector.

On a side table next to his desk was a framed photograph of Lieutenant John Van Ness Philip, the copy that my mother sent him. This portrait of John Van Ness in full naval officer's uniform had been taken at the Rowles photo studio in Hudson, the same camera shop where as kids we eagerly took our rolls of film taken with Brownie Instamatic cameras and later picked up the white envelopes of out-of-focus prints. Gold stars gleamed on the sleeves of Lieutenant John Van Ness's dark uniform, indicating that when the photograph was taken, he was the commanding officer of a ship. That ship was the USS *Cuyler*, which, during the early years of the Civil War, chased and captured Confederate ships seeking to cross the Union blockade, which stretched a thousand miles along the Atlantic coast. The USS *Cuyler*'s mission was to prevent supplies and arms from reaching southern port cities.

Later Mr. Moser figured that given the star on John Van Ness's sleeve and the location of the photographer, the photograph would have had to have been taken in June or July 1862, when John Van Ness returned home for the last time.

That July, on the twenty-third, the *Cuyler* steamed south again, returning to blockade duty off the coast of Florida, and the next month, somewhere near Key West, John Van Ness was bitten by *Aëdes aegypti,* the kind of mosquito that carries yellow fever.

Their first mission was to steam to Havana to inspect a fast-sailing British steamer, the *Oreto,* which had docked there and was being refitted with armaments. Intelligence had reported that the notorious Confederate Captain Raphael Semmes arrived in Havana at the same time as the *Oreto,* indicating that it was probably being refitted as a Confederate ship. John Van Ness and his crew arrived in Havana without mishap, but since the authorities there had refused to allow them to inspect the *Oreto,* they steamed out to wait for her in nonneutral waters. Meanwhile they were on the lookout for two other Confederate steamers, the CNS *Florida* and CNS *Tennessee.*

The *Cuyler* had been on a terrific run since April, capturing first the *Grace E. Baker,* carrying fifteen tons of cotton, then the *Jane,* a twenty-six-ton schooner loaded with pig iron. The *Cuyler* had also chased a large side-wheeled steamer for four hours, but she had slipped into the Bahía Honda under British colors and escaped. In late August, at latitude 30 degrees 23' N and longitude 75 degrees 24' N, the *Cuyler* had captured the *Anne Sophia,* bound for Baltimore and also flying the British flag.

Then, on August 20, just off the coast of Key West, their luck turned. Within two weeks the *Cuyler*'s captain, Francis Winslow, then the ship's surgeon, then John Van Ness Philip succumbed to yellow fever.

In 1860 yellow fever was a gruesome way to die, and even

today there is no cure for the disease. It took scientists forty years to conclude that it was carried by mosquitoes and begin to control its spread. As the virus multiplied in the body, it attacked liver cells, producing jaundice, a yellowing of the eyes and skin. In their final days, patients began to bleed internally, vomiting dark, altered blood. Meanwhile patients were dosed with whiskey and brandy to alleviate the pain of their high fever and kept in quarantine. Two days after his death, John Van Ness's sword and his dog, Cuyler, were shipped upriver to Hudson by steamer, but I had not found a steamer receipt for the transport of his body. Possibly it was cremated in New York City as part of yellow fever quarantine. The family held a funeral, however, and had a stone marker erected in the cemetery of the Dutch Reformed Church just down the road. For the next 111 years, his sword rested on the mantel in the library at Talavera. I must have seen it countless times during my childhood but never noticed it.

Not long after Mr. Moser contacted my mother, he had begun to dig up files on John Van Ness in the National Archives and in U.S. Navy records. That fall he drove north to meet my mother and visit Talavera. She told him where he could find John Van Ness's grave, and he went there as well. Next to the portrait of Lieutenant John Van Ness, I could see a color photograph of the tall white stone spire that marks his grave. In the sunny picture, you can clearly see the carved letters of his name and an unusual design of a cross overlaid with a fouled anchor.

My mother's generosity toward Mr. Moser when he visited and Talavera's tall white columns left him with a deep impression of my family. Where I began to see decrepitude, neglect, simply too much to take care of, he saw history. "It's incredible, the stability in your family. People move, and houses get torn down, but Talavera is there. You've got a gold mine of history there, you really do. It means so much more when it's your own family."

But standing there in his study, a part of my family's history enshrined here, I found myself thinking surprisingly opposite thoughts. I glanced over at the sword now on the table. It had been taken down from the library mantel at Talavera during a division of family property after my grandmother's death and had disappeared. I could have felt robbed, either directly or indirectly by the sword's loss, but at that moment I was aware of the sword's meaning, not to me but to the man who now owned it. For Mr. Moser, this sword represented things I could only guess at: tradition, service, the sentimental rituals of the military, patriotism and a way of life he clearly believed in, his own memories of service as a U.S. naval officer on the open sea.

A new story had become folded into that of John Van Ness. The sword had moved from being an object of my family to an object in the world. Questions of ownership suddenly seemed irrelevant. I couldn't help thinking again of those gnawing questions of tradition and history. When did a family's allegiance to a place last so long that it began to suffocate everyone involved? Was hanging on to Talavera really the right thing to do? I wondered if I was practicing a larger lesson for letting go of Talavera. I didn't feel the desire to own my great-great-uncle's sword. What I wanted, now more than ever, was to know his story. There, on Mr. Moser's side table, John Van Ness stared out from the photograph, his eyes as dark as the black waterfall of beard that cascaded from his chin.

"John Van Ness is one of my heroes," Mr. Moser said simply when he reentered the room, carrying a plate of sandwiches. He nodded toward the photograph. "He was so patriotic. I've had his picture here in my study since your mother sent it to me. I really admire him and what he did and what he sacrificed. He left his happy life and his family. He didn't have to do that. He had served for fifteen years."

While we ate the sandwiches, he explained the substitution system in place during the Civil War, a practice whereby for three hundred dollars you could pay someone to take your place. "He wasn't going to be drafted," continued Mr.

Moser, "and even if he had been, he was rich enough to pay the three hundred dollars to buy a substitute. Lots of people in his class did just that."

Again, Mr. Moser pushed the plate of sandwiches toward me. Only when he was sure that I had indeed eaten all that I could did he put the plate away, and we resumed looking at the Van Ness sword. I asked him who would have carried swords on ships like the *Cuyler*.

"A jack-tar would not have had a sword like this," explained Mr. Moser, "definitely not, only midshipmen. There was no ROTC then; midshipmen were like officers in training. Enlisted men, they were the jack-tars, would have had cutlasses. Here I'll show you."

He walked over to a rack of swords and pulled out a long blade. He pointed at its curved handle. The sword was as long as an officer's sword but had no ornamentation. Over the handle was a curved brass bar to protect the knuckles. He handed it to me and explained, "Here is a cutlass with the standard soup kettle over the handle. The men who went ashore in boats with John Van Ness when they chased the *Wilder* would have carried these. Maybe Tom had one too. They would have had pistols too, of course."

I recognized his mention of the *Wilder,* a Confederate ship, that John Van Ness and his servant Tom had encountered off Mobile Bay. When I asked Mr. Moser if he had any pistols, he nodded. The next thing I knew I was holding an 1846 single-shot pistol, the heaviest, most primitive-looking gun that I had ever seen. I looked over the slender barrel and dark wood, wondering first how a person could ever fire such a weapon with any accuracy and second, how he could load up in time. To fire the pistol, a man would have had to pull a percussion cap and a ball out of his ammunition bag, slip the cap on the mount and the ball into the short muzzle, then pull off the ramrod to pack the ball in tightly. Only then could he have taken aim and fired.

I handed the pistol back to Mr. Moser, and he held it up to the light. "For all I know," he said, squinting at the burnished pistol in his hand, "Van Ness could have used this in 1846, when he talks about sleeping on the beach with a pistol under his pillow in California."

He chuckled then, clearly enjoying the time we were spending with his collection. For him these weapons opened up times and places in American history. I remembered reading a long letter that John Van Ness wrote home about his 1846 mission to the Monterey Bay. In the navy for only five years at that time, he was proud to have just passed the rigorous midshipman exams. In Monterey, he landed with the naval mission that helped plant the U.S. flag on California soil, establishing its statehood. The legendary General John Frémont had impressed him deeply. So had the reports of Indian scouts that motivated the sailors to sleep on their pistols.

Before I knew it, I was getting a lesson on firearm technology. To illustrate his point, Mr. Moser brought out a Brown Bess, one of the flintlock muskets that were used in the Revolutionary War. When he handed it to me, I was again stunned by its weight. How could anyone stand still for long holding up, arms extended, ten pounds of iron and wood, much less shoot with accuracy? The gun was even more primitive and slower to load and fire than the 1846 pistol. I began to understand why the development of the rifled musket, in which a ball followed grooves carved into the barrel, shooting out straight and fast, was considered the most important innovation of the Civil War. Accurate at 250 yards, the rifle could kill from a half mile away. I also began to understand why the Civil War was called the first modern war. The difference between a flintlock musket and a rifle was like the difference between a bicycle and an automobile. Little wonder that the war left six hundred thousand men dead, 2 percent of the entire population.

Three hours have passed like minutes. As I packed my briefcase to go, Mr. Moser pulled something off the shelf and showed it to me with a grin. "Before you go, look at this," he said, and handed me what appeared to be a brass belt buckle. I turned it over in my hands and read the bold letters *SNY* inscribed on the face.

"A belt buckle?" I ventured, handing it back to him.

"Yes," he replied, "some states had them. It stands for the State of New York." He looked at me a minute, then added with a chuckle, "But of course here in the South we don't call it the State of New York. We say it stands for snotty-nosed Yankees."

I blinked for a split second. How was I supposed to take these words? Then I saw the laughter in his eyes and laughed out loud. I understood his joke for what it was, a show of trust, of our developing friendship. For the first time since I arrived, Mr. Moser had shown me, the snotty-nosed Yankee who had come south to see him, a glimpse of the man behind his southern hospitality and graciousness. He was born and raised in Charlotte, North Carolina. If he'd had ancestors in the Civil War, they would have fought on the Confederate side.

✤

95

We were driving up into the airport dropoff line when I asked Mr. Moser the question that had been perplexing me ever since our talks began. Why collect military items from the Civil War?

"Oh, I began only about three years ago," he said modestly, then added, "These people made huge sacrifices for us. When you die for your country, you have made the ultimate sacrifice and the Civil War was such a defining moment. . . ." His words trailed off, and we drove for a few moments in silence. I waited, letting him assemble his thoughts. When he spoke, it was clear that he had considered the subject deeply. "I guess we've had three holy wars," he said, "the Revolution, the Civil War and World War II, but the Civil War, well, that was the war that settled once and for all the way we were going to be."

As my plane back to New York took off, vaulting into the clouds, Washington and its landmarks—the domed Capitol, the Mall, the tall white needle—soon shrinking into patterns of green and brown and houses and trees, I thought about something else Mr. Moser said as I was leaving: "You know, you've got a gold mine to write about. You've got John Van Ness fighting off the coast, William Henry fighting down in Yorktown and their mother back at Talavera. If you can connect all that, you've really got something."

That was the question. Could I connect it all? A letter, then a sword had brought me south to Virginia, and I had spent the day talking to a man with whom, before writing this book, I would have had little in common. Now I was heading north again, but it was clear that I couldn't understand the present without diving further into the story of Talavera during the Civil War, the war that tried to settle once and for all the way we were going to be. A war fought so far south had changed forever the configuration of a farm and a family five hundred miles north. A family that had once owned slaves had joined the fight to abolish slavery. The contradictions made my head spin. How to go forward from here? How to begin?

CHAPTER NINE

Writing to the Wind

APRIL 1861

Acoating of fine snow hid the green fields, rippling white across the front lawns and gardens, but Catherine Douw noted in her diary that it was not very cold. All the sleighs had been washed and stored in the barn loft, while below the newborn calves, their legs buckling, tried to stand, wobbled, but fell. On the ridge across from the meadow, the apple trees set out by Hoffman were swelling into green tip, and down in the meadow the peepers had begun.

Catherine Douw started each morning as she always did with prayer, then waited eagerly for the newspaper and its daily column of war news. On the seventeenth, William Henry wrote to her from Washington, D.C.

My dear mother,
We have got War at last. I presume you keep well posted but you can form but little idea of the excitement here. This city now is going to assume the appearance of a vast camp, orderlies are flying about,

thickets of soldiers are galloping in different directions and posting themselves on all the thoroughfares and bridges leading into the city.

. . . There is a rumor today that martial law will be declared tomorrow, but I do not believe it. It is possible we will come to that but not yet. I fear the south will bear a terrible destruction before this is over. It seems to me perfect insanity and madness on their part to inaugurate a war which in all human probability will lead to such fearful results.

A few days later he listed the following in his account book—uniform coat, $25; epaulets, $18; pants, $11; vest, $6; sword belt, $6.50; shoulder strap, $6.50, laying out $73 on his Union army uniform. He had Willi, the large horse that John Van Ness had recently shipped down to him from Talavera, outfitted with an army saddle and gear. William Henry's letter confirmed Catherine Douw's worst fears. A few days earlier, on April 15, President Lincoln called for seventy-five thousand volunteers to support the Union. She knew now that two of them were to be her sons.

John Van Ness was busy for days, preparing to reenlist in the navy. He wrote William Henry, urging him to appeal directly to Mr. Lincoln to see if the president would commission him to his old ship, the USS *Mississippi*. Still on the sea after its dramatic voyage into the Tokyo Bay under Commodore Perry, it was, by John Van Ness's reckoning, one of the most powerful vessels in the navy. In the weeks to come, William Henry did what he could to get his brother aboard his old ship but did not succeed. In addition to land attacks, the federal government was formulating a plan to use the navy to surround the South by way of the sea. John Van Ness received orders to serve as second-in-command of the USS *Cuyler*, a steam-powered fast frigate being refitted for blockade duty along the Atlantic coastline.

If he was disappointed in his commission to the *Cuyler*,

John Van Ness did not say so. He wrote William Henry that he was getting ready to depart and planned to take with him into the war Tom, the slave he had inherited and freed. "I am getting ready as fast as possible, making underclothes to [sic] and when my orders come I will leave on the next train. Tom goes with me as my servant. He is crazy to go."

That Tom chose to follow the man who once legally owned him into the effort to fight slavery may seem the ultimate of historical ironies. Only five years earlier in Maryland Tom had been listed in the inventory of Chancellor Johnson's property. It had taken me almost a year to track down records of Tom, for Lieutenant John Van Ness's father-in-law had died intestate. But I was determined to find him. If my family had collaborated in reducing a man's humanity to a figure of cash on a page, I wanted to see it. Tom was at the bottom of the estate list after a lengthy accounting of bond holdings. He was the first entry under the heading "Sundry household and kitchen furniture": "Negro man, Tom, slave for life, 21 years of age—$850.00." Reading those words would leave me feeling sickened.

John Van Ness had decided to bring Tom north to Talavera. Tom's valuation of $850 was subtracted from Laura's inheritance. John Van Ness's decision probably freed Tom for slavery had been abolished in New York by then, and he mentions wages for Tom, but whether Tom felt able to leave Talavera and strike out on his own was another matter. It seems clear from letters that the family wanted to believe that Tom's desire to serve in the U.S. Navy was a faithful slave's desire to further serve them.

When Tom was wounded after a particularly fierce skirmish with a Confederate ship, John Van Ness wrote his family often to detail Tom's recovery. In a letter to his brother some days after the event, he recounted Tom's desire for revenge.

Tom is getting along very well. There is no danger to be apprehended from his wound. I went to see him

99

this morning and asked him how he was getting
along. He said "first rate." He would like to be on his
legs so that he could "go at em again." But Tom, said
I, you must not feel so. You know the bible says you
must forgive your enemys. "Love, sir" answered
Tom—"I'll forgive the rest of em, but I'll never forgive the fellow that shot me." But, said I, you can't
tell exactly who shot you. "But I must shoot somebody else. I got to shoot one of em" said Tom.

I saw that he was bent upon spilling an equivalent
amount of blood so I discontinued the conversation.

John Van Ness's letter went on to express concern for Tom
but he clearly viewed Tom's role in the navy as an extension
of family service. When I read the letter, however, I had to
assume something different. Tom wasn't serving in the war to
serve John Van Ness, or the family, he was on board the
Cuyler to serve himself—to fight for the idea of the Union
and freedom for all slaves.

In the larger context of the war, the practice of black servants, some of them freed slaves like Tom, following their
masters into Civil War battles was not uncommon. Black soldiers were prevented from enlisting in the Union army until
1863, but they could sign up in the U.S. Navy from the start.

Within two years of the start of the war, 339 blacks from
New York were listed on U.S. Navy rolls, most of them on
the lowest rank as landsmen. Tom was registered as Thomas
W. Johnson, using the surname of his previous owner. In the
1862 naval report submitted by the *Cuyler*'s captain, Francis
Winslow, Tom is registered as a landsman on the USS *Cuyler*.
As far as the family was concerned, Tom's loyalty to John Van
Ness, in wanting to follow him into battle, earned him an
even more cherished place at Talavera. When John Van Ness
wrote of the war news and his own situation at sea, he almost
always mentioned Tom. Similarly, when Catherine Douw
wrote to William Henry with news of John Van Ness, she
often mentioned Tom. The anecdotes were full of conde-

scension but also real concern for how Tom was faring so far from home and at war on the sea.

John Van Ness was eager to be off but concerned about his mother. "Write as often as you can," he urged William Henry when he wrote him next, "and when you do tell Ma that there is no danger of Washington being attacked. She is continuously afraid about you." He was also clearly worried about leaving their younger brother, Martin Hoffman, in charge of Talavera and the farm in which he had so much invested, but as if to reassure William Henry and himself on this point, he wrote on the thirtieth of the month: "I have talked with him very seriously and if the crops will do well I hope he will get along."

Most of John Van Ness's time was spent readying for departure and worrying about how the farm and Laura would get on in his absence. But one Saturday evening distraction appeared in the form of a troop of cadets from the Hudson River Institute in Claverack. They marched up to Talavera along the Old Post Road. It was Laura who spotted them first, proceeding up the driveway to where they assembled and stood at attention on the front lawn. She stepped out to inform them that the lieutenant was not at home. Just then his carriage began its ascent up the front drive.

When the carriage came to a stop between the columns of the porte cochere, the boys waited eagerly. Then they caught sight of Lieutenant John Van Ness Philip stepping out, and they began to cheer. They wanted a speech, a speech. A speech from the great patriot. According to the newspaper accounts the next day, "an intense degree of patriotic feeling was manifested." The mood would have been set by the sunset, by the front porches with their commanding white columns. Perhaps already in U.S. Navy attire, John Van Ness, his black beard flowing, must have seemed a schoolboy's dream of valor. One of the cadets returned to the institute to write a poem "in honor of the occasion." On Monday, April 22, along with a description of the event, it was printed in the *Hudson Daily Star*:

Raise our country's tri-hued emblem,
Let its blendings proudly fly,
'Twas its like that led our fathers
When the battle tide was high.

'Twas bequeathed us; and to keep it
We will fight like royal sons
Who have never learned to tremble
At the boom of rebel guns.

But John Van Ness's mother, Catherine Douw, widowed at thirty-two, knew death as more than a schoolboy's abstraction. She was the mother of three sons in a nation about to make war upon itself. Such displays of patriotism were lost on her. Not even the sight of John Van Ness several weeks later with his glorious sword, the embodiment of the community's wholehearted support, cheered her up one bit. On June 4 she entered only two lines in her diary: "The Cuyler sails today, and my dear Van Ness is gone. May the Lord bless him and keep him as in the Hollow of his Hand."

JULY 1861

William Henry returned to Washington after having taken sick on the battlefield. John Van Ness was cruising off the Florida coast near Tampa. The hayfields at Talavera rippled with gold, and Hoffman began the yearly haying. Not even the impressive new mower, which John Van Ness had purchased for $120 a few years earlier, made the job any easier for Hoffman to supervise alone, and much of the farm's income depended upon a successful harvest of hay. Catherine Douw wrote to William Henry that all was well at Talavera. Pippins and Baldwins were turning red-gold on the trees. They should have a good crop of cider. Meanwhile, deep in the apple wood, next year's crop of fruit buds was growing and setting with each day of hot July sun. Even so, she believed that "Hoffman has entirely too much for one person." She awoke several times at night and, upon hearing the wheels of a carriage, rushed downstairs, thinking that it was her dear William Henry returning home. Each time the sound of wheels turned into the barnyard, and she knew he had not come. The relative calm, both at home and with her sons, seemed to allow her to express her frustration at the war in general and at a neighbor named Mercer in particular: "I feel so provoked at those southerners for forcing us to all this expense and trouble. Mercer is the greatest secessionist you ever saw. he talks like a fool. he would have rejoiced if they had taken Washington. I tell you he gets it hot and heavy if he talks secession over here—"

The summer continued uneventfully for John Van Ness. The *Cuyler* had some rough cruising off Cuba, but for the most part, he wrote, he was bored and beginning to worry about affairs at Talavera because Hoffman had not written. He complained to William Henry, but in a typically protective manner: "So anxious I was to hear everything about the farms, the horses, cows and the milk business.... It was duty to write to me. It is inexcusable. Of course he will say he is very busy, but I know it is only his intolerable habit of laziness and procrastination. Don't say anything to him about it."

Of equal concern to John Van Ness was the way in which Laura's southern cousins began to slight her because of her northern alliance. In a rare burst of anger he cursed them soundly when he next wrote William Henry: "I don't care about what they say of me, but for them to treat Laura with neglect. Confound their rebellious skins. It will be a long time before I forgive them. Poor Laura."

103

DECEMBER 1861

By winter John Van Ness was even more worried about affairs at Talavera and wanted Hoffman to find a man to help him with the farm at Talavera. Near the Ship Islands he wrote Hoffman a letter wishing him a Merry Christmas, then gave him detailed instructions about the place:

I hope you will get a good man to work the place on thirds. Then for mercy sakes, sell some of those horses. What will you do with Bill? I think upon the whole, the Raspbury's herd better go. You can't attend to them and situated as you are they will only be a bother and an expense. Make a nice patch at the bottom of the garden below that grape arbor where we have corn and potatoes for family use and let the rest go.

. . . Make a good bargain with whoever rents the farm and make him understand that he is to be responsible to Laura and pay the money regularly to her. I can scarcely afford to let the whole thing lie idle another year. If I can make anything out of the Navy, I will of course use it for the good of the family, but I want Laura to have the benefit of whatever comes from Talavera.

As for news of the war, he mentioned that 570 houses in Charleston had been burned. "Confound their rebellious skins."

JANUARY 1862

By the end of the month Tom had been seriously wounded, a minié rifle ball cut out of his upper thigh by the ship's surgeon after a skirmish with the *J. W. Wilder* of Handsboro, Mississippi. The *Cuyler* had come upon the schooner in the morning, fifteen miles east of Mobile Bar, at anchor after having slipped the blockade by flying the British flag. When they steamed toward it, the *Wilder* attempted to flee. They saw it slip, make sail and steer toward the beach, where it grounded almost immediately on a sandbar. The crew and captain quickly fled, disappearing onto the shore, and the *Cuyler* went on with the business of securing its prize undisturbed by enemy fire. A small boat was put over the side, and Lieutenant John Van Ness led a boarding party, armed with pistols and cutlasses in case the *Wilder's* crew should return.

By two o'clock in the afternoon they had managed to make the *Wilder* fast by securing their largest hawser to its foremast. John Van Ness ordered the men to load into the small boats and return to the *Cuyler*. It was then that the enemy decided to attack, opening fire from hiding places in the sandhills. John Van Ness managed to make it back to the *Cuyler* unhurt, but Tom, who seemed to have insisted upon accompanying his master as part of the boarding party, was wounded.

John Van Ness wrote to William Henry about the skirmish five days later: "I am almost afraid to write to Laura and tell her the whole truth, but the ship has anchored now. It was no trifling matter (to secure the schooner) But I returned to the ship without accident. Our boat is riddled with ball and the schooner galley and foucsle is filled with holes. It looks like a pepper box."

As usual, he included mention of Tom in his reports to the family. And as usual Tom was seen through the lens of the idea of the faithful slave whose every action was motivated by service to the master.

> When I left in the same boat in the morning, Tom came down the side ladder with a large box of ammunition buckled around his waist and a musket with a huge bayonet on the side. Said I, "Where are you going?" "I want to go with you sir. I want to go where ever you go."
>
> . . . You can imagine my feelings when the boat came alongside to see Tom lying among the wounded, stretched out on the bottom of the boat. They were covered with blood and as we hoisted them out I could not prevent the tears running down rather freely because I knew that it was only the poor fellow's devotion to me that led him to volunteer. I had him carefully carried to the guardroom and to my

great relief the surgeon soon examined him and found him shot in the thigh. The ball had gone up ten inches and he made a counter incision below his ribs extracted a large Minié rifle ball which I have in my possession. He is doing very well and is in no danger whatever. It is only a flesh wound but the surgeon says there is no other portion of his body where a ball could have gone that distance without touching some mortal part.

Four days after the incident, John Van Ness wrote to his brother William Henry, asking him to inquire about the possibility of a pension for Tom, given his wound. He kept the conical-shaped bullet with him and brought it with him to Talavera when he returned. I was pretty sure that Tom's bullet was still in the house, for in the dining room curio cabinet, nestled in its own cloth bag, was a Civil War bullet. And if that was Tom's minié ball, enshrined like a talisman next to Mohican arrowheads, bits of Roman tile and a rock from Pompei, it was further proof that to John Van Ness and the family, Tom was not seen as an independent person but an extension of them all.

Once Tom and the two seamen and one other landsman who had also been wounded in the skirmish had been cared for and ordered restored to the *Cuyler,* the crew had time to search the *Wilder.* In the ship's hull they discovered valuable medicines, a Confederate flag "ingeniously secreted in a bag of coffee" and, to everyone's delight, a huge cache of Havana cigars. "She was the J. W. Wilder bound from Havannah to Mobile loaded with coffee, cigars, medicines and a thousand other little things which we know our citizens are much in want of. There were many loose boxes drifting around in the cabin and among the baggage, which was apprehended. . . . I will send home by the Connecticut about 4,000 or 5,000 of the *very best Havanna*'s worth $800. I will tell Laura to send you as many as you want."

William Henry, a heavy smoker, much to his mother's disapproval, delighted in the expectation of Havana cigars. He received the letter in Washington, where finally restored to health, he was contemplating which army regiment to join. He must have written to his brother for advice, for at the end of his letter John Van Ness encouraged him to consider joining General John Grubb Parke: "I am anxious to hear your decision about Gen'l Parke. I think it would be a good thing and it certainly would be a good position for you. It seems almost as if I would accept as I think we will all have to fight before this confounded war is over. I am only thinking of poor ma. It will pain her so much . . ."

While John Van Ness described his skirmish with the *Wilder* with great detail and excitement when writing William Henry, the last few months had clearly sobered his thoughts about the war. When he wrote to Martin Hoffman three days later, still off Mobile, it was to urge him again to find a man to run Talavera.

My Dear Brother,
I was really very glad to receive your letter. I think
you are getting to be quite a respectable decent sort of
a white man. After you once get fairly started you do
pretty well. I am glad that you are getting along so
well and to hear also that you will be able to make all
your payments and expenses. I think that will do very
well. I hope you will secure a good man for Talavera.
It is too much for our man to do justice to, and besides I hope to have something from Talavera
although I don't know whether I will get more than
enough to pay the interest.

He went on to ask about the horses. He was clearly trying to be positive about Hoffman's general lack of communication, but it irked him that he had recently learned from Tom, who received word in a letter from Bill, another servant at Talavera, about a recent transaction of horses. Apparently the workhorse, Old Squire, had died, and Hoffman had traded the horse, Tom, for a black horse called Dandy. "You do not speak of it. You must have had a busy fall and I would have liked to have been there to have helped you. I think that was a good operation selling hay and buying stalks. Don't go it too strong. Keep within bounds. You know there is such a thing as running any business into the ground."

His main point, however, in writing to his youngest brother, was to insist that he not consider also enlisting: "William Henry talks of 'pitching in' and as I am already 'pitching in' I think you had better content yourself with pitching hay and corn stalks."

APRIL 1862

This time spring came on slowly, the cold hanging in a dreary progression of rainy days. The news from down south was equally chilly. On April 4 General George McClellan had shipped 121,500 troops and 14,592 horses south to Fortress Monroe in preparation for his campaign to capture Richmond, the Confederate capital, by way of Yorktown. William Henry and Willi had boarded one of the army steamers shipping troops south for this Peninsula campaign. Catherine Douw sat at her little round table by the library window and could think of nothing but the war. When she wrote to William Henry, she penned in large dark letters across the small envelope "Colonel William Henry, c/o General Franklin, near Yorktown" and prayed that the letter would reach him.

> My dear son,
> Where you are and how you are, I do not know. I feel almost as if I am writing to the wind. Still I think of you so much, that it is some comfort to write you.
> I have not heard from Van Ness, I saw in the Herald last evening that the Cuyler had taken another prize in Cuba. I hope he will be home soon. I am watching the papers daily. I do dread the Yorktown

battle. It is life and death with the rebels now and they will not have any thing undone.

As the letter progressed, she did her best to report on events at home and even to amuse him by relating an anecdote of Tom's recovery aboard the *Cuyler*: "Van Ness says that Tom is well again and getting quite hardy. He said one day that Van Ness said, 'Tom, why is it that you are not down with sea sickness?' 'Oh, Tom says, Sir, it does no good to be sick for every little swell.'"

Only in her closing did she again reveal her anxiety, urging him to pay close attention to his duties to God: "My dear son, May god bless you and keep you in the hollow of his hand is my ever constant prayer. Commit your way unto the lord so as not to neglect your duty to God. May he keep you from every ill and give you faith, fervent and abiding—write as often as possible, good bye your affectionate mother, Catherine D. Philip."

By mid-April General McClellan had still not begun his attack. Fooled by the Confederates, who marched the same regiment in and out of cover, around and around, so that it seemed as if their army were much larger than it was, McClellan sent word to Washington that he faced an army of 120,000 strong, and he requested more reserves. He was beginning to earn his nickname, the Virginia Creeper. Meanwhile, between the rain and the heat and the unfamiliar terrain, Union troops were falling sick to waves of pestilence and disease. Soldiers had a one in sixty-five chance of being killed in battle, but one out of every thirteen died of sickness and disease: cholera, dysentery, malaria, measles, smallpox and yellow fever.

Catherine Douw no longer had the heart to describe events at Talavera when she wrote to William Henry. She was so beside herself with worry that even her Christian imagery became infused with her motherly instinct to hide her son. She closed her letter, "May the lord bless you and protect you and hide you under the shadow of his wings."

Again, she beseeched him: "PS—Do not let anything draw you aside from your duty to God whatever else you omit or neglect."

In contrast, Martin Hoffman, the son who stayed behind, wrote three weeks later to tell William Henry how much he had enjoyed his brother's descriptions of sleeping within range of Rebel guns near Yorktown. They received little real news from the papers, Hoffman complained. But apparently there had been much talk: "What seems to be the opine of intelligent men. The idea is gaining ground here that it will be the greatest battle ever fought in the world."

In typical Philip family fashion, he went on to inquire about William Henry's horse: "How does poor Willi stand the racket? I am afraid it will be the last of him. I wish you could have had old Bill. He would had endured the hardship well and if you ever got in a tight place and meant to run away he could have brought you out one mile or twenty, it would be all the same to him. Or if you just ever wanted to catch a flying rebel. . . ."

A few weeks later he wrote again to say how much he would have liked to witness the battlefield. "How I would like to look upon such a scene. It must be an awful thing to listen while there is such a battle proceeding. The country is looking splendidly now on account of a fine rain. Goodbye. God bless you and keep you is my constant prayer."

MAY 1862

The apples were in full bloom when Catherine Douw sent her next letter to William Henry, addressing it to Franklin's Division, Army of the Potomac, near Yorktown. She clearly tried to cheer him up with news of events at home but was too worried to mask her fears. The Battle of Shiloh with its horrific casualties had sobered the entire nation, and the irony of the battle's name would not have been lost on her. A fervent student of the Bible, Catherine Douw

110

would have known that Shiloh in Hebrew means "place of peace": "Hoffman laying out a great many trees, intends to set out more. I am setting out flowers. I have very little ambition this spring, but I must keep doing to keep my mind occupied for it is too much to think of you and Van Ness both being away. I have no news. Nothing seems of any importance nowadays but War—War and unknowns of war."

Her concern was no longer with the progress of the war, but with her sense of its spiritual corruption. Before closing her letter, she warned William Henry about alcohol and tobacco: "This war is so demoralizing, it stains everyone, to beware, 'he that thinketh he stands, to take head, lest he fall.'"

JUNE 1862

After eleven months at sea, John Van Ness finally returned home for six weeks of leave, while the *Cuyler* docked in the Boston Naval Yard to undergo repairs. On the fourteenth he wrote to William Henry, still south near Yorktown, sending news of home and of Hoffman's first child, Catherine, who was born earlier that year.

111

> The country here is looking beautifully. I never saw anything like it. It is almost impossible to realize it. I have not seen a blade of green grass since I left. You can imagine how I am luxuriating in these green fields. I am also laying back on green peas, asparagus, lettuce *and strawberries* by the bushel. Poor soldier think of that and think of a fellow after a year keeping on beans and salt horse. What a quantity he is naturally consuming.
>
> . . . I found ma in a pretty good stew. Somewhat excited but I have cheered her up. Baby is great.

The next time he wrote to William Henry, on the twenty-fourth, it was to send news of Tom, who, recovered,

was fully enjoying life back on land: "The country is looking very lovely and Talavera is in all her glory. It is like drawing teeth to leave again. Tom arrives home on Sunday having
lost all of his money $120.64. It is too bad. He is always so
careful of my things that it never occurred to me that he
could lose his money. Hoffman seems to be getting along
very well but you must certainly send him the money for
those notes. The baby is certainly the most engaging little
thing I ever saw."

JULY 1862

Catherine Douw wrote to him on the Fourth of July during a quiet moment when John Van Ness, Laura and Hoffman and his wife, Sarah, had all gone into Hudson, where
John Van Ness was to give a patriotic speech.

My dear son,
My eyes have been so very weak and inflamed of late
that I have not written at all, or read any thing. They
are better now. I will write a few lines to you today
and then finish tomorrow. I am all *alone* in the house
today, everybody is gone to Hudson to spend the 4th.
I feel extremely anxious about you today my dear
dear son *where* and how you are. I cannot think of
anything else—various unknowns are afloat—one,
that our army has been replenished—next, that Mc-
Clellan is in Richmond, then that he has retreated. I
do not believe them but still it makes me *hold my
breath*. I hope and trust in the lord.

The next morning, still inspired by the tremendous ap-
plause that he received the night before at the Hudson City
Hall, John Van Ness also wrote William Henry. By now even
those as far north as Talavera had heard news of the recent
skirmish at Yorktown. Newspapers had termed it the Seven
Days Battle because it began on June 24 and ended exactly

one week later. John Van Ness shared his mother's concern. "My Dear Brother, We are filled with the most painful anxiety and suspense for the last week in fact the whole country has been in a most terrible state."

Three days later Catherine Douw wrote again, echoing these sentiments: "Words cannot express the anxiety that we all feel about you my dear dear son." Later that month the family at Talavera heard that William Henry was dead and waited anxiously for a telegram. But it turned out to be a rumor. William Henry had again become ill, probably with a recurrence of undiagnosed malaria. He was sent back to Washington, D.C., where this time his health prevented him from returning to the battlefield for almost a year.

SEPTEMBER 1, 1862

On August 30 the family received a telegram informing them that Lieutenant John Van Ness Philip was aboard the *Florence Nightingale,* a hospital ship stationed in New York Harbor. The *Cuyler* had been taking prize after prize off the Florida coast when somewhere near Tampa a mosquito carrying yellow fever found its way on board. By August 26 the captain of the *Cuyler,* Francis Winslow, had died and John Van Ness as well as the ship's surgeon were also sick. Despite his weak condition, John Van Ness took command, steaming the ship north to New York as fast as he could. But within three days the ship's surgeon also died and John Van Ness fell into a raging fever.

As soon as they heard the news that John Van Ness had been transferred to a hospital ship near Staten Island, Martin Hoffman and Laura rushed down to New York City. On a stormy night they made it across the harbor to board the *Florence Nightingale.* The next morning Martin Hoffman sent word to William Henry. The doctor had informed him that John Van Ness probably would not live long: "the doctor filled him with brandy and champagne hoping that he would hold out to see some of us as that seemed his *great burden,* for he longed to see some homeface before the struggle came. . . . Of course he was much changed but still his voice was clear and while he was able to talk spoke only of home and all the loved ones there. He seemed so grateful to see me and said he knew that some of us would break through and come to him."

Laura spent that night at her dying husband's side. The next morning, at age thirty-nine, Lieutenant John Van Ness Philip, second-in-command of the USS *Cuyler,* was reported dead.

Lieutenant John Van Ness Philip, 1823–1862
Photograph taken at Rowles Studio in Hudson, New York
when he returned home on six weeks of leave in 1862. He
holds the sword presented to him by the city of Hudson.

Colonel William Henry Philip, 1824–1881
Photograph taken soon after his marriage to
Eliza Worthingon in 1865.

Eliza Worthington Philip, 1842–1896
Photograph taken about 1865. She is wearing
a dark purple dress that during my childhood was stored
in a trunk in the barns at Talavera.

Elizabeth Worthington Philip, 1876–1967
Aunt Bessie. Here she is depicted with her brother's
champion steeplechaser, "Hari Kari" and one of her dogs
in Leicestershire, England. Photograph taken in 1903.

Herman Hoffman Philip, 1872–1951
My father's uncle. Photograph taken in Gibraltar in 1904.

Family photograph taken about 1890 at Talavera
From left, Aunt Bessie, Uncle Gaston, unidentified groom,
Uncle Hoffman, unidentified groom, Eliza Worthingon,
John Van Ness Philip (my grandfather) with armful of puppies.

Campaign poster for John Van Ness Philip, 1866–1949
My grandfather, when he ran for
New York State Assembly in 1903.

Helen Munroe Stott (Mrs. J. Van Ness Philip), 1883–1973
My grandmother photographed about 1915 soon
after she returned from Egypt.

My grandmother with my father and his baby sister
Photograph taken about 1925. Leila Stott died two years later.

My grandmother with my father and his younger brother
Photograph taken about 1932. My father is on the far left,
my grandmother center and my uncle, Nicholas Worthington,
is holding a ball. Danny, my grandfather's hunting spaniel
is in the foreground.

My father riding "Lord Hun"
In this photograph my father was riding a family friend's
horse at a horseshow in Baltimore, Maryland in 1936.
He was 12.

Family photograph next to Talavera, 1943,
just before my father shipped out as a marine.
From left, my father, his father, his mother.

Major John Van Ness Philip, 1866–1949
My grandfather during the years that he worked in
Washington, D.C. for President Roosevelt.

Lieutenant John Van Ness Philip Jr., 1922–1992
My father; photograph taken when the war ended in 1945.

Julia Somerville Willis, born 1924
My mother, photographed during the late forties
when she was working in Manhattan.

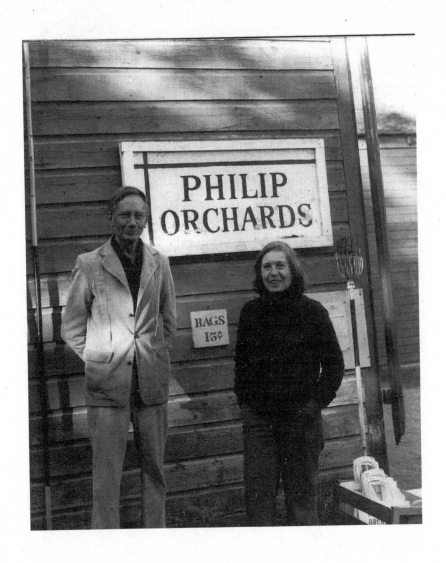

John Van Ness and Julia Philip
My parents down at the barn in 1980. My father was living at
Talavera full time, running the farm while also publishing his
business newsletter.

Sorting apples, about 1950
In these pictures, the crew is sorting apples on the apple
grader in the barn. The woman in the top picture is
Betty Scofield, who would end up working at the house;
when I was a child she ran the kitchen.

Anna Van Ness Post 1916–2008
Photograph taken at Rowles Photograph Studio
in Hudson about 1934.

Talavera on a summer day

Julia Willis Philip *(top)*
This photograph ran in a local newspaper that featured her as
the first woman to be listed as fruitgrower in
Columbia County, 2008

The front hall at Talavera *(bottom)*

Talavera, 1866

Once again April had arrived, bringing with it the welcome spread of green at Talavera. On the twenty-fourth, Laura Johnson Philip, by then an official war widow and receiving the standard thirty dollars a month, sent a hasty letter to William Henry, congratulating him on the birth of his first child, a son. The news brought great renewal to everyone at Talavera, for they had had a long, sad winter. In early January, Catherine Douw had died. She had anchored the family for so long and through so many changes it was hard for any of them to know how to proceed. "And now it is all over. We have lost her and shall now hear her good words of counsel and motherly advice no more. Yet our loss is her gain, and this must be our great consolation," wrote William Henry to his wife Eliza after arriving home at Talavera.

Two years earlier William Henry had written to his mother to announce his engagement to the "sweetest, best and nicest girl in the world," Eliza Worthington. He had made sure to note to his mother that his fiancée, whom he called Lilah, was educated in Europe and could speak several languages, then closed his letter mischievously: "The only objection is her rather advanced years, she is actually over twenty one, although I am happy to say she is not quite twenty two. Still, one can't have everything you know." As soon as Laura heard the news, she had made a package of the family's lace shards to send to the young bride and in great excitement had traveled to Baltimore with several trunks filled with her own finery so as to be on hand to help with preparations for the wedding.

Now Laura wrote to send her thoughts to dear Lilah, whom she was glad had "come through the ordeal safely." Laura noted how moved she was to hear the baby's name: "Like you I cannot help thinking of one who would have rejoiced so much at his birth."

The baby was not to be named after his father as was the custom, but after his father's brother. Christened John Van Ness Philip, he bore the name of the family's fallen hero and grew up to become my grandfather.

Three years later William Henry, now the father of two more boys and well established as a successful lawyer in Washington, purchased Talavera and the farm from Laura. She soon remarried and moved north to the town of Ghent. By 1871 Martin Hoffman and his family had moved to Titusville, Pennsylvania, where he became a partner in an engineering firm that produced engines and steam boilers. No doubt he was glad to leave agriculture and finally be allowed independence from the family.

Tom disappeared. For a time after John Van Ness's death, family letters mentioned concerns about him. He had traveled to Boston with a woman whom the family believed was no good. Martin Hoffman tried to find him but failed. In the 1865 census, three adult black servants were listed along with family members. Two of them were from Virginia, bringing up the question of whether they had been other freed slaves, but Tom was not mentioned, so it seemed he was gone.

The horse Willi, by then retired to Talavera on a special diet of grain and hay, had a luxurious box stall near where

the cows had once been stationed. When the new farm manager, Leroy Van Hoesen, wrote to William Henry about "the
place," he did not fail to mention Willi, the dark horse that,
like Lieutenant John Van Ness, had left Talavera and traveled
south to participate in the Civil War. For two years, Willi had
carried Colonel William Henry on and off southern battle-
fields.

Household Accounts

When I open the slim Chinese red journal, three parched sheets of paper fall out: an 1873 bill from a Paris dressmaker, an 1874 receipt for children's clothes from the Lilliputian Warehouse on Regent Street in London and a bill for $93.84 from a shipping company in New York City, dated February 15, 1882. The bills interest me, for they are addressed to Mrs. William Henry Philip, my great-grandmother, but not as much as the volume in my hands. I push them aside and look inside the cover. There I find what I am looking for, a familiar spidery hand that reads "Eliza W. Philip, Accounts at Talavera 1869." In my hands, light as an old-fashioned paperback, rests the journal that my great-grandmother began the year she and my great-grandfather bought Talavera from Lieutenant John Van Ness's widow.

I close the cover for a moment to read the spine. Along its half-inch width large gold letters spell CASH. I flip quickly to the back and see that the last page is dated 1896, a mixed entry describing my grandfather's emerging role in politics, his younger brother Gaston's first job as a geologist and engineer and seasonal work done on the land: "Gaston went to the Adirondacks on a US. Geological Topological Survey Tour. Left early June from Washington. John Van Ness sent as a delegate to a democratic conference in Chicago, also as Representative to a Democratic Reform Convention in Indiana. Mrs. Folger set out for me heliotrope, verbena, balm and scarlet geraniums, featherfew, cypress, marble petunias, hydrangea and passion vine."

Twenty-seven years of entries on the family's visits to Talavera and the time they spent there. I can't believe my luck. When the journal begins, my grandfather John Van Ness is three years old. By the time it ends he is a young man, almost thirty. The journal in my hands, along with the four others kept by Eliza Worthington while mistress of Talavera, open a window onto life there for my grandfather, his two brothers, Gaston and Hoffman, and their sister, Elizabeth—the generation that lived at Talavera after Catherine Douw and her three sons.

119

As soon as I begin reading, however, I am caught by another surprise, one so clear and ironic that before I can stop myself, I have laughed out loud, a startling sound in the dimly lit library of the New-York Historical Society. The reference assistant, whose job it is to protect the archives against possible manhandling by researchers like me, gives me a sharp warning glance. I smile at her, a "don't worry, everything's fine" kind of smile and turn away from her gaze, but I can still feel the beam of her watching eyes. I try to ignore it. I know she is only trying to do her job. Each year the archives in the New-York Historical Society suffer from theft. As the director kindly explained to me one day, the staff believes that some of the worst culprits are researchers whose own families' pasts are housed there. In other words, as soon as the assistant reads the name Leila Stott Philip on the call form for the Philip–Van Ness papers, I am a prime suspect.

I try to behave so as not to alarm the assistant, but the

more I read, the more I want to hoot. I can't help it. Eliza Worthington's journal could be the wall above my desk at home, plastered with yellow Post-It notes about meetings, and research leads, the name of the antibiotic and the date it was given to my son for bronchitis, a taped-up coupon for orange juice, the phone number of the art shipper who will be picking up some of my husband's work. Everything I need to remember and can't gets taped to the wall. My generation calls it multitasking; my great-grandmother called it household accounts.

Eliza Worthington ordered her journal carefully, however, and that is not at all like my haphazard bulletin board of a wall. The first pages list an index for entries in specific areas: "Butter, Eggs, Chickens, Raspberries, Vegetables when sown, Wages to Servants, Flowers." When I turn to those pages, I find seasonal and yearly accounts for the market garden, poultry output and butter production at Talavera, areas of the farm that she seemed to have managed in addition to supervising the care of the house and grounds, tending the children's needs and managing their busy social lives. Her journals record seating plans for dinner parties for twelve and a constant flow of visitors.

Under wages for servants she records whom she has engaged to cook, clean the house, keep the gardens and nurse the children. Flowers were her great joy and extravagance. She might only give fifty cents to the tea peddler and do so grudgingly, but when it came to her ordering flowers, the list blooms. Geraniums, pansies, pink masses of them, featherfew and summer and fall blooming roses, sweet alyssum in a variegated flock, lemon verbena and heliotrope, her list goes on. Individual orders for flowers to set in the gardens or cut flowers for the house could run as much as ten dollars, as much money as four barrels of Seckel pears could bring when shipped downriver to the New York City market.

But the body of Eliza's journal, like the three others with it, reminds me of the mosaic of Post-Its on my wall; the range of her duties and concerns is dizzying. She kept chronological entries for purchases "$1.75 for bronze candlesticks" (they still sit on the library mantel), "$2 for boots for John Van Ness." She noted the seasonal comings and goings of family and friends from Talavera—"Arrived June 5th and found the house in order"—and kept a running list of whom she visited and when—"visit to Livingston Manor, up to Ghent to visit Laura H." (John Van Ness's widow, now married to a Mr. Harrison). She jotted brief notes about adventures with the children: "lovely picnic to lake Chalotte, took boys fishing on the back farm, little Johnny caught five fish." She kept notes on the house and grounds: "Contents of linen closet, winter 1876" and "elms doing well, but grow slowly, set out nine white pines measuring the ridge between the house and barns, afterwards twelve more." She suffered from headaches and also made careful note of them. "I was taken with one of my bad headaches on that Sunday before Easter, directly after Church and was obliged to go to bed and remained there until the following Saturday when I sat up for a brief time."

There was the occasional recipe. One recipe for oyster stew has been carefully backdated December 6, 1864. Eliza was a bride that year, and given the family penchant for oysters, the recipe probably came from her new mother-in-law, Catherine Douw, then still alive and living at Talavera. I don't particularly like oysters, but I make a note to try it: "Oyster Stew—2 quarts oysters, 1 quart milk, ½ lb. butter, spoonful of flower, mace, salt and pepper to taste."

At times Eliza Worthington would paste in newspaper articles, mainly beauty tips and housekeeping ideas:

Sleep's Time—Sleep obtained two hours before midnight, when the negative forces are in operation is the rest which most recuperate the system, giving brightness o the eye and a glow to the cheek.

The Uses of Borax—The washerwomen of Holland and Belgium so proverbially

clean, and who get up their linen so beautifully white, use refined borax as a washing
powder instead of soda, in the proportion
of a large handful of pulverized borax to
about ten gallons of water.

Or she would write notes on watercoloring techniques.
Occasionally, half-finished sketches of people and places appear. But mainly, braided into her collection of daily and
weekly notes, is an ongoing record of the children's heights
and weights, their accidents—"Hoffman fell from the banis-
ter about the fourth step from the bottom and broke his collar bone . . . two weeks in bed was prescribed"—and their
childhood illnesses. The dates of scarlet fever, measles and
whooping cough are all carefully recorded. In an unusually
reflective entry in 1874, Eliza records the birth of her fourth
child and the family's first girl, an infant she will name Elizabeth Worthington Philip after herself, but the family will always call Bessie. "Bessie was supposed to weigh 12 pounds
when first born but the old nurse Aunt Martha, thinking it
unlucky to weigh her, it was not done accordingly. A number of bouquets were showered on the young lady during
the first week of her existence and many little encum-
brances, socks, blankets. Everybody seems so glad that it
should be a dear little girl. For her own sake she is most precious to us, but so wedded have we been to boys that it feels
a measure as if I had been disloyal to them."

Before the journal comes to an end, Eliza Worthington
will lose three children: her handsome eight-year-old,
Charles Worthington; then sunny William Henry, born at
Talavera, and finally the baby, William Houston. In one entry she proudly described this last baby, who was also born at
Talavera only to succumb to illness there fourteen months
later: "Houston weighed thirty five pounds when one year
old—had also both upper and lower front teeth and several
back. Up until this time he has never taken a dose of medi-

cine. Fresh cow's milk from one cow was his only food until a year old—then a baked potato and slice of bread in milk was given him at four o'clock in the afternoon."

Several pages later she records scarlet fever moving throughout the nursery, beginning with Hoffman, and pens her stark, final entry for William Houston: "Precious Houston taken sick on Thursday afternoon at half past five."

In 1881 antibiotics had not yet been discovered. The baby probably died from the same illness that made his older brothers and sister ill but from which they recovered. Eliza Worthington will not mention him again, either in letters or in her journal. I had discovered his place in my grandfather's family only by accident, the day I was browsing through the family Bible and found his date of birth and death carefully recorded. His name had given me a shock, for the only family person named William Churchill Houston Philip that I knew about then was my older brother Bill. But it wouldn't be the first time that I would discover that names in my family were like revolving doors. One generation had them; then the next generation took them over.

Kept with Eliza's journals are some odd papers, including a long elegy to a lost child titled "Poem for My Brother Charles." The poem was dated 1875, and I wondered if Eliza had written it herself as an antidote to her grief. The other likely candidate for authorship, my grandfather, would have been only nine years old at the time, and while he was already pretty good in Latin and geography, the five stanzas of metered verse could not have been his. Eliza had clearly grieved deeply when she lost her first child. That year her mother had sent her a palm-sized volume titled *Consolation for Those Who Mourn*. She kept a marker on page three: "Not my will, but thine, be done" (Luke, 22:42). I would find that small green volume among scores of other books on theology and Christianity that had been carefully packed in wooden trunks and stored in one of the barn lofts. Almost all the books were signed "Eliza W. Philip." Like her mother-in-law, Catherine Douw, Eliza was a devout Christian who read avidly. She was catholic in her taste, reading meditations and lectures from a wide range of scholars and preachers, including those of the evangelist preacher Dwight L. Moody, whose seminary later became the Northfield Mount Hermon boarding school where I had finished high school.

"Multitasking," "household accounts." The range of Eliza's duties, concerns and responsibilities was impressive, but I can't help being disappointed at first by the brevity of her entries. After a while, however, I begin to realize that their short length, like the way they jump from notes on watercoloring to a record of the December pork killing, tells me something important about her. She wasn't a writer, for one thing. Unlike her mother-in-law, Catherine Douw, whose ability to turn a Christian image on the page made words leap, Eliza Worthington wrote in a sparse, matter-of-fact style. Even the elegiac poem to her lost child, while touching, was formulaic and predictable. For her, keeping a journal must have seemed like yet another of her many pressing duties. Probably the few daily lines that she did write were an exercise in self-discipline, especially as her life would become busier, more complicated and increasingly filled with financial worries.

In the first years of her marriage to my great-grandfather William Henry, Eliza spent only summers at Talavera, enjoying city life the rest of the time, but as the number of children multiplied, her journal described increasingly long stays at Talavera. They would leave for Washington as late as December and return while there was still snow. William Henry was often detained by his law practice in Washington, and she would travel on alone with the children and the servants. She did not seem to mind the arrangement, especially as it was not long before her parents were coming to stay at Talavera on extended visits as well. Slipped between journal pages for the year 1872 is a Western Union telegram sent by William Henry from Baltimore on February 21. "Will not return until tomorrow," he wrote, "detained here." Eliza and the family were at Talavera that season, a good two weeks

124

before even the robins and red-winged blackbirds had returned from warmer climes.

It was not unusual that Eliza, as mistress of Talavera, managed the market garden and estate grounds as well as the house, but as time went on, she seemed to take an increasingly active role in overseeing the work on the larger farm as well. When William's brother, Martin Hoffman, decided to leave Talavera and seek his fortune in the manufacturing business in Pennsylvania, William Henry had decided to sell most of the dairy herd and find a farm manager to run the land as crops and hay, which until the turn of the century and the advent of motorcars would bring a good price. That January a Claverack neighbor wrote to recommend a man for the job. "Col. Philip, My Dear Sir," began the letter's author, a Mr. J. Philip, "I think I have found a first class farmer for you. His name is Leroy Van Hoesen. I knew him personally some years ago as an excellent man."

Leroy Van Hoesen and his wife and child soon were living in the tenant house just up from the barns. While he ran the crops, oversaw the haying and tended the small but profitable apple and pear orchard just down from the garden, his wife took over milking the remaining cows, making butter and caring for the poultry. For the next eight years Van Hoesen ran the farm, writing regularly during the winter months of events on the place, usually including mention of Willi, William Henry's mount during the Civil War: "Everything is right about the Place. We are having nice wintry weather not much snow. I will send you a box of poultry so you can have them by Christmas. Old Willi is fine, I think he will winter. The children are all having the Hooping coff."

Some years earlier the house had been broken into, but nothing had been taken. When he went to look for the robbers, Van Hoesen found a pair of demijohns that someone had left on the floor. "Your haus is all right and everything is well. As soon as I sell the corn and hay I will deposit your portion in the bank." He and my great-grandfather were apparently sharing portions of the land and school taxes on the farm, for in that letter, dated January 15, 1873, he informs my great-grandfather that his share of the bill will be $95.65 in land tax, and $7.50 due for the school tax.

Tucked in with Eliza's journals and papers are also several handwritten sheets of directions for work to be done on the place that my great-grandfather had clearly given her, not Van Hoesen, to oversee. For October 1879 the list contained twenty-five items, including "paint waggon and buggy, continue stone wall in back lots, dig out and lay foundation for stone gate posts, straighten farm road and cut down the edge of the woods, draw manure regularly from rear of stable to bring for compost, make a keg of cider." That spring Eliza was busy overseeing a few remaining items on the list. Most of her letters to her husband during the 1870s are full of cheerful descriptions of their life at Talavera and a wish that he rejoin them soon, but on March 27, 1879, she has a bone to pick with him. She begins with news of the place. The peacocks that a Mr. Miller has set aside for them will be coming soon, and a man has come by trying to sell Eliza a large milk goat. "He asked me to come see a goat that he has for sale, half deer he says. I fear it will be too large and expensive, but I will see it tomorrow." She is following her husband's instructions and has two men busy putting in the new cistern while a man named Stickles is at work on the orchard trees. What concerns her is her belief that Van Hoesen may be taking liberties. She chides her husband for not making his arrangements with the farm manager clear. "Van Hoesen wants to keep three pigs. He took off a load of undivided hay to Bristol to sell. Was that right? You ought to have been clear with him before you left."

Apparently, the carting off of the undivided hay was not quite right, for within four days Van Hoesen has been released as the farm manager of Talavera. On April 1 a new lease has been drawn up for a local farmer named Andrew Stickles, probably the man who had been working on the trees. Stickles will get a half share of the potatoes, grain, hay and corn grown at Talavera, including the land planted in potatoes last year by Van Hoesen. In the terms of the lease, which runs for two years, he has been given an area to plant as his own garden and use of the hogpens and hogyard. He and his family will live in the tenant house.

While I would learn to surmise something of Catherine Douw's emotional state by her use of Christian metaphors and imagery, "May God Bless you and keep you as in the hollow of his hand," reflecting quite a different mood from "May God Bless you and keep you as in the hollow of his hand . . . and hide you in the shadow of his wings," I could find nothing similar in Eliza's journal until I began to read more carefully her pages of the poultry and vegetable accounts. I saw a dramatic shift in the 1881 entries.

In 1880 she records proudly that she sold $58.69 in vegetables and seems happy with this sum. She does not bother to break down this income into categories but merely comments, "Aside from this, fresh vegetables enough to bountifully supply our table for a large family." One year later, however, she is working the garden with much more ambition, almost doubling her profits to the sum of $113.80, carefully noting that this was accomplished by the addition of turnips, cabbages, carrots and two barrels of pears, which brought $2.25 each. The next year she increases her profits to $162.46, raising her take by sending apples downriver: two barrels of Baldwins at $6, two barrels of Greenings at $4.50 and two barrels of unnamed apples for $4 each. She also sends corn. Her accounting for the sale of eggs and butter becomes similarly more meticulous: "Eggs, spring 1882, 96 dozen, butter 43 lbs." She begins to keep a notepad on which she records which hens are setting and the number of their eggs: "Hens Setting—Game hen 13 eggs, Spanish hen 13 eggs, Dominique 14 eggs, Brahman 14 eggs." She also records the amounts of poultry meat sold: in 1882, eighty-nine pounds at fifteen cents a pound and eight pounds of turkey. The sales figures are small, yet so carefully noted. Was this the same woman who only nine years before had confidently ordered the latest of Paris fashions?

The spring of 1881 had come on early, a rush of light across the valley, setting the fields ablaze with green. The river opened quickly, flooding its banks. Only a few years earlier they had resilled all the barns, but still the runoff from a sudden snowmelt was terrible. By the first week in May, the perfection potatoes that Eliza had planted on April 26 had sent up feathery green shoots. You could stand by the hawthorn hedges in the center of the garden, look down over the terraced slopes and the fields and grow dizzy from the many levels and hues of green. Just east of the gardens, the hundred apple trees set out in 1866 were wild with bloom. Already the two hired men who helped Stickles were out with the teams, plowing and planting the back fields.

Eliza had journeyed north to Talavera as early as she could that year. My grandfather was enrolled in Claverack College, better known as the Hudson River Institute, and was bringing home perfect marks in Latin and English, Declamation, Astronomy, Arithmetic and Military Drill. William Henry had left Washington several days earlier with a cough, not unusual for him. His bouts of malaria during the Civil War had left him prone to illness. He was a tall, thin man, and when he was not well, his hollow cheeks and deepset eyes gave him a Lincolnesque gauntness. By the time William Henry had reached New York City, his cough had become runaway pneumonia. On May 7, still waylaid in a New York City hotel room, he suddenly and unexpectedly took his last breath.

For Eliza Worthington and for her children, nothing at Talavera would be the same again. She would never stop missing William Henry, but more immediately she had become a widow with four children and a large estate to maintain on an insufficient income.

⁂

By the time I reach the last pages of Eliza's journals, I am sorry to put the slim volumes away; so much life is compacted in those hastily written five-by-seven pages. But it is almost closing time in the Historical Society's library, so I close the red and black account books and take a quick look at the receipts that I had set aside earlier.

On October 31, 1874, Eliza ordered clothes for the children. I have only to glance to see that neither my grandfather nor his brothers or sister wore the equivalent of Old Navy. At the top of the ornate stationery for the Lilliputian Dress Factory is printed the proud disclaimer "Manufacturers and warehousemen to Her Majesty the Queen of Great Britain and Ireland, the Prince and Princess of Wales, Grand Duchess of Russia, Princess Frederick Charles of Germany, Queen of Denmark and the leading families of Europe, Asia, Africa and America."

My grandfather, John Van Ness, was eight by then; his younger brother, Hoffman, just six. Bessie and Gaston and William Houston were not yet born, and Charles Worthington and William Henry had not yet died. For the children, Eliza Worthington ordered Irish balbriggan stockings, British wool socks, Segovia wool undervests and dogskin gloves and gants de suede.

The next receipt is from a Paris dressmaker to whom she sends $240 for two dresses, two sets of gloves and a matching bonnet, the equivalent of two years of monthly wages for her servant girl, Lucie.

The final receipt is a receipt for transport from New York to Washington. I see train fare for "remains and self," ferry tickets, then the cost of reboxing and disinfectant. Tucked into her red journal, Eliza had saved the undertaker's bill for transporting my great-grandfather's body from New York City to Washington D.C., where it was interred in the Van Ness mausoleum. The bill is dated February 15, 1882. For Eliza Worthington, used to dressing her boys in the garb of princes and herself in clothes of equal finery, the hard times have begun. No more $240 bills from Paris dressmakers, no more gants de suede for the children.

The extra income she could earn from vegetables, dairy and butter helped cover Talavera's bills, but soon their previous lifestyle is beyond her means. By 1887 her account in the Farmer's National Bank of Hudson is only $457.99. Eliza Worthington makes a critical decision: They will spend summers at Talavera, but during the rest of the year they will live in Europe to save money. My grandfather had already graduated from St. Paul's Academy in Long Island by that time and Hoffman was almost finished with his studies at St. Lawrence Academy in Lawrenceville. No one quite knows exactly where they lived and when, but letters and a trail of dressmaker and pharmacy receipts seem to indicate that aside from frequent travels throughout France and Italy, Eliza Worthington based the family in Dresden until 1894.

Eliza's headaches apparently returned. Even back in the happy times at Talavera her journal records her taking to her bed for as long as five days to recover—migraines in the days before Imitrex. She has trouble sleeping and begins to travel to various spas. When she is not taking a cure, she is often traveling to churches and cathedrals. Like her mother-in-law, Catherine Douw, she fears Catholicism and is careful not to visit cathedrals on the Sabbath for fear of angering what she believes is the one true God. But she collects a great quantity of prints, etchings and lithographs as souvenirs: *Capella del Principe di Sansevero, La Madone de Saint Sixtei* and an enormous engraving of *Cardinal Guido Bentivoglio.*

Still a young girl when they leave for Europe, Bessie learns to be unusually independent. In an undated letter from their early years in Europe, Eliza Worthington writes to her daughter from somewhere in France, where she is convalescing. "Darling Bessie, Your postals have given me a great deal of pleasure and have conveyed a great deal of news in the short space. Only I beg of you, eat no more *candy+cakes* as you will *surely* be ill." Eliza is staying in a hotel taking a cure. She mentions that her sleeping is getting better, but that her doctor wants her to stay another week. She is not sure if she will do this but explains that if she does stay, she will write for Bessie to come. The plan is for her to send a servant girl named Marie to go fetch Bessie, then bring her back home so that

Bessie won't miss school. As in her opening, Eliza closes with motherly concern: "Lock the house up when you leave and put some water on the ferns. Your devoted Mother. E. W. P"

By the time Bessie is fifteen, she and her mother seem quite settled in Dresden. They have just celebrated Christmas when Bessie sends the following letter to my grandfather. "Dear Van Ness.—It was awfully kind of you to send me that beautiful little brooch. It was just what I wanted and have seen nothing like it over here. We go to the opera quite often and I enjoy it very much, it's rather nice having it so early for then it doesn't prevent me from getting up early and going to school the next morning. . . ."

My grandfather, who had graduated from Princeton three years earlier and then gone on to study law at Georgetown, has begun studying at the École de Droit in Paris. Hoffman has come to visit for the holidays, as has Gaston, their younger brother. Just seventeen that year and busy studying at the University of Heidelberg, Gaston Pearson has already demonstrated the kind of original, creative thinking that often marks the second and third born. He is studying geography and engineering because he plans to explore the South American jungle and bring home emeralds.

Gaston was one of those children in whom the faces of both parents are so perfectly blended it made you gasp. He had inherited something of his father's gaunt solemnity, but overlaid with the sparkling, slightly imperious beauty of his mother. His face was a gravity of angles—the strong forward nose, the decisive chin, cheekbones that soared—but this was offset by his unruly, dark, almost black hair and his unforgivably rakish eyes. It was as if his face contained opposite forces, both duty and abandon, but held in perfect sway. Women found him irresistible.

Bessie adored and idolized her older brother, but Gaston was in trouble again, spending too much time with the pretty fräuleins of Heidelberg. Already he is showing the penchant for good times, beautiful women and liquor that will end in tragedy.

In her letter to my grandfather, Bessie, cheerfully rambles on, talking about her drawing lessons as if her aptitude for art was already well known in the family. "I draw four hours a day twice a week. I think my master is a very good one. Gaston arrived on the 23. (late at night as usual). Dresden has the most dismal damp and foggy atmosphere of any place I was ever in. The skating promises to be pretty good if it stops thawing every other day." Bessie had begun to show talent and a determined interest in sketching and drawing. Probably she had been encouraged by her mother, a lady watercolorist of no particular talent but considerable interest. Reading along in one of Eliza Worthington's account books from her travels in Europe, I often come across half-finished sketches of people and places. Tucked away with her miscellaneous papers—calling cards, dinner invitations and party lists, bills and articles from *Harper's* and *McClure's*—are several sheafs of delicate, accomplished watercolors, all landscapes, deftly touched with washes of green and yellow and cerise, pale blue.

By 1894 mother and daughter are corresponding about which art school Bessie should attend. Just eighteen, Bessie of course wants to study art in Paris. In 1894 the lure of Paris for young aspiring painters was like nothing that had come before. With its prestigious government art school, the École de Beaux-Arts, its spring salons and many private academies, Paris had become a mecca for young artists from around the world. Bessie can't study at the government École because women are not allowed, but she can enter one of the many private academies, which had admitted women since 1870. She has two of the most famous ones in mind: "As for the studio, of course it would be splendid if I could get into Duran's but I have rather counted on going to Julien's. Every one says that the first thing to consider is the distance of one's studio from one's home because they are generally too fearfully far away, and as one has to be there at 8 o'clock in the morning, distance has to be considered. I have heard of two different branches of Julien's, one on the Rue Vivienne and another at Rue de Berri. Both are said to be very good.

With love to Hoffman. Ever your loving daughter, Bessie W. Philip"

While the atelier of Charles-Emile-Auguste Duran, a popular painter of society portraits, had gained notoriety for the presence of rising stars such as John Singer Sargent, who studied there for two years, Julian's was the most popular, distinctive and successful of the private art schools. At the Académie Julian, students learned that correct draftsmanship was fundamental. Before being allowed to draw from real life, students had to first master drawing from engravings, then from casts. Each week a subject for composition was given to students to work up in their own studios, and once they had progressed to drawing from real life, they drew and painted from the model.

Within this strict progression, however, Julian's stressed innovation and fostered an atmosphere of fierce competition among students. For Rudolphe Julian, who had founded the school in 1868, an artist's success depended upon dedication, the study of appropriate masters and the forging of an emotional toughness that would allow an artist to persevere in the face of adversity and criticism.

In following her desire to pursue a career in painting, Bessie was probably inspired by early women painters like Mary Cassatt, who had arrived in the 1870s and become a sensation, in part because her family's support of her talent was unbelievably unusual. But the wave of women studying in Paris would have peaked by the time Bessie arrived. And studying at an *académie* did not mean that women received equal treatment. Bessie may have chosen Julian's for reasons other than its many locations. Its admission policy did not discriminate against women, and while it continued the Parisian custom of having women pay more tuition than men (at Julian's a man paid twenty-five francs a month for one half day of instruction, while a woman paid sixty), this was still much less of an inequity than at Duran's, where women paid one hundred francs instead of the thirty required for men.

That Bessie was considering the branch of Julian's located on the rue Vivienne was also interesting, for this studio had been created in 1877 only for women. Whatever location of Julian's that she eventually chose, however, and it seems likely that she ended up there rather than at the studio of Carolus-Duran (Charles Duran), Bessie would have enjoyed what became a renowned camaraderie among the large group of Americans studying there in the 1880s and 1890s.

Pharmacy and dress receipts from Paris for 1895 indicate that by that time Bessie's mother had joined her there. But the following spring, when, as usual, they return to Talavera for the summer, Eliza stays on through the fall. She is not well. On October 28, at the age of fifty-four, she dies in her sleep. The next day the *Hudson Gazette* prints the following obituary: "The sudden death of Eliza Worthington Philip which occurred last evening at her summer residence near Claverack has overwhelmed her friends with sorrow and filled them with sympathy for those dear ones to whom she was so devoted." Interestingly, within a few paragraphs, the obituary focuses upon memorializing her as a wife and a mother and as the mistress of Talavera. Her years of travel in Europe are not mentioned. "Mrs. Philips was entitled by birth to a high position in society and through her many graces she was widely known and much admired. While the social side of her nature was marked still she especially shone in her home life. She was devoted as a wife and bore with patience and submission the bereavements that came to her in the death of her husband and children and to those who are left she has been a loving and devoted mother. Her house reflected her beautiful, enthusiastic and lovely nature. It was full of cheerfulness and comfort and in it she dispensed a gracious and generous hospitality."

The glowing mention of Talavera I found particularly interesting, for only seven years earlier, F. H. Webb, in his local history titled *Claverack, Clover-reach,* had described the long, illustrious history of the Philips and Van Nesses at Talavera, then made a delicate allusion to Eliza's difficult financial state by noting that the house was "at present in a state of neglect."

After her death, my grandfather gathered up his mother's collection of religious prints and, unwilling to throw them out, but unwilling also to have them hanging in the house, carried them up into the cathedral heights of Talavera's upper attic. There the large sheets, including the enormous engraving of *Cardinal Guido Bentivoglio,* flopped down like great white leaves and rested, gathering dust and darkness.

For my grandfather and his brothers and sister, a new era has begun. Bessie makes her way back to Paris, where out of grief or rebellion or simply giddy with her new freedom, she throws herself into the life of a Paris bohemian and moves to the Left Bank. Within two years she has begun to study painting with the bad boy of the Paris art world James Abbott McNeill Whistler.

Exactly how and even if Bessie ever studied very closely with Whistler is not clear, but when she recounted those years in interviews later, she emphasized that he had been her teacher. At least one of the paintings done by her that remains could be said to be Whistlerian, for it is a sparsely painted beach scene with a spare composition and an emphasis upon tonality rather than detail. And Whistler had returned to Paris in 1898, to found an art school, which he named the Académie Rossi, after his model Carmen Rossi, who ended up running the school, but which was popularly called the Académie Whistler.

Twenty years earlier Whistler had gotten into a bitter fight with the art theorist and critic John Ruskin, and his reputation had for a long time flagged, something he blamed on Ruskin and every other figure of the art establishment. Whistler had reacted to Victorian painting and its moral agendas by rejecting narrative and refusing to paint in a detailed, finished manner. In his portraits and seascapes, he was interested in what he called harmonious totalities rather than adherence to realistic details. Ruskin had accused him of throwing paint on his canvases. But for students wanting something progressive, Whistler was an icon, a James Dean–like figure of rebellion. He argued with critics, squabbled in public and was known for his hot temper.

In 1898 Whistler's career was on the rise again after years of bitter nonattention, and he was in Paris, but he rarely took on students. It is possible that Bessie studied at the Whistler Académie and caught his eye. It is also possible that she had minimal actual contact with him but chose to identify with him as the primary influence of her Paris days. By twenty, when she would have studied with him, she was already demonstrating what would become her lifelong trajectory of rebellion against Talavera and her family background.

Yet perhaps she really did study with Whistler, and he had recognized her talent and tough original spirit and encouraged her. Among the few scattered papers about Bessie that I could find was an interview that she gave to the *Florida Times-Union* in 1964. About her studies with Whistler in Paris, she said, "He was a strange little man who wore a little black velvet bow in his hair. He was very angry most of the time and very sarcastic. He wrote a book called 'The Gentle Art of Making Enemies' and I daresay he was good at it. He was such a fine painter; I remember his portrait of Thomas Carlyle, one of the finest things he ever did. Roman style, very classical. And I remember he permitted me to study with him only after he learned that I had won a gold medal for my work in Washington at the Corcoran Gallery."

After their mother's death, my grandfather took an almost fatherly concern and interest in Bessie, something she clearly did not appreciate. If he had known the details of her Paris studies, I doubt that he would have approved. But as luck would have it, as far as Bessie was concerned, he was conveniently busy in Cuba and then the Philippines. That same year both my grandfather and Hoffman signed up for the Cuba campaign. Hoffman was soon accepted into Roosevelt's elite New York troop, the Rough Riders. Bessie continued living on the Left Bank without either of her older brothers there to tell her what she could and could not do.

Soon Gaston leaves Europe as well, accepting a job on the Isthmus of Panama Canal. The letter, which comes directly from the secretary of the Canal Commission in the Department of State, is strangely worded for a job offer. Gaston will receive ninety dollars a month and expenses, but the letter goes on to set out strict terms for his conduct: "If your services prove satisfactory, your return passage from Darien will be paid when the commission no longer needs them; but bad or unsatisfactory conduct on your part would result in your discharge without payment of passage home." It seems likely that either my grandfather or Hoffman had pulled strings to get their brother the job but had warned the commission of Gaston's need for discipline. He does not seem to mind, for at last he is headed for South America.

Bessie continues on in Paris. Then, in the winter of 1900, my grandfather receives word that she is dangerously ill with typhoid fever. Still stationed in the Philippines, he contacts Hoffman, who has just accepted his first diplomatic position, deputy consul to the embassy in Tangier. Hoffman rushes to Paris and takes Bessie to Tangier, where he believes the warm sun will help her convalesce. She seems to make a speedy recovery, for within months she is photographed riding Pedro, one of the two Barb stallions that Hoffman had purchased from a village headsman so that he could play polo with the Tangier Tent Club and, in keeping with the local sport, chase wild boars through the brush with long spears, a pastime called pigsticking.

Aunt Bessie would not have been allowed to join the bloody sport, even if she had wanted to. But in keeping with the tradition of turn-of-the-century lady adventurers in the Arab world, she is dressed like an "honorary male" in men's pants and blousy man's shirt. She sits forward in the saddle, a style of riding still considered unladylike in England, where for women, riding sidesaddle was preferred. In the photograph, her face has almost disappeared beneath her huge grin. She and Hoffman spend several months together in Tangier before Bessie makes another bold move, one that supports the idea that she really has studied with Whistler. She leaves for Tokyo to study wood-block printing.

Forty years earlier it had been Japanese wood-block prints, considered valueless in Japan and thus shipped to Europe as wrapping for ceramics, that had caught the eye of French artists, who began to collect them. Among painters of his time, Whistler had been one of the first to be influenced by these prints and evolve a distinctly Japanese style. From 1900 through 1902 Bessie would reside in Tokyo, studying traditional wood-block printmaking and living an expatriate life about which little is known.

CHAPTER TWELVE

Hardly a Hasty Word

B y May 1903 my grandfather, Bessie and Gaston all had returned to Talavera. In a slim journal that he titled "Farm Diary, Talavera," my grandfather recorded five busy months when they lived there together, in apparent harmony, although they had come home for different reasons. Gaston seemed broke. He had apparently behaved well enough in Colombia to remain at work for the U.S. government on the isthmus canal for some time, but by 1902 his brothers were worried about him again. That October, Hoffman, still happily posted in Tangier, wrote my grandfather about Gaston's unsettled ways, which more and more often involved various women. "I hope you let me know your first news of Gaston. I hope he does not go and get married on that $100. If he could find the right sort of girl. I believe it would be a capital thing for him in many ways." Soon Hoffman was commenting that he supposed low finances had brought Gaston to Claverack. My grandfather responded with discouraging news: "It is very disheartening to feel that Gaston has an idea apparently but to spend what money he can get his hands on but I believe that is the worst he would do."

Perhaps Gaston had already gotten into his infamous "trouble." One family story recounts that he got into a fight with a man over a woman and shot the man. The man died, and Gaston was sent out of the country for a while until the affair settled down. He was also known for keeping company with the illustrious architect and notorious woman chaser Stanford White and was with White one night in a New York City club when the architect supposedly shot a man. The family didn't want Gaston called as a witness and so had him conveniently sent abroad for some time. It is impossible to track down which, if either, of these stories is true, but what is clear is that just as their father, William Henry, and his brother Lieutenant John Van Ness had spent years sorting out the screwball finances of their younger brother Martin Hoffman, so they cared for the handsome ne'er-do-well of their generation, Gaston Pearson.

Bessie was delighted that Gaston was returning home. She was also returning for unclear reasons, probably some of them financial. In November 1902, she wrote my grandfather from Tokyo: "I have at last really decided to leave Japan, but I can't resist the temptation of going home via India and Tangier. Train from Calcutta to Bombay. I will send a cable from Calcutta." That February Hoffman traveled to meet her in Gibraltar. He and my grandfather were still trying to convince her to settle down to a respectable life in Washington, D.C., where I imagine they hoped she would have some chance of finding a husband and getting married. But Bessie would have none of it. She promptly informed Hoffman that she planned to journey on to southern Spain. Half apologizing for his failure to influence her, Hoffman wrote my grandfather that he had heard Bessie had been quite a *hit* in India, then explained: "She has done all this *by* herself and I suppose it is wonderful that *nothing* has happened. . . . I can say that I seem to have no weight with her."

By early spring of that year Bessie was writing to my

grandfather from England, where she was staying with a Lady Cecil of Stockton Hall. She was thrilled with the horses, which she described as "perfect marvels of endurance" and had been enjoying the attentions of a young man who had offered her the pick of his stable so that she could follow the hounds. She proudly described how she was also being provided with horses by a renowned horse dealer in Leicestershire who had no doubt drummed up some business for himself by telling her that "the bold and determined way I ride over the country necessitates the very best."

No doubt my grandfather would receive the bill. He had returned home to take over managing the farm and sort out the family's affairs. Hoffman, my grandfather, Bessie and Gaston all had agreed that it was time for them to create independent finances. Up until that point, whenever Bessie or Gaston needed funds, they would write my grandfather, who would forward the bills to an agency called Fishers, which handled whatever funds they had inherited from their mother as well as their jointly owned property in Washington, D.C.

In October 1902 Hoffman wrote from Tangier, where he was still deputy consul to approve my grandfather's decision to introduce beef cattle. Money was apparently tight all around. "I think your action in buying the cattle for us was good business—especially considering the poor quality of hay this year. The price you paid not too high. I see old Snyder still draws his advanced wages. I sincerely hope that an extra man's wages will not be added for the care of the cattle through the winter. Has Peyton S. paid his pasture bill?"

By the summer of 1903 my grandfather had quit his position as chief of the War Department's Bureau of Insular Affairs, the plum he had received after returning home from active service in Cuba and the Philippines. From that point on, everything he did was shaped by the volatile economics of agriculture in the valley, by the sprawling yellow house and by his role as eldest son and caretaker of the family. When I finally put the pieces of my grandfather's life together, it was amazing to me to consider how much his decision mirrored the path of the family's dead war hero, Lieutenant John Van Ness, after whom he had been named. Like his uncle, my grandfather had ascended rapidly in a military career, then in his thirties, while enjoying that success, had abruptly left it behind to live at Talavera.

In 1902 my grandfather headed home a confirmed bachelor, not the delighted husband of a beautiful heiress, as Lieutenant John Van Ness had been. But like his uncle, he showed a great love for the land at Talavera and became interested in the larger social and political aspects of agriculture.

In many ways, my grandfather was more of an eccentric in his decision than his uncle had been. In 1902 agriculture in the valley was not booming the way it had been in the years leading up to the Civil War, and the romantic era model of the gentleman farmer, with its moral and political agendas, held little popular appeal.

Still, my grandfather headed home, stubbornly, or nostalgically, or out of a sense of family duty, right back into history, back to tradition, back to Talavera, back to the land. For several years he had been serving long distance as the vice president of the Columbia County Agriculture and Horticultural Association, that vestige of scientific agriculture founded by his uncle. Now he entered politics, running as Columbia County's Democratic nominee for the state assembly. He lost the election and the money he had spent financing his campaign, but in the photograph of him taken for his 1903 campaign poster, he looked out with vision and optimism, his blue eyes keenly focused on an unseen target, his entire then-youthful face, with its strong eyebrows and long, slim nose, a study in classical symmetry and pose.

When I opened the small black book that recorded his months at Talavera from that time, I saw his evident pride in his Dutch heritage, for pasted inside the cover was a black-and-white image of the Van Ness coat of arms, with its silly knight's helmet, three stars and the words *Pro Deo Et Nobilissima Patria Batavorum*. The first pages recorded the names of people he was then employing to work on the farm: Fred Snyder as "head man and farmer," Sidney Kells as "second man and laborer," John Schram as "laborer—no rent, farmhouse" and William May as "ditcher for 1.25 per day plus board." The advanced wages that Hoffman complained about for Mr. Snyder totaled thirty dollars a month with house and garden and board for one cow and one hog. Mr. Snyder's wife cared for the chickens, did the milking, made butter and could earn an extra ten dollars a month by boarding workmen. The second man earned twenty dollars a month with room and board.

Then my grandfather described the busy, varied and cheerful life he enjoyed as the twentieth-century version of the gentleman farmer, as busy with the landscaping of Talavera's grounds as he was with overseeing the planting of young trees and crops on the farm. His journal began:

143

MAY— Weather cold and season backward. Planting began

MAY 16 Set hedge of honey locust in West side of garden—2 men and 3 horses

MAY 26 Finish planting young orchard

MAY 29 Leave Talavera at 7:00, arrive Copake Flats 9:00 (a distance of 21 miles) trout fish on Roleff Jansen kill

In addition to introducing beef cattle, my grandfather was expanding the orchards. To the one hundred trees planted near the gardens that his mother noted in her journal to be "doing nicely" in 1888, he added a new orchard, which he called block eight: "Baldwins, Newtown Pippins, Bellflowers, Seek No Furthers, Crabapples and Greenings." Next to the volumes on agriculture and landscaping collected by his uncle, my grandfather carefully collected the latest reports from the Department of Agriculture as well as important new works such as S. A. Beach et al.'s encyclopedic *The Apples of New York* and Jesse Buel's *The Farmer's Companion*.

As important to my grandfather as his records of the growing number of apple trees, the types of sheep, cattle, hogs and poultry kept at any given time and the progress of various crops were his notes about his riding horses, Freeship and Hari Kari, and his two white pointers, Lady and Jumbo, which he kept to hunt partridge and woodcock. The journal records his many trips to visit friends, to fish for trout and to attend meetings. He might ride to Hudson to board the *Ontario* and steam downriver to New York City to shop for a new hat, then, given the sartorial standards passed on to him by his mother, complain about it soundly: "Could not find but one hat at all smart in the whole town and that I found at Brooks. We are about two years behind the English styles that we try to copy." He might oversee the planting of corn one day, then leave for Washington, D.C., by train to visit President Roosevelt at the White House and travel back to New York with Mrs. Roosevelt, journeying back up the Hudson by boat.

On June 3 he delivered a lecture titled "Farming in the Philippines, the Moro Tribe, etc." for the Claverack Grange. That week brought on a typical burst of June heat in the valley, and he noted: "Heat more oppressive than in Cuba or Philippines." Bessie and Gaston were soon off in the runabout, heading the two driving horses, Toma and Talavera, toward the cool shade of the Catskill Mountains. My grandfather, ready for any excuse to go fly fishing, used the rationale of the terrible heat to hitch Hari Kari to the rubber-wheeled wagon and, once the cool of the afternoon began, set out with his fly pole for the Copake Flats or the Greene River. On June 10, heat or no, he drove twenty miles north to Chatham to attend a reunion of the Grand Army of the Republic and Spanish War Veterans.

A heat wave in early June is not uncommon in the Hudson Valley, and that year it must have been followed by just enough rain, for by July 16 my grandfather recorded thirty-one loads of hay brought into the barns, along with six loads of rye and four loads of potatoes. Two days later he rode to Hudson to pick up twelve hundred cabbage plants and had three men set them out along a ditch. Soon good news surfaced on the family front as well: Gaston had received a telegram from the U.S. Panama Canal Commission asking if he could be ready to leave for Panama in a week. He had been offered a position as one of the assistant engineers for the Panama Canal.

On August 2, Bessie and Gaston left Talavera in the morning. Bessie was to accompany Gaston to New York City and see him off. My grandfather was clearly very proud of Gaston and probably relieved: "Gaston will be one of the Assistant Engineers on the Panama Canal—the largest artificial waterway ever undertaken by man." He added: "We have lived together for a year here without hardly a hasty word between us."

In another month my grandfather was busy with harvest preparations for second crops of hay and rye and corn, for plums, cabbage, apples and pears. On September 7 he took a break to ride to Lenox and participate in a gymkhana there. On Hari Kari, he won first place in "slicing three lemons in succession cut with a sabre at a full gallop." Then he rode home to oversee the planting of twenty-six bushels of rye in the nine-acre "Pine Tree Lot," where a spreading Carolina hemlock, planted by his uncle forty-six years before, still punctuated the view, rising as an emblem of that once-wild American land.

My grandfather's interest in agriculture and commitment to farming Talavera did not seem to waver even throughout those years of agricultural slump in the Hudson Valley, but by 1909 things had begun to look up. Hay was no longer profitable, since cars and trucks, tractors and streetcars were replacing horses in the city and country alike, but again cities like New York and Boston needed food.

Many of the valley's farms had gone belly up in the wake

145

of the agricultural depression that followed the Civil War, but now cities had grown to the point at which once more population had outpaced food production, and prices were good for those farmers who had managed to hang on. Apples shipped to New York City from Talavera began bringing twenty-two cents a pound on the barrel, and that year Talavera apples were of high enough quality to be shipped via the FK Fisher company to London, England. Prices for sheep were also rising, for the journal recorded Talavera sheep bringing forty cents a pound per head in the nearby town of Philmont.

By 1909 my grandfather had expanded his farming operation to include six hundred acres in the Old Forge area, his favorite trout-fishing ground. He had purchased five farms there on which he ran sheep. That year, from a herd of 227 ewes, 185 lambs were born. He had also added sheep at Talavera, for his farm journals from that time noted the transfer of ewes and lambs between the two locations. Soon, in complete faith with the rustic tradition of English landscaping, when you stood on the front porches at Talavera, you could look out across the lawns to front meadows dotted white with the bushy, woolly shapes of Shropshire ewes. My grandfather continued planting and shaping the grounds at Talavera throughout his life there, but in 1909 he set out a record number of ornamental trees, on April 12 alone, a hundred European larches, a hundred catalpa speciosas and a thousand honey locusts. In May he set thirteen arborvitaes along the farm drive and planted two magnolias, one by the house and one down by the recently constructed tennis court. A small berm rose up on the far side of the court, so identical to one landscaped at nearby Olana that several horticultural historians believe the berm at Talavera to have been influenced by Frederic Church's design. On the house side of the berm, my grandfather planted another stand of pine, creating a green wave of trees.

It would never occur to me when I was growing up that someone had deliberately planned out, then planted the many nooks and crannies, sudden glens and secret sheltered places that we ran through and hid in as part of our games. But all these improvements took money, and how my grandfather acquired such lavish amounts of it, I am not certain, but spend he did. By 1909 he and Hoffman had taken over full ownership of Talavera. Although Bessie and Gaston continued living at Talavera, they had relinquished their share of it years earlier for one dollar, the equivalent of the British peppercorn. An act of self-sacrifice, necessary to keep the family homestead intact, or an act of relief? From that point Gaston and Bessie were free of any financial responsibility toward Talavera. Only Hoffman, whose diplomatic career did not bring him back to the United States to live until 1950, remained on the deed of Talavera as a long-distance partner. For the next five years he helped finance the orchards.

Presumably Gaston was still working in Panama in 1905, the year the deed was signed, for a Washington lawyer signed on his behalf. Soon after, my grandfather deeded to Gaston and Bessie Pierce Place, a thirty-acre piece of land that bordered Talavera to the north. The property came with a lovely white house and magnificent horse barns, and Bessie seemed happy with the arrangement. No doubt, after traveling the world on her own, she was not about to keep house for her brother, especially not a house like Talavera, which had become the vocation of many women in the family before her.

The years 1910 to 1914 came to be called the golden age of agriculture in the Hudson Valley, and a large part of what contributed to the return of good times for farms there was the newly discovered cash crop fruit. For some time apples grown in the valley had held a reputation for exceptional flavor. As Hudson Valley fruit growers would have it, the popular expression *okay* evolved from the Old Kinderhook fruit stamp *O. K.* that labeled boxes of apples grown just north of Claverack in the Dutch settlement of Old Kinderhook. Buyers reached for the fruit boxes marked "OK," and the expression became synonymous with anything that was good.

By 1914 hundreds of farms were raising apples and pears up and down the temperate Hudson Valley.

My grandfather clearly believed in the future of this trend, for by 1909 he recorded planting 1,864 apple and pear trees. On July 5, 1910, he sent Hoffman a detailed list of the trees he put in—"Yellow transparent, Greening, Northern Spy, Pewaukee, Baldwin, Clapps Favorite and Kieffer selected"—and a bill for Hoffman's share of the cost of tree purchase and planting, which came to $389.33. My grandfather outlined his plan to begin producing a new apple that he believed would do well: "The McIntosh Red is an apple of excellent flavor and color and sells extremely well, but is hard to grow from the stock obtained in nurseries; therefore it is better to graft it upon a thrifty growing variety like the above." My grandfather was convinced of the economic viability of fruit and clearly wanted his brother and business partner to be convinced as well: "If the trees are brought into proper bearing conditions and bear, the return from them will be many times greater than anything else that can be put on the land; and therefore everything should be done to further the interest of the trees."

It seems that Hoffman was easily convinced, for my grandfather moved ahead on his systematic plan to transform Talavera's farm from cattle and crops to fruit. These first orchards were interplanted with alfalfa, buckwheat, yellow flint corn, turnips and beans, but gradually, as the number of trees increased, he planted only ground cover crops like clover and buckwheat, Japanese millet and rye that were plowed back with the Clark cutaway harrow to condition the soil. The next spring my grandfather had three men clearing land of rocks and stumps with 40 percent Red Cross dynamite in order to plant 760 more trees, creating two more orchard blocks. This pattern continued until the entire farm, save for two small hayfields and the designated twenty-five acres of "park" around the house, was planted in apples and pears, with scattered blocks of peaches, cherries and plums.

Talavera, 1913

The fall of 1913 promised to be a good harvest at Van Ness Orchards. The older trees were bearing well, and the one- and two-year-old plantings, benefiting from the hot summer and my grandfather's insistence upon regular watering, had grown beautifully. The younger trees had been hard hit during July by a typical midsummer flare-up of mites, but my grandfather had gotten them under control through regular applications of pesticide, usually one gallon of lime and sulfur concentrate, mixed with one pint of black leaf and a hefty five pounds of lead arsenate.

But there was trouble on the family front. Bessie had decided that she was sick of living in the Hudson Valley. She was also, it seemed, sick of Talavera, sick of her brothers and sick of being a Philip. She held a public auction to sell off her share of family possessions, which, because she was the only girl, meant most of the silver, crystal, furniture and even some of the family portraits. Later, in a slim memoir, she wrote how she "despised the Hudson Valley Aristocracy." By then she had a plan that she knew she should keep secret from her brothers.

Appalled and outraged by what they considered an act of family treason, my grandfather and Hoffman bought as much as they could of the family things which Bessie put up for sale. On my wall is taped a Western Union telegram that Hoffman, then the secretary of the embassy in Constantinople, sent to my grandfather: "Must have sideboard." The same summer that he sent the cable, Hoffman was busy helping save lives in the midst of the growing human tragedy around him. He had already been awarded the Red Cross Balkan War Medal for his work bringing relief to victims of cholera and Turkish aggression. Still, while engaged in humanitarian efforts across the globe, well aware that that part of the world was about to erupt into further violence, Hoffman felt keenly the need to preserve the family place, with everything just as it had been at Talavera.

My grandfather managed to buy most of the Dutch silver, the portraits, the dining room set and the sideboard that Hoffman wanted. Then, on September 7, Bessie initiated stage one of her larger plan. She hired a young German couple to help her and prepared to drive south to Florida, where she intended to buy some property and move. She loaded up her seven horses and three dogs and set out in a reconditioned school bus.

My grandfather was soon busy, not only with the upcoming farm harvest but with his decision to run a second time for the state assembly. However, after his recent expenditure of funds to buy back the family things from Bessie, he did not have enough money to finance his campaign and took a four-thousand-dollar loan from a friend along the river who accepted his portrait of his great-uncle General John P. Van Ness as collateral. The portrait, a handsome rendering done by Gilbert Stuart, was a family heirloom, but my grandfather clearly assumed that he would be able to pay the loan back shortly, for the two friends did not bother to draw up papers. The deal was completed with a handshake.

Then October arrived with multiple shocks. Gaston, perhaps floundering without the company and watch of his younger sister, became sick and died. The stated cause was pneumonia. The unstated cause was alcoholism. Gaston had begun to exhibit a family intolerance for alcohol that later surfaced in my father. There was speculation that my grandfather too had begun a habit of drinking, for eventually we found mountains of glass whiskey bottles hidden under the outhouse.

One month after Gaston's sudden death Bessie sent my grandfather a letter from Haycross, Georgia. "Dear Van Ness, I forgot to tell you in my last letter that I became Mrs. J. Peter Stark. . . ." She had eloped with Jacob Peter Stark, the man who had been taking care of her horses at Talavera. Unknown to my grandfather or Hoffman, he had traveled south to meet up with her. They planned to buy land in Florida and build a winter resort there for people who liked riding and fishing.

Uncle Jack, as he came to be called by my father and his brother, seems to have been accepted by my grandfather. Perhaps he and Hoffman were simply glad to see their sister married at last. They may also have known Jack Stark for years. One of the names in their mother's journal under the list of Talavera servants was one Louisa Stark, probably Jack Stark's mother, if not another close relative.

My grandfather was soon distracted by another problem. He lost the election and could not pay back the four-thousand-dollar loan, especially as Hoffman had decided that he would like to withdraw from partnership in the farm. Busier than ever in Constantinople, where a cholera epidemic was leaving thousands dying in the streets, Hoffman did not demand half the value of the farm and estate, which technically, as half owner, he was entitled to. Still, my grandfather was hard pressed to find the five thousand dollars that they agreed upon.

The winter of 1914 my grandfather closed the south wing of the house and lived on the north side to save money. He rearranged the portraits in the dining room, removing Marcia Burns, General John P. Van Ness's widow, so that she would not stare across at the shamefully empty space where the portrait of her husband had hung. To fill in the gaps on the walls, he brought in the elegant Ammi Phillips portraits of his grandmother and grandfather and shifted the more elderly rendition of Catherine Douw and her three sons a little to the left along the walls.

The kitchen was still in the cellar, but my grandfather had a dumbwaiter put in so that he could live there with minimal help from servants. Before the cracking of green in early spring, it was not uncommon for at least one ice storm to thrash against the house. By the time the storm was over, such a thick coating of ice coated the trees that when even the gentlest of winds blew, the drooping fronds of pine and hemlock that surrounded the house tinkled like bells. Alone at Talavera, how could my grandfather avoid thinking about the wasteful, sad demise of his younger brother, the infuriating flight of his younger sister? Meanwhile, after an ice storm, the young apple and pear trees became icicles, their fragile fruit buds, already swollen, waiting for spring, next year's crop safe in their ice cocoons.

It was six years before my grandfather married the daughter of the wealthy Stott family just up the road. The winter of 1914 the lovely Helen Stott was still far from Columbia County, traveling through Egypt, where she was photographed in great style on the back of a large camel.

CHAPTER FOURTEEN

The Lives of Aunts

The wild aunt, the radical aunt, the aunt who had been forgotten altogether. My family didn't talk about these women, so of course I was keenly interested in the shadowed, slightly forbidden topic of their lives. I knew their names: Aunt Bessie, Aunt Leila Stott, Aunt Lee. But what I learned about them I often discovered by accident, coming upon a campaign poster, or a gold-tipped riding crop, or a newspaper article, or a photograph, or, while sorting the linen closet one day, a beautifully embroidered tablecloth from Vienna. These aunts all had lived at Talavera and had left their mark there: a random possession now enshrined, or a photo, or a favorite chair, so that they became part of my childhood there, part of what I would discover as I explored the old house and barns or overheard while taking in fragments of adult conversation in the formal dining room. But these were just fragments of whole lives, lives that, for the most part, had been lived off the record.

Aunt Bessie was the only girl in the family and as such pretty much did as she pleased. Fate had granted her tremendous independence and a definite lack of guidance. Her misbehavior and lack of reverence for family connection made her an appealing role model in my mind, as did her freedom and general boldness. When I was nine, ten, eleven, I was most in awe of her because she was famous for fox hunting sidesaddle. I could just see her astride one of the large dark warm bloods with which she was often photographed in full riding habit, her gold-tipped riding crop held nonchalantly at her side. When the powerful horse rose up and over the fence, her long black dress swept out behind. Then they were down and galloping after the hounds, racing and roiling just ahead. Later I would go to live in Japan, just as she had done.

While my grandfather, as the eldest son, fashioned a life with Talavera as its center, taking over responsibility for the house and actively farming the land, Aunt Bessie seemed to spend her life fleeing it, a kind of heiress on the run. Only the problem was, even then the family finances were limited. She would write to my grandfather from Calcutta, from Tokyo, from Tangier, from Paris, ignoring his pleas that she return to Washington. Usually these letters, filled with her plucky descriptions of people and places, ended with an address where—could he please send her a line of credit? She seemed to be running low.

While Aunt Bessie seemed to fall in love with her expatriate notoriety, her maid, Isabella, was rightly mortified. In her slim self-published memoir of her travels, *Around the World in Three Years*, Bessie proudly describes how a policeman had to be called to break up the crowds that had come to watch them cross the street. No doubt the Japanese stared agape at Isabella with her black skin and Bessie with her red hair. Isabella soon returned to the United States, but Bessie stayed on, living in a traditional Japanese house with her bug-eyed Japanese spaniel. Clearly, she had loved reinventing herself in foreign terrain. Even when I had gone to Japan during the 1980s, people there had stared at my blond hair and blue eyes. Sometimes on the train I would feel a hand stroking the fine blond hairs on my arm. I had only to open my mouth and speak fluent Japanese to astonish. I felt I un-

154

derstood something about Aunt Bessie's reluctance to go home.

I never got a chance to meet my aunt Bessie because she died when I was eight, but my oldest brother and my oldest cousin had. In the photographs of their trip to visit her in Florida, she is keeping company with a fine-boned collie. Her once-red hair swirls around her face in a white flame. She died on the edge of a trailer park in a tiny house. By then she was a devout vegetarian—living on a diet that consisted mainly of nuts and grains—impoverished but seemingly unperturbed.

Although I grew up worshiping the idea of my aunt Bessie and her exploits as a kind of childhood hero, she was a distant figure to me, someone whom I felt I should not imitate, even though I wanted to. In contrast, my other aunts, especially the radical aunt, the political one, my aunt Lee, came to represent a kind of role model, a possibility, even an obligation for a way to be. This feeling was no doubt accentuated by the fact that we both were named Leila. I assumed that I was named after her.

Actually, as I would discover, this was only partly true. I had been named more directly for another Leila in the family, Leila Stott, my father's little sister, who had died from meningitis when she was three. Apparently my grandmother, a superstitious person, had not wanted me to be given this name, but when I was born on April 18, my grandfather's birthday, she had decided that the coincidence was auspicious. I suspect that for my grandmother, the sight of three-year-old me tumbling on the lawn must have been a poignant déjà vu. But she never mentioned that Leila when I was growing up, nor did she keep a photograph of her in the library, where we always gathered.

I found out about Leila Stott in high school when one day I noticed for the first time the black-and-white portrait of a little girl resting on the bookshelf in the far sitting room. I asked my mother who she was, and I don't remember feeling any surprise when my mother told me that my father had

had a little sister named Leila Stott who had died. Such silence toward the past was typical of my family, and I never thought to question it.

In the photograph, Leila Stott is looking down at a white ball resting by her feet. She is dressed like a princess in a white frock, white bonnet, white stockings and white shoes. Her face a hazy study of three-year-old glee. When I look at the photograph now, I think not so much about her as about my father. He had been seven when his little sister died, and in the flurry of letters from that time, uncles and aunts express concern at his enormous grief: "How is young Johnny doing with the terrible shock? It must seem to you all, just too much to bear."

Leila Stott had been much beloved, but she was of the past and had been deliberately left there, so that she did not seem part of the family's history. The aunt whom I thought about the most from high school on was my aunt Lee, Leila Vanderbilt Stott. She floated in the background of my emerging sense of who I was so strongly that once I had begun my quest into the past, she was one of the family members that I most wanted to find out about. So far with little success.

My childhood memories of her clustered like stars, but as with all the aunts and even my grandmother, the rest was dark space. She remained as much of an enigma as my debonair grandfather, perhaps more. I had tantalizing bits of information about her. I knew that she had studied in Vienna at the turn of the century when it was still Europe's intellectual hotbed, that she had been an early suffragette, that she had run for political office in the American Labor party, that she had been a union organizer and a teacher and that she had helped found a school in New York City. I knew that she had never married. But I had no details about any of it.

My mother remembered that two boxes of my aunt Lee's personal papers had been kept in the downstairs bedroom at Talavera, but during the property division in 1973, these papers along with her campaign poster had disappeared. I had

searched everywhere, especially through family papers
housed in the New-York Historical Society, but could find
nothing. In some ways I was not surprised. Aside from short
diaries, shopping receipts and correspondence, little remained to document the lives of any of the women in the
family. While my grandfather was a stranger to me because I
had never known him, I could look up the facts of his early
military years in the Spanish-American War and World War I,
his political life in various Roosevelt ministries in Washington and his involvement with the farm at Talavera by reading
through the boxes of his papers.

In contrast, nothing was on file about my great-aunt. Was
it because the family felt her work had been insignificant, or
had there been a conscious or unconscious effort not to preserve her active, somewhat radical past? I couldn't say, but I
wanted to know more, especially after I found in the library
closet a deed in which she lent my grandfather and grandmother thirty-six thousand dollars. The deed was dated
1936. Times were bad for the farm, agriculture in the valley
having peaked, then busted during the Depression. But Aunt
Lee had thirty-six thousand dollars to lend my grandfather,
money that kept the farm at Talavera solvent. I am pretty sure
that she was never repaid, for in the letters between her and
her sister, there is no mention of the loan, nor is there a receipt of repayment.

Both my great-aunt Lee and my grandmother dressed in
similar versions of fine cotton dresses with soft floral prints,
always in colors of purple and blue. By the time I was six
they were old and frail. Betty made them soft-boiled eggs
and toast for breakfast, and when I think of them, I can see
still the bits of dried yellow egg that would often remain at
the corners of their mouths, the white Kleenex tumbling
out from the edges of their sleeves, the white paper skin of
their hands. Both wore glasses, the pointed kind with shimmering rhinestones in the corners. But my grandmother often took hers off, and I remember the startling Caribbean
blue of her eyes, which even later, when her speech had be-

come a tangle of guttural sounds and the blue clouded with cataracts, continued to send out waves of interest and love as if she were marooned in her failing body, shipwrecked, but still hopeful, her eyes beaming out signals, a steady, hopeful SOS: "Here I am, here I am."

Unlike my grandmother, whom I remember mostly sitting in the library, Aunt Lee liked to sit and read on the south porch. She was a fixture of our summer days, an accepting and benign presence that seemed to welcome our constant interruptions. My mother remembers her patience with me one summer, when too young to go to school yet, I pestered her to teach me how to read. I recall her large old-lady shoes crossed at the ankles, the book on her lap, her eyeglasses hanging from a chain around her neck. She would sit there, steeped in sun, framed by splashes of red and purple and white, the geraniums and petunias that always filled the long window boxes along the edges of the porch. When I was very little, I would pick berry boxes full of yucca pods down in the garden, then walk carefully back to the porch and carry my pretend cucumbers up to sell to her. How the long white fingers would struggle with the clasp of her black purse, eventually fishing out a dime. Then how eagerly the thin arms would reach out and grasp me, a hug so faint I felt enclosed in a circle of air.

In the horse stables I would catch sight of her campaign poster, which had been tacked on the wall by the crossties. Since I was always down there doing one thing or another with the horses, I saw it often. In the black-and-white photo, she looks much younger than when I knew her, a vigorous, confident-looking woman who stares ahead as if to say, "Here I am, take it or leave it." But what I really liked was the caption underneath, the large black Roman letters that proclaimed "Vote for Leila V. Stott." When I bent over to pick stones out of a hoof or to stab at piles of the pungent sweet manure with my pitchfork, I could feel the power of those words and her unknown story. She had been a teacher and a spinster, her loves and desires kept secret from her family to the end. Had her role model been her forebear on the Livingston side Elizabeth Cady Stanton? Stanton had shown the possibilities of resisting, yet making good use of the landed patriarchy into which she had been born.

I once tried to ask my father about my aunt Lee. I was seventeen at the time and feisty with my newfound awareness of feminism. When I asked him why he thought my great-aunt had never married, he answered that she had been beautiful and that several men had wanted to marry her. He didn't talk about her political activism or her dedication to her work. He wanted to impress upon me that she had not been a spinster by default, that she could have married if she had wanted to.

The blank spaces. These erasures of personal history that time and my family had wrought upon these women's lives was in such stark contrast with the detailed way the lives of the family's men had been recorded that I wanted to recover these women, my aunts, my past.

159

✌

It was my mother who suggested that I call Janet Chester to see if she had known my grandmother or great-aunt Lee. Mrs. Chester had belonged to the Ladies Democratic Club o f Columbia County at the same time that my grandmother and aunt had been members.

"Sure I knew your grandmother," Mrs. Chester said easily when I called her on the phone. I could hear her take a breath before she began. "Your grandmother, now she was something. What a charming, adorable lady. And I knew your great-aunt Lee as well. The sixties was our time. Yes, it was. I would pick your grandmother up and drive her to the meetings. Dinner was at six; then there was a lecture. Every month we would go. Sometimes Lee was with her. She was something, they both were, those Stott girls. Oh, the times we had . . ." Mrs. Chester's voice trailed off for a moment, then came back. "And you're Julia's daughter? Isn't that

something. I knew your father too, what a wonderful man. I
love to talk about old times, I really do—"

I quickly interrupt and ask when I can interview her. She
can meet me the next week, if I will come to her house. She
and her husband have sold their place in Taghkanic and live
on upper Warren Street in Hudson.

JULY 20, 1999

By the time I arrive, the main street is glazed with sun.
Kids in shorts and tank tops mill about stoops and entryways
or wander, rubber-thonged, aimless in the heat. Hudson, a
sprawling river town, once so depressed that it seemed to be
folding in upon itself, was undergoing a revival as an antiques
center. Lines of antique shops faced out along the street.

At the stoop of a large town house, I adjust my bag, checking that my tape recorder and list of questions are in place,
then reach for the doorbell. There is none. I try the door
handle, and it turns, the door opening into a narrow foyer
and a curtained inner door. Again, I look around for a doorbell and find none. Then I notice that the inner door has
been left ajar. I push it open slowly, calling out, "Hello. Mrs.
Chester? Hello?"

My words are soon swallowed in a flood of wind and
sound, the slurring roar of a fan on high. No one answers. I
call again, louder this time to be heard over the roar of the
fan. Only then does a clear voice answer. "I'm in here."

I turn to the left, following the voice and the noise, and
find myself in a sunny front room crammed with bookshelves and dark furniture. A large woman in a casual but
carefully pressed white blouse and light slacks sits facing me.
Mrs. Chester. Although two red armchairs and a couch are
arranged nearby, she sits on a hard wooden chair, bolt upright. At her feet I notice a half-empty glass of iced tea. By
one of the red armchairs, I see another glass of iced tea still
full. Beads of cold sweat jewel the glass. She has been waiting

for me. As soon as I step in, she stares at me intently, her arms extended sphinx style along the sides of her chair. She does not get up but leans forward slightly and begins to speak. Her voice is muffled by the roar of the fan, but still I hear each word.

"There are things that I know that I am *not* going to tell you." She says this not unkindly but very firmly, emphasizing each word as if she has been pondering this decision for a long time but is still uncertain if she has made the right decision. The fan whips her brown curls forward around her ears. I stop in front of her and stand still while her large brown eyes focus on me so intently I think I can see them beginning to bulge.

"You see," she begins, her voice softening, putting her hands in her lap, "there are things about the past that are"— she stops for a moment to choose her next words carefully— "things that are personal."

I stare at the large woman seated like Hitchcock himself in an opening scene.

Personal? Things she is not going to tell me? Perhaps it is the heat, my having rushed so as to be on time, the melodrama of her words, but for a few seconds I struggle against an impulse to giggle.

Then she breaks the silence, waving me in with a friendly wave of her arm. "Come on in, sit down, anywhere," she begins, her voice loosening from its previous resolve. She gives me an easy, generous smile and points around the room. "Look at this mess, such a clutter. We had to move everything in here from our old house. We've been giving furniture to our children, but there's still so much to move, but really, this heat is terrible, just terrible."

I glance briefly around the room crowded with dark furniture, bookshelves and books, then concentrate upon introducing myself and asking her permission to tape and use my conversation with her. When she nods yes, I quickly flick on the small tape recorder and sit on a nearby chair. I don't want to lose a word of this conversation. She has snared my interest, as I suspect she knew she would.

"Are you writing a book?" she asks me directly. When I say yes and explain that it is about my family and the land at Talavera, she nods approvingly. Now it is my turn to lean forward and to try to capture her attention with my gaze. For some reason I suspect that this secret she has declared but withheld has little to do with my grandmother or my great-aunt. Perhaps she knows something about my debonair, enigmatic grandfather.

But I ignore her opening statement, at least for now, and begin by asking her to tell me what she remembers about the Ladies Democratic Club and about my great-aunt Lee and my grandmother. Mrs. Chester smiles. Her beaver-bright hair shines in the light. She begins to speak, again choosing her words carefully but without hesitation.

"She was very involved with, well . . . the past. I met her when we were trying to get new members for the Ladies Democratic Club. We had a wonderful organization. Absolutely wonderful. It was a social gathering, but everyone was interested in politics. Politics was fun then; it was social. Not like today. Anyway, I would pick your grandmother up, and we would go to the meeting, and we would visit all the way there and all the way back. I always drove. She could drive herself, but I always drove her to the meetings. Then when we drove back I would visit with her, you know, before saying good night. She would tell me lots of things about her husband, about the property, all down and around. They had lots of acreage. I don't even know if they even thought about where the boundaries were. She'd just say, 'Way out there, you know, all the way to Lake Taghkanic.'"

Mrs. Chester pauses for a moment and laughs, a fond, sentimental laugh. "That's it. And she would talk about her boys. Your father, she called him Van Ness and then Nicholas. She would say, 'Van Ness is coming this weekend with the children,' well—" Mrs. Chester laughs and looks at me "—that must have been you she meant. I know she loved it when the grandchildren were there. Do you have lots of brothers and sisters?" She waits a minute for me to nod, then returns to her memories. "Your grandmother would tell me about her mother and father, how they had owned the Stottville mills, and I remember that she told me about being involved in women's suffrage. That was very important to her."

I interrupt her reverie, to ask her again what she remembers about my grandmother. She replies easily. "She was a wonderful, wonderful lady. She was adorable, really she was. She always wore lace collars and had handkerchiefs, small leather pocketbooks. Blue dresses. I think she liked everything she did, but women's suffrage, that was big for her. You know I picked your grandmother up one night, and it was stormy. Your grandmother said, 'You know, my sister and I went out on a night like this. There was a women's suffrage meeting across the river in Athens, and we went, unknown to our parents. We got over there and had a wonderful, successful meeting, but then, when we went to come back, the river was freezing over. And oh, my, there we were in a rowboat, rowing through the ice.'"

I hear again the family stories of how my grandmother and great-aunt would sneak out at night to attend suffrage meetings. How they would tiptoe past the rooms of their sleeping parents and the servants, then step over the lolling dogs to slip out of the house. How one night they crossed the river as usual in a rowboat to get to a meeting in Athens, but when they headed back across, they discovered that the dark, flowing river was beginning to crust with ice.

I imagine my grandmother and her older sister in their long close-waisted dresses, tiny buttons up and down the front. My grandmother's blond wavy hair was coiffed and piled upon her head, a gentle confusion of rolled hair and tortoiseshell combs. But my great-aunt had already begun to keep her curly blond hair short. Glasses rested on her short nose, making her square chin seem even more pronounced. They had loved crossing the river at night, the miles of dark, flowing water, an endless freedom. But on the way home the ominous crunch of the oars breaking the dark ice had scared them. The hard row back across the channel, a one-mile width, seemed much longer heading home. Even traveling together in Egypt, they had been more chaperoned than now. By the time they finally made it back to the shore, their feet in thin leather boots were soaked and freezing, and they still had a long walk back up the hill from the landing. All across Stottville the lawns were shadowed with blue predawn light, the night dew having frozen into a sparkling sheet of white. As soon as they crossed their own lawn, they quickly called the dogs to keep them from barking. My grandmother's white bull terriers would have leapt at her in delight. But perhaps the family's St. Bernards, tongues lolling, were still asleep on the carpets inside, too lazy to be roused by the rustle of their skirts across the porch, the click of the latch on the front door. Those Stott girls. But once again they had made it home.

My grandmother seemed to have let her political activism for women's rights cool after her marriage to my grandfather in 1921, but Lee went on to organize union strikes at the Stottville mills, at times donating large sums of money to the millworkers' cause. She and my grandmother both had traveled to Italy to study with Maria Montessori, but while my grandmother used that knowledge for her family, home schooling both my father and uncle until they were ten and seven, Lee carved out a career as an educator in New York City, helping Caroline Pratt found the progressive Play School, later renamed the City & Country School in the hope of attracting more students. Later she returned to politics, running for state assembly in Columbia County on the Democratic and Labor party tickets, a campaign she lost.

Mrs. Chester clearly enjoys talking about the times she met my great-aunt, but her memories only confirm my sense that my great-aunt was an earnest, forceful and somewhat distant figure. "Lee was different," Mrs. Chester continues. "Your grandmother was a homebody, you know. She loved her home. But Lee was different . . . and she loved to travel. I am sure that your grandmother wanted her sister to come live with her at Talavera, but Lee would have none of it."

No matter how persistently I try to tease out of Mrs. Chester her secret, the mysterious story that she knows but has decided not to tell me, she holds firm to her initial resolve. I decide to shift my approach and begin asking her to tell me what she remembers of Talavera.

"Oh, the house was beautiful. Not crowded, you know, but kept. It was like Olana or the Roosevelt home in Hyde Park. It was nice, but it was old. It felt like an old home. In those days I don't think they replaced things. If something was broken, they didn't go buy a new one; they covered it. If there was a hole in the drapes or something. I can't explain . . . You just didn't go out and buy new things like today. Things were tasteful, sometimes severe, the chairs and things.

Olana, Frederic Church's gorgeous house and carefully landscaped estate. Hyde Park, the extensive Vanderbilt and Roosevelt mansions. As Mrs. Chester speaks, I find myself stunned by her comparisons. The Talavera I remembered has always been just home, maybe even a bit threadbare. But the house that Mrs. Chester remembers belonged to a golden era of wealth and taste in the Hudson Valley. I find myself leaping to embrace her vision, even though I suspect she is exaggerating.

"I remember one Sunday afternoon your grandmother was going to have several of the officers of the Ladies Democratic Club over for tea. Your grandmother had asked me to come over on a Saturday to go over little things with her about the cookies and where to set up the tea service and so forth. She was telling me about the wallpaper. She wanted to do something about it. She was upset about it, it was kind of like ready to come off, but I said, 'Oh, don't change it, don't ever do anything to it, it's tradition. And I like it just the way it is, and that's all that counts, you know.'"

Mrs. Chester laughs a little, thinking back. I can just see

the wallpaper that she is mentioning. The year after my grandmother died, a huge section had fallen off the curving back wall of the dining room. My father had climbed up a twenty-foot ladder to nail the thick sheets back on, but not before my mother had cut out a foot-square swatch and separated the layers, discovering eight layers of paper underneath. No matter how faded and torn it became, everyone hated the thought of taking the old paper down. On all sides of the elliptical dining room, ornate flowers and vines twisted up tall blue poles. The twilight colors of the room— the muted reds and purples of the flowers, the dusky greens of the vines and the soft gray tones of the background— made it seem as if you were not in a room at all but, rather, sheltered in some primitive forest. Even though the room looked glorious when it was finally repapered, we all felt so sad to see the old wallpaper gone that my mother framed a section and hung it in the sitting room.

166

"So then Joe Resnick was going to run for Congress." Startled, I realize that Mrs. Chester has been talking all this time, and I have been hardly listening. I glance down at the tape recorder, relieved to see the steady spin of the tiny tape wheels.

"We were talking about doing something, and your grandmother said, 'Well, I could do something on the lawn,' and I said that would be absolutely lovely. And it was. Before I knew it, I was going there, and we were doing it. We had a wonderful gathering. Lots of important people came from Albany and New York City."

Once again, Mrs. Chester's memories collide with mine. I remembered that gathering vividly because during it I had learned how to ride a two-wheeler. The morning of the event, enormous white tents had mushroomed up across the lawns. By late afternoon the meadows gleamed with chrome, cars parked bumper to bumper. Big people, big tables, big chairs, trays of food, endless white teacups. The lawn had become a maze that we kids had to weave through to find our parents. I was mad because I had to wear a dress that itched terribly

all around the neck, where it was stiff with smocking. I soon
gave up tasting the doll-size sandwiches and ran down to the
garage. No one was around. It was my chance to pull out my
older brother's small red bicycle.

My plan was simple. I would start on the drive behind the
back steps to the kitchen and ride the slight incline down to
the barns. At some point between my hauling out the bicycle and actually trying to ride it, a tall man with a graying
beard appeared from the cedar walk and was beside me. I
don't remember any conversation, I don't, even now, remember his name, although when I recounted this memory
to my mother she believed he must have been my uncle Bill
Whitney. Soon he was patiently keeping the bike steady
while I got on, holding it for a few steps while I pedaled, then
letting it go. I'd waver for a few pedal turns, then fall
over, pick the bicycle up and bring it back to where the man
stood, ready to help me get started again. Finally, one time,
his large hands pushed me off down the drive, and I didn't
fall right over, miraculously, the wheels kept turning, my feet
kept pedaling, and in a wavery line, I made it all the way
down to the barns before crashing into the packinghouse
doors.

"Your grandmother was a dear. I enjoyed every minute
that I spent with her. She had a lot of get-up-and-go. There
were so many times, so many, many times." Mrs. Chester
continues to talk, again clasping her hands. "Your grandmother would talk about Lake Taghkanic. She told me about
that, and it was called Lake Charlotte or Charlotte's lake, after an Indian person or something. She always talked about
acreage. Franklin Roosevelt was running for office, and he
knew your grandfather, and he would visit. So would Clif-
ford Miller, he was another landowner."

I interrupt to ask if Mrs. Chester thinks Talavera was
much bigger then.

"Oh, yes, well, of course," she says, looking at me with some
astonishment, as if to say, "Don't you know that?" "Talavera
was just the beginning. They owned all the way down to the

Old Forge. A lot of those people over there were just share-croppers really, the Coons, the Orsteds, they were people from Denmark. Then"—Mrs. Chester pauses for a split second—"eventually they became the owners of the land."

Mrs. Chester's voice carries on gaily, but then she falls silent. She knows that I have heard it, that glimmer of hesitation. She isn't certain anymore of what she wants to say. She purses her red lips as she thinks of how to proceed. *Things that are personal. Things that I know that I am not going to tell you.* I had heard stories about the Old Forge as the place that my grandfather had apparently loved to go to fish for trout. Had he owned much more land and lost it?

"I have always wondered about my grandfather." I probe, deciding that it is time for me to work more actively to flush out her secret. "My father didn't talk about him very much at all. I mean, I wonder what he was really like."

Mrs. Chester's voice leaps to life again, quicksilver, a trout flashing. "That's why I don't want to talk about it. I don't want to say anything about it. I don't want to be the one. It isn't something that was awful. It's something wonderful. I was surprised that so many people knew, not just the old generation, people like my daddy. And it's nothing bad. It was, well, just not so wonderful for your grandmother."

She looks at me quickly as if to register the impact of her words. "I heard he was just wonderful, this young, handsome guy and in his riding boots, and on his horse he was just great. And your father, he was such a nice man, he really was, a wonderful guy."

Mrs. Chester's voice trails off. She is pulling away again.

"I don't know that much about who my grandfather was." I continue, pushing harder. "My sense is that he was perhaps distant from his family."

"That's because he had interests other than home interests." Mrs. Chester says firmly. "So he would be out and about. You know, there are lots of people like that. You can't find fault with it."

"Do you mean out and about for work or socializing?"

"Well, it was that," says Mrs. Chester evasively, "but I think he had interests in his farms and I think he had interests in the people *of* the farm. You know . . . They said he was great. My daddy lived in Taghkanic; he remembered him riding through."

I listen quietly, but I am no longer buoyed by the initial hilarity of our meeting, no longer flushed with the chase. Clearly, she is trying to tell me that my grandfather had an affair, or affairs, perhaps even while he was married to my grandmother. I can see the photograph of my grandfather that sits in the library, dressed as always in beautifully tailored clothes. Waves of shock flood through me. Was this the dark wing of a dream that I have always felt flying over Talavera, the mystery that surrounded my grandfather and propelled my father to believe even more fervently in those old values of honor and family and land? A bone from the past has been flung my way, and suddenly I am not sure that I want it.

"People knew that he was very interested in his acreage," Mrs. Chester continues. "He was always around and about. What do you call that Hudson Valley landowner who was always out there and had all these people under him?"

"A manor lord?"

"Yes, that's what it was in those days. He was interested in his farms and in the people on his farms. There are photographs of him on his horse. That's the way it was. That's how people lived."

Mrs. Chester continues to look directly at me, but with these words she announces that she has closed up shop. At least for now she doesn't want to talk anymore, and her cheeks go slack with relief when I finally give up prodding her into further conversation and begin to thank her for her time and gather my things to leave.

"I don't care what you say," she tells me as I am walking out. "Those were wonderful days. I look back and think over all the times with those people in the twenties and thirties. I've read Edith Wharton. I love her books. I do. She'd sell something and pack her trunks and live for two years in Europe on two thousand dollars. Can you imagine? How wonderful. Money was different then. It takes people like you and me to keep those things alive. To say, 'Oh, I remember,' and to write them down."

Her voice gathers under her, racing forward. "I love the past. So many people are going forward, but I'm not like that. I love it, the past, the nostalgia. Do you know I have never forgotten anything?" I decide not to interrupt, to give her room to tell me what she knows when she decides she can. There is nothing else I can do. It is when I have packed up my tape recorder and am half out the door that she throws me another clue. "If you could get some pictures of your grandfather," she says coyly, then pauses. "Sometime we'll take a drive to the Old Forge. If I could only show you how he looked on his horse, how dashing he was, and we could drive to the old places.... Then I could tell you." She clasps her hands. "Oh, if you could see it, there is someone in the county who looks so much like your father. If you could just meet this person, I know you'd see it. Then—"

My face must be giving away some of the shock that I feel, for Mrs. Chester breaks off in midsentence and shakes her head vigorously. I watch the brown curls of her hair fly around her head like meadow grass in a storm. "No, no," she says, retreating to her previous position. "If you don't know, I'm not going to tell you."

But she has told me. She believes that my grandfather had an affair and that the relationship produced a child, a man now living in Columbia County who resembles my father. But how can Mrs. Chester be sure of all this, unless— I am struck by an even more uncomfortable thought: Mrs. Chester is related to this person. Could he be her husband? That would explain how she had seen photographs of my grandfather. But then why not just tell me, why the melodrama? No. I decide that as compelling as this story is, Mrs. Chester must be making it up. The question I need to answer is why.

I stagger back out into the heat, wondering what I have

170

begun. That night I dig out a picture of my grandfather on Hari Kari, the champion steeplechaser that his brother Hoffman had bought and that he had raced in the Maryland Steeplechase in 1902. Many horses had fallen during the race, some had broken their legs, but Hari Kari had come in the winner, taking home the enormous silver punch bowl that each May we filled with punch or pea soup (depending on the weather), then loaded onto the flat wooden trailer. Surrounding the punch would be food for seventy, the usual number of guests who came to my mother's annual apple blossom picnic.

In the photograph Hari Kari shines in the sun, his muscled haunches ready to leap the heights for which he was famed. My grandfather wears a bowler hat and, in the style of the day, sports a curled black mustache. To me the mustache looks like a thick black caterpillar, and Hari Kari decidedly more dashing than my grandfather, but I decide that the photo will have to do. I put it in my bag to take to Mrs. Chester. But when I call her the next morning, no one answers the phone. It rings and rings until I hang up. Throughout the day I keep trying. Still no answer and no machine to say that they cannot come to the phone. Days go by, then weeks. I call at all hours to see if I can reach her but have no luck. Mrs. Chester begins to seem like a mirage, appearing, then transpiring.

What did I know of my grandfather anyway? I knew his saddles. I knew the elaborate lines of riding boots and bridles that filled the tack room in the barn. I had seen his VN 49 plates for the Packard and letters written to him from President Roosevelt filed among the pedigrees of his purebred hunting dogs. I had found the letters that he had written back and one note asking if Johnny, my father, then a student at the St. Albans School in Washington, be allowed to research an article for the school newspaper in the White House library. One afternoon, while rooting through the tack room, I had pulled a crumpled newspaper out of my

171

grandfather's Chilean riding boots and found a newspaper article dated 1903 describing his run for the state assembly.

I knew what he looked like from the photographs of him on horseback appearing stern and accomplished, or handsome in evening clothes, his eyes flint blue, staring ahead with a steady, unwavering confidence. But I also knew my own father's reluctance to say much when I sometimes asked him about his father. "Your grandfather was very outgoing and accomplished. People liked him a great deal" was the kind of answer he would give me. In the white silence of what was unsaid, I understood that my grandfather had remained a distant figure to my father and his younger brother.

A slender thread from the past had come unraveled. I kept calling Mrs. Chester. Each time I listened, disappointed as the phone rang and rang and was not answered. Then one day, eight months later, a familiar voice answers the phone.

"Well, yes, hello. I saw your mother last week at a meeting of the Fortnightly Club. Your mother is so nice, she really is, then doing all those apples, I mean, really, she is something." Mrs. Chester and her husband had been away, first to Georgia, then to North Carolina. "We're back now," she explains, "and you know, I'm glad you called, I've been thinking, *Oh, I should call her,* but I didn't. I have something to tell you." We arrange to meet for lunch in Hudson in two weeks.

JP

"I am going to tell you everything," says Mrs. Chester brightly as we sit down to lunch at a restaurant across the street from her house, "because there comes a time." I lean forward, straining to hear over the clatter of dishes and conversation in the busy restaurant. "But first, tell me, how is Mother? Are the apples okay?"

"She's fine," I say. "Getting ready for the blossom."

That morning my mother and I had driven through the orchards to check bud stage. In the young trees damage from deer was terrible. Throughout the winter she had seen their tracks, and now we saw where they had grazed on the tree buds, a sweet carbo-load for them and death for many of the year-old trees. As usual, they had ignored the bars of soap, the bags of human hair and lines of cassette tape that were supposed to scare them away. Recently it had been mentioned that the thing to keep deer away was lion dung. Nobody had any answers to the deer problem, except for fifteen-foot-high deer fencing, which costs over a thousand dollars an acre to install.

The sap was rising quickly, though, and my mother was sure that green tip would come on early. Sure enough, on our way back we had watched a flock of small black birds descend on the meadow, the telltale glints of red on their wings. The red-winged blackbirds had returned. Deep in the woods, the skunk cabbage would soon unfurl, along with pussy willows, bloodroot and yellow marsh marigolds, purple hepatica. Spring was on its way.

We order quickly, coffee and cake, and then I wait for Mrs. Chester to begin talking about my grandfather. Instead, she begins to describe the land and a road that leads east just five miles south of Claverack, the old Churchtown-Taghkanic road.

"Now," she says when the waitress leaves, "you follow that road, and you know those red barns when you turn at the corner? Yes, that's right, the Merrifields; of course, they grew apples, so your mother probably knows them. Well, there's a woman in her sixties, Sarah Orsted, and she has a cousin, Anna, who is in her eighties. The Orsteds were a family from Denmark. . . . I don't know how they came to live there. But Mr. Philip would ride all over. The Orsteds had a daughter; she's Anna's mother; I don't know her name. . . ."

As she speaks, I strain forward to hear and write notes as fast as I can. She clearly thinks it important to describe each farm along the road.

"Then, over the hill, you pass a beautiful old colonial and another house. Then you get to the Posts' farm. Now, Mr.

Post worked on the railroad. He had five boys. They bought a farm there and had a family, you know." I nod, but I don't know. I have no idea what she is talking about, and already I am confused by the litany of names, people and their farms, the farms and their people, so mixed together that they seem to blend. But I keep writing as fast as I can. I don't want to interrupt the way she chooses to tell me her story. Gradually Mrs. Chester describes the road as it passes through the modern townships of Churchtown, West Taghkanic, East Taghkanic and Ancram, the area local people call the Old Forge. Taghkanic had been one of the original seven towns that made up Livingston Manor, and the first lord of the manor, Robert Livingston, had built two iron forges along the Taghkanic Creek, some of the first industry in the county.

Geologists refer to this area ten miles east of the Hudson River as the High Taconics, a series of landslides that slid off the Berkshires during the creation of that range 460 million years ago. A natural division between High and Low Taconics left a perfect situation for the formation of waterfalls. Over time, creeks broke through the faulted rock, cascading down. Farmers had little use for the area's rocky scenic beauty. They mainly knew it as hardscrabble farmland, thin-soiled and dank, good for grazing and sheep, but too rugged to crop out, completely different from the rich, loamy soil that made up vast stretches of land closer to the river. Still, acres and acres of this land, which stretched east toward Massachusetts, were originally attached to the Livingston Manor as tenant farms.

As Mrs. Chester continues to describe this countryside, she begins to weave in this early colonial history, when most of the valley stretched up and down the river as a system of manors run by lords who had been granted many of the same lordship privileges as lords back in England: jurisdiction over the tenants and the right to determine and collect taxes. Not surprisingly, the lords accumulated great wealth, while the tenants lived in subsistence conditions, impoverished by high rents and poor land. Rents paid not in cash but in chickens and wheat and labor.

"Back then Lake Taghkanic was called Lake Chalotte," she explained. "Your family's property went all back there, acres and acres back to the Old Forge. Your grandfather would ride back there. Miles and miles. Everywhere on his fine horse. It was nothing to him. People said he was a sight. I bet he was."

Mrs. Chester stops for a moment and leans across the table so that her face is even closer to mine. I stop taking notes for a moment and bob my head vigorously, anything to keep her from getting off the track of her story now. She seems encouraged by my interest and continues.

"He rode by to see the land, to check on things; he had people working for him, you know, sharecroppers really. There was one family that had come from Denmark. Their name was Orsted, and they worked on his land in the Old Forge. The family had a beautiful daughter. She was seventeen, eighteen. Your grandfather would ride by, his horse prancing, the sun glancing off of his beautiful boots." Mrs. Chester slows her voice, building the suspense. "He was dashing. She was beautiful. He became smitten with her. I mean, why wouldn't he? They had an affair. She became pregnant, and they had a baby. She was named Anna."

Mrs. Chester looks at me now to see how I am taking this news. I stare back at her openmouthed. "You mean the same Anna that you mentioned earlier?" My ears are ringing slightly as I flip back through my notes to find the names I had jotted down.

Mrs. Chester ignores my question. "Her mother and father were probably proud of the baby," she says, "and they got the farm."

"Here," I say, squinting down at my notebook to read my penciled notes, "you mean, Anna Post?"

"Yes, that's right. And she grew up and was beautiful. She must be eighty-seven now, but she lives right there on the farm that was given to her because of who her father was. Right there in the Old Forge. If you could just see how much she looks like your father."

"Anna Post." I repeat the name. "You mean, she would be my aunt then, right? A half aunt?"

"Exactly. And the thing is I bet she knows who her father was. I mean, come on, she got this farm that had belonged to the Philips—your family."

I continue to stare at her in some confusion. I had gotten used to the idea that I might have an uncle out there somewhere, someone who looked like my father. I had it all worked out to ask her if this man was her husband. But of course a woman could look like my father. I had just made the wrong assumption. Still, I feel thrown into darkness all over again. I had wanted to talk to Mrs. Chester to find out more about my grandmother and elusive great-aunt Lee. I knew that my great-aunt's story was only half told by what the family chose to remember or record, and I was eager to be surprised, even shocked, by what I might find out about her. But I hadn't been prepared for this, the discovery of an aunt whose life had been left out of the family history altogether.

"An aunt," I say again, as if to get used to the idea by saying the words.

"Oh, I can just see it," Mrs. Chester continues. She clasps her hands so that her bracelets jingle. She loves the romance of the story she is weaving. "How dashing he was. How he fell in love with that beautiful girl. The family was given a farm, to take care of the baby. That's the way things were done then. Look in the courthouse, you'll see it on the deeds. I'm sure it's there."

I still don't know what to say. According to Mrs. Chester, my father had an older sister, whom I have never met. That she is only a half sister does not make her seem any less important. Not only is she still alive, but if what Mrs. Chester has been telling me is true, a vast class divide has kept her a secret, even now. But not a secret to everybody.

"How did you know this?"

Again, Mrs. Chester answers me easily. "Oh, lots of people knew, at least in Taghkanic they did." This time, when she leans toward me, she lays one hand on the table and beats a light rhythm to emphasize her words. "Anna had class; there's just no other way to describe it. You could see it right away, oh, the way she looked, the way she moved, her face. She carried herself with such poise. That's something in the blood, I don't care what you say. She had a sister because her mother married Mr. Thorpe and had another daughter, but that sister looked completely different. Anna was so beautiful. She was, well, just aristocratic, that's what she was. Breeding, you know, the family you're from . . . everything is in breeding."

Mrs. Chester looks me dead in the eye. I suddenly feel uncomfortable, wondering what she sees in me, but I return her gaze, all the while thinking that I have somehow fallen into a Charles Dickens novel. More unsettling yet, Mrs. Chester's words confirm so much of what I had lived and grown up with that I know she speaks a truth that is rarely discussed. Class lines do exist, and in Columbia County, as in most of rural America, they have always been based upon the ownership of land.

Even though my family, as early Dutch New Yorkers, were never as rich as the original Livingston Manor lords that Mrs. Chester describes, so that their actual wealth, like that of all those in the middle ground, has been unstable over time, prone to dips and rises, they did own land, land that was further signified by its houses and farms, Talavera and the farm there, farms in Taghkanic, the old Van Ness mansion in Washington, D.C. Talavera was not just an agricultural enterprise; it was a country seat, the homestead and rural retreat of men who spent winters in cities like Washington, D.C., and New York. Geographically, Talavera was only ten miles from East Taghkanic, but socially it was as far from that community of small, once tenant-owned farms as Mars. I think of the child Anna, my aunt perhaps, growing up ten miles from her father, from her stepbrothers and from their grow-

177

ing families, but kept apart, so that none of us could benefit from what the other might have to offer. The lines of class appear for what they are, a harsh, superficial grid.

The coffee and the lemon cake that we have ordered arrive. We drink and eat without talking for a few minutes. Then I am bothered by a new question. "How old were you when you first heard about this Anna?"

As before, Mrs. Chester answers me easily, almost cheerfully, clearly relieved to have gotten this secret off her chest. "I was probably seventeen. It was a family gathering of some sort, and I said something about Norman Post's wife being so beautiful. Then I said something about how she didn't look anything like her sister. That's when my mother said, 'That's because she had a different father. It's a long story, but she is the daughter of the landowner Mr. Philip.'"

"Do you remember what you thought about it at the time?" I ask.

"Never gave it a thought. Never. Never."

So Mrs. Chester knew this story, the people of East Taghkanic knew, but my own family did not. Or did they? Was it possible that my father suspected that he had a half sister but never talked about it? I ask Mrs. Chester if she will help me find Anna and try to contact her. Mrs. Chester says that she will try. I will have to wait, but she will make some calls. Her uncle is Anna's husband's brother. She will ask him some questions. Before we leave I ask Mrs. Chester again if she thinks Anna knows who her father is.

"Oh, I think so. I mean, there's the farm. Come on. The land, that tells it all." Then she leans toward me conspiratorially and adds, "Anna had a daughter, and what do you think she named her? Valerie. Think about that name, Valerie, Val. What does that sound like? Talavera. I think she named her after Talavera. I think she must have known about her father and named her daughter after the family place. Yes, I do."

"Do you think she will agree to meet me?"

"I don't know," says Mrs. Chester. "It must have been hard. But I think she would. I really do. I think she knows who her father was, and I think she would be really happy that you wanted to meet her. Go look in the courthouse. I'll check also. Then you and I will take a drive to the Old Forge so you can see everything."

A daughter named after Talavera. Family land deeded to an illegitimate child. The plot seems to be racing forward ahead of me, and still I have no idea how much of it is true. As soon as I can, I search the courthouse for any deeds of land transfer between my grandfather and a family named Orsted. Since Anna is by Mrs. Chester's reckoning about eighty-five, five years older than my father would be if he were alive, I look for the years 1915, 1916. Eagerly I flip open the heavy deed book and scan the page. The only land transfers for my grandfather, however, are for lands transferred between him and a woman named Alice Rockefeller, and they are not for lands located in the old Forge. If anything, her name only adds another complication to the story. I had found an accounting for the farms on the Old Forge property and at Talavera typed up and signed by Alice Rockefeller, who had presumably been working in a secretarial capacity for my grandfather. Either that, or they had been business partners. But Alice Rockefeller was not a secretarial type. In high school I had hung in my room a photograph of another Alice that my grandfather had known. She intrigued me with her Chekhovian air of studied elegance. Years later, when I read "The Lady with the Pet Dog," I would imagine the protagonist to look like the woman in that photograph with her plumed hat, the dark fur lining her coat as glossy as her dark, distracted eyes. The photograph had been signed "Alice Roosevelt." Had my grandfather kept close company with beautiful women at both ends of the social spectrum?

I knew that my grandfather had indeed owned land in the Old Forge area, for I had found the farm logs that recorded sheep pastured there. By 1915 he was planting orchards there as well and had set out thousands of fir and pine trees and a handful of ornamental trees that showed he was interested in landscaping those farms as well as Talavera.

One faded blue map had clearly penciled boundaries: Scism Place, Cronk Place, Shaugnessy Place, Banner Place—a total of six hundred acres along with houses and outbuildings. Finding out what had happened to that land had been on my list of things to do. Perhaps now I had a partial answer, but if acreage had been given to Anna's family to provide for the baby, why was there no record in the courthouse? As often has happened in the course of my research on my family and its land, I have made progress only to hit a dead end. So many riddles in the past. Pandora's box, letting loose confusion. I would have to wait until a way forward opened.

◈

"All I do is live in the past. Isn't that awful?" says Mrs. Chester when I phone her the next month to arrange a time for us to drive through the Old Forge. "But I grew up in a wonderful home with wonderful parents. I remember when my father got the first hay-loader. It was the first in the area. All the other farmers came to watch. It was great, and after that everybody bought one. Everything was just a few hundred dollars back then." She is surprised to hear that I can't find the deeds but admits that she hasn't had a chance to look herself.

One week later, we are driving east along the Churchtown-Taghkanic Road, past Churchtown, past West Taghkanic, then across the parkway, east toward the border with Massachusetts. Within minutes, rolling farmland gives way to woods and hills, dark green stands of conifer. Here and there the woodlands and fields give way to a farmhouse, newly renovated and landscaped. Most of the farmhouses along the road have left their history as struggling tenant farms long behind. Now they shine with fresh paint, firm-timbered, beautifully landscaped. Some have swimming pools, gardens, riding horses—the old farms transformed into weekend retreats. Mrs. Chester, whose family still owns several hundred acres in East Taghkanic, seems to know each one.

"I'm going to take you there via the Old Forge road," says

Mrs. Chester, "because then you can see everything. Where he used to go, where Anna's mother lived, everything. But first, tell me, how is Mother?"

"Fine," I answer, "busy."

"Oh, yes," says Mrs. Chester, "What she manages, that house and all the apples, I can't believe it, really. Did you get that terrible frost?"

"No, we were lucky, no frost."

"Oh, good," says Mrs. Chester, and sighs loudly, relief. "Honestly, I just don't know what these farmers are going to do. They can't make any money. They just can't. Now with this freeze, I tell you, it's tough."

I nod. The bloom had come a good two weeks early this year, and several days ago, right when the flowers were in peak bloom, temperatures along the river had dropped as low as twenty-eight degrees. Most orchards had suffered big losses, especially in pears, but for the second year in a row we have been spared. My mother and I had driven out to look over the blossoms and found only scattered brown ones. Petal damage had occurred in some low-lying blocks of apples, but my mother was pretty sure that the pollen was still good and that the bees would find it, for only about half the white petals had withered. The next day a sudden wave of heat had sent the damaged petals stretching. The day before, we had held our annual apple blossom picnic, but it was so hot we had picnicked along the garden's outer edge, enjoying the cool of the cedar walk. When I had left this morning, the orchards were a haze of pink, each tree buzzing with five or six bees just as they should be.

"I had always heard that my grandfather loved the Old Forge," I muse. "I think he would go there to trout-fish."

"Exactly," says Mrs. Chester. "You see, there was nothing here before, just property. It's amazing really, to think about it, all that land and no houses. This was all rural. There was nothing here. Not a thing. I remember this road. It was all dirt."

I look out at the landscape, surprised to see how many of

181

the trees are still tightfisted, the ground a winterish brown. All along the road leading out from Claverack, the trees are budding out, the land sloughing off its winter colors and beginning to shine green. We must have driven into higher elevation. I comment that riding from Claverack to Copake was quite a ride for my grandfather, but Mrs. Chester shakes her head.

"Oh, no. When you're riding in the country, hill and dale, miles and miles seem like nothing. He would have ridden across the fields anyway, and this was all property owned by the Philips. The Livingstons originally, but then somehow they had married or whatever, and people got some here and there." She sighs. "He must have had a good life . . . really."

We begin to pass farms and old houses. Mrs. Chester seems to know each one.

"There, see that farm." Mrs. Chester points to a complex of tumbledown barns on a hillside, a family-owned farm that has clearly not yet changed hands. Fanning out in all directions are lines of old stone walls, sheep fence. The weathered barns look flung against the hill, like driftwood. One has caved in completely, and the front porch of the small house slants so severely it seems to be falling off.

"Oh, that was a beautiful old farm." Mrs. Chester continues. "Again sheep. My father used to tell me the name of the people, but I've forgotten now. What a shame. Here, now we are coming to the next place; that's the farm that the Posts bought. Mr. Post worked for the railroad. Anna married one of the Post boys, Norman."

Soon woods begin to spill down closer and closer to the road until we drive through a forested canopy.

"Here, now we're coming to it. See that up there. That is the road your grandfather would have ridden down; we will turn down there." She points to a narrower road leading off to the right. I turn the car, and we are soon driving deeper into woodland. "Yes, this is it. Back then it would have been a dirt path."

I can imagine the joy of riding along such a road, the sun dappling the leaves, the cool forest air and the steady, spirited clop of the horses' hooves on the cool packed dirt all conspiring to make one feel as if it were a perfect moment. I try to imagine this new grandfather, the one who would have been riding through a green field of joy, each leaf buzzing with desire as he rode toward his Anna, a woman he must have known he would never marry. How long had they been involved?

"Now, this was all open property, okay. Nothing here. Now up ahead we're going to come to the Old Forge Road. This would have been Van Ness Philip property, all of it."

What we have driven through is more like a thousand acres rather than six hundred, but I have come to see that for Mrs. Chester, the story of my grandfather meeting Anna's mother is a romance without bounds.

"And this is where—" Mrs. Chester interrupts herself to crane up through the woods on the left. "Interesting. People have bought this property and built. Look up there. I tell you, really." We both look at the modern house peeking through the trees.

"You see, it's never been settled. It's always been kind of wild like this. Now this was all covered with heavy forest, lots of pine trees and oak trees. You have to imagine that. It was all trees, trees, trees. And up in the hills were the bushwhackers. Those were the people who whacked the bushes and made baskets. In the spring they would come out and buy everything they needed and sell all their baskets and live for another year."

I drive on slowly, listening as Mrs. Chester continues. "What history, what incredible history lies here. I mean, this was really, really backwoods property. And this is where your grandfather used to ride. It's wonderful, isn't it? He would ride up here to the lake. Come on, he would spend the whole day, riding along, going up to the lake—"

Abruptly Mrs. Chester stops talking and peers ahead.

When she sees a turn, she gestures with great excitement at a narrow dirt road leading off to the right. "There, there is the road. Turn right there."

As soon as we make the turn, it feels as if we were driving back in time. We pass a farmhouse, but it has clearly not yet changed hands. The next farmhouse is the same. House walls need paint; barn roofs sag. Then we come over a hill, and tucked into the side of the hill stands a newly built beige house. Across the road from it is a complex of three barns.

"This is it," says Mrs. Chester suddenly. "This is the place that your grandfather gave to them." I look at the modern house in some confusion, but Mrs. Chester explains, "The original was old; it was a lovely old colonial, set back a little more. This was the Orsted home. Mr. Thorpe used to have his horseshoeing business in the barn. But nobody is home. They are in Florida."

I point to the drive, where a car is parked, but Mrs. Chester only says, "Yes, isn't that amazing," and keeps driving.

184

I want to stop the car. I want to get out and knock on the door, at least to walk around the place that links Anna to my family, but it is clear that Mrs. Chester feels we must not stop, at least not today. I remind myself that we haven't made contact with Anna yet.

"No," says Mrs. Chester, as if reading my thoughts. "Today we are going to go all the way through. I want to show you everything here. All where he used to go. This was all property. All of it. All of it was Van Ness property."

Within minutes we are back in conifer stands. Beside the road a creek rushes by, and soon I am guiding the car slowly across a single-span pony truss bridge. Underneath, the creek, called a kill, follows the Taconic fault line, plunging down, the water falling 100 feet in less than 250 yards. Waterfalls. Waterpower. A small green state sign on the other side names it the Old Maryburgh Iron Forge at Ancram, founded in 1772 by Robert Livingston and kept in operation until after the Revolution.

When I see the sign, I can't help thinking it ironic that the

Livingstons, like the Philips and the Stotts, all families to whom I am related, helped found the iron, carpet and textile mills that by the middle of the nineteenth century were transforming the purely rural landscape of Columbia County into an industrial one. While my great-grandfather on my grandfather's side, William Henry, had headed south to fight in the Civil War, my grandmother's family had been busy up north, overseeing the Stottville mills that were prospering under Union army contracts for woolen clothing.

Columbia County's transformation from a rural to industrial landscape, a process that gathered warp speed after the Civil War, was heralded by most as great social progress. Of course fortunes were made along the way. But my own family's involvement in the building of iron forges and carpet and wool mills could seem ironic, at least when I considered our current status as agricultural preservationists, struggling to keep a farm intact and one small spot of land free from development.

185

"Look at those waterfalls, isn't that something?" says Mrs. Chester. "You know, whatever you want to write about, it is here."

"Have *you* ever thought of writing a book?" I ask.

"No," she says emphatically. "No, no. As much as I love history and everything, no." We drive along, saying nothing for a while, the silence comfortable. We have shared something now: this drive, the story of Anna and our interest in opening up the past.

"When did you last see Anna?" I ask casually.

"Thanksgiving. I saw her at the Merrifields getting pies. Don't you think I thought, *Oh, if I could just tell her?* She carries herself so nicely, the way she speaks, her face. You know, every time I'd see your dad at the train station going back to the city I'd think, *Oh, they do look alike, they do,* but . . ." Mrs. Chester looks out the window and falls quiet.

I think of my father then and how he and Anna could never meet and feel a wave of sadness and fatigue. Now that I have seen her house, the land in the Old Forge, it seems impossible that the story of Anna might not be true. But even if I get to meet her, what then?

"What made you pull back last summer from telling me about Anna?" I ask Mrs. Chester.

"Well," Mrs. Chester begins, still looking out the window, "I thought, as much as people know, maybe I shouldn't say anything. I can be very closemouthed anyway, you know. It's just something. I don't know. But I wonder if your daddy ever knew. You know. Those are things you wonder."

"I wonder that too," I say. "Were you surprised when I called you last summer?"

"Yes," says Mrs. Chester, "yes, I was."

We both fall silent for the remaining miles. When I let her off at her house, she sits in the car for a moment before getting out. She says philosophically, "Well, I am glad that we had this time together and saw these things." She gets out of the car slowly, as if something were still on her mind. Then she turns to me and flashes a mischievous grin, her red lips glowing. "Wouldn't it be great if we find out all about it, then discover that everyone knew anyway?" She waves gaily and shuts the car door with a slam. I drive off, down the long center street where in a few blocks I turn back up through side streets to Route 23 then Route 9H, the Old Post Road, where today the land stretches out on either side, a great shout of green.

186

Mrs. Chester's plan is to ask her friend Sarah, Anna's cousin, to call Anna and find out if Anna will speak to me, or at the very least to get Anna's address from her so that I can write her. But she has to wait until Sarah comes back from Florida, where she goes each winter, and to find a way to have that conversation. She can't just call Sarah up; she has to find the right moment. But first she has to run into Sarah. It all takes time. Days, then weeks go by. Each time I call Mrs. Chester, she says, "I haven't seen her yet." Then, one week in early June, when I phone, Mrs. Chester has news.

"I found out everything," she says, "We were at the beauty parlor and heading back out. I said that I had always admired her cousin, that she had so much character, so much poise, and Sarah said, 'That's the Philips.' And Sarah should know. She is a very busy person, and she knows everything and everybody, and she is going to call Anna up, how about that?"

Mrs. Chester is going to call Sarah to set up a time for me to meet her so that I can get Anna's address from her. Then I will write to Anna myself. Mrs. Chester lays this sequence of events out for me, then coaches me on what I should say when I write Anna. "You will have to say, 'I've been writing this book, and I would like to ask you some questions about things I've been reading about. I really would love to meet you. . . .' You'll know what to say."

Two weeks later, when I call Mrs. Chester for an update, I discover great news. "I called Sarah," Mrs. Chester says excitedly, "and do you know what she said? She said that Anna would enjoy it much more if she could meet you. Isn't that perfect? She wants to meet you, and she knows. All these years I wanted to tell Anna, but I didn't want to embarrass her. But she would have wanted it. I have her phone number. You tell me when you want to come over, and I'll call her and we'll set something up."

While I wait to hear from Mrs. Chester, I consider talking to my family about what I have learned but decide to wait. Even though I had begun to believe that Anna was my aunt, it was still possible that much of this story, like the six hundred acres of family land that had grown into thousands, was not true. I had found nothing about her in family papers or in the county deed books. If the story was true, this was a family skeleton that had been skillfully hidden. I knew that I could count on my mother's being gracious, and upon my oldest brother to be interested and warm, but I wasn't sure about how everyone else would feel. I decided to wait until I met her.

187

When the day comes, a Sunday in June, the heat begins early. I dress carefully, an indigo blue shirt, a dark cotton skirt with a pattern of small flowers and a blue cotton blazer. I don't want to appear too stylish, but I want her to know I have made an effort. It is too hot for stockings, but I wear my best slip-on shoes. I realize that I am nervous. What if she doesn't like me? What if I don't like her? As I glance in the mirror, wetting my short, unruly hair, it occurs to me that when I meet Anna, I will be representing my whole family. I rub in some hair gel to paste down any loose ends.

By the time we drive up, she is leaning out over the rails of the porch. The first thing I notice is that like my father, she is tall. But I can't tell if she looks like him because all I seem to notice is her dress, not the design, which is simple and elegant, but the colors of the floral pattern—turquoise, teal, violet and navy—a spectrum of blues, the same old-lady colors that my grandmother and great-aunt had always worn, a field of blue that pulls me from the car.

188

When I step out, I leave my notepad and tape recorder behind. There she is, my would-be aunt, leaning out toward me with such expectation, such openness. I am on the porch and see her strand of white beads, her shiny white hair, her wide smile. The strongly defined nose that, yes, could remind me of my father. Hello, we both say, and then she clasps my hand between both of her own and holds it tight, a clasp that seems to say everything. She sees me as a niece she has never met and she knows this and she is so glad that I am here. As I look at her, I feel my doubts dissolve. I stand looking at a generation that I had thought, with the death of my father, was gone. But here she is, my father's half sister, and our meeting, only now, but still not too late, has stunned us both. I have so many questions to ask her. But first this moment, when I feel that the past has opened its door. We keep holding hands. I had not realized how worried I had been that I would discover an aunt who was bitter about the past, but if anything, Anna seems to shine with joy.

As soon as we have finished our greeting, Mrs. Chester,

who has come with me, walks into the house with Anna to meet her husband. They are just back from church, Anna explains. I fetch my notepad and tape recorder, take a deep breath and walk in. As soon as I enter the sunny living room, I hear Anna saying, "My mother never lived it down, she never did." Anna is talking to Mrs. Chester. I shake hands with her husband, who has seated himself in a nearby chair, and ask Anna if I can tape our conversation and include her story in my book. She nods.

"I think it is time that things were out in the open and talked about," she begins matter-of-factly, her voice surprisingly soft. "It's time." She looks at me for a minute and laughs. "You know, I always felt I must never bother them. Mother said that she had promised that she wouldn't ever bother. I felt that even though I had never made any such promise. Oh, I was curious, but I tried to put it out of my mind. They don't want to be bothered with me, I thought. They don't want to know about me."

Never bother them. Writing this now, I think back on that moment and wish that I had followed my impulse to get up and hug her, responding to the wound that was rising beneath those softly spoken words, a lifetime of grief at being forgotten, of knowing that her father and his family were living ten miles away but, as far as she could tell, wanted nothing to do with her.

Instead of getting up, I sit very still. Was it to respect her dignity or protect myself? I don't know what to say, but I must say something.

"That must have felt just rotten," I murmur.

Anna laughs, but not unkindly, and looks at me. "I was christened Anna Van Ness Philip," she says, her voice tinged with pride, " but later my mother changed my last name to Orsted like her."

As Anna speaks, the story unfolds. At each turn of events, I keep reminding myself this is true. I would have to write a novel to begin to understand the complex knot of duty and desire, human passion and frailty that set Anna's life on its trajectory. But at least I can sketch out the facts as they were related to me. Anna's mother, also named Anna, had apparently worked at Talavera.

"Well, she was the maid, I suppose," explains Anna, after a pause. "She took care of the house. My uncle Floyd had worked there, he was the chauffeur, and I guess she started working there too." Anna doesn't know how many years her mother worked there before 1916, the year Anna was born, but she thinks it was several. As she talks, I am wondering if her mother had begun working at Talavera that long winter of 1914, after Gaston had died and Bessie had moved away. If so, might not Anna Orsted, with her clear, laughing features, have seemed to my grandfather, alone at Talavera, nursing his losses and defeats, an angel who had walked in just in time?

The brother and sister must have lived for periods of time at Talavera, for it was too far to commute by wagon each day. And there was a large family at home. Anna's grandparents had come from Anslat in Denmark and been married in the Copake Church. Many children were born, and many died, including twins. When it was clear that Anna's mother was pregnant, my grandfather arranged for her to go to Albany to have the baby. Nobody knew. Not her parents. Not her brother. Not even her best friend Lizzie.

"My mother would tell me the story. How she told everyone that she was going to Albany to study to be a milliner," explained Anna. "Then one day, oh, about nine months later, Lizzie saw her go by in the wagon, a tiny baby in her arms." Anna laughs. "She never sounded upset about it."

Anna also remembers her mother telling her stories of my grandfather's taking her to dinner at Keeler's, the Albany restaurant where still today people dine to be seen, of visiting friends with him and taking a trip to Massachusetts. According to Anna, my grandfather had wanted Anna's mother, then twenty-six, to go to college, but she had refused.

"I was supposed to be educated too," Anna says, "but I was too scared to go. My mother said, 'You are supposed to go to college,' but I just refused. And I had met Norman by then, and we were very much in love." She looks over at Norman and smiles. He nods but remains quiet, his silence protective. He seems happy that I am there but clearly does not want Anna hurt. They have been married for sixty-four years.

"I met Norman when I was nineteen," continues Anna, "and we were married when I was twenty-one."

Again she laughs, a soft, gentle sound that waves across the room, strikingly free of bitterness or regret. "When I was little, I used to like to draw pictures. I guess I began to show that I was good at it, and my mother used to say that there had been someone in the family who had been a painter. I forget who it was now."

"My grandfather's sister painted," I say quickly. "Did she ever mention meeting a Bessie?"

"Yes, that was it." Anna's eyes flare open in surprise. "Yes, a sister, she must have meant her. My mother talked about all the people she met at the house. A sister who was very accomplished and a brother who got into some trouble, I think. The Roosevelts would come to visit. Dinner parties and things. My mother was probably serving them."

191

"Do you have any of your paintings?" I ask.

Anna gives a little laugh. "Oh, some watercolors and things. Most of them got burned up in the fire. Our house burned up three years ago, everything. But my daughter, Valerie, brought these back."

She points to several framed watercolors on the opposite wall. I get up to take a look. The watercolors are all landscapes and barns, country roads, snow scenes, nothing like what my outrageous aunt Bessie would have painted, but still, the coincidence seems fantastic. Each one is lovely. When I look at them closely, I see that most of them are studies of her house, the barns, the wooded road that leads here. The colors are serene; the brushstrokes, so precise yet tender, show her great love for this place, her home.

"Did you ever study art?" I ask, sitting back down.

"No. Oh, no, I just did it as a hobby. And I haven't painted now in a long time. I can't see well enough anymore."

I ask her if she remembers my grandfather, and she says no, but that he must have visited for a while because he brought her a silver cup, a silver knife and fork and a pearl-handled rattle with silver bells, all from the best stores in Washington, D.C. He also brought her a pink dress, which Anna remembers well.

"Oh, I remember that dress!" Anna exclaims. "I loved it because it was so beautiful. It was pink and had all smocking on the front, you know. But one day I cut holes in it. I remember my mother was so upset."

"Did you cut the holes on purpose, do you think?" I ask, thinking about the kinds of things my own toddler would do if he was mad, but Anna shakes her head.

"Oh, no, I think I was just cutting paper dolls or something. I think I was,"—she laughs a bit, embarrassed—"I think I was sitting on the potty at the time. My mother was so upset."

According to Anna, my grandfather also brought her mother gifts. "Mother had an elegant locket with pearls on it and a gold watch pin with her initials engraved on it. She had dresses and suits that he must have bought her."

But by 1917, when Anna was just beginning to toddle across the room, her light brown hair flying, he stopped visiting. Then the money he was sending became infrequent.

"There are letters about it somewhere. Norman had put them in a tin box along with the deed to the property, so when the fire was out, we dug through the ashes and found them. Nothing romantic, just how was the baby doing, you know. Then my mother sued him for money in 1920. I don't know how much money she got, but she did get money from him, but I don't think she heard from him after that. They were just living here after that. Then, when Mother remarried, she asked him to sell her the farm so that she could have the title in her name."

"She bought the farm from him?"

"Yes, she wanted everything clear."

I feel my heart sink. Not only had my grandfather abandoned his baby daughter, but he had not provided for her the way Mrs. Chester had thought.

"You know I looked for deeds in the courthouse," I say to Anna. I am sure that my voice reflects my confusion. "I wonder why I couldn't find anything."

For the first time Anna's husband chimes in. "He didn't want nobody to know about it. Someone else's name is on the deed."

I look at him startled. So much intrigue. That was why there were no deeds in the courthouse. He had transferred the property to Anna's mother through a third party.

"Do you have them?" I ask.

"Yes." He nods. They were saved from the fire. "I can find them; they're here somewhere."

Again I think to myself Why? Was my grandfather just a scoundrel? Had he fallen on hard times? I recall the thick files of letters between my grandfather and his sister and brother; letters posted from my grandfather around that time came from Claverack, Washington and then France. Where had he gone in 1917? Was he running from the grief of a love he had decided was not possible or trying to disentangle himself from an affair that he felt had gone further than he intended? By 1921 he was back at Talavera and about to marry my grandmother, Helen Stott of Stottville, just up the road.

193

"We'll find the deeds," Anna says. "You can make copies of them if you want. My mother always said to me, if we hadn't sued him, maybe we might have seen more of him. I heard that his mother had someone picked out for him to marry and that he eventually did."

When Anna says this, her voice sounds sad. She clearly blames her uncle for forcing her mother to hire a lawyer to pursue my grandfather. But I point out that her mother must have needed money, she had a baby to support. Anna nods and remembers that yes, they were very poor. Her uncle was supporting them, and then he became ill. "She thought the world of him," says Anna suddenly, and again I hear the sadness in her voice. "I know that. Even before she died, she said he was the love of her life."

"How long do you think they were involved?"

"I don't know," Anna answers, "long enough for him to take her on trips, I know that. And he took care of her in Albany, of course. But Valerie knows more about it than I do. Mother loved to talk about him and the things they did, but I guess she knew it upset me, so she didn't talk about him much around me. I just wanted to get on with my life. I tried not to think about things, I guess."

Again, I make a mental note to try to find out where my grandfather was from 1917 to 1920. I hate the grandfather who seemed to have turned away from his baby daughter. Even when I remind myself that I know too little about what happened to judge, instinctively I take the woman's side.

When I ask Anna what her mother would say when Anna asked who her father was, she answers thoughtfully, "My mother told me what my father's name was, but she also told me, 'Never tell anybody.' Sometimes she'd say Mr. Philip, sometimes she'd say captain. Mostly Mr. Philip, never by his first name. She'd say, 'If anyone asks you who your father is, say you don't know.' So I learned to lie when I was a little kid. I didn't like the sound of 'I don't know.' So I'd say, 'He was here, but now he isn't, so I don't see him anymore.'"

Anna laughs, thinking back on those days. I continue to be amazed by her lack of any evident bitterness.

"Kids would tease me terribly at school," she continues. "I was always crying, coming home crying. Then one day, a little boy who was always getting picked on terribly said to me, 'You mustn't let them make you cry, you mustn't. You don't see me crying, do you?'"

"He was trying to help you out."

"Yes," says Anna, "yes, he was. I will never forget that."

Anna leans back on the couch and looks at me. Even at eighty-five, she is poised and gracious with me and my questions. She is clearly shy and making a great effort to tell me everything she can remember. She wants me to know her story, to be sitting right where I am, listening.

"You see, back in those days, my mother had the idea that she had sinned. She'd say, 'I have sinned.' You see, my grandmother had been rather preachy. And Uncle Floyd, he was always throwing the Bible at you."

"That must have made you feel even worse," I say.

"Well, yes, I suppose it did," says Anna, "One time my mother and I were looking through a catalog, and there was this red dress that I wanted. But later I overheard my mother say to my uncle, 'Well, not for her anyway.' I remember feeling that I mustn't stand out in any way. Sometimes when people came over I would hide under the table, I felt so inferior."

A heavy silence fills the room. I do not want to dismiss the gravity of what Anna is saying by small talk. But as I sit there, I can't help thinking that my own father would have wanted to know her. And as Anna talks, I begin to see another grandfather, one who could be heartless. No doubt he told himself he was acting out of a sense of honor. But honor to whom? What a paradoxical, contradictory thing that sense of honor was and how it had wounded someone he probably never meant to wound.

Mrs. Chester breaks the silence, speaking hurriedly. "And the thing is, today it would be no big deal. Everything has changed. But he must have cared for her a great deal. I think that. Otherwise why bother? She was such a beautiful girl. Don't you have a picture somewhere of your mother?"

At Mrs. Chester's insistence, Anna gets out a photo album, compiled of pictures that Valerie had been keeping and so were saved from the fire that burned their house to the ground three years earlier. I look at the small photographs of her mother and see that even in the grainy prints Anna Orsted is radiant.

"Mother always said that he was the love of her life," repeats Anna, "even right up until the end. She was never angry, even up until she died. She died in 1987. She tried not to talk to me about him much because she knew that it upset me, but I gathered from her that he felt he couldn't marry her because he would be marrying beneath his station. You know . . ." Anna pauses here, then chuckles, "I remembered once overhearing people say that here in the United States there aren't any social classes." For the first time since she has begun talking, Anna's voice becomes heated. "But sure there are. There's the lower class and the upper class. I always felt that there was."

I glance over at Anna and realize that her large figure has begun to slump down into the cushions of the couch. She is growing tired. "Would you like to see the photographs that I brought?" I say quickly.

Anna nods her head eagerly and leans forward in anticipation. When I turn over a photograph of my grandfather, taken about the time she was born, she looks and looks. "Oh, my," she says.

"Does he look the way you imagined?"

"Yes," she says slowly, but I hear a long "but" in her voice, "sort of."

I wonder if she is disappointed in what she sees. But then I pull out a copy of his obituary, and Anna brings the clipping with its photograph up close to her face and studies it for a long time.

"Have you seen that before?" I ask.

"Yes, Mother sent it to me, I think. I can't remember. Mother was very upset, of course, very upset. But I guess it was then that—" Anna looks down and is quiet for a moment, collecting her words. "Well, I had my own life and everything, but that was when I knew that I would never meet him." Anna wipes a tear from her left eye, and I am reminded that for her, this is all she will ever have of her father.

"Did your mother have any photographs of him?"

"Well, Mother had a photograph of him on a horse, I think, and there was a silhouette, but they all burned in the fire. We lost everything except a few letters and the silver cup and spoon. We found those in the ashes. Valerie has them. But you know, one day—it was quite a few years ago now—

I opened the paper, and there was a picture of someone from your family, could it have been your brother? And I looked at it and I said to myself. 'I look like him. That's who I look like.'"

We work back through the years, and I realize that the photograph that she must be referring to was a publicity shot of my eldest brother, blond and handsome, taken during his acting days, when he had achieved local notoriety for his roles on television soaps and in the Merchant-Ivory film *The Bostonians.* Probably she had noticed the photograph because of the name under it, John Van Ness Philip, my grandfather's name. She had carefully cut the picture out of the paper and saved it.

"Would you like to see a picture of Talavera?" I ask, and when Anna nods yes, I pull out a large black-and-white glossy print.

Anna pulls it toward her quickly. Her eyes travel up and down the white pillars. Then she sighs. "Oh, my," she says, then puts it carefully down.

197

"Have you ever seen the house before?"

"Well, Valerie drove me by there once. She has done some research. And once there was an open house, the local historical society or something, and I thought of going, but then I just felt too awkward."

"Would you like to see it in person, to visit?"

"Oh, yes," she says quickly, "I would like that very much."

I glance over at Mrs. Chester and suddenly remember her speculation that Anna's daughter had been named after Talavera. As I begin to gather my things, I ask her how she chose the name Valerie for her daughter.

"Oh." Anna laughs. "Valerie was a girl in my school. I always thought she was so beautiful. So I chose that name."

I click off the tape recorder, and we begin our good-byes. Anna says that she will have Norman find the box of letters and deeds, and I promise to make Anna copies of pictures that I brought of her father. We agree to meet in Hudson soon.

It is clear that Anna wants to meet my family, that for her, walking into Talavera would be like walking into a fairy-tale version of her life. I walk out thinking about how to make that happen. This time, when I leave, I give her the hug that I had wanted to give her earlier. As I come forward, her smile opens like a bird's wings. I feel her large arms folding around my back, protective, hopeful. Anna Van Ness Philip. She is the lost aunt. Found.

Anna

That night I told my mother about Anna Post. We were sitting on the south porch after dinner, enjoying the cool night. When I looked up at the tops of the fluted Corinthian columns, I could just make out the shadowed patterns of palmettes and acanthus leaves. The moon was still low and hazy. My mother responded with a shocked silence at first, then wanted to know everything I had found out about this would-be aunt. She was sure that my father never knew that he had a half sister because if he had known about her, my mother was sure he would have tried to find her. I asked her if she would be the one to tell my brothers and sister that they had an aunt they never knew about, and she said yes. Then she said she had to think about how to contact Anna.

One month later, when the busy harvest weekends were winding down, my mother called Anna Post and introduced herself. She invited Anna to Talavera that Saturday so that they could meet. My oldest brother, whose picture Anna cut from the newspaper and saved for many years, was up that weekend, helping with the harvest, and so he met her too.

They had tea in the dining room, sipping hot tea out of my grandmother's Dresden china, stirring with the little silver spoons that belonged to General John P. Van Ness. All around Anna, the family portraits bore down, but she was not alarmed. She was delighted by everything she saw: the candles lit at noon, the fire sparkling in the grate, the curio cabinets packed with souvenirs from generations of grand tours, the mahogany table where on many occasions her mother must have served my grandfather and the Roosevelts, perhaps even Gaston and Bessie, their own cups of hot steaming tea.

A few weeks after her visit Anna told me about it on the phone. "I was overwhelmed. It's so large and . . . but your mother was so nice, and your brother. I kept thinking I should write you. For a long time I've wanted to tell you how much this has meant to me. That you wanted to meet me, that was what was important. It's like this huge weight has been lifted. . . . A few weeks ago my granddaughter called me. She had decided to look up her birth parents— she's adopted, you know—and finally she had met them. She said to me, 'Grandmother, now you know how I feel. I feel complete.'"

Anna had laughed, another of her gentle, unassuming laughs, which by then I knew conveyed much more than she could say. I was glad then, for her, for me, for everyone.

What I discovered when reading through the deeds and letters was also surprising. The Old Forge property—a house, three barns and five and a half acres—was indeed transferred to Anna Orsted via a third party in 1926. Across the top of the deed was written in pencil *not for publication*. Even that transfer was not recorded in the courthouse. In 1926 my father was four, and my uncle just two. My grandfather was clearly trying to hide any connection to Anna Orsted and his illegitimate daughter by her. But Mrs. Chester was right about the farm's being given by my grandfather, for he handed it over for one dollar, a token amount to make the gift a legal sale.

When I looked through the papers and deeds that Anna saved, I saw that although by 1920 he had paid in full, initially he had had great trouble coming up with the five thousand dollars that he had promised Anna's mother in 1917. Letters to Anna's mother from the Hudson lawyer she hired to represent her case, however, urged her to be patient. At one point the lawyer relayed to her a letter that my grandfather, whom he referred to as Major, had sent him. My grandfather wrote: "These notes are alright and perfectly good. I am only too anxious to pay them in full and will do so at the earliest opportunity. Is there any distress at this time that has to be relieved? I am just at that point where everything practically is outgo, but this condition will shortly change to the reverse."

The letter was dated August 5, 1917. My grandfather wrote from France, where he was still on active duty as an officer in the Fourth Division of the U.S. Army. That July the Germans initiated their last major offensive of the war, and the Fourth Division had been ordered to attack the German main line of resistance between Rivière de Cligon and Ruisseau d'Alland. By August 6, when the offensive ended, the Fourth Division had lost 53 officers and 1,357 enlisted men. Another 179 officers and 5,296 enlisted men had been wounded. Despite heavy bombardment, the Fourth Division established and held the first bridgehead across the Vesle River.

As I discovered, my grandfather's involvement in World War I started as early as 1915, when he began helping with the Plattsburgh training plan, becoming a sergeant major in the First Provisional Plattsburgh Regiment. He remained in France some months after the end of active fighting.

While he was away, Alice Rockefeller was handling the farm accounts for the Old Forge properties and Talavera. In November 1917 she typed up an inventory of the Scism House, the farmhouse next door, which was almost identical to the one in which one-year-old Anna and her mother were living. The list held twenty-seven entries and described a life stripped down to the essentials:

Bread box
Water pail and dipper
Kerosene can
New broom
4 oat meal dishes
3 cups and saucers
5 soup plates
5 plates
salt and pepper shaker
water pitcher and 5 glasses
Lantern
Tea kettle, dish pan, tea pot, kettle and cover, 2 frying
  pans

In 1939 my grandfather began selling his Old Forge lands to finance the college educations of his two sons. That year my father was at the top of his class at the St. Albans School in Washington and about to enter Princeton, where a few years later his younger brother followed.

CHAPTER SIXTEEN

Another War

In 1941 Germany invaded Russia, and Italy and Germany invaded Egypt. In the death camp of Auschwitz-Birkenau, the mass executions of Jews were soon to begin.

By winter my grandfather had sold most of his Old Forge lands. My father was busy in his second year at Princeton. With his blond hair and gray-blue eyes, his tall good looks, my father looked like a Scott Fitzgerald version of a Princeton boy. He was already passionately devoted to orange and black, the Gothic buildings and walkways tumbling with ivy, the cheerful lines of shops along Nassau Street. On a letterhead headed "8A Holder Hall," he wrote to my grandfather that he was trying to get on the staff at the *Daily Princetonian*. He was on break but working as hard as he could to collect enough interviews to get an editorship. Every day he rushed out with his pad and pen, then typed like mad. He thought the interviews were going well and that he had a shot, but the best news of all was that out of the blue, Mrs. Roosevelt had called him up personally to invite him to dinner at the White House.

My father figured that he could justify the trip to Washington, D.C., since he could conduct more interviews there. Written after the event, his letter brimmed with excitement: "Dear Daddy, The President was there, Mrs. Knudson, the secretary of the Navy, Harry Hopkins and Justice Douglas— and we sat through jokes, discussions, and stories about everything inside and outside the New Deal, the defense program, the war—not for publication of course, but quite an experience for me." My grandfather would not have been surprised. Only a month earlier he had written the president directly: "Van Ness jr. is trying for the Princetonian and has to get certain interviews . . . It occurred to me you might see him for a minute or two . . ."

By that point the family sleigh that had belonged to my great-great-great-grandfather Martinus Hoffman was on display at Roosevelt's Hudson River estate in Hyde Park as part of an exhibit of the early Dutch culture of the valley. It seems that after dinner, that night in the White House, the president took my father upstairs and showed him the presidential library.

My father made it onto the staff of the *Daily Princetonian*. Within a year he worked his way up to the position of managing news editor. He decided to major in the School of Public and International Affairs, in large part because my grandfather envisioned a career for him in politics or government service. But already my father had other ideas: He wanted to be a journalist and in that way to travel the world.

On December 7 all that would change, but not for the reasons anyone might have expected. On that day the Japanese bombed Pearl Harbor. Within twenty-four hours the United States joined the Allied powers in declaring war on Japan. Then Germany and Italy declared war on the United States. Another war. Like his father before him, my father would graduate from Princeton and go directly into the military.

There seemed to be no question that my father would enlist as soon as possible. His first choice was the marines, but he applied too late and was told that the quota had been filled. In a letter to my grandfather, he railed: "If I had just acted a month ago (and realized the necessity) I could be in the Marines now, and could just kick myself for not doing so. . . ."

In the same letter he asked his father if he should give up his first choice and join the navy, something he clearly did not want to do, but a move that would get him into action sooner. He added that in any event, he needed my grandfather to send his birth certificate and a letter stating that his parents were permitting him to enlist. That April my father turned twenty. In May the quota was increased, and he entered the Marine Corps as part of the Reserve Officers' Training Corps. From that point on, his studies at Princeton became a funnel, channeling him toward the war. He took five classes a semester to complete requirements in three years instead of the usual four. He and his fellow editors on the *Daily Princetonian* worked around the clock, filing the latest news briefs on the war. In addition to these university commitments, he began courses in officers' training.

When I read over the mimeograph of his academic transcript, I saw that, not surprisingly, his grades soon crashed. But he completed his senior thesis on time, and it must have been considered better than adequate, for he graduated with honors. I had found a black-bound copy in the barn loft, and read the title with surprise: "A Study of the Price Mechanism of the New York Apple Market." Had my father even then been preparing himself to take over the farm? His thesis in the almost two-hundred-page economic history was that the Hudson Valley apple industry was headed for trouble because of its poor marketing practices. His conclusion, although vague, was prophetic: "A long period of hard times will probably be required before producers and dealers are induced to take decisive action in making necessary improvements." I heard the same sorts of comments fifty-five years later at meetings of the Columbia County Fruit Growers Association delivered by Cornell University professors brought in to try to help the troubled fruit industry. While they spoke, the audience glared.

In a photograph of the commencement services of 1943, more than half the graduating class was wearing khaki, my father included. Two months later he began active duty training and spent thirteen weeks in Camp Lejeune and twenty-four weeks at Quantico. At that point he was considered ready to ship out. A photograph was taken of him then: First Lieutenant John Van Ness Philip 039636/0302 USMCR. In the picture his face looked butter soft, so full of hope it made you wince. He had inherited nothing of his father's cool detachment. The eyes that looked toward the camera were so earnestly looking forward, trying so hard to hold their gaze steady, that you could tell right away he was shy. When I looked at the photograph, I saw another one, a picture of my father aged five, playing with his toy farm by the smokehouse at Talavera. In his recruiting photo he was twenty years old but looked like a boy. He *was* a boy, and he was about to go to war.

Ten months later his division was preparing for a special assignment. On the Hawaiian Islands they practiced beach landings. As soon as the amphibs reached the shore, they ran like hell in choreographed patterns to trick the enemy. They learned how to camouflage themselves with sand and seaweed, how to fight from "spider holes," basic foxholes with camouflaged lids, how to attack heavily fortified positions and how to streak across beaches riddled with minefields. They didn't know it yet, but they were headed for Iwo Jima, considered the most heavily defended island in the Japanese archipelago. Twenty-two thousand Japanese, commanded by Tadamichi Kuribayashi, were waiting for them. While the marines trained, the Japanese dug thirteen thousand yards of underground tunnels and fortified the hospital and four-story gallery they built within Mount Suribachi, a volcanic crater that dominated the island's tip. By D-Day the sides of Suribachi had become an invisible grid of pillboxes, one thousand of them, some with concrete walls five feet thick, and the rest of the island was similarly fortified. The Japanese soldiers on Iwo had been told that the marines soon to land on their island were murderers, lunatics and felons, freed from institutions on the condition that they fight.

As the Fifth Division Marines trained for Iwo, they knew that they were headed for a terrible situation. Newly revised navy standards on journalism allowed an unprecedented amount of coverage in the weeks building up to the attack. Some of this news filtered to the waiting marines, so that well before D-Day they knew that Iwo's defenses were lethal. They also knew that 40 percent casualties were predicted. Iwo was to be a classic amphibious assault: men put ashore to kill or capture anyone who stood in their way. The marines, playing cards, swabbing the deck, studying again and again their rubber maps of Island X, looked at one another and knew how to figure the odds. For every three of them who dropped down into the landing boats, only two would come out alive.

Not surprisingly, the mood in the transport ships as they headed for Iwo was tense. The marine chaplain reported outbreaks of ghoulish black humor. Periodically, one marine would play taps at dinnertime. For the umpteenth time, the units were drilled on their assignments, but once Island X was identified as Iwo, the regimental surgeon reported an outbreak of diarrhea. One seasoned reporter, who traveled with them, commented: "The marines bound for Iwo spoke more flatly . . . of the expectation of death than any assault troops I had ever been with before."

After I had read about the situation for the marines heading for Iwo, I was confused when I sat down to read through my father's letters from that time. In all of them, my father never mentions Iwo or his fears about going into action. Instead, he describes in upbeat detail attempts to go fishing while at sea, the quality of meals and the occasional movies that play on board. I read the letters through carefully several times, confirming that they were indeed addressed from Lieutenant John Van Ness Philip of the Fifth Division Marines and dated just before the invasion of Iwo. Only from his letter of January 29, two weeks or so before D-Day, do I understand.

In that faded blue letter, my father began as usual asking for news of his younger brother Nick, whom he had just written advising him to take up a specialty to stall being assigned to the Pacific. He was very worried about that possibility and went on at some length to persuade my grandfather to advise Nick of the same. Before closing, however, he changed the subject: "At last I am permitted to say that we are at sea and that we are going into action. Where or when I am not really certain myself, though the scuttlebut has been flying about, naturally, and we have certainly planned long enough and thoroughly enough....After I have been in action, I will be permitted to write you about the many places I have been since coming here. Your devoted son, Van Ness jr."

Only two days earlier, he had sent a similar, although markedly more descriptive letter in which he alerted his mother to the news of pending action, but then did his best to reassure her. "Dear Mummy, After we have been in action, I will be able to write about many of the places I have seen. The sea is very calm, a pale blue in the bright sun, broken only by the white foam from the tow and the green wake. No whitecaps but small ripples atop the swell, which rolls the ship very quietly from side to side. It is quite comfortable aboard, the Navy chow the best I have had anywhere except at home since I joined the Marine corps. I hope all is well. My love to Daddy. With love as always, Van Ness jr."

It was like my father not to complain or to want to worry his elderly father, but his complete silence on the issue of Iwo had been navy censorship. In his next letter, four days later, he again wrote of his great concern that Nick stay out of active service. Then he asked about recent reports from Talavera. My grandfather was serving on the Pan-American

Highway Finance Committee then and he and my grandmother had closed Talavera for the winter and were living in
Washington, D.C. My father reported that life on ship was
not unpleasant, meals good and lots of work to keep them
busy. Only that it was hard to keep track of days and time.
They had to keep changing their watches as they proceeded.
And then there was the annoying voice of Radio Tokyo,
which they picked up on the air every day saying that
MacArthur was being led into a tremendous trap.

Only in his close did he again mention his situation. By
that point, they were close to Iwo, some 750 miles from
Tokyo. "Dear Daddy, I suppose you are up on the news and
realize why this letter was so long in getting to you. Remember, I will always write when I can, if only a few lines,
so expect to hear from me again soon. There will also be a
time when I can tell you where I am, where I have been,
what I am doing."

By February 11 he could see Tinian Island from the ship
and he described it to his mother, carefully withholding the
name.

209

Dear Mummy,
Soon I will be able to write and to explain many
things. . . . This island is more formidable than some I
have seen, but it is new and strange in a way—different shades of green and different shapes from the
other islands of its size, though it is misty and overcast
with some rain and the view is none too good. Still
quite warm, though, and peaceful, with hundreds of
lights twinkling on shore.

The ship rolls impatiently at anchor in the swell, and
the little boats have the devil of a time coming up to the
gangway, and launching themselves off for the mail and
messenger runs, etc.

I hope you and Daddy are in good cheer and health
and finding everything is satisfactory at Talavera.

The war is personal to us all, of course, as you say, but

it is good to look over the big picture and see how well
it is turning for the best, and realize that happier days
may not be too far off. My best to you and Daddy,
     your devoted Van Ness jr.

Then it was February 15, less than twenty-four hours to
D-Day. As if in preparation, my father sent his sixty-five dollars of spare cash home to his mother via registered mail,
telling her that he had "no way to spend it and I fear it getting lost." Again my father wrote of everything he could
think of that would entertain his parents. He described how
marvelous it was to stretch his arms out into open ocean on
the occasional times they were allowed to swim off the small
boats, and the great beauty of the South Pacific, "calm,
bright sunshine, a fresh breeze on deck, and only the gentle
motion of the ship in the swell. Lagoons fringed by coral
reefs and little islands that seem a pleasant oasis." Perhaps
D-Day had already been announced for quite suddenly, before he closed, my father burst into an uncharacteristically
open disclosure of yearning for his parents and for Talavera.
"How I wish that I could be there with you and Mummy, if
only as few times as I got home last spring. But perhaps by
next spring, who knows. I will be at least beginning to think
of real possibilities of getting home."

On D-Day the sun broke cleanly over the blue horizon.
Visibility perfect. Operation Detachment began at 0500. The
men ate steak and eggs, traditional landing day fare. Then, by
0640, the guns of heavy transport ships boomed into action.
While the prelanding bombardment continued, the Third,
Fourth and Fifth Marine divisions got ready. The transports
eased into their assigned areas, and at 0805, seventy-two
fighter and bomber planes roared toward the island to attack
the eastern and northern slopes.

At 0830 the first wave of armored amphibians, loaded
with marines, headed for the shore. Each one had been al-
lotted thirty minutes to reach the steep beach, a distance of
four thousand yards. At 0902, only two minutes off schedule,

it was H hour. Orders came bawling over a loudspeaker from the control ship for marines to get down into their boats. Minesweepers had already cleared pathways, carefully knifing the sand for mines as the marines crawled forward. The plan called for the Fifth Marines to cut off Suribachi and then pivot north. As soon as the Fifth splashed ashore, climbing up onto the black beach, the men began to run as they had trained, as fast as they could across the beach and toward cover. But something was wrong.

The sand on the beach was not at all like the sand on the Hawaiian beaches where they had trained. One step and they were ankle deep in black volcanic ash, fine as cake flour. They couldn't run. They could barely walk. Miraculously there was no fire from the Japanese. The marines struggled forward, more and more of them becoming mired like ants in honey. Only when seven battalions of marines were struggling across the dark sand did the Japanese rise from their hidden positions and open fire. Some marines panicked and tried to dig foxholes, but it was impossible, like burrowing into a bag of wheat. Soon, among urgent calls to the control ship for mortar shells, stretchers and plasma, there were cries for sandbags so that the marines, pinned down on a beach that was being raked by enemy fire, could build cover.

At 1130 Associated Press photographer Joe Rosenthal was still waiting in a landing craft. The waterline was choked with the wreckage of boats and vehicles trapped in the sand. He could barely see the beach so much black dust was being kicked up by shellfire. Enormous spigot mortar shells called flying ashcans and rocket-boosted aerial bombs were especially scary. Then there was Mount Suribachi, bathed in an eerie fog. In an interview, Rosenthal recounted: "I kept thinking. 'Here are guys who haven't lived yet. . . . If I'm killed it will be no great loss, but these kids haven't had a fair chance, and we know the odds. The odds mean that four out of five of them are not coming back. . . .'" When his boat touched the shore, Rosenthal stood up and snapped two pictures of "kids" racing down the ramp lugging their mortar carriages behind them. A few minutes later, onshore, he saw a picture that for him seemed to sum up the nightmarish quality of the landing. A dead marine was lying on an uphill slope, his gun ready, frozen in the act of charging forward. Struggling past him were newly landed marines, one of whom could have been my father. Rosenthal crept up the beach until he could get an angle on the shot. Then, just as a marine lurched by, he clicked the shutter. By nightfall the press plane had left for Guam carrying his film. By Wednesday his image of the dead marine standing guard for his comrades as they ran through enemy fire was on the front page of every major newspaper in the United States.

Regular airmail was not allowed in combat zones, but soldiers could send and receive V-mail, brief personal letters reduced onto microfilm to save precious cargo on ships and airplanes, then developed and enlarged to fit a 4½- by 5-inch sheet of paper. My father's first V-mail was just a paragraph that he sent his mother. "Dear Mummy, I am fine, unscratched and in good health and intend to stay that way. . . . Hope you and Daddy are both well. You must not worry over what you read in the newspapers, it is always exaggerated. Be sure that Nick sticks to that sea duty. It is fine, as you know. All my love to you and Daddy, Van Ness jr."

Three days passed before he could write again. This time he sent a V-mail to his father, urging him to ignore the newspaper accounts of the invasion and repeating his concern that they try to keep Nick from active duty. "No air mail facilities but I wrote Mummy yesterday I was O.K. and well. We are enjoying fine hot meals, hot coffee, butter, etc. . . . My main worry is that you and Mummy will worry unnecessarily from reading exaggerated accounting by newspapers. . . . You know I can take care of myself and will continue to be O.K. love to you and Mummy and Nick, steer him to sea duty by all means. VN jr."

In the next V-mail to his mother, sent out the same day, my father tried to make light of his situation: "Rumor has it that our General has bet someone $1,000 he would get us back to the States within a year."

What he did not tell them was that his colonel, operations officer and sergeant major had already been killed and that the fighting was not yet over. He also did not mention that his battalion had actually been part of the heroic charge up Mount Suribachi to plant the American flag or that on D plus 5, or February 24, while pursuing two powerful cross-island defenses, hills 362 and 362A, he had been wounded in the head by shellfire.

Only my uncle, still stationed at Parris Island, knew that my father had been hit. As soon as letters came in, one arrived from my uncle, who assured my father that he would honor my father's request not to tell their parents about what my father had called his "Hollywood Wound." Nick went to assure my father that if he were assigned to Princeton that summer, he would visit Talavera on weekends as my father had done, that my father should not worry about the place. Again, he asked my father about his hit, but my father didn't seem to answer that either, for in letters that followed, my uncle repeated the question and commented that their parents had written to say that my father's surviving Iwo had changed their whole view of life.

On March 11, my father wrote again but still did not mention his hit. He seemed intent upon deflecting his parents' concern and made fun of the newspaper coverage of the war.

Iwo Jima, March 11

Dear Daddy,
All is well and I hope you have been getting my letters. When you get this letter of course, it will all be over long since, as it is almost over now, and you and Mummy will not be worrying anymore....
I have seen mainland news accounts reported in our paper over here. The latest one to give us a good laugh

was about nurses and doctors being rushed to Pearl to devise means to protect us from the "deadly sulphur fumes" of Iwo. This is ridiculous. While the dust does get in our weapons, the hot sulphur smoke coming out of the earth is often one of the comforts of this island as it keeps you warm at night and literally furnishes steam-heated foxholes.

...I hope all is well with the fruit and that the pruning is coming along okay. No doubt the snow is melted by now. All my love to you and Mummy,

your devoted son, Van Ness jr.

Only in a letter to his uncle Hoffman, written that same day, did he describe something of what he had been through.

Dear Uncle Hoffman,
I have seen plenty of action. We are the "George" company of the 3rd and the policy around here seems to be "let George do it" for my company has seen more time on the front lines than any other company in all 3 Divisions. Now we are in a rest area. The big Japanese mortars and artillery are pretty well silenced. . . .

Those Marines in the assault platoon certainly have guts—I never believed such courage and heroism as I have seen right before my eyes time and time again. Well, I will tell you about it when I see you. . . . I have not told Mummy and Daddy about the action and perhaps won't for a time.

Your devoted nephew, VN jr.

Only on March 27, when guns on Iwo finally went silent, did my father send some news of what he had survived. His letter, written on Red Cross stationery, not the usual marines' letterhead, implied that he was in a "resting area," if not a hospital. As usual, he started with assurances: "Dear Daddy, I hope that you and Mummy are well and have been getting my letters, and of course realize that Iwo Jima is a thing of the past for us now." He went on to describe recent skirmishes with Japanese who had come out of hiding to try to steal their water and K rations, but nothing serious. His main complaint was with what he considered media mongering by the Twenty-eighth Battalion, which was photographed planting the American flag on Mount Suribachi, although his battalion, the Twenty-sixth, had fought with them to gain that ground. "Our battalion took the last pocket of resistance on the island—a fact which will probably not be recognized afterwards by anyone but us, as the 28th Marines, the Suribachi outfit, had a company right behind us (which was supposed to be on our flank) which rushed up as soon as we had taken the last hill and planted the flag on it in the name of the 28th Marines right in the middle of our leading companies—It seems they had a lot of cameramen along and after Suribachi, wanted to leave no doubts as to who were the champion flag-raisers on the island. So, if you see the 28th again, you will know the true story."

He did not admit, even then, that he was wounded but wrote about the strange, hollowed-out feeling of returning to life after Iwo: "Now that it is all over, it will seem strange to go back to the old routines—wearing uniforms, holding inspections, calling captains and majors 'Sir' or 'Captain'— all the things so utterly foreign to what goes on in action." He added that it would take him some time before he could see a Japanese person in civilian clothes and not instinctively grab for a rifle. He wondered if he would ever be able to smoke a cigarette without cupping his hands around the tip to hide the glow at night. Some of his comrades were exhibiting classic effects of shell shock: "It is probably lucky that none of us goes to civilization too soon after these operations. Everyone would think us crazy. I know only last night somebody sleeping next to me in a nice safe bed with sheets woke up screaming bloody murder and woke everyone up." The marine had apparently been dreaming that a

Japanese had jumped into his foxhole. He could not stop screaming for a long time. This was all my father said about life in the camp, except to repeat his strange disbelief that he had come out alive.

Looking back on it curiously though, I know all of us still here can only reflect that we will never again have the right to complain, no matter what befalls us in the future. We are lucky, that is all, and it is hard to understand why luck runs as it does.

I hope you have good reports from Talavera. I know we can look forward to a good year to make up for the "hail luck" of last. We are due for one. Hope the Mexico business goes O.K. Anxious for news of Nick. My love to Mummy as always.

Your devoted son, VN jr.

216

For the first time upon my reading the letters, it hit me with some force that I was reading about my own father. I knew those words. I had heard them myself, or something similar, because when I tried to ask my father about the war, all he would ever say was something mumbled about how he never understood how he had come out alive. "I just came back and the others didn't. That's the thing, the only important thing." Not talking about his wound had become a habit, so that even when his children asked about his being shot, he would wave his hand dismissively and say, "What I got was nothing. There were lots of soldiers braver than me." Talking about Iwo at all seemed to make him angry, and he refused to associate with anything to do with World War II veterans. At one point he had written his uncle Hoffman that he intended to save his helmet with the four bullet holes in it as a souvenir of Iwo. But he had either changed his mind or disposed of the helmet when he returned. For him, that time was over, and he didn't want to think about it, especially not in terms that made it seem heroic. But he hadn't left the war behind, not really. Like thousands of men who came back from World War II to found the blue dream of the American suburbs, he was haunted by it. For the first time, holding his thin letter, tender as a new leaf between my hands, I felt I understood something new about my father. The sadness that could creep up on him at odd moments was a form of survivor's guilt. He had survived Iwo Jima.

On Easter Friday, my father attended services (later his parents received a letter from the marine chaplain to say that their son had attended Good Friday service) and wrote to his mother. He thanked her for sending him a compass, a camp stove and heat tablets, apparently things he had requested, and described in detail how good the meals were on Iwo, which he called the Rock. "Always when things were not too active, the front lines would get hot coffee twice a day, often with doughnuts and white bread, so all in all the living conditions were not what I expected."

He asked about Talavera and the place and responded that he had not been able to check on the status of a friend's son in the Twenty-eighth Battalion because censorship did not allow them to mention casualties. "If he were wounded, I wouldn't be able to say." As usual, one of his main concerns was the status of his younger brother, who by this point was working hard to try to get V-12 status and enter officers' training: "I am particularly anxious to hear about Nick. I do hope he has gotten the best that luck and opportunity could afford, over and above his own earnest efforts."

Again, his letter was written on Red Cross stationery, implying that even as late as April, he was in a resting area, but neither my grandmother nor my grandfather queried him about his location or condition. Only my great-aunt Lee, clearly suspecting something, tried to get him to reveal his situation. On April 8, she wrote innocently: "It was wonderful to get your letters of March 28 and 29 and know that you had actually left Iwo. . . . I can understand your not wanting to write much about details of your experience on that '7 miles of hell' as the correspondents put it, but I would like to know what you did about sleep! It seems you would have to catch a few winks to keep up the fight . . ." She sent him news of Talavera and how they were all on the usual spring tenterhooks because of the coming bloom: "This week we had a cold snap again for two days and the question of damage to the fruit trees is acute."

In her next letter, along with sending him the great news that Nick had made the V-12 and the sad news of President Roosevelt's sudden death, she raised the question of his status: "Where ever you are in your 'rest area.' It is wonderful to know you are enjoying the luxury of sleep and cleanliness and rest. And yesterday came the news from your mother that Nick has made V-12. It brought some cheer into the terrible gloom in which we have been since the news of the President's death stunned us Thursday evening."

Only gradually did she disclose how worried they had all been, how they had spent the first terrible days before his first V-mail arrived listening to the radio every hour. In her next letter, her usual description of the land and the trees at Talavera soared with relief: "It is like the spring when you were born and the apple blossoms and lilacs were in bloom. Your father actually picked some apple blossoms and took them to your mother in the hospital. She was more impressed than she would have been by jewels."

She included a letter from a cousin, Bill Whitney, stationed in France. But as she ended, she admitted that they had all been trying to figure out where he was by the speed at which his letters were reaching them. They were reaching Talavera in two days, as fast as when he had been stationed in California. She closed: "PS I can't figure out at all where you are. Can you mention any clues?"

My father was probably not allowed to mention his location at this point, and he stubbornly and poignantly refused to reveal that he had been wounded. He would rather write about the latest news of Talavera. At times, reading his looping hand, I thought of his great-uncle Lieutenant John Van Ness, who, while chasing confederate ships off Mobile, was constantly thinking about Talavera and worried about affairs on the farm. In between brief descriptions of ship life, my father spoke to his father about the labor shortage caused by the war, about the falling price of apples, about the frost and early bloom. Even then his faith in the land was complete. "In the meantime though, I don't see how we can help but have better luck next season than we did last."

Miles from any tree, still at sea in the Pacific, my father clearly cheered himself up by thinking of spring in the orchards, even mud season. "All goes well, and I am looking forward to the next mail which should not be too long from now, to hear about the latest word from Nick and your and Mummy's spring plans. I imagine now that the country is thawing so that you or Mummy or Nick have been able to get the Chevrolet out in the orchards."

Only a week before his birthday, as April came to a close, did my father reflect upon what he had been through. For the first time, he alluded to his own father's war experience in the trenches of World War I:

219

It was fine to hear about the place looking well and Danny in fine form. I trust that there is no frost damage. It is grand to return here, but the associations only make us think more keenly of those who will not see it. I know you can appreciate this from experience. . . .

Our own Colonel was killed, also our operations officer, and the Sargent major, and the executive officer evacuated—all within 48 hours of the landing of the battalion. . . .

But it is over now and I hope there will never be any more Iwos for anybody.

On August 6 an atomic bomb decimated Hiroshima. Three days later another bomb destroyed Nagasaki. Within twenty-four hours the Japanese surrendered. VJ-Day.

On April 22, 1946, my father was released from active service. Three weeks later he received what was probably a form letter of official thanks from General A. A. Vandegrift, the commanding general of the Marine Corps.

My dear Lieutenant Philip,
Your readjustment to the life of a civilian has, I hope, been fully accomplished, and with as little difficulty as you experienced in adapting yourself to military life when you came on in active duty.

No one is more familiar than I with the essential role which you of the Reserve assumed in the war. Together we accomplished our missions, however difficult they may have been. Together we developed the Marine Corps into the finest of all fighting forces. It could not have been done without you. Your patriotism and your fine devotion to duty have been an inspiration to the Officers and men who shared the responsibilities for final and complete victory.

... We always think of you as one of our own.

Please accept my personal and official thanks and my best wishes for your continued success.
Sincerely yours,
A. A. Vandergrift
General, USMC
Commandant of the Marine Corps

By the time my father arrived back at Talavera, the apples had bloomed and a fine crop of button-sized fruit could be seen throughout the trees. My father folded his wool jacket and pants, and one of his better khaki shirts and placed them carefully in his wooden U.S. Marines trunk along with his hat, his medals and various papers. His Purple Heart medal and Purple Heart ribbon for wounds received at Iwo Jima had been tucked into a separate envelope. He wrapped the entire package in newspaper. Before he closed the trunk, he threw in his dog tags and another mysterious pair, not his own. Then he closed the lid and dragged the trunk up into the barn loft. He did not place it with the other trunks of family things, however: the Civil War correspondence of his great-uncle and grandfather or the boxes of books on Christian readings collected by his grandmother and great-grandmother. Instead, he pulled the trunk across the aisle to a corner under the eaves where it sat, collecting mice droppings and bat guano, for the next fifty-three years.

That fall my father entered Harvard Business School, where he completed a master's in business. When he returned, he went to work as the editor of the *Princeton Herald*. There he met a vivacious young reporter with glossy dark, almost black hair and a wide smile. As with all the young women he met then, she dressed like a movie star, the most notable influence being Joan Crawford. Even her hair, cut so that it swept the shoulders, was gently waved and parted to one side Crawford style. She wore the latest fashions, tight-waisted dresses with padded shoulders, strangely reminiscent of military wear. Her slender legs touched the floor in high-heeled pumps. She smoked. Now that the wartime shortage was over, she wore silk stockings all the time. She loved a good time. In fact, she had been living on something of the wild side, cohabiting a brownstone in New York City with several other women and men. They joked that their establishment was a commune. No, the young woman my father fell in love with was definitely not a rich debutante, although she had gone to Vassar.

She was the daughter of a Princeton professor. Both her parents were from Virginia and had soft Culpepper accents and a strict Baptist view of the world. But my parents negotiated these differences. They were in love. With my mother's natural appetite for risk and my father's love of tradition, they balanced each other like yin and yang, light and dark. In Cary Grant fashion, my father's tall, broad shoulders filled his well-tailored jackets. He sported a fedora ever so slightly tilted at the brim. In my mother's closet were emerald evening gowns, a color that made her eyes flash. On what was then a wild open beach in Jacksonville, Florida, my father proposed. In 1952, they married and joined the rest of the country in trying to forget the war.

By 1957 two of my older brothers had been born, and a third baby was on the way. My father had risen in his chosen career of business journalism to become the managing editor of a magazine titled *Industrial Distribution,* published by McGraw-Hill. His younger brother had also done well as an agricultural engineer working for a large international firm. Together the two brothers pooled resources and bought a brownstone on East Eighty-fourth Street in Manhattan. My family took the downstairs apartment with its backyard, and my uncle and his family the slightly larger upstairs apartment with its grander front entrance. Both families were happy with the arrangement. By the time my sister and I were born, joining our three older brothers, we had three cousins living upstairs and kids all up and down the block to play with. My parents rarely locked our door. If we came home from school and didn't feel like playing at home, we walked into someone else's house. Everybody's mom was always home.

Every Friday without fail we drove to Talavera, where my father and at that point his younger brother Nick were running the farm. My grandmother lived at Talavera and managed the house. The orchards planted by my grandfather now produced twenty thousand bushels of apples and pears. Both brothers were clearly knowledgeable about the orchard business, for when one of them had to be away, the other kept him up-to-date with detailed information about sprays, blossom counts, pollination, picking and shipping schedules and many other details of ongoing farm work. It was the heyday of postwar technology and a typical curculio spray was four parts lead arsenate, three parts Ferbam and four parts DDT, chemicals that would not be banned until the 1960s. Willard Swartz, my grandfather's valet, then the general handyman at Talavera, had retired, but his nephew, a young man named Mike, had begun doing some work on the place.

In addition, my father and uncle had hired a headman named Adam Keeler, who oversaw and did much of the orchard work, bringing in extra workers to help with big seasonal jobs like winter pruning. During the harvest a crew from Jamaica, led by a crew leader named Reginald Small, drove up from Florida in a blue school bus to pick and pack out the crop.

As early as 1957, however, a pattern began to emerge whereby my father was at Talavera overseeing work and my uncle was traveling. When a sudden freeze threatened the crop, it was my father that my grandmother wired at his editorial office at McGraw-Hill: ALL APPLES SAFE IN BARN BEFORE LAST NIGHTS FREEZE. Most of the letters that I found were written by my father to his brother. On February 17, 1959, my father wrote to my uncle, away on business in Chicago: "Dear Nick, I spent yesterday with Adam—pruning about half way through no. 7, or more, and Adam wants to finish it before pushing brush. We have spent nearly $1,000 on the work for 1957 following harvest—but if he gets other work done economically we had best go ahead with it I think." The farm seemed to be paying its bills and supporting the house, but only barely, for my father went on to discuss their decision to buy a new sprayer and ways they could finance it temporarily by using personal capital. "Delicious are sold but only half paid for. Macs selling very slowly. We are shipping some this week. . . . Please let me know about gas papers, expense account and the literature on the sprayer. Yours, VN"

By 1963 letters from my father to his brother about farm activities were being sent to Kuala Lumpur, where my uncle was working. We no longer trooped upstairs to play with our cousins because they were living in Malaysia. My uncle had an active interest in affairs at Talavera, and my father wrote him regularly and received detailed letters in reply, but my father had assumed de facto responsibility for the farm and increasingly for management of their shared brownstone in

Manhattan. My uncle had tenants who lived in his half of the house while he was away, and my father served as land-lord.

My father did not complain about his increasing workload of their shared property, nor did he seem to consider how work spent maintaining Talavera was time he did not have to build his career. Within a year he had convinced his brother to purchase the farm just south of Talavera, a 150-acre fruit orchard that they call the South Place. They closed the deal in December. My father was thrilled with the decision, fig-uring that their total bushel capacity had just been expanded to close to fifty thousand. They would still produce some of the old favorites like Baldwin and Northern Spy, but most of the production would be in the popular new breeds: Royal Red Delicious, Rogers McIntosh and the newly developed Ida Red, a cross between a McIntosh and a Rome. They would also market young pears and plums.

But it was much more than the commercial opportunity that excited my father about this purchase. Our farm now stretched for almost a mile south along Route 9H, the Old Post Road, toward Claverack—all original Van Ness lands. The north and south sections of the first Van Ness farm, founded in 1732, had been reunited. The original Van Ness house had been sold to new owners, but the land and the original barns were back. My father clearly felt he had ac-complished something important by restoring the farm to its original size, for in his papers I found a press release typed by him which began "Historic Farm Reunited" then briefly outlined the farm's eighteenth-century founding and more recent past.

My uncle also seemed to have been excited by the pur-chase, although that summer hail thrashed through the or-chards, scarring the fruit so that the best price my father could get was eighty cents a box for hail-hit Macs, but that seemed good to them at the time. Not enough profit to ser-vice the large mortgage that they had taken to purchase the south farm, but even so, their excitement over the new land persisted. The following fall my uncle sent my father a detailed letter outlining improvements he thought they should make to the land on South Place. These included the plowing, debrushing and seeding of meadows and the bringing in of new water by enlarging the existing pond and digging out some swampy aquifers. Before they could start on these improvements, however, they faced another bad hailstorm, which again ravaged the crop.

By the fall of 1966 my parents had begun a new marketing strategy which they believed would help solve the farm's financial problems. It was called Pick Your Own. Instead of paying a crew to pick and pack the fruit, then paying a distributor to store and ship it, my parents planned on having people come to the orchard to buy the fruit directly. If all went as planned, they would triple their profits and cut out the high costs of middlemen entirely. My uncle endorsed the idea, calling it their bright hope. But since they had had two bad years in a row of losses from summer hail, he thought they should not concentrate all their land investment in fruit. His suggestion was that they begin plantings of oaks and maples along the road frontage and think about selling sections of the land, at least the more valuable road frontage property.

225

Here I begin to read a division of thought that grew over time, eventually dividing the two brothers. For my father, Talavera and now the older Van Ness lands of the South Place were not just home, but the family homestead, their place in the world, their identity. He didn't seem to mind doing the maintenance work of upkeeping while his younger brother was off making his fortune in the larger world, because he was the older son, and keeping Talavera together was his duty, just as it had been his father's before him. He couldn't think of the land as an asset because for him it wasn't. Since it could never be sold, it had all value and no value at the same time. He believed in farming because he believed that the land would never let them down. It was his great strength and his Achilles' heel. They had just righted an ancient wrong—the sale of the south section of the farm by cousins at the turn of the century—and he couldn't embrace thinking of the land in terms of development. But far away, involved in large-scale international development projects, my uncle could.

By 1969 my father and his brother had sold most of the road frontage property, but they still needed cash to finance improvements on the land. They decided to sell the old Van Ness barns and fifty acres of land around them. Within weeks of their being put on the market, four doctors from New York City bought the old barns to make a weekend retreat. I remembered that year as an especially exciting time because my cousins had returned from Malaysia and the family was together again. Talavera was in constant commotion. Every day Betty was on the verge of quitting and my father or my uncle, both of them charming and handsome, would convince her to give it one more day. When Mrs. Patzwahl, the local woman who did errands for my grandmother during the week, drove up in her baby blue Impala, we were ushered out of the house. Miraculously, the house was cleaned, and fresh flowers filled the vases in the dining room, the library, the parlor, the south hall. When I look at pictures of that time, I see that the house was even then in need of repair. But I never noticed the worn rugs or the fading wallpaper. The mysterious rhythms of the house, rhythms that had to do with caring for my grandmother and caring for such an old and large house, were strange but comforting.

I didn't know any of the land's long history then. But I must have overheard something or at any rate felt my father's enthusiasm because I vividly remember the day the four doctors arrived at Talavera to visit. They had already agreed upon the land deal. As one of the four doctors later recounted, "We met at the Princeton Club in New York. I'll never forget it. Your father and your uncle came. They were both wearing tweed jackets. We had a concern because in the deed they specifically stipulated that we could not develop the land for any commercial use but there was no such constraint on their land. Our lawyer had told us to have this changed. But when we mentioned this concern to your father and uncle, they looked at us sort of shocked. 'This land has been in our family for over two hundred years,' they said; 'it will never be developed.'" Apparently the four doctors were satisfied, because by the end of the conversation they had agreed upon the price and the terms. The old Van Ness barns became the 4 Docs Place.

The day the doctors arrived was a rainy day and cold. I remember this because I had gone out riding anyway, and now I was back inside, deliciously warm. Lunch was creamed chicken over rice. For some reason we all had been sitting in the parlor, plates on our laps, eating, when the doctors arrived. I remember the warm room, the hot food, a fire in the grate, my brothers and sisters, maybe my cousins too all around and the rain pouring down outside. Above the black marble mantelpiece in the parlor hung a large portrait of William of Orange dressed in slate-colored armor, a long white wig curling down from the top of his head to the bottom of his breastplate. For years I assumed he was some sort of ancestor, like the other portraits that lined the house. Especially as the long Dutch sword that rested on the baby grand piano on the other side of the room was just like the one in the portrait. Until they were told that having a portrait of William of Orange was an eighteenth-century Dutch fashion, most visitors to the house thought so as well.

I remember the doctors stopping and staring at the portrait, peering out in some kind of disbelief. I don't know that what they felt was awe. Perhaps they were simply perplexed. Here were people living in a suspended state of history, caught like ants in amber. Maybe it was comical even to see us all there acting like gentry while we ate creamed chicken on plates seated cross-legged on the floor, on our already worn rugs.

I didn't care about my ancestors or William of Orange. The portraits looking down on us were simply extensions of the house, of my parents, of everything I took for granted. I was busy eating my lunch, trying to figure out if I could get away with saddle soaping my tack there in the warm parlor after everyone had gone.

But something made me look up, and when I did, I saw the doctors there, hands in their pockets, heads upturned. Their voices were hushed, almost as if they were in a museum, and perhaps it was that which made me take note. I remember looking at them while they looked at us and feeling for the first time a sense that we were different from other people and that somehow that difference, which had to do with the old portraits and the way people stared at them when they came into the house and sighed when they looked up at the white columns outside, had to do with the past, a past that made us special. I knew as well that to talk about this would have made my father frown. Talking about yourself was rude, and anyway, you didn't have to. Talavera spoke for us all.

The sale of the barns didn't seem to bother my father. The land was what mattered, and now he and my uncle were running almost two hundred acres of it in fruit. By 1969 Pick Your Own had proved such a success that within a few years the entire crop was sold directly to customers who came to pick. In his own career my father made a bold move, leaving the steady paycheck of McGraw-Hill to found a specialized business newsletter titled *Modern Distribution Management,* which he published biweekly. From now on, when I walked home from school, my mother was away at a job and my father was the one at home, writing in his office.

A year later something wonderful happened. The heirs of the man who had lent my grandfather four thousand dollars in 1914, a loan that had never been repaid, called my father to say that their family wanted to give my father the portrait of General John P. Van Ness.

That July 4 my father and mother drove down to the river estate where the painting had been hanging for more than fifty years, wrapped it gently in a blanket, placed it in the backseat of our old VW sedan and drove the general home.

Once the portrait had been returned to the dining room at Talavera, the room seemed to glow. Even when oil prices soared and the recession hit, causing apple prices to crash and small farms to falter all across the nation, my father did not waver in his belief that the land and the family would make it through.

But in 1973, when my grandmother died, a cavern opened. My father and uncle disagreed on the future of Talavera. My father envisioned a land trust, keeping Talavera together and preserving the land for the next generation—my brothers and sister, my three cousins, me. My uncle wanted to divide the estate. My father was clearly not prepared for this. All the years of caring for Talavera while his brother was away had set a dangerous precedent. He must have assumed that, as had been the case in previous generations, he and his brother would work together to keep Talavera intact or that if one stepped out, he would do so in a way that did not threaten Talavera's continuity. Even Aunt Bessie's histrionic sale of 1912 had been done with the full knowledge not only that her brothers could afford to buy all the family possessions she put up for sale but also that they would. It seemed likely that she and Gaston had felt they got the better deal when they unloaded any responsibility toward Talavera for a dollar.

But this moment of generational transfer had no precedent. My father and his brother went back and forth about possible lines of division. My father wanted Talavera, and my uncle wanted the brownstone in Manhattan, already a valuable income-producing property, although nothing like the multimillion-dollar real estate holding that it would become. The division should have been easy, but it wasn't. They couldn't agree on how much land should go with each house. Finally, my father proposed that they make two equal parcels and flip a coin to see who got which one. He figured that way they would both work toward a division that was fair. But then my uncle told my father that if he got Talavera on the flip, he would sell it. My uncle must have known the effect that his words would have on my father. His words were like lightning. From that point on, my father agreed to almost everything my uncle and his wife wanted in order to be the one who inherited Talavera.

My father could not imagine what had come over his younger brother. But my uncle was already unwell by that time and perhaps even then knew that he had cancer. He was driving such a hard bargain that by the time my father took over ownership of Talavera, our family resources had been so diminished that years of hardship followed as my father and mother doggedly set out to preserve the family place.

My father was the third generation of men named John Van Ness Philip to leave a career in the larger world to return to Talavera. But while Lieutenant John Van Ness had come home to follow the moral agenda of nineteenth-century scientific agriculture, expanding the farm and the estate, a process that fifty years later, my grandfather echoed when he too retired from a rising career to return to Talavera, my father was heading back on different terms. He left New York City and moved his publishing business to Talavera, not to seek his fortune in agriculture but to preserve the farm from disappearing altogether. Yet from that point on, he followed the family tradition of men named John Van Ness by concentrating more and more of his time, effort and energy into restoring the farm.

Soon my family was packing up and moving out of our house on East Eighty-fourth Street in Manhattan. Rugs and furniture, silver and portraits were being carried out of Talavera. Then my uncle died. For my father, it had been loss after loss, and it was not over yet. Soon after my uncle's death, his widow sold their share of the family land to a developer. The bulk of the original Van Ness farm, which my father had tried to preserve twelve years earlier, became Orchard Estates, a 1.5-acre sudivision of prefabricated houses. It felt like the end of the farm, the end of the family.

But the following spring the land woke up as it usually does and sloughed off winter. The apple trees burst into bloom. Another season began. And it wasn't the end of the farm after all. In some ways, for my own family, it was a new beginning. My father replanted the orchards with a hardy semidwarf rootstock to try to make the farm, now half its size, profitable again. The era of Paris fashions and gants de suede was long gone. That summer one of my older brothers woke at 5:00 A.M. to drive the spray rig through the orchards. My sister and I weeded and watered baby trees. We headed off to boarding schools to finish high school and, on vacations home, pruned and pulled brush and helped plant more young orchards. Within the next five years, my brothers, my sister and I were at various stages of entering or finishing college. With my father concentrating so much of his time on the farm, income from his newsletter declined. Even with my mother's job, they didn't have enough money to pay for Princeton, Columbia, Vassar and Smith, the colleges we all attended. We got scholarships, held down jobs and took semesters off to work, then went back to finish. This had become our life now. Good harvests and bad. On my eighteenth birthday, we celebrated in the April wind by planting an orchard of Japanese Mutsu trees, a new variety that my parents thought would sell. When thunderstorms shook the French wallpaper loose in the dining room, my father, getting stiffer now, climbed the rickety wooden ladder and hammered it back on.

Talavera was not sold. The apple trees produced, and the farm survived. But there was a price. Like his father before him, my father spent too much time alone at Talavera. My mother was there on weekends, but we needed the income from her job, so she continued her office job in Manhattan, boarding Amtrak for Hudson every Friday. In the evenings, before catching the news, my father liked to sit for a while in the dining room, facing the portrait of General John P. Van Ness. Even when it was cold, he sat there, hunched in his tweed jacket, taking some sort of strange comfort in the portrait before him.

I didn't like his sitting there. I could tell by the way one of his large hands was fumbling with the dog's soft retriever ears, and the other was wrapped around a drink, that he was thinking too much about the past, brooding, sitting alone, as *his* father had done, following that other family tradition, of stiff evening drinks.

It was terrifying to watch the father I loved become someone else when he was drunk. But in some ways it only made me love him more. What I hated was the sadness that, loosened by the alcohol, would slide over him, so that his talk became sentimental and maudlin. "You know, I love you all so much. . . . You do know that, don't you?" All the things he felt and couldn't say rose up to the surface. Just as bad was his guilt the next day, a force that made him leap out of bed in the morning so that long before anyone else in the house, he was already bent over his desk, writing as if he had gone to bed at nine instead of at two.

For years I connected his drinking to the portraits. I didn't know any of Talavera's past then, but I could feel it all around me, and it felt like a prison sentence. I was jealous then of Talavera, which, like some aged and imperious diva, furiously past her prime, demanded so much of my father, so much of us all. Because I had no real knowledge yet of the long past that my father saw himself part of, I didn't understand how so much of that past was a history of military service and land—the sword and the plowshare—and that for a long time, drinking had served to mediate the inevitable conflict between the two. Or, even more confusing, how for my father, the lean, aristocratic face of General John P. Van Ness, like the stern visage of Catherine Douw, could be like the evening light, streaming in through the soft gauze of the long curtains, offering him solace.

Strangely, this direct hot wire that my father had to Talavera and the family's past there seemed to make him modest rather than proud. It was as if like people who work outdoors or who live in direct contact with the wilderness, living with all that history, he was forced to realize his own insignificance on a daily basis. As a teenager I had begun to feel Talavera's influence too, only I fought it. So much history flowed in and out of the house, swirled across the land, that the balance could become swayed, so instead of just keeping you from becoming conceited, it made you feel irrelevant. It took me years to be able to stand between Talavera's columns and not feel that the past was something grander, better, more important than the present. Sometimes I even wondered if sitting there alone, my father wasn't stumped by the past too. But for a while anyway, the face of his great-uncle there on Talavera's wall seemed to offer him moments of peace and resolution.

But unlike a mountain or a river, a house, even one that has lasted so many generations, is a risky place to find solace. Within two years, my uncle's widow, who by then owned the Ammi Phillips portraits of my father's great-grandparents Colonel Henry G. Philip and his wife, Catherine Douw, sued for half ownership of the Gilbert Stuart portrait of General John P. Van Ness. When I asked my mother about the event, for I knew enough never to try to discuss it with my father, she said that they had hardly taken the suit seriously, assuming that they would win. They had a letter written by the heir of the man who had wanted to give the portrait to my father, stating her father's intent, and since the loan had never been repaid after so many years, they had assumed that their family owned the portrait and could give it to whomever they wished.

Even without that letter, my father could not believe that there would be any question that the portrait belonged to him. General John P. Van Ness, his great-uncle, was one of his namesakes. That the portrait was intended for him was as natural as the fact that because his brother's middle name was Worthington, he had been given their grandfather's pocket watch. Initially, my uncle had wanted the portrait to be included in the things they divided, but just before he died, he had written that he had changed his mind and considered the portrait my father's.

My parents did not think to use my uncle's letter of understanding in court. They hired a local lawyer who offered them cheap rates. My father refused to do more than make sure that when the day came, he remembered to show up. This was his mistake. The prosecution came well prepared, arguing on the basis of New York State debtor-pledger laws that the subjective intent of the donor was irrelevant. Rather, they argued, the donor held only possessory interest in the portrait and thus had had no right to give it in the first place. It didn't matter that he had had the portrait for more than fifty years and that the loan had never been repaid. The court now considered the portrait part of my grandfather's unsettled estate.

Friends and relatives urged my father to appeal, but he wouldn't. Going to court over a family matter had been shameful in the first place. He wanted it to end. The portrait was put on the market and bought by a well-known collector who hung it in his Hudson River estate. My father was relieved that General John P. Van Ness would remain in the Hudson Valley, but he never went to see the portrait in its new home.

234

My mother moved the portrait of lovely Eliza Worthington, my father's grandmother, into the empty space between the windows. She found a decorator who specialized in period restoration and showed her the many layers of hand-blocked French wallpaper in the room. In exchange for copyright use of the original 1812 patterns, the decorator had the pattern reproduced and gave my mother enough wallpaper to redo the dining room and the parlor. My mother had the bright new paper put on the walls. My father went back to sitting in the library.

🙟🙠

When I began my search through Talavera for papers and letters that might open up the family's past, my father's wooden army trunk was one of the first things that I found. The day I located it was hot and muggy, and I was ready to quit my prowling through the dust-ridden dark when the green trunk caught my eye. Glimmers of light were streaming over it from the small dovecote holes under the eaves. I could just make out the letters printed neatly on the side:

"J. Van Ness Philip jr. Lt. US Marines." Of course I made my way toward it, pushing through the piles of broken metal garden furniture.

I opened the box slowly, curiously afraid. When I pulled back the dusty layers of newspaper, I saw my father's wool uniform, the manila envelope with his Purple Heart medal and ribbon, then a small brown book in which he had listed the shoe and uniform sizes of all his men, then a pocket-size army primer on conversational Japanese and a folder of discharge papers. As I lifted these things, his dog tags clinked against the bottom of the trunk, and right then I decided to close the trunk. I didn't want to know any more. I was overcome with a desire to repack the trunk, to leave the barn, to let my father's war years lie, to be done with my quest for the past. That was when I heard the second clink. Dog tags. But not my father's. I picked up the silver tags and fingered them, reading the name embossed in the thin steel: Robert Calvin Smith. I could feel my throat go dry. Who was this person? It was as if I had discovered the secret clue, the final piece that pulled the story together, something, but I didn't know what, that explained everything. I was as shocked as if I had just discovered that my father had had a secret lover, this marine, Robert Calvin Smith, whom he had never mentioned, but whose tags he had carefully packed away in his trunk.

When I asked World War II veterans about the mysterious dog tags, ex-marines answered that they were probably the tags of a buddy, the man with whom my father had shared the war until that man had been killed. When they heard that my father had been at Iwo Jima, they speculated that Robert Calvin Smith had been killed there. My father would have been twenty-two, his short hair bristling, sweat pouring down his sides, waiting for the order to leap ashore.

In late August, when my father was hospitalized for the last time, we had a brief, urgent talk about the farm. I arrived at the hospital just in time. My father was storming down the corridor, his IV clanking behind him. He had his boots on and was looking for someone to check him out.

"Where are all the damn nurses," my father exploded when he saw me. "I'm getting out of this hospital, and I mean now."

It took me some time to convince my father to let me page his doctor. We went back to his room and my father agreed to get back in bed and rest for a moment while we waited for his doctor to arrive. I had brought my father a box of sugarless chocolates and I opened it and offered him one. I sat on the edge of his bed, and we ate chocolates and waited. My father was in a single with a large window on one side, but still the bitter smell of hospital disinfectant filled the room. We talked about how the crop was looking, then my father interjected.

"One of you needs to get involved in the farm."

I nodded slowly, stiff with apprehension. My father continued.

"You could make a go of it because you would not assume that you know anything. You'd research it and learn about it just like you were writing an article." My father stopped to take a breath. "Fruit growing is all new ideas now, it's changing fast. You all have to realize that. What we did made sense, but that was then. The farm has to make money, otherwise you might as well forget it."

"Dad, I know, but . . ." I stopped, then took a breath and blurted out a rush of words, "Dad, I'd love to run the farm, you know that, but I want to write. I don't know if I can do both. You of all people know how hard it is."

My father didn't say anything. He nodded.

"Let me think about it, I mean, let me try to learn about it this year. If I could spend a year learning about what is involved, I don't know, maybe I could make it work."

"Okay."

I continued to sit on the edge of the bed, stunned. My father had never spoken so directly to me before. Perhaps he had talked to my brothers and my sister this way, provoking us to decide upon our commitments, but at that moment I

236

didn't think so. What I thought about was all the time I had spent helping my father on the farm as a young girl, as a teenager, as a young woman. I thought about standing in the freezing winter wind, trying to learn how to prune apple trees. I knew then that it had been my first apprenticeship.

I closed the lid on the box of chocolates and looked at my father. He had shut his eyes and was leaning back on the stiff white pillow. His doctor walked in and began to speak. The doctor's words were swift, focused on one point. My father was going to die unless he could get more oxygen into his lungs. They didn't have any other treatments to try at the hospital, so my father could go home if he wanted, but he was going to have to accept almost complete rest. No more driving through the orchards in the pickup. If he would spend one more night so that they could check the oxygen level of his blood in the morning, they would release him.

My father listened quietly and accepted the doctor's terms. When it was time for me to go, he watched me leave in a mood that seemed content.

I went home and wept. I cried for a long time, for him, for myself. I knew then that my father was going to die. In that stammered response to my father I had uttered something I had always known but never said out loud. I had inherited his dream of holding on to Talavera. Like many people, I realized only with the death of a parent that I had been running from a childhood that I did not understand and had ignored. Instead, I had traveled, farther and farther west, until as Thoreau would say, I had finally arrived back where I started, in the east, my home.

First the study of ceramics, then work had taken me to Japan. But maybe it ran in the family, for like Aunt Bessie, I had loved my expatriate life there, had reveled in the sudden expansion of everything unknown. Also like Aunt Bessie, at every opportunity I had traveled: through Japan and China, Korea, then later south to Thailand and Malaysia, Indonesia, Bali, Singapore. When I looked back, I could see that all over

Asia I was fascinated by the things that reminded me of home. Asia in the twentieth century was synonymous with traditions trying to persevere, to adapt or simply not to be wiped out in the crush of everything new.

In Bali, I had met a prince swatting flies in the swirls of red dust left by a roaring bus. His gaze from his aluminum lawn chair had been regal, even despotic. If he was ashamed that his family's once-resplendent palace, half of it in ruins, was now an overnight stop for tourists, he did not show any signs of this. His dark eyes, the gaze that looked right through and beyond the scraggly tourists who came stumbling off the bus, knew who they were by what his family had been. He was a prince whom, in all his absurdity, I could not mock. He was too familiar.

The summer that my father's lungs gave out, I was working in Japan. In July I had traveled to a mountain in the far north named Osorezan. The Japanese believe that when you die, your spirit travels to this mountain. For forty-nine days your spirit wanders there, or longer if it becomes waylaid because of your misconduct in life. Osorezan is a topography of hells, each one a brightly colored mineral pool bubbling with hot spring water. Only after successfully passing through the mineral blue hell of avarice, the sulfur yellow hell of drinking, the orange hell of adultery and, the biggest hell of all, the blood-red hell of murder does the soul reach the shores of heavenly paradise, a large lake on the far side.

I watched pilgrims wandering through the mist, slowly navigating the paths of black volcanic sand. Contemporary pilgrims picked up maps at the entrance so that they could leave incense, food, liquor, water and sandals at the particular hells where they believed their loved ones might have become waylaid. Kneeling by the bubbling sulfur springs, they placed their offerings on the sand and prayed. Crows circled and cawed, waiting for the pilgrims to leave so that they could dive-bomb and pillage whatever food had been placed there.

I had come to Osorezan to watch the blind shaman

women who were allowed to set up booths outside the walls of the Buddhist temple there for four days each July. As part of their pilgrimages to Osorezan many visitors engaged shamans to contact the dead, tell their fortunes or give them advice about the advisability of various plans. A Japanese anthropologist had come with me to translate the shaman's rough Tohoku dialect into Japanese that I could understand, and I engaged a shaman, asking her if she could tell me something about my future.

The old shaman chanted and shook, then rattled her wooden beads near my face and, in bursts of rough guttural dialect, began to speak. "I hear a voice calling me, it is very faint, but I can hear it calling. It is calling you, it needs you to hear it, it is calling, calling. The voice is telling me, it wants you to go home, to go home. . . ." I didn't think much about what she said. I had listened to shamans doling out what often seemed like canned versions of the same advice to the lines of pilgrims that waited for hours to enter their white tents.

As I rode the train back to Tokyo, the next day, it wasn't the shaman's words that had me thinking. While I watched the landscape flash by, the rice fields glazed with sun, the sea's gray, broken edge, I wondered if the Japanese people, through centuries of superstition mixed with Buddhist and Shinto thought, had shaped Osorezan's fantastic landscape, towering and volcanic until it was in fact a pretty great rendition of hell. Or perhaps things had worked out the other way around, and the mountain itself had been what shaped the Japanese.

It took me all day to travel by train from Osorezan back to Tokyo. By the time I arrived, a fax was waiting for me. My father had had his first mysterious collapse. When I stared at the thin transmission paper, I saw the shaman as she had looked the day before, her thick wooden beads clacking as she rocked back and forth, her unseeing eyes staring straight at me as she told me to go home.

In the Orchard

We are standing in the thick orchard grass, my mother, her dog, Danny, and I. My mother and I are hunting *Psylla pyricola,* the dreaded psylla fly. Danny is hunting mice. Despite the already hot morning sun, we are clothed in long pants and long-sleeved shirts. My mother wears a bent straw hat, and I wear a similar but more ragged version, frayed at the brim where Danny chewed the edge. Entering the orchards in June is to enter an insect kingdom. We need all the protection we can get. Even now the whirring and buzzing, clacking and colliding of wings and mandibles, so many legs and pincers, rises into a sea of sound. I listen for a minute while the insect noises build to a shrill crescendo, then just as suddenly subside. A crow's sharp rasp breaks the droning; a ground dove starts her long, gentle moan. Down by my feet, Danny scratches industriously in a patch of yellow vetch at the base of a tree.

My mother needs to know how many psylla flies are in her pears so that she can determine if and when she needs to apply a spray. Psylla is a predacious insect whose nymphs, encased in beds of sticky insect spit, called honeydew, devour pear trees. They begin by sucking the nutrients out of the leaves but then move onto the fruit. A pear where psyllas have been is not a pretty sight. Blotches of black mottle the surface, and the skin is as rough as sandpaper. Meanwhile, as they feed, the nymphs spread their honeydew, which is toxic to bud formation and thus destroys next year's crop as well. But psylla flies, which overwinter as eggs and hatch out with the first of the blossoms, are hard to kill. Even so, my mother is trying to control them with the mildest of chemical sprays. Four days ago, when she shook a limb and several adults came zooming out, she applied Mitac, a fairly weak insecticide. She hopes that it has done the trick. I have never seen a psylla fly, but my mother knows their wretched habits well. Last year over fifty bushels of pears from this block were so scarred from psylla that they had to be dumped. Nine hundred dollars of income gone.

"See anything?" my mother asks, pushing back her hat.

"Nothing that's moving," I say, and grab another branch.

"Get 'em, Danny boy," my mother says to the dog. Encouraged by her voice, he paws the ground harder. Spatters of dirt flick my calves.

"Check a terminal; they like soft new leaves," my mother says, looking across the tree. She reaches over and pulls down a young branch of sucker growth that is shooting straight up. I take the branch from her and position my magnifying lens over the young leaves at the tip, turning them so that the undersides come into view. Two weeks ago this tree was a white froth of blossom. Now the leaves are as long as my thumb, and the blossoms that survived the sudden frost in early May have swollen into perfect doll-size Bosc pears. The leaf in my hand has a reddish tinge, so new that it hasn't produced much green chlorophyll yet, the cells still full of carotene. I stare down into the magnifying lens, and my view constricts to a red-green blur. Then the leaf comes into focus. Unlike the apple leaf whose underside is woolly with fine hairs called trichomes, pear leaves are as shiny and smooth as holly. The serrate leaf that rests in my palm is full

grown with intricate yellow veins fanning out in all directions from the midrib. I start in the center of the leaf and
move outward, scanning for insects. A tiny dark spot comes
into view, and I move the lens closer. The spot sharpens. I
see a black insect with an ugly, blunt head and lacy, transparent wings.

"Got one here, I think."

"They look like tiny cicadas," my mother says, her arm
still extended, helping to hold down the branch. When I
hear her description, I know that I am staring at a psylla,
which, if left unchecked, will produce as many as eight generations in one summer.

"One, two, three, four." I begin counting off the number
of flies that I see holding on to the leaf. Then I stop, amazed
and horrified. My lens has come across a mass of orange eggs
stacked in overlapping piles as if the leaf had grown fish
scales. I lose count at fifty. Then I see a fly with what looks
like a clear orange substance emerging from the tail. It is long
and oval, already twice the size of the huge head: a female
laying her enormous brood. Instinctively I shudder.

"What do you see?" my mother asks, moving closer so
that she can look over my shoulder.

"I think it's psylla," I answer, not mentioning the egg-
laying business, "and eggs."

"Let me take a look."

I hand her the lens and let go of the branch so that she can
bring it down closer to her. She stares hard, then stops for a
moment to push her straw hat back farther so that more sun
falls on the leaf. She studies it again.

"Yes," she says suddenly, "those are psylla all right, and lots
of eggs. Dammit, the Mitac didn't work."

"How many eggs did you count?"

"Too many." My mother let the branch snap back, hands
the lens to me and starts to walk away from the tree.

She does not need to count the exact number of eggs to
learn what she needs to know. The Mitac application did not
work, and she now has a well-established infestation with at

least two generations present on the leaves. If the problem were something like thrips, my mother could consider importing enough aphids or ladybugs to control them, but psyllas are the sharks of the insect world; no one eats them. My mother can try Mitac again or go for a stronger chemical like Pyromite, which will wipe out her beneficials—the ladybugs and predacious black mites she has been trying to cultivate for the past three years. I watch my mother walk back to the truck, swinging her stiff left knee as she crosses the thick orchard grass.

My mother is eager to get going and complete the scout. She sits in the cab of the truck, one hand on the key in the ignition, waiting for my return.

"Be right there, Mom," I call, and take a last look at the leaf in my hand. The past two weeks of rain finally let up, but since then the temperatures have been in the eighties. Around me the trees seem to heave like sweating horses, their hundreds of leaves pulsing with the force of energy being released.

I keep staring at the leaf beneath my lens, trying to visualize what a botanist must see. Deep in the mesophyll layers of the leaf, the football-shaped mitochondria are thrumming with the force of molecules splitting and rearranging. $6H_2O + 6CO_2 = C_6H_{12}O_6 + 6O_2$. Photosynthesis, the mystery upon which all life depends. Here in my hand, light is being converted into chemicals that will rapidly combine to form sugars—plant food. My mind balks. How can this basic fact of life be? A botanist, intimate with the chemical transfer of energy into food, the shattering of molecules and the forming of ions, probably sees this mystery before even the leaf. In the same way a physicist might see molecules racing at two thousand miles an hour where I see a match being struck. What we see depends upon what we know. Here in the orchard what I see is how much there is to learn. Later, tucked into bed with a heavy book on plant physiology across my knees, I will read about the complex chemical reaction called plant respiration, the carbon cycle and the oxygen cycle that makes plants the link between the living and the dead, the organic and the inorganic worlds. If plants stopped breathing, all life on earth would suffocate within a matter of days.

I take another deep breath, one of the sixteen I will take each minute, one of the twenty-three thousand that I require in the course of a day. I let the leaf drop and move my mammal bulk down the row and toward my mother, all fifty trillion cells of me, including the ones that must be expiring in the heat.

"Let's check the young pears," my mother says when I slide into the truck next to her. "The psylla might not have crossed the road yet. I'm not sure where they come from. The hedgerow, I think."

We drive across the road into block nine. This hillside orchard was the first orchard that my father replanted when he and my mother took over full ownership of the farm in 1975. I remember a windy spring day, me standing up to my calves in the newly tilled dark soil, trying to keep a guide string steady while my parents sited the rows. My parents put in mostly apples: Empires and Macoun, Ida Reds, Red Delicious and a scattering of Romes on the top of the ridge. But at the very top and bottom of the orchard, they planted pears— Boscs and Bartletts and Seckels—pulling out the Clapps, which ripened too early to sell to our Pick Your Own crowds. Orchard nine was also where my mother planted trees the first spring that she began managing the farm without my father. Along the top ridge, where some open space remained, she set out two rows of Harrow Sweets and Anjous, new pear varieties that she and my father had talked about planting.

My mother parks at the far end of the young Harrow Sweets. When we shake the terminals, psylla flies tumble out. Through our lenses we find eggs, some already into the nymph stage, the leaves tacky with trails of clear goo. But what bothers me even more than the psylla are the piles of green aphids feeding on the tips of the new growth and the tree's slender leader. On some of the terminals, the tiny leaves are so studded with green bodies that the aphids pile up upon one another like nursing pigs. At fruit-growing school this past February, my mother and I had listened to Cornell pomologists lecture about the importance of a young tree's first three years. Trees were not unlike humans in that the first three years of development were key. Whatever happened during that time would be reflected throughout the tree's entire fruit-bearing life. I can't stand looking at the infant trees so burdened with intruders.

"Mom," I almost shout, "what can we do? I see psylla everywhere, and aphids."

"Nothing," my mother says bluntly. "Wait."

"Wait?"

I am thinking, *How can we wait? The trees are being devoured.* And it is as if my mother can read my thoughts because when she answers this time, her voice sounds irritated. "You can't just kill psylla. It doesn't work that way. I don't know the timing exactly, we'll have to check, but you have to wait until they hatch into nymphs."

"But what about the aphids? Mom, we have to do something."

My mother sighs. "I don't think they're such a problem. There's always somebody ready to eat an aphid. Look, there goes a ladybug now."

I look where my mother points, and indeed, several ladybugs are climbing up the stem of the young pear tree in front of us. But three ladybugs seem no match for the crowds of psylla and aphids cutting into the terminals.

"Look for ants," my mother continues soothingly. "They get the aphids too. Look, there's an ant now. Attaboy!" She points to an ant traveling quickly up the terminal and gives a short chuckle before turning back toward the truck.

I check a few more trees and see many ants and several more ladybugs, but I am still worried about the young trees. As we head down the hill, I ask my mother how she knows when aphids are a problem.

"Oh, you can tell. You'll see yellow leaves curling. The tree looks sick."

"I see," I say. But suddenly I am trying to remember the times that I had scouted the orchards with my father. Had we ever seen aphids this numerous? When we did see pests, what sprays had he chosen? All the hours that I spent with my father in the orchards, but I realize suddenly how little I really had learned about fruit growing. My family seemed to have owned the land since forever, but as for actively working on it, that was a new story. We weren't a midwestern farm family. In fact, as far as I could tell, it seemed that my father had been the first generation to make the uneasy transition from gentleman to farmer or at least, the first generation to work the land directly in many generations. Even Lieutenant John Van Ness, who had dedicated himself to running the farm, relied on the yearly income from his inheritance to fund his many farm improvements. Women in the family had always been mistresses of Talavera, keeping kitchen gardens and overseeing the sale of butter and eggs, but my mother was, I believed, the first woman to run the larger farm as well as manage Talavera. Would we learn how to run this farm in time? Even if we could, should we be trying to raise apples on this scale in the Hudson Valley?

Two weeks ago our closest neighbor to the north set out For Sale signs. His orchards were on the market as five- to twenty-five-acre lots. It wasn't just our farm that was struggling. The entire fruit growing industry in the Hudson Valley was in a state of crisis.

My mother and I walk over to look over the Bosc and Anjou whips that my mother planted this past May. Several trees have curling, blackened leaves. My mother fingers them silently, letting the dead leaves crackle between her fingers.

"Fire blight?" I ask my mother, thinking again of fruit school, where a Cornell scientist had lectured extensively on the recent emergence of this disease in the Hudson Valley. Fire blight is a systemic disease that will kill a tree in one season if left untreated. The only cure is to cut off infected areas and bathe the wounds in a copper solution. Infected wood had to be burned immediately or the disease could spread throughout the orchards.

"Could be," my mother answers glumly.

"Mom, do you mind if I call the fruit agent?"

"No. Sure, that's a good idea."

*

We drive back via the sod, a square of orchard at the top of block thirteen in which we had planted the first Mutsu apple trees one April weekend. According to the family lore, this area just beneath the hedgerow had been cleared by hand by my grandfather, after his first year at Princeton. He had apparently been bullied all year, and he spent the summer bodybuilding to make sure that it not happen again. His self-imposed Jack Armstrong routine was to spend weeks clearing the land of trees and brush. It is almost impossible for me to imagine my grandfather sweating in the hot sun, working off his frustrations by cutting trees and underbrush with ax and saw. But then, despite all that I had learned about what he had done and where he had been, he had remained a mystery.

Back when my grandfather founded the first orchards, the farm produced apples with enticing, old-fashioned names like Opalescent, Baldwin, Wealthy, Spitzenburg, Newtown Pippin, Seek No Further, Northern Spy. They were early apple breeds that had been replaced on our farm in the 1930s by more contemporary stock like McIntosh, Red Delicious and Macoun. The oldest apple tree on the farm was a seventy-year-old McIntosh that my father kept for nostalgic reasons, but also for grafts. These he sent to the nursery, where they were grafted onto vigorous, fast-growing rootstocks for re-planting as semidwarf trees. We called the old tree the Captain Mac and kept it alive, although these days it is a gnarled and bent affair.

You never knew with apples what would become fashionable again. In the late eighties my parents had begun to

247

plant small plots of "old-fashioned" apples for fun. Customers enjoyed rediscovering sentimental favorites like Greening and Northern Spy. These days you could special order gift boxes of these antique apples from catalogs like Williams-Sonoma that marketed country nostalgia. Balducci's in the Village carried "heritage" brands for twice the price of regular apples. But my mother was skeptical of increasing her antique orchards too rapidly. There were reasons why the older breeds had been replaced. Northern Spies, for example, had a tendency to bear biannually. Once the trees got into this habit, you had to put up with it, which meant a crop every other year, instead of fruit each fall. Also, trees take at least five years to mature and begin serious bearing. The enthusiasm for antique fruit could end as quickly as it had begun, leaving my mother with bushels of eccentric fruit to try to sell.

As we head down along the meadow, we pass block ten, a small grouping of Northern Spy and Greening at the edge of the meadow, one of our youngest "old-fashioned" blocks.

"Look at those trees. Dammit, something is wrong," my mother says suddenly, slowing the truck as we pass by. "Mites are in there, I just know it."

"How can you tell?" I ask, surprised by my mother's vehemence.

"Look at them. Those trees are just plain sick. They haven't been looking right, and I don't know why, I just don't know. It's not too wet there. They just never have been right. No, I'm afraid they were just too damaged by the time they arrived."

The spring that the trees arrived, a UPS strike virtually stopped deliveries for weeks. My mother's trees, boxed and ready to go from the nursery, had been stuck in transit so long that by the time she opened the boxes, new roots had sprouted from the trunk.

"Oh," I say. I had not noticed before that the trees were sick. As I drove by, they had seemed fine. One or two were crooked, but that wasn't unusual for a dwarf rootstock. Each limb was spread with new growth and a fine covering of leaves. But when I look closely, I see that none of them have much fruit growing on the limbs.

"Spies can't take much," my mother adds. "That's part of why everyone stopped growing them. And mites are bullies. They go for sick trees that can't defend themselves. That's just what bullies do."

We drive in silence around the bend and up toward the main pond. I am absorbing this new information when my mother stops the truck again, this time to peer into the woods that line the road on my side. Earlier in the spring this spot under the trees had been spotted with yellow turk's heads and the ivory tufts of wood anemones. It is also one of my mother's favorite spots for cutting the early pussy willows. When I ask what she is looking for, she answers, "My new cash crop. Ramps."

"Ramps," I say, amused. "Isn't that some kind of hillbilly food?"

"Was," answers my mother. "Now brings twenty dollars a pound, and I have lots of it."

Earlier that spring my mother had sent three hundred dollars' worth of lilacs down to New York City with a local berry grower who was making trips to the Union Square farmers' market. He had wanted more, but my mother didn't want to harvest any more blooms from the lilac walks that lined the west edge of the garden. Planted in 1857, when Lieutenant John Van Ness, inspired by Andrew Jackson Downing, had reshaped the gardens at Talavera along visions of the picturesque, the lilacs were now a cash crop. Instinctively, my mother was returning the farm to an older pattern of diversification. *Alternative agriculture, ethnic markets, direct marketing* were the new buzzwords at the yearly meetings of the Columbia County Fruitgrower's Association. That, and the one billion apples now entering the global market from China each year. The Asian markets had gone with these cheaper Chinese apples, and there were reports that Chinese Fujis were beginning to appear in London as well.

New York State had traditionally competed with Washington State for shelf space in East and West Coast supermarkets. But now the competition was global. Even with the cost of shipping fruit grown seven thousand miles away, large chain stores believed they could get a better deal with apples from China and New Zealand. Already most of the nation was drinking apple juice made from Chinese apple concentrate sold on the world market.

Our customers would be those who could afford the higher price of food grown locally with a minimal use of pesticides. My father had predicted that the New York State apple industry would lose its markets unless it radically reorganized. Only gradually were growers realizing that if they were going to survive, they were going to have to work together and develop a plan for regional marketing. Meanwhile, my mother had plans to supplement apple sales by planting raspberries and gooseberries, maybe late-blooming strawberries as well. Now lilacs and ramps. No significant income, but it all helped pay the bills.

"Look!" exclaims my mother suddenly, and reaches over to point toward the woods. A large dark bird walks out of the underbrush, its huge dinosaur feet jerking up and down in exaggerated, cartoonlike motions as it begins to cross the road: a wild turkey. Behind her ran six half-grown chicks.

"How grand!" my mother exclaims, and for the first time since we have been in the orchards, her face beams.

Unlike most farmers, my mother delights in the presence of the wild on the land she farms. For her, the orchards are a meeting ground of things she should not control and things she believes she must.

Western civilization has romanticized the beauty of agrarian life since the time of Virgil, but all fruit growers know that during the early summer months what they are engaged in is war. A Darwinian struggle, if you will, but one that nonetheless relies on brutal tactics, even softened by strategies like IPM. The very chemicals and fertilizers that we were using had been developed from domestic applications of military technology, spin-offs from major world wars. Parathion, used as a cover spray for many insects during the sixties, had been derived from nerve gas. The nitrogen fertilizer that we needed to increase fruit production could be traced back to a World War II process for making explosives.

But even in this state of "war" with insects and disease, every time I drove over to scout the orchards with my mother, I found myself falling back in love with the land. It was not hard to do. Apple and pear orchards in April, May, June are a sanctuary of sun and green. No wonder the Roman poets eulogized the orchard as prototype of that first garden, a counterpart to urban confusion, the great human mess. But the fact remained that much of our work as fruit growers was hardly lyrical. Unlike the Roman hero Cincinnatus, whose world was neatly divided into the roles of warrior and farmer, establishing that division for Western literature, my mother's life on our farm was a constant war. She couldn't trade her sword for a plowshare because her battles happened on the land. They had to do with figuring out how to make broken-down machinery keep running, how to kill off waves of insects and disease, how to anticipate changing weather, fickle markets, and her worst enemy of all, the bottomed-out price of apples and pears.

I loved scouting the orchards with my mother, getting to know the trees in that way, but I was suspicious of our cultural romance with the family farm. If we assume that agriculture is an inherently good practice and way of being on the land that is noble, then we have to ask an uncomfortable question. Just where does this romantic idea come from? For that matter, who gets to have this kind of relationship with the land in the first place? Thomas Jefferson's vision of the new Republic was as a democracy of independent yeoman farmers, but that history of landownership would not include women for a long time.

In Columbia County, farming is still a man's world. When my mother and I take our seats at fruit-growing association meetings, a sea of worn visors turns to stare at our white stick-on labels that read "Philip Orchards." She is the only woman fruit grower in the county, and although several of the growers are accompanied by sons, we are the only mother-daughter team. We are not unwelcome exactly, just not what anyone expects to see.

⳹

Two days after our scout, the county fruit agent arrives and diagnoses possible fire blight in the young pears. He takes several leaves to send to the experimental station for testing. He recommends that we spray the psylla as soon as possible with Pyromite, a much stronger chemical than Mitac. Reports are coming in that Mitac hasn't been working this season; possibly the psylla have become resistant. He suggests we try using Agri-Mek next season when we put on the oil spray to coat and suffocate overwintered mite and psylla eggs. Agri-Mek not only is a contact killer but has a kickback as well, meaning that it is absorbed by the vascular tissue of the tree and will be there waiting to poison any new insects that begin to feed. The only problem is the cost.

Agri-Mek sounds like the answer to all our problems. As I watch my mother listen to his recommendations but say little, I am overcome with a sinking feeling. I knew why my mother hadn't gone with Agri-Mek: It was too expensive, and she had not wanted to spend the extra $1,000. She was trying to make do on an undercapitalized farm that couldn't pay all its bills. Only the week before, we had confronted another tractor breakdown. The John Deere needed an engine overhaul that was going to cost $500. Meanwhile, we would have to rent a tractor at $250 a day. My mother had hoped to get by this year without borrowing against the harvest, but the John Deere's collapse erased that hope. Last week she went over her outstanding bills to calculate her debt load and then called Production Credit to get the necessary paperwork moving for a $10,000 loan.

Tractor disasters were a familiar story at Talavera. There

had been three tractors on the farm when I was growing up, a powerful red 2010 that pulled the spray rig and pushed brush, a green John Deere with cheerful yellow trim that my father hitched up to the cutter bar for mowing and a rusty old red Case that was used for odd jobs. What I remember most about them was that they were always breaking down. To me, tractor disasters were a fact of life on a farm. So was being late for wherever we were going if the weather was good and my father could get in a few more hours in the orchards. We would be all dressed up and waiting on the porch, ready to head out for a family outing, when someone would realize that my father had not been getting ready all that time but was still down at the barn . . . working on a tractor.

My favorite had been the Case with its long old-fashioned nose. It looked as if it belonged in a junkyard, but I liked the way the tin can tilted to one side over the exhaust pipe, keeping the rain out, the way the grid of tree wire that covered the radiator had rumpled into an abstract pattern. I could still see over the hood when I slipped down a little to get my foot all the way down over the clutch. Most of all, it didn't bolt away from you like the fast 2010.

When I was fourteen, my father decided that I should learn to mow. That my brothers and sister and I work on the farm was part of his vision of running Talavera as a family business and part of his training for me as well. It occurred to me now that part of my ostensible rebellion against girlhood—my obstinate tomboyishness that went on and on—had another dimension. From the time I had been little, my father had been giving me lessons in competence and self-competition usually reserved for boys.

At first I was thrilled to handle so much raw power. The John Deere moved with a smooth, coiled energy even in first gear. When I engaged the mower gear, the blades whirred menacingly and ripped cleanly through the stiff orchard grass. Along the bar twenty serrated triangular knives were flicking back and forth with enough speed to cut even small bushes and scrub. I nosed the tractor into the waist-high grass and watched it fall. We pushed into a yellow chaos of drying grass and weed, leaving behind a rich green carpet.

But the whole time that I was mowing, I was worried that I would encounter a hidden stump or steer incorrectly into a small tree and get the mower stuck. Not long before, I had almost jackknifed the Case while coming up a steep hill with a load. The tractor had begun to slip on the incline, sliding back into the trailer, which immediately began to twist. Miraculously, I had managed to jam it into a lower gear just in time. But my near accident had given me a case of the willies that stuck. By the end of a mowing session I would slump off the tractor, too exhausted to speak. The meadow looked wonderful, a parkland of mowed grass, but I didn't feel the rush of satisfaction that I had figured I would. I had been terrified but was too proud to admit it, and I didn't want to risk letting my father down.

254

*

By the time she calls me five days later, my mother has solved her tractor problem. She and Willi found a second-hand Ford that the dealership was willing to let her take on credit until the production loan came through. That morning she had sprayed for psylla, another round of Mitac. She hadn't wanted to use Pyromite because she thought it too rough on her aphids and ladybugs. To be safe from chemical poisoning, I will have to wait ninety-six hours until I can reenter the orchard, but then my mother would like me to do a scout. The timing of a psylla spray is key. Nymphs could be killed only when they entered their last instar and were in the hard-shell stage. But if you waited too long, they would hatch out, another generation ready to lay thousands more eggs within three days. The heat that week had risen to record highs, and it was still hot at five when I set out to walk through the pears. Every leaf tells me the same story: a carnage of withered black psylla bodies. Scattered eggs remain, but most of them seemed to have hatched out.

I walk on to inspect the young pears across the road. They had tested clean for fire blight. My mother now thought the damage had been caused by splatters of weed killer that Willi had applied to the bases of the young trees as mouse control earlier in the week. I turn over the young leaves and examine terminal ends. What I see surprises me. The aphid population is about half what it had been. But it is the apple trees in block nine that I find the most mysterious: no red mites, even in the Red Delicious.

Back at the house, as I sip iced tea and recount my observations to my mother, she grins when I mention the mites. "See what the beneficials can do!" she exclaims. "You have to give them time."

"I can't believe that they could have eaten so many mites. It's tremendous," I say.

"Yes, well, that's why I don't use Agri-Mek. You use that in the beginning of the season, and it kills everybody. Then you are just stuck with spraying away. I want the beneficials to do the job."

"Why did you wait so long with the Mitac?"

"I can use it only twice a season, so I wanted to wait until the population of psylla was the highest." My mother looks at me and smiles, "You don't go in to get the enemy until you see the whites of their eyes."

I say nothing but tell myself to remember this moment. My mother had been raised in an era when direct competition with men was not tolerated. She masked her competence, but when she set her mind to it, insects that invaded our trees didn't have a chance.

Still, running an orchard with an integrated pest management approach could end in disaster. Unchecked psylla could not only ruin a pear crop but hamper a tree's productivity in the coming year. Left to propagate, the shy and highly camouflaged oblique banded roller cuts a young tree's growth in half. No one wants to eat an apple after a snout-nosed plum curculio larva has hatched out, leaving a wide brown scar where it has bored its way out from the core. When the most serious and common pest, European red mites, get out of control, they prey on trees so rapaciously that it is not long before the leaves are completely sucked dry of nutrients and begin to yellow, a condition called bronzing. Severely bronzed trees lose their leaves and cannot store up enough carbohydrates for the winter. Come spring, the chemical reactions that triggered up through the xylem, telling the cells to initiate fruit, will not occur. Instead the cells inside fruit buds will vegetate in an attempt to replace the lost leaves and keep the tree alive.

By using IPM, my mother saved significantly on her spray bill. She also protected the environment from pounds of unnecessary toxins. The underlying philosophy was appealing. IPM was an insect version of *High Noon*. A farmer tried to pit the good guys against the bad guys and trusted that the good guys could win. There was truth to this. By our not spraying a continual regimen of toxic chemicals, beneficial insects flourished. These "beneficials" could have huge appetites for such pests as aphids, thrips, leafhoppers and, the bane of all apple growers, European red mites. The innocent ladybird beetle, *Stethorus punctum,* dines on mites three and four times a day then snacks on mite larvae. Her own alligator-shaped brood could eat even more. No one knew how many aphids the orange syrphid fly larvae ate in a day because no one had been able to keep count.

Only when my mother identified harmful numbers of insects like European red mites, rosy apple aphids, green aphids, leafhoppers, apple maggots, leaf miners, plum curculios, scales, coddling moths, oblique banded leaf rollers or psyllas on her pears would she spray. Monitoring the orchards in this way took time. Since mid-May my mother and I have spent hours each week tramping under the hot sun to study leaves for insects and disease. Each month brought a different insect plague and a different fungus or disease. Scab ascospores, which overwintered in the fallen leaves, were mature and ready to fly by the end of March. Right on the heels of the prime scab infection period came danger zones for powdery mildew and black rot. May is when the first generation of the insects begins to hatch out as well, the overwintered eggs of "rosies," or apple aphids, and mites and psylla.

My mother was willing to risk pest damage because she figured that what she lost in damaged fruit, she saved on her spray bill. Our orchard required six to ten tanks to cover completely, and one tank of spray cost up to two hundred dollars. But her decision to manage the orchards this way had as much to do with her attitude toward farming as it did with her desire to save money. One August day, when the spray representative advised her to go after her leafhoppers, warning her that they would fly out and bother her Pick Your Own customers at harvesttime, she answered promptly, "No, thanks, my customers like it wild."

꿇

Three weeks later at four o'clock in the afternoon I pull into the driveway right on time for the first of the July mite counts with my mother. Last week European red mites had flared in the two back orchards, especially in the Red Delicious, and my mother applied Kelthane, a fairly weak miticide that tended not to harm the beneficial mites like *Amblysieus fullacis* and *Ti pyri* that feed on the damaging ones. Today I have brought my fifteen-month-old son, Rhys, with me. When I stop the car, he throws down his bottle and shouts, "Oooh, oooh, oooh." Danny leaps up and down at the car, his long ears flying like sails.

We begin in the new land, a corner block of Jonagold, Mutsu and Marshall McIntosh trees. Most growers are scornful of Kelthane, thinking it not powerful enough, but even when fighting a July flare of mites, my mother wants to give her beneficials a chance.

My mother parks in the shade of a large pine tree. It takes me a minute to pull Rhys out, slap Skin-So-Soft on his arms, pull a hat down on his head firmly enough so that he can't pull it off and set his favorite toy, a yellow bulldozer, down on a shady patch of orchard grass. "Uh, oh," he says when I

257

put him down, and immediately he starts out, walking un-
steadily toward the young trees where my mother is already
standing, peering at a leaf. The grass comes up to his waist,
so walking is hard, but he makes it to the young tree just as I
do, then belly flops down into a tuft of grass and laughs.

"See anything?" I ask my mother.

She shakes her head. "You look."

I take the magnifying glass and pull a leaf out from a fruit
cluster. The woolly underside feels like velvet in my hands. I
peer down at the top surface first, beginning at the midrib
and moving the lens carefully out over the leaf blade. The
warm leaf is midsize, fully veined and clear of blemishes like
apple rust and scab. My mother must have gotten the timing
of the fungicide sprays perfect because this is a bad year for
scab in the valley. No mites on the smooth leaf top. I turn it
over and study the underside, where a dozen crumpled black
mite bodies are stuck to the fine hairs. Near them is a sprin-
kling of orange dots, at least twenty mite eggs.

"Kelthane worked," I say, "lots of dead ones, but I see a
lot of eggs too. How long does it take for the eggs to hatch?"

"I'm not sure," my mother answers. "We can look it up
back at the house. Did you see any predators? There's one
that looks like a shiny black dot. Look for those."

"I'll look some more," I say, "I want to check some trees
down the row."

My mother stays behind to keep an eye on Rhys, who has
begun poking the dirt under the tree with a small stick. A
brown ring surrounds the base of the tree where weed killer
was applied earlier in the spring. All commercial weed killers
are derived from chemical weapons, such as Paraquat, which
defoliated much of Vietnam, and I wonder if I really should
let a baby play in chemically burned grass but decide to let
him be. Down the row, I check leaves on the four quadrants
of four trees. Each leaf tells the same story: a high concen-
tration of dead mites but also a new generation of eggs that
will hatch out, meaning another mite spray will be needed
when they hatch. Mites are like psylla in that the eggs cannot

be killed. I haven't seen any black dots or the delicate lacewings or grublike syrphid larvae, which also feed on mites. No ladybird beetles. I walk back and give my results to my mother. When he sees me, Rhys looks up at me excitedly, then turns his head back down to where he had been looking in the grass and shouts, "Buh, buh, buggh."

"What you got, baby?" I say, and bend down to look where he is looking. On a blade of grass near his foot, a large *Stethorus punctum* is crawling up the stem.

"Rhys found a predator," I say and point to the large ladybug that Rhys is now reaching out to try to grab with his small hand. My mother and I both laugh.

In the next block, the far end of number thirteen by the pond, we stop to check the Spartan trees. A cross between McIntosh and Newtown Pippin, the Spartan has never really caught on with Pick Your Own customers. This year we have a fair-size crop, but the set was so heavy that the size is small. We had thinned them with acid after petal fall, choosing a warm day. But there had been days of rain the week before, and the apples, still thimble-size, must have carbo-loaded in the cool nights before we applied the thinner. They held on despite the thinning acid, which usually makes the surface cells on the epidermis of the fruit stem constrict, causing the stems to fall off the branch.

"Dead ones?" asks my mother hopefully, as I leave the tree to walk back toward her.

"Live ones too, I'm afraid," I answer. "Twenty dead, but about five live on each leaf that I checked."

"The new generation must have hatched out." My mother sighs. She is losing her war with the mites. "We need another spray. Let's check the Ida Reds and Goldens on the other side."

I take Rhys onto my lap, and we bounce across the grass to the other side of the orchard, where a young orchard of Golden Delicious lines up in beautiful, even rows. Five years old, this block of semidwarfs produced a beautiful crop last season, and the fruit set was again good this spring. Unlike in

259

the Spartans, here in the Goldens, the thinning took, so the fruit is evenly spaced, already the size of tennis balls.

This time my mother wants to get out of the truck and scout, so I try putting Rhys on the grass by my feet while I begin studying the leaves on a nearby tree. Each leaf has a scattering of dead mites and lots of eggs but no live adults. Then I begin to see the baby mites, tiny crablike specks, their four legs already poking out of their rosy bodies. More and more of them. I had read that left unchecked, two mites become thirteen million in six generations alone. No surprise that mites are the most numerous animals on the earth. More serious for fruit growers is the emerging fact that they are becoming resistant to the only five pesticides approved for use to kill them: Kelthane, Apollo, Savey, Pyromite Vendex and Carzol. Of these, Carzol and Pyromite are rescue sprays, meaning that they are so powerful they can be used only twice during a growing season. If they are used more often than that, the mites could easily become resistant to the pesticide, leaving growers with no means of control. There were some new chemicals on the market, like Agri-Mek, but the best hope for fruit growers and the environment alike was for the valley to achieve biological control through the cultivation of mite predators.

"Babies," I say when my mother returns. She bends down to sniff the piece of clover that Rhys is holding up for her to smell.

"Lots?" she asks.

"Baby mites galore," I answer.

"Baybee," Rhys suddenly says emphatically, as if to join the conversation. He holds up his arms and chants, "Baybee, up, up." I ignore him and try to finish examining the leaf in my hand. His small fists begin to pound my calves. Then he stops. "Baybee?" he asks inquisitively. When I look down, he gives an enormous chipmunk grin.

"Okay," I say, "you win." I scoop him up and balance him on my raised knee while I do my best to keep studying the leaf by placing it on a bare spot on a nearby limb. Rhys screeches with delight and pulls a fistful of my hair.

"Fruit set looks good, Mom," I say, letting the leaf drop and turning to my mother.

"Yes," she says. "But I don't know whether to blame the spray rig, which hasn't been working properly, or Willi, or myself. This mite situation is bad. Bronzed trees . . . it's shameful."

"You'll get them this time. I'm sure you will," I say, and although the sight of the trees with yellowing leaves had startled me too, I believe that she will. We pile into the truck just as a familiar rumble sounds along the road. As soon as he hears the noise, Rhys scrambles up until he stands his full height against the truck door to get a better view.

"Traktah, traktah," he shouts excitedly. Soon we see Willi on the new blue tractor driving by. Now that the terminal buds have set, he can begin the summer pruning. My mother turns the key in the ignition, and the truck roars to life, then heads forward with a jerk. We are soon racing along the orchard rows. It occurs to me that these trees, which, through their mysterious ability to photosynthesize light into food, link the organic and the inorganic worlds, have also forged another kind of link, a new way for me to be with my mother. Not inside the house making beds or preparing one of the many meals that seemed to keep us perpetually busy there, but here, bouncing along in a silver truck, outside, in the orchards.

261

"Look at that size," I say, pointing to a large Ida Red as we pass it by.

"That one's headed for the fair," my mother says decisively. She strains to see over the top of the steering wheel as the silver truck bounces along, her straw hat tilting like a windmill.

ॐ

We had won. When my mother and I walked into the apple booth at the county fair that fall, we saw a huge purple ribbon clipped to the sign for our farm. We could hardly believe our eyes. Philip Orchards had been designated the grand champion fruit grower for Columbia County. We had received blue ribbons for individual fruit categories before, but never had we won so many blues that we came in first over all. My mother was typically wary of accepting praise, but she couldn't hide her delight either.

"We just took the prize because so many farms got knocked out with hail," she said when we went to look over our displays of apples and pears lined up on the shelves around the room. "But those Ida Reds, I just knew they would win."

It was true that my mother had been lucky with the weather. Only a month earlier the *New York Times* had reported that the July drought, then scourings of summer hail had destroyed the Hudson Valley fruit crop. Fruit growers were applying for federal disaster relief. My mother's was one of the few orchards in the county whose pears had not been completely shredded by the bean-size hail. Some of our fruit had been scarred, but overall we had a gorgeous crop. In fact, it looked as though we just might have a record harvest.

When I had driven through the orchards to do the fall check with our spray representative, Gil Lasher, even he had clucked over my mother's success. "She just got the timing right on everything," he said, giving one of his big belly laughs. "These orchards are clean, cleaner than I've ever seen them. Your mother got lucky with the weather with those psylla. The heat breaks 'em. They just can't take it. But she knew to figure that, and then she just got the timing on everything else just pretty damn perfect."

Gil advised us on what pesticide to use and as a service routinely scouted our orchards. A large, quiet man, he rarely paid this kind of compliment, especially because he was lukewarm about the pest management strategies that my mother was using. Once during the scout, I'd brought along a new IPM publication from Cornell, and he'd snorted. "I don't use IPM guidelines. I use my onboard computer," he had said, tapping his head to emphasize his point. "I look until I think I know what's there. Then I stop. Even when it looks like I'm not looking, I am. You've got to see the whole picture; then you can step back and look for specific problems."

Gil had been scouting orchards for thirty years, and he was good at it. I had watched him glance at a block of our trees from a distance and, just by the particular hue of green in the leaf canopy, predict with accuracy how many leaf rollers were there. As he would say, "By July I know what's out there. From that point on, it's all inventory." Although my mother didn't always follow Gil's suggestions, she knew she could trust him. Gil was too smart and too ethical to recommend unnecessary sprays to boost sales for his company. And he knew only too well how quickly growers were going out of business.

"Once I'm on the property, I'm working for the grower. The last thing in the world I think of is that I'm a salesman. The most important thing you can do for a fruit grower these days is make sure he survives. Then you have a customer next year."

On the way back from our late fall scout after the fair, we had stopped to look at a set of trees by the garden where I had released a colony of voracious beneficial mites called *T. pyri*. At the February fruit school, I had heard about an experiment that some scientists at Cornell were running to try to combat red spider mites with predators. Everyone knew that it was just a matter of years before the current population of red spider mites became resistant to the current sprays. Chemical companies were working furiously to develop new chemical weapons. Meanwhile researchers at Cornell were trying to reintroduce natural red mite predators to the valley to achieve biological control. You could receive as many as six hundred female mites for release if you wanted to become part of the experiment.

When the Styrofoam box marked "Living Organisms, Refrigerate Immediately" arrived, I set to work as soon as I could. The three hundred leaves with *T. pyri* on them had to be stapled to the shady undergrowth of apple trees that would become the mites' new home. My mother and I chose six Lady Apple trees by the garden because they tended to be hardy against red spider mites and were slightly isolated from other trees. The *T. pyri* could eat mold until they were strong enough to begin moving to other trees, where they would find plenty of red spider mites to eat. Meanwhile, the incubation trees would protect them, for the sprays that killed red mites would also kill the *T. pyri*. We would have to hold off on spraying those trees for the rest of the season.

I eagerly crunched numbers. Adult mites lived for twenty days, and the females laid one egg a day. Those eggs took one to three days to hatch out and matured in about thirty days. Then the process began again. You could count on at least three to four generations of mites in one season, and in some years, as many as nine. That was why they could become such an epidemic so fast. In two generations, my 600 mites would become 120,000, but by generation four, they'd be up to 48 million. I had a vision of my *T. pyri* spreading out over our orchards, feasting on the dangerous red mites for breakfast, lunch and dinner—saving us.

Gil wasn't so optimistic. Lab trials were one thing, but the field was another. He had looked at the trees and nodded, but then added, "I don't know about these *T. pyri* fellas, maybe they'll take off in the valley, but I can tell you, right now, the only predator I have any respect for is *Stethorus punctum*. Like this one right here." He had laughed, then pointed to the ladybird beetle crawling up his hand.

❧

After the fair the harvest began in earnest. Even the weather cooperated so that the first weeks in September were sunny and bright, perfect for apple picking. Except that pickers were not arriving. Every Saturday my mother looked at the thin trickle of cars pulling into the barnyard and frowned, remembering the days when so many customers came at once that the line of cars had reached almost out to the main road. The customers who did arrive couldn't believe the fruit. "It's like a candy store in there," one man said, loading bags of enormous Golden Delicious into his trunk. He still picked for his extended family, and his wife still baked pies.

The apples began to drop. My mother sprayed the Macs with Naphthaleneacctic acid (NAA) in an attempt to hold them on the trees. NAA was an acid that kept the fruit from releasing hormones that caused the cells in the stem to constrict. When those stem cells constricted, the apple fell from the tree. But ten days later the sprayed apples also began to fall. Usually, Willi trucked bins of fallen Macs to a local cider operation and sold them as cider fruit. But the mill had closed after a recent E. coli scare. New pasteurizing regulations meant expensive new equipment that the mill couldn't yet afford.

By the time the first frost hit, my mother had calculated that only 60 percent of our fruit had sold. The ground under the trees was red with rotting fruit, our farm was ten thousand dollars short of paying its current bills and the barn shop needed a new roof.

That November, at our yearly postharvest meeting, when my brothers, my sister and I sat down to review the harvest and affairs at Talavera, tempers flared. No one wanted to admit it, but the Pick Your Own business seemed over as a means to market all of our fruit. Pick Your Own had worked dur-ing the seventies and eighties, but families no longer had the time to pick and store fruit. We had a loyal core of customers, many of whom had come to pick apples at the farm for two generations, but they came more as a form of recreation than as serious pickers. They picked a half bushel of fruit where their parents would have bought four or five. Some farms had adapted by developing what was called agritourism, offering hay rides and petting zoos and special programs to attract weekend customers. Other farms closer to the city had adopted a park mentality. You paid an admission fee to enter the orchards in addition to the price of the fruit.

Agritourism brought snorts of derision from my mother,

265

and I could see her point. When you worked hard all year to raise the best fruit you could, it seemed nothing less than demeaning to have to entertain your customers too. What was the line between agritourism and running a farm museum, a kind of Sturbridge Village of farm life? We wanted to sell fruit, not market ourselves. But the fact was, Pick Your Own was no longer profitable. Packing out fruit for stores was even more dim. Our closest neighbor had put his orchards up for sale, or rather the bank had. Three other farms had likewise folded. Down the road at the old Estok farm, Paul Estok carried a piece of paper in his back pocket with the previous year's apple tally. Ask him how business was doing, and he'd give you a lopsided grin, then pull out the paper, which showed that his entire crop, planted to help diversify his dairy—fourteen thousand dollars' worth of apples—had netted exactly two thousand dollars once the cost of picking, packing, storage and shipping had been factored in. His father had bought their-two-hundred-acre farm with four hundred dollars in the 1920s. The orchards, just south and west of ours, had gorgeous views of the Catskills, and it seemed as if a crop of houses would be going up there soon. Commercial fruit growing in the Hudson Valley was becoming a thing of the past. We were not the only farm whose books were coming up red. Most farms were being subsidized in one way or another: The wife of the farmer took a job, or the fruit grower did, or the land was bought by someone who made money in the city and enjoyed the farm on weekends.

Our farm was being subsidized by my mother's free labor and her inputs of cash, and it couldn't go on. More troubling, we didn't have a clear idea of how we would take the farm over when my mother no longer felt she was able to run it.

We spent a restless, anxiety-ridden winter. Only my mother, busy with the present tense reality of life on a small farm in an enormous house, seemed characteristically nonplussed.

She had kept the farm going for more than five years, and she was not ready to give up on it yet. Meanwhile, out in the orchards, the trees, irreverent to history, were already gearing up to produce next year's seeds, which would be genetically distinct, a completely new generation. While in winter sleep, they had chosen which cells would turn to flowers, which to wood so that when spring began, they were ready for those chemical changes that deep in the vascular tissue signaled the fruit buds to grow.

Before we knew it, the trees were in green tip, silver tip, tight cluster, bloom. As usual, those of us who could gathered to help my mother put on her yearly apple blossom picnic. This year something wonderful happens. A sudden heat wave has made the orchards too hot for the picnic, so we have gathered in the garden, backing the wooden trailer up to the cedar walk.

A few years earlier my eldest brother and my mother had widened the cedar walk and cut an opening in the eastern side so that right in the middle was a shaded area that looked out over the meadow, the pond and the upward swell of hills on the opposite side, a hillside now frothed with white pear blossoms and pink apple blooms. Because the spot afforded one of the best views of the farm, the family's dogs and horses had been buried there for some time. My father's childhood horse, Little Dan, had been buried there, as had his father's horse, Big Dan, and my horse, Peter, although luckily, I had not been there to watch the backhoe dig Peter's deep grave.

Lieutenant John Van Ness's formal gardens were smaller than they had once been. Instead of six garden beds of flowering plants and roses, my mother and eldest brother maintained only the long main bed and one other. Similarly, the terraced vegetable plots that had been there when I was a child had been mostly seeded over as lawn. We had a few raspberries growing at the bottom of the garden along with peach, cherry and plum trees, but the lines of grapes and berries had been discontinued. Still, one could see the outlines of the old plan. The long lilac walk, the cedar walk, the hawthorn hedges with their shiny thorns still outlined the whole, while the bottom of the garden area was now outlined with a bushy hedge of bridal veil. Here and there a carefully placed hemlock or spruce or white pine, now grown into a towering tree, broke up the symmetry of walkway and lawn. But still, walking south from the house you felt as if you were entering and leaving a series of green rooms.

As the picnic started, guests wandered across the lawns, enjoying the masses of purple lilacs, then slumped down in lawn chairs to escape the heat. We brought bowls and platters and baskets of food out and arranged a picnic on the trailer. It was while people were still gathered around it, helping themselves to the piles of food and glasses of lemonade from the silver punch bowl that Hari Kari had won, that a family friend walked to the edge of the garden and waited there. Beside him was an object draped in my grandmother's wool throw. Behind him the meadow dipped down and the orchards began, a haze of pink and white bloom.

He stood for a while until people noticed him and began to quiet down so that they could hear what he had to say. He had a gift that he wanted to give to Talavera in memory of my father. Ever since he had heard of how a piece of Talavera was missing, he explained, he had wanted to do something to try to bring it back. While we watched, he removed the blanket from a large, beautifully framed portrait of General John P. Van Ness. Everyone stared in amazement. There stood such a stunning rendition of the original Gilbert Stuart that had hung in the dining room it hardly seemed a copy. Someone shouted, "He's back. The general's back," and then everyone was clapping. I was astounded that someone else had understood how my father had been wounded by the portrait's loss and even more amazed that he had wanted to try to address that hurt. My eldest brother hung the portrait in the dining room between the two windows where the original had been. Immediately the room seemed to glow.

After all the guests had gone home, I walked through the dining room. Evening light was falling, and through the windows I could still see the pink haze of orchards. When I looked at the portrait, itself a work of art that had taken almost two years to complete, I thought about how in some ways the copy was even better than the original. A new story had become woven into that of Talavera, that of the portrait's return. All the stories that I had worked so hard to collect—Lieutenant John Van Ness, Tom, Catherine Douw, Eliza Worthington, my grandfather, my great-aunt Lee, my lost aunt and Aunt Bessie, Uncle Gaston, my father—seemed to reach out and hold me. I had begun my search for the truth about the past convinced that unless I did something, I would lose Talavera, lose my home. But the portrait's return crystallized for me the realization that what was here was more durable than I had thought. And it wasn't all up to me.

I had traveled a long journey to root out Talavera's past, to turn that past over, trying to make sense of previous lives, to weave those stories into narrative, giving them shape. Like any journey, the traveling out had been accompanied by a parallel journey in. I understood better now who I was and what that meant. I was not a fallen version of some previous generation because the idea that we had lived at Talavera like lords and ladies of the manor was a fiction. There had been periods of wealth, but we were my father with his grease-stained khakis and Brooks Brother jacket, just as we were my mother with her tilted straw hat, me with my magnifying lens and dog-chewed cap. The truth was, we never had been an elite, landed gentry for whom the farm was a passing distraction. That was a story of the Hudson Valley, but not our own story here. As much as it was *Talavera*, the house that anchored my family to this place, it was the farm.

Wealth and social position were a large part of the Van Ness legacy in the Hudson Valley, but it was not the almost mythic wealth of manor families like the Livingstons, whose river estates still lay along the eastern banks of the river just south of here. According to the earliest tax records, Catherine Douw's grandfather Peter Van Ness had been the richest man in Kinderhook by the end of the Revolution. His brother David had built a similar fortune south in Red Hook. Both of them acquired their wealth as merchants and traders and had built fine houses. Peter's sons had gone on to political acclaim. General John P. Van Ness became one of the first mayors of Washington, D.C., while his brother Cornelius became the governor of Vermont. But William's family had chosen the quieter path of carrying on the Van Ness lands in Claverack. His son, Judge William W., had been a distinguished lawyer and become prominent in federal-era New York politics but we were still a family for whom the farm was central.

I remembered something that my mother said when I asked her about the difficult years that followed my grandmother's death.

"Your father felt the land was what was important, not the house. It was why I suppose we concentrated on the farm and didn't worry as much about keeping Talavera up as we might have...."

Her voice had trailed off then, part apology for the peeling wallpaper, for the yellowing curtains. Then she burst out chuckling, "This was built as a foolish house back then and it's still a foolish house now!"

We both laughed. What she said was so true. William W. had built his elegant, exotic mansion as much to display his wealth as his patriotism. He probably never noticed that by the time you shuttled food from the kitchen to the dining room, it was cold.

To me, Talavera, our foolish house, was the keeper of previous lives, but the land had been the constraint that had shaped them.

What a relief it was to accept who we were and had been. It didn't mean that I too now had to commit to staying here. But it did mean that if I left, I would know what I was leaving, and that knowledge seemed to equip me with a way to make a choice. I didn't want to live under the shadow of regret. Perhaps the most important lesson offered up by Chief Keesieway was not to become seduced by one firelock gun. If we sold Talavera, or developed rather than farmed the land, our burden would be lifted. But each century of my family's tenure here had revealed the same truth: Once you stopped working the land, you lost your connection to it.

Meanwhile, when I looked across the dining room and saw General John P. Van Ness's aquiline profile, I had to admit that Talavera had not given up all its secrets. They still swirled around the house like dust motes, bloomed and fell, falling, like the apple blossoms, like the falling evening light. And while I sat there, watching the light fall, listening for the far-off silence of the river, I was glad for all that I did not yet know.

Epilogue

Sixteen years have passed since my father died, starting this story, sixteen years since my mother, steeling herself, had promised to keep the farm going for five more years. When I wrote this book, it was during one of the darkest hours for fruit growing in the valley, and when it was first published in 2001, farms, including our nearest neighbor, were folding at an alarming rate. To carry on seemed in equal parts foolish and necessary. I was determined to collect the stories of the land, the house, and the many lives entwined with this place because whether we could continue to hold on was an open question. It still is. Philip Orchards is the last remaining fruit farm in the township of Claverack, an area which had listed more than 315 farms in 1875.

And yet, if I had written this book in part thinking that it would free me from the past; as if by sweeping up the random bits of history and fact and myth, sorting papers and disentangling legend and fact and tale, then sitting down to pull it all together into one long narrative I had hoped to free myself of the past, I was wrong. It would never be that simple. Once I had discovered so many characters—generations of ancestors who had struggled or not to hang onto this family place—well, it didn't make sense to walk away without first exploring options of hanging on. Luckily, my mother was managing to keep the farm going long enough to see an upswing for agriculture in the valley, or at the very least relief. Small farms, many of them much smaller than ours, that grow specialty produce and fruits, are on the rise in the Hudson Valley. Thanks to my mother's commitment and work, my oldest brother's unwavering belief in the value of hanging on and our ability to put our differences aside, we had kept the place together by simply carrying on. It hadn't been easy, but by the time the first edition of this book was published in 2001, my mother had passed that five-year mark; there was no question of her waking up one day and saying she had decided that Florida looked good after all. For better or worse, Talavera and the cycles of fruit growing had become her life.

When a local paper did a story on her last year, I looked at the photograph they ran of her—the first and still the only woman fruit grower in Columbia County—and the face on the page startled me with its farmer's gaze, a look that said nature could be a damn fool and kill your whole crop with one sudden frost then just as quickly surprise you with its glory, and by the way, people could act just the same. Her look was that of a farmer or rancher—unsentimental about nature, aware of just how hard things could get—but in contrast, her smile beamed. No, there was no question of my mother quitting the farm now. My mother loved her life at Talavera even when the electricity went out and the well failed, even when the stove broke or the hot muggy nights in July made sleep impossible. The paint could start to peel on the kitchen ceiling after a spontaneous roof leak, but until she had the money to get it fixed, my mother would ignore it; instead, she'd stare out the window, marveling at the sight of chickadees, their impossibly small feet leaving delicate tracks in the snow. At eighty-four, she'd rather make her slow way through thick orchard grass with a ski pole than stop running the farm. That didn't diminish all the questions. How many more years could she carry on? What about when she herself needed care? We hadn't answered these questions because my mother's plan was simple: do what I'm doing for as long as I can. How could you argue with that? In the past seven years I'd watched her attend the funerals of most of her lifelong friends. Once you got to be her age, who was to say what was practical or what made sense? If my mother still wanted to face the risks and discomforts of living on her own, I was ready to help her. Throughout the harvest, my siblings and Rhys's cousins would be in to lend a hand as they could. The anchor would be my oldest brother, John, who works in Manhattan; he would be at Talavera every weekend until the harvest was done.

The test, of course would be that time, coming, when my mother would be unable to live here alone or run the farm. We didn't have a plan in place for that moment, even though we knew it was coming and we felt we should. Talavera, such as it was, was still a *villa rustico,* a self-sustaining agricultural estate. Until one of us began running the farm, or we found someone to run it for us, once my mother could no longer manage the business we would be at a whole new juncture.

◈

October 10, 2008. Another harvest. By the time I head out for orchard check, the sun has spread a wide band across the tops of the trees. The air feels cold and sharp, still far from the bite of winter but chill enough to bring color to the fruit. In the two weeks since I've last been home, the older maples have shifted orange, red, and russet brown, the tree by the back door now a shock of yellow. Columbus Day and at six a.m. the weather radio blasted out zero precipitation, meaning we should have a busy day of Pick Your Own. Down at the barns, my oldest brother, the next in the line of men named John Van Ness Philip to devote themselves to the task of maintaining Talavera, is pulling out wooden apple boxes, and my son, Rhys Philip, now eleven, is lifting them two at a time onto the bed of Willi's truck.

Rhys is a typical boy of his generation: his idea of a good time is surfing the album covers and hit songs on iTunes. He'd rather text than call his friends and can Google with the best of them, but I watch how Talavera and the farm, maybe because it is so far removed from the technology that dominates his world, intrigues him. I remember my own childhood here and how navigating between our weekday world of school and friends in Manhattan and the weekend days of Talavera felt like time traveling or at least left me with the feeling that I was moving between worlds, not just city versus country, but being of this moment and yet not. I wonder sometimes if Rhys feels the same or if, given his generation and the vast speeding up of time that has occurred alongside the speed of information, the differences feel even more acute. This fall Rhys wanted to help regularly on harvest weekends, and as parents we were glad. Like many kids of his generation, he is so busy that he barely has time to do a few chores, let alone experience the lessons to be gained from sticking to a job. Rhys has five cousins and hopefully, if my own generation can keep the farm going, they will have the chance to sort out their own relationships to this place and to each other and shape its future.

Meanwhile, Rhys and my brother have already loaded onto the truck bed the small table, chairs, and other supplies, including the money bag with thirty dollars in change that they will need for the Pick Your Own business today. Customers will drive in and get a map of the orchards and picking directions on a spot along the farm road just down the hill from the barns. When they are done picking they will pay from their cars on the way out. No one wants to wait in line on a beautiful weekend, especially not our pickers, who, in addition to coming from the immediate tri-state area, routinely drive two hours and more to pick fruit here, many making yearly pilgrimages from as far as Long Island, Queens, and New Jersey. Columbus Day weekend has continued to be one of our most important harvest weekends, for by October, each of the eighteen varieties of apples we grow is ready to pick; some early varieties such as McIntosh, Cortland, and Macoun will have started to drop, but the later apples, the Empires, Jonagolds, Red and Golden Delicious, Mutsu, and the relatively new apple, Honey Crisp, which my mother began planting five years ago, are at their peak. This year, we have been surprised by the number of new customers, many of whom have moved to the Hudson Valley in the last five years, an ongoing exodus from New York City since 9/11. Our loyal customers, those who have picked here since they were kids, are driving in but also a surprising number of customers who are picking apples for the first time.

Sales receipts are bigger, too. Where five years ago even those who arrived in minivans with two, three, four kids in tow picked only a half-bushel of fruit, this fall they are picking two bushels and more. Apples to eat, apples to cook, apples to store, and apples to give away. I've answered ongoing questions about how to store apples and which varieties are best for keeping and are best for cooking. Perhaps the buy local movement has begun to sink in, perhaps the recent scares about food safety and food security have convinced people that buying direct from farms isn't just about saving money, it's about eating healthy food. Certainly, the carbon footprint of an apple grown here in the Hudson Valley is nothing like one shipped almost three thousand miles from Washington State or another nine thousand from New Zealand. And the suddenly skyrocketing cost of oil this fall has raised prices on all food shipped to even the usually cheaper chain stores. For the past ten years there has been a growing awareness of the need to preserve open space in the Hudson Valley, although nationally the American Farmland Trust estimates that the United States loses 125 acres of farm and ranch land every hour. One positive response to the tragedy of 9/11 seems to be an awakening to our need to connect with the places where we live. Or perhaps the weakening economy is encouraging a return to simple pleasures; an afternoon with the kids picking apples costs far less than taking them to Six Flags of New England. Whatever the reason, we are seeing more and more customers drive in this year.

At breakfast, while we jostled for space around the small table, eating yet a bit more of the bacon, eggs, and toast, my mother had gone over the day's plan. John and Rhys would do barn set-up. At ten o'clock the two teenage girls she had hired to help for the season would arrive to help them at the barns until four. Various family friends were coming and going throughout the day. I was to do an orchard check and then roam the orchards to help customers and direct traffic. John and Rhys would oversee close-up at six. Under no conditions should we sell the bushels of Jonagolds on the front porch: they were being donated to a local fundraiser for elderly care. A bus group was arriving from a Brooklyn Church at ten. She and Willi would manage that. Dinner was pot-roast. Oh, and by the way, we needed a record weekend, the first payment on the spray bill—eight thousand dollars—was due in two weeks.

Once I am certain that my mother's chickens are safely at the barn, I cross the back lawn, almost sliding down the slope when I reach the edge where the land drops toward the meadow. So many catalpa leaves have fallen during the night that the short lawn grass is awash with them and my feet slip on the slick, heart-shaped leaves. Beside me, my son's dog, Coda, a young golden retriever, chaser of chickens, prances, trying hard not to strain against her lead. As soon as I see that the coast is clear, I unsnap her lead. She runs toward the pond, a streak of red and gold, and for a moment I am back in time and watching Danny, my father's Springer Spaniel, make that same mad dash, his short Springer body leaping to clear the grass, his huge brown ears sailing. Danny, who had accompanied me in many scenes of the book, died five years ago. My mother thought about replacing him with a dog but then decided she would try living pet-free. Within a few months, her chickens, led by their fearless rooster, George, began coming closer and closer to the house, drawn to the kitchen door by her treats of fruit and other scraps.

One evening I came home to find a large Araucana hen sitting on the front porch near one of the tall white columns. When she saw me she cocked her head, staring at me with a cautious yellow eye, then shook her neck, rustling her gold-brown feathers. It wasn't long before the chickens were regularly visiting the back porch in search of cat food, for my mother had rescued a litter of kittens left in the barn and was feeding them. When they felt like it, some of the hens, especially the elegant long-necked Araucanas, would settle on chairs near the columns on the front porch. Meanwhile, the kittens chased one another through the trees around the house. My mother allowed her favorite, a dark grey tabby with black stripes, which she named Scooter, to come inside. Part mischief-maker, part thug, Scooter is now a big fat cat who jumps to the back of my mother's arm chair as soon as she sits in the library. There he will nestle against her neck, his large body draped across the back of her chair, one paw dangling free so he can bat at anyone who walks by.

278

Soon I am at the fork in the road where one way leads to the pond and the other into the orchards. I bear left following the bend in the meadow but not before I see an unusual shape glide across the pond, moving quickly on the surface of the still water and into the irrigation ditch that runs through the meadow. A great blue heron, its tall head erect, is hiding there among the thick grasses, that black eye watching. I run ahead across the meadow, whooping now and making noise, trying to distract Coda from the pond, but she is a water dog and while I'm still running I hear the splash. Too late. The great grey wings begin to flap and beat the air, the bird rises, its long legs dangling like sticks as it swoops across the meadow. Thrilled at what she has discovered, Coda now runs along the side of the ditch, chasing the sight of the bird, airborne and now well ahead of us. My mother's way of managing this farm is still to revel in those places where the wild and the domestic meet. Her chickens run loose and she lets the meadow grow all summer instead of mowing it for mulch or hay so that by fall the tall grass, home to many birds and rodents, becomes entwined with black-eyed Susans, chickory, daisies, wild asters, and columbine.

Following the guidelines of IPM, Integrated Pest Management, she only sprays for pests or disease when she absolutely has to, and as a result her apples sometimes have cosmetic blemishes. She wouldn't be able to ship out fruit touched with something like flyspeck, but over the years her customers have begun to appreciate her approach; they come here because they want good fruit raised with a minimum use of commercial fertilizer and pesticide. For years fruit growers scoffed at my mother's practices, but now, with current concerns over food safety, global warming, and energy independence, her practices locate her quite ironically at the cutting edge.

Even though it was hot, dreary work, the insect scout was one of the things that I missed the most about working on the farm on a daily basis. First, leaves had to be collected from sample trees in each block, taken at just the right height from all four quadrants of a tree's leaf canopy. Once you finished the collection, each leaf was examined with a hand lens to identify and count both advantageous and disadvantageous insects. A typical summer scout took most of the morning, and by the end of the season you really knew the trees with all their quirks and idiosyncrasies, and the fruit, well, it wasn't just bushels of apples anymore. No, the crop was the block of Red Delicious you had saved from plum curculio, the Jonagolds that suffered frost ring but on whom an early application of Captan had prevented scab. The Ida Reds, ever hardy, were those trees at the top of block thirteen that had suffered through a mite infestation, but we hadn't needed to spray because, in the end, just as my mother had predicted, the predacious bugs had finally gotten the upper hand, killing the mites before they had completely sucked the nutrients from the leaves, a phenomenon called bronzing. No, once you did the scout week after week the orchards became loud with tree types, tree quirks, tree enigmas, and so many shades of foliage you never again could call an orchard just green.

The Bosc pears, for example: now why didn't they bear this year? Was it the early frost, or was it an insufficient bloom caused the summer before by an infestation of psylla that had stressed the trees in July when the cells were dividing and specializing as floral initiation? Or was the lack of fruit due to a potassium deficiency in the soil? Did the abundance of rain in July wash out the soil so that my mother's gamble that she could get by without spending money on fertilizer had lost the crop this year? Or was it perhaps, and most probably, a combination of all three, so that the many elements that needed to line up for a good crop were each a little bit off, resulting in disaster? These were well-pruned trees in the prime of their bearing life, planted in good soil with adequate circulation of wind to prevent frost. The only consolation was that up and down the county everyone was complaining that they had no pear crop to speak of this year. That fact didn't replace the five thousand dollars of lost income they would have brought in, but did keep my mother from fretting overly about what she might have done wrong.

During the 2008 growing season, the main challenges had come from apple and pear diseases rather than insect invasion. Early rains from petal-fall onward had left moist conditions, ideal for scab, sooty blotch, cedar apple rust, mildew, and frog's eye, and had made it impossible for Willi to spray. While some diseases, such as fly speck, which shows up as tiny black dots on the fruit near the stem, only mark the fruit with superficial blemishes, other problems, such as mildew, attack the tree and consequently limit next year's crop as well.

Most of my mother's customers would tolerate fly speck in return for less spray. They also came here for the freedom of being able to drive into the orchards and, for the most part, pick where they choose. Many Pick Your Own fruit farms have begun charging parking fees, then running shuttles to the orchards, or if they allow cars to enter, inspect them carefully on the way out for fear of theft, often selling by the pound instead of by the bag to make sure that the customers are not overloading. A bushel of apples weighs between forty to fifty pounds depending upon the variety, and this season my mother is charging an average of twenty dollars a bushel, which works out to about forty cents per pound, less than a quarter of what supermarkets or even farmers' markets charge. Even with these low prices, my mother would rather see a bit of waste, or even lose a few bushels to theft, than deny people full access to the orchards—now some sixty plus acres of trees and another forty of woodland and meadow. A few years ago, when other farms closer to New York City began the practice of charging entrance fees to allow customers in to pick, I had raised the idea with my mother. It made a certain kind of sense to charge a usage fee given the cost of maintaining the open space that people enjoy when they come to the farm. But my mother was vehemently opposed. "You start charging people to get in and just watch, they'll expect all kinds of things," she had warned; then, as if the very thought insulted her, she retorted, "I raise apples and pears. If people want entertainment they can go to the zoo!"

Already a few pickers are taking advantage of my mother's philosophy and have spread out blankets and food on the top ridge of block nine, the first orchard that my parents planted when they took over full management in the early seventies. I can see their cars parked to the left and kids running around among the trees. Once I am back on the road, Coda catches up with me, grinning foolishly and giving me one of her "you are hopelessly slow" looks before loping ahead between the two bridges. Two springs ago Rhys, my husband, and I walked on this road in late April and been amazed by the sight of crayfish migrating slowly up the hill, crawling through the wet mud by the dozens, claws waving, desperately trying to get to the upper pond to lay their eggs. Crayfish crawling out of the ditches, up and along the dirt road, up and then further on, uphill! The sight was bizarre and almost eerie; it seemed apocalyptic, like freaky warm weather in January, but later we would read that this was their practice, to seek another body of water in which to lay their eggs. How they knew there was a pond on the top of the hill was my question. Nothing but dust underfoot today.

On one side of the road are two apple trees, tagged white to indicate that the apples filling their limbs are Greening apples. These two trees are all that remain of the heritage orchard that my father and mother planted ten years before my father died. My mother calls the soil here just "sour hardpan" and doesn't plan to replant the trees that one by one have died. Soon I am walking up past the section of block nine where seven years ago my mother began planting more pears along the bottom edge, with more added two years later. This year those newer trees, all of them Anjou, Buerre Bosc, and Harrow Sweet, began to bear in earnest. Here at the top of the hill and the top of orchard eleven is where my mother plans to bring the bus later. She will have them park beneath the large white pine that, planted more than a hundred years ago, still punctuates the view. I check to make sure that the garbage can is in place and walk on. I still have to work my way through orchards eleven, thirteen, fifteen, and sixteen before working my way back to orchards ten and four, then out to the front where we have a block planted beside the entrance to the farm. In the past sixteen years since she has taken over full management of the farm, my mother has continued my father's practice of planting at least fifty new trees each spring. She now has thriving blocks of Jonagold and Honey Crisp and hopefully will soon have success with Gala.

Thus, with each year that my mother ages, the orchards, at least in part, grow younger. For the coming spring she will plant mostly Gala and Fuji apples but also more plums. Deer love the sweet buds of apple trees and for the past three years my mother has planted young whips only to have the deer completely consume them. This spring, Willi plans to tie rags dipped in hogsblood near each young tree. My mother tried that with this year's young trees and it seemed to actually deter them, unlike everything else we've done. My mother has removed almost half of the older trees in orchard thirteen, but the old captain Mac, one of the original trees planted by my grandfather when he set out the first orchards in 1911, is still alive. She has also begun removing the long rows of McIntosh and Cortland in blocks fifteen and sixteen and replanting with smaller, semi-dwarf stock. Those older trees, planted by my father when he was a young man, still line up in long rows looking like apples from a storybook, but they are expensive to care for, requiring large amounts of spray, and are not as productive as smaller stock. They are what is left of the large, old-style apple trees, great for climbing and lovely to look at with their classic large gnarled limbs. Once the leaves have fallen each one spreads out like a weathered hand, the bent fingers clutching the land.

Twenty-first-century fruit growing is all about raising productivity on less acreage. The most up-to-date methods of high density cultivation called trellis-axis planting involve close planting methods and spindle pruning, where trees are literally trained to grow along wires, not unlike grape vines. Even our farm, which at this point is planted primarily in semi-dwarf stock set twelve feet apart along the rows, has only three to four thousand trees spread over its sixty acres. In contrast, this newer planting method means a farmer can fit as many as fifteen hundred trees per acre. Each tree is planted next to a pole and wires are strung pole to pole, creating a kind of fence or trellis that the trees are then pruned to grow along. Given adequate water through a drip irrigation system, this style of high-tech orchard will produce fruit within a year. While the up front cost of planting this way is very high, the yields are large and the orchard is easier to spray, maintain, and harvest. Professional pickers can move from tree to tree, picking fruit that is all within arm's reach. But even if we had the substantial capital it would take to plant trees in the trellis-axis method, it is hard to imagine Pick Your Own customers getting much fun out of picking apples from what look like high-tech grape vines roped with wire and irrigation pipe.

I stop at an apple tree and reach up through its limbs to grab a red apple, then bite, savoring the burst of sweet tang

283

flavors. Despite the extreme and volatile weather patterns this
season—the sudden spring that came on too fast, the killing
frost that left growers worried that they might lose their crop,
the rain-filled July, and the hail—the fruit has been remarkable. The worst of the bad weather had been hail. Hail in June.
Hail in July. Hail as late as August. Hail like freezing rain and
hail so large it had ripped the still-green apples to shreds; hail
like no one had seen in more than forty years. Despite these
weather-related disasters, the apples that survived had size,
color, and especially rich flavor, for August had come on with
unusually cool nights, so that the flavor zesters multiplied.

Frost had probably played a role in our losing our entire
crop of Bosc pears, and some of the Jonagolds were also damaged, leaving brown frost rings in scattered areas, but we were
spared the devastating hail. Among the apples, our only real
casualty was the Red Delicious. Always difficult to rear to
size, the Red Delicious were affected by the sudden frost and
responded by not producing enough seeds. The result was
that the apples refused to grow, even when other varieties just
two rows over swelled with the days and inches of July rain.
But overall, the strange weather has heightened each apple's
natural flavor. This fall I tasted Cortlands so sun-baked they
melted under the tongue like garden-ripe melons, Macintosh
apples whose scarlet red skin was all tang but whose white
flesh was so sweet crisp it was like biting into a candy apple
in reverse. My newfound favorite for cooking, the Jonagolds,
have come through with a rich yellow meat this year and are
the size of small grapefruit. Meanwhile the Empires, especially the young trees on the top of block nine, are covered in
deep red, almost purple fruit. Apples such as the one I am
eating have an unbelievable crunchy sweetness and a taste so
smooth that to bite into one feels like biting into some kind
of large pungent sweet.

Soon I am over the ridge in block thirteen, walking past a
stand of Mutsus and Golden Delicious that were planted almost thirty years ago on the April weekend we celebrated my
birthday. I see Willi's black truck parked to the side of the

road, and his tall lean form leaning against the back of the truck bed. John Willi Thomas was raised in Georgia, but he has been on his own since the day his stepmother tried to poison him by putting arsenic in the flour of a cake. Willi spent two years in the hospital and when he was finally recovered he left home and found work as a fruit picker in Florida. He was fifteen. The fruit picking crews traveled north to New York State each fall, following the apple harvest, and one fall Willi came north and stayed. He never learned to read but he was a skilled and gifted mechanic, a hard worker, and soon he learned to drive the spray rig and prune, and in general discovered he had a feel for the trees. He had several offers of work and tried out different situations but as he put it to me one time, as an African American man growing up when he did, he learned to size up quickly if a situation was going to treat him well or not. If he felt he was being treated unfairly because he was black, he'd leave and never return. Willi came to work for my father two years before my father died, and as Willi remembers it, he liked something about my father right away and knew that working here would be a good job for him. That was eighteen years ago. These days Willi oversees the pruning or does it himself, runs the spray rig and does the other work of maintaining the trees. He mows and plows snow and maintains the machinery. Even when there is no work to be done, he checks in daily with my mother.

This morning he looks over the loaded trees with a satisfied smile. This is his crop, the result of a spring and summer of working with my mother, who oversees planting, the harvest, and, most important, throughout the season decides what to spray and when. While we all depend on our mother to keep the farm going, she depends on Willi. She could not continue if he chose to retire, which one day he will do. Willi is a handsome man, trim and fit, but although he looks young, he is sixty-eight.

I stop to talk to Willi for awhile, exchanging information about the fruit, the weather, the season, politics, and one of our favorite topics of conversation, dogs; Willi raises hunting beagles. When another car rounds the bend, heads up the road, and crosses over into the back orchards, Willi gets in his truck to take ladders to them and I continue back toward the barns.

Soon I reach the pond. Morning has begun on Orchard Estates, the development that sprang up on the southern end of the farm after my uncle's widow sold her share of the land. Cars drive in and out. Orchard Estates has become something of a poster child for development in America. The entire hillside is a grid of houses pressed into 1.5-acre lots with no plantings or open space to break up the pattern. All that remains of the orchards are the apple variety names posted on the streets. I don't like the high intensity lights that flood the land at night or the wide stretches of tarmac that now punctuate the view, but people live in those houses now and they are our neighbors.

I turn away from Orchard Estates and head up the hill to the barns. When I arrive, Rhys and my brother have loaded the truck with signs and are about to drive out. I quickly fill them in and they grab a few more signs, then head off. I wince when I see the open packing-house door and the open lot behind the barn. We lost the back barn two years ago. If we'd had about forty thousand dollars to spend we could have fixed up the old nineteenth-century barn with a new foundation, new corner beams, a new tin roof, new siding, and paint. But our small farm generated no such profits; we were lucky if it paid its bills and that was with my mother donating her own time to running it. We found a barn carpenter who carefully dismantled the old barn, saving what timbers he could to be used for repairing the other barns still standing, or if any one of us had a windfall, for one day rebuilding the old barn. Like most small farms, we are faced with an aesthetic dilemma. We'd like to save the historic outbuildings, but the fact is that we can replace them with much cheaper tin or plastic shelters.

I walk slowly back to the house, kicking through the fallen leaves, Coda once again on her leash by my side. My mother is sitting on the back porch making a grocery list and watching the cars pull in. Behind her the house beams with its new coat of yellow paint. This past summer she had the gutters fixed and the entire house repainted sunflower gold. My mother and I look at it for a minute and smile; this is still William W. Van Ness's foolish house, still the keeper of previous lives, and, for the moment anyway, her home and our evolving present.

ℐℐℐ

When I give readings from *A Family Place* or do book signings, people almost always ask me three questions: How is your mother? Do you still have the farm? What will happen next?

The first and second questions are easy to answer. My mother is doing well. At eighty-four she finds everything a bit harder to manage, but all things considered, she is lucky. She still sits on the board of the local historical society and does volunteer work for a charitable organization, RSVP, helping to drive seniors to doctors' appointments. In late August, she writes the flier for our customers, updating them on this year's harvest and letting them know the dates by which each variety will be ready to pick. We not only still have the farm, she still runs it.

My mother no longer drives the silver pick-up: instead, she heads out to check on the orchards in her small, fuel-efficient Aveo which is low enough to the ground for her to get in and out of. She can't walk as steadily or as far as she could eight years ago when she and I were scouting orchards together regularly, so she relies on the representative from United Agri Products, UAP, her spray supplier, for reports on what is in the trees. Gil Lasher, the UAP representative who taught me so much about scouting years before, died suddenly of cancer and a new man, Jay Matthews, has taken over to help my mother scout. Like Gil, Jay is kind and jovial, and my mother trusts his expertise and his honesty. Jay won't oversell spray material to my mother or fool her into spraying when she doesn't need to; his goal is to help keep her in business so that she will continue to be his customer. While spray coverage cost something like three hundred dollars per acre in the late 1980s, that same protection now costs more than seven hundred dollars. My mother runs sixty-plus acres of fruit; she can't afford a forty-two thousand dollar spray bill and isn't interested in growing cosmetically perfect fruit. As much as possible, she will follow the IPM strategy of only spraying for the most virulent of pests and diseases, relying on her resident populations of helpful insects to kill the destructive ones.

For the past five years, my mother has been letting several of our fields lie fallow, or has had them sown with buckwheat, which Willi plows back into the soil to enrich it with nitrogen. Given the number of customers that my mother can manage without hiring significant outside labor, she grows plenty of fruit. As it is, she figures she loses twenty percent of the crop to waste; she sells an annual average of three thousand bushels of apples, pears, and plums. Willi used to gather and sell windfall apples for cider, but new health codes prevent this, as fallen apples cannot be sold for juice. In the future, these fields might be planted over in cover crops again, or high-end vegetables, or become pasture for range-fed beef. Farms in the Hudson Valley only began to specialize in fruit in the early 1900s. That system of intensive monoculture worked for many decades, but to survive into the twenty-first century, Hudson Valley farms like ours may need to return to an older pattern of farm diversification.

According to the latest census in 2002, Columbia County, which covers some 586 square miles, has thirty fruit farms; combined, they farm a total of 2,018 acres, on which are planted 441,314 trees. The top five apples grown are Empire, McIntosh, Rome Beauty, Red Delicious, and Cortland, in that order. Most farms are quite small, listing fewer than 350 trees, while a few, such as Yonder Farms in Kinderhook, which has taken over the acreage of many of the smaller fruit growers around us, manages tens of thousands of trees. My mother's orchard consists of several thousand trees, so by to-day's standards she is now one of the larger growers.

So in response to the third question—What will happen next?—I have no answer. The larger picture for agriculture in our county and for the Hudson Valley in general is either bleak or optimistic, depending upon how you define agriculture. The Hudson Valley is made up of ten counties on both sides of the river and covers an area of roughly nine thousand five hundred square miles. Only seventeen percent of the land remains in use for agriculture, but this still amounts to over one thousand square miles of farmland, a significant figure considering the density of population in the valley and the development pressure from cities like New York, Albany, Kingston, and Poughkeepsie. There is no question that the model of fruit and diary farms that existed when I was growing up is a thing of the past.

When we'd set out riding as kids, we'd cover miles of open land. Sometimes we'd head our horses into the small "development" off the Fish and Game road just for the novelty of walking along the tarmac, listening to the sharp clop of our horses' hooves on the paved road, looking with interest at the carefully mowed lawns, the shrubs, and the basketball hoops, each suspended over a glistening plane of black tarmac. This was our little glimpse into suburbia, and although the "development" was only one street with about ten houses lined up along it on either side, we'd feel as if we had ridden into a strange new country. The horses would sense our excitement and snort and prance and sidestep or shy at lawn ornaments. In about two minutes we would have reached the end of the small strip of houses where, in a burst of relief, we'd let our horses go at a gallop into the next field, over that and down into the woods, back to the old railroad bed, through the woods, and then, if we felt like it and the day hadn't grown too hot, we could ride as far east as Philmont or head south to the center of Claverack. Once in the village, we'd take turns holding the horses while one of us went to get an ice cream or a Coke at Hickey's, the small grocery store. Once when I stood there by the side of the road, holding my pony and my cousin's horse, a knapsack on my back to hold our anticipated Cokes, the woman who cleaned for my grandmother came driving by. By the time we got home she had called to report that she'd seen me trying to run away from home. Little did we know that by 2008, when we let people ride horses across our hundred-plus acres, they would revel in what for them were wide-open spaces.

Many of the growers I met with my mother at fruit meetings in 1999 and 2000 are out of business. Some have sold their orchards to larger growers, others have sold their land. From 1997 to 2002, the Hudson Valley as a whole lost record numbers of farms, and the greatest losses were in fruit and dairy farms. Yet, the number of farms in the valley has held relatively stable in the past two years, in part because the threshold for declaring an agricultural operation has been lowered to only one thousand dollars in sales. Similarly, the face and shape of agriculture has shifted toward a pattern of smaller farms with increasingly diversified activities. One now sees farms raising horses, running game preserves, raising alternative vegetables on a smaller scale, but with the net effect of an agricultural sector that looks relatively viable, and the mood is optimistic. Groups like Scenic Hudson have identified some 45,000 acres of land, much of it agricultural, which they hope to preserve and keep as open land in the future. This activism is happening across the country as more and more communities are talking about the need to protect farmland. There is a general awareness of the need to create tax structures that allow farms to compete with development, and as history has shown, public awareness and grass roots movements are the first wave that leads to the creation of public policy; those bumper stickers that read "no farms no food" help make change happen.

These days the median size for a farm in the Hudson Valley is about eighty-seven acres, but more than half of the farms are now under one hundred acres and list sales of less than ten thousand dollars. The lesson of our family's farm is perhaps just one of tenacity. Maybe the best answer to what will happen next is my brother's usual response when passers-by ask the same question. He will point to the flag above the farm gate. The large white banner says "OPEN" in bold red print, waving as if to say, *We are still here.*

I sometimes get letters and emails from people who have read my book. Civil War buffs send me information that they have uncovered about the USS Cuyler, Lt. John Van Ness's ship during the Civil War. Farmers send me photographs of their land and trees. Genealogists and historians of all kinds send me bits of information that they think I will enjoy. But most write to tell me that the book touched them in some way, that it got them thinking about their own family histories, and then they end up telling me stories of their own family places. Most of these stories are about loss, of the home they once had on a lake in Vermont or New York, that house on the bluff of the river or around the corner from the most marvelous dune. It is just a small house—a bungalow, a summer cottage, a farmhouse surrounded by corn in Michigan, Minnesota, or Iowa—but to them it is their family place, the place where all their childhood and family memories lie. They had to sell it, and they have accepted that but they still they miss it, or they regret not having worked harder to find a way to hang on.

Not all of the stories are sad. Some readers tell me about their decision to return to a family place, a farm that they have tentatively begun to work again, starting with some acres of hay. Next year they are going to try berries and corn. One man proudly wrote that he'd moved back to his family's farm. The place had been divided among him and his siblings; the siblings had sold their shares, but he had held onto his fifty acres and was living there now, renovating an old sap house, teaching at a local college, making his u-turn back to the family farm work. Some admit they are glad not to have the albatross of a family place to care for anymore. Then there are others who write about how moving it was to read about a family with so much remembered, traceable past. Their own family history is one of war and genocide, Holocaust, limiting their past to one or two generations, beyond which the family record stops. A great yearning for the past is expressed in many of the letters I receive, and a great nostalgia for place. Surely, Gaston Bachelard touched a nerve when he wrote, in his famous *Poetics of Space*, "In order to sense across the years our attachment to the house we were born in, dream is more powerful than thought." I love getting these messages from people I have never met. When I read them I am reminded of why I write in the first place—to try to make a difference, to reach across the void.

Sometimes people ask me if I am still in touch with Anna Van Ness, my father's half sister, the aunt I found. I did keep in touch with Anna in the years after the book was published. She came to the first reading that I gave in Hudson when I read the section from "Lives of Aunts" for a large audience at the Hudson Opera House. Mrs. Testa had not come; she was ill and, in fact, not long afterward died of cancer. But Anna's family was there, along with many of her friends. More than once, she had told me how my finding her had changed her life. Last winter, after a brief illness, she died. She was ninety-two.

At her funeral, my mother and I saw an old woman in a wheel chair in the aisle of the small church. On our way out, she caught my eye, and when I came close, reached out to grab my hand. "I am Ann Drumm," she said simply, "I was Anna's best friend. And you must be Leila Philip." I nodded, almost apprehensive. Would I discover that Anna had not been pleased by what I had written even though I knew that she had loved being found by me? "Yes," I stammered as she grabbed my hand. Her skin felt fragile to my touch but her grip was surprisingly strong.

"Thank you," she said, clasping my hand, "Thank you for finding Anna. You did a wonderful thing."

"You knew Anna when she was young?" I managed to ask.

"Well yes, since she was eight years old," she said, "Anna was my best friend!"

Before we could continue, the church began to empty, and a younger woman came to wheel her out. She introduced herself as Ann Drumm's daughter, greeted us warmly, and said she had loved my book.

"Call me, or come visit," Ann called from her wheelchair, " I live at the Pine Haven nursing home now. We can talk about Anna."

Outside in the small cemetery I watched the dark casket being lowered and felt tears welling up in my eyes. I had treasured meeting Anna and once I had gotten to know her I had hoped that what I had written had indeed touched her life as she claimed, but a part of me had always worried that she had just said that because she didn't want to hurt my feelings. She was, you could tell right away, a deeply kind person. But her best friend would not have lied. Now I could hold onto that knowledge and have no doubt about it. Something for Anna had been redeemed through the telling of her story, through the acceptance she felt at being included in the larger family.

Months later I called Ann Drumm. At ninety-seven, she was as Anna had been, never complaining, always so pleased to talk. "I wake up every morning," she said into the phone, "and I say, 'Please, Lord, make me be happy, thank you for this day.' I have to stay up, you see. My granddaughter visits me and I don't want her to be upset."

For a moment I was taken aback; it was as if were talking to Anna, for, like her, this Ann had a deep faith in the goodness of the world. I thought of her and her determination to remain cheerful at the nursing home, living out her days among the old and dying, waiting for visits, and I made a mental note never to complain about my life again. She told me about her childhood days with Anna, and how the kids had been so cruel to Anna because they knew that she was an illegitimate child, born out of wedlock. Ann thought that they were extra cruel because they were jealous. As Ann remembered it, the other kids were mean because Anna was smart and pretty and good at art even as a child.

"I knew her in school." continued Ann, " And I knew how much she had suffered. When she was up here you know, she wanted your book read to her, even when she couldn't see. I have your book too, right here in my bedside table." She laughed with so much happiness that, again, I was taken aback. Then, missing Anna, I asked her a question that I wasn't sure that I fully understood.

"Why did it mean so much?" I asked, "the book I mean, my finding her."

"Well," she stopped for a minute. "You have to understand that she had felt so rejected."

Again Ann paused, "She felt the burden of being, you know, illegitimate, was finally gone. She was accepted. That just meant everything."

Soon after, I asked Anna's daughter what she could re-member of her mother and grandmother and she wrote me a long letter and included a copy of Anna's baptismal record. There on the page I saw again proof that she had been rec-ognized by my grandfather, for her name was recorded as Anna Van Ness Orsted Philip and my grandfather was listed as her father. Anna's daughter went on to say that her grand-mother had loved talking about her days at Talavera and her time with my grandfather and seemed to do so without re-gard for the way it must have made her daughter feel. For Anna, the child of that affair, how could the question not have surfaced—Why had this man, her father, who had clearly loved her mother, opted not to love her? Again, Anna's daughter emphasized that it was her grandmother who had promised not to visit once my grandfather had married and would not hear of her daughter breaking that promise. But the story was more complicated, too, because it seems that my grandfather had wanted Anna's mother to get an educa-tion and had offered to pay for her to go to college. Had he, then, hoped she would find a way to raise herself up from her recent status as a first-generation Danish immigrant and join him in his social class? Was it she who broke it off, feeling that the gap was too great?

Some time after my mother learned the story of Anna, she said she thought she finally understood something of my grandfather's great grief when Leila Stott, my father's little sister, had died of meningitis. Leila Stott had been three, the same age as Anna Van Ness when my grandfather had last seen her. My mother's theory was that my grandfather, who was, she said, very superstitious, must have felt that, in some way, losing little Leila was a kind of punishment for having abandoned his first daughter. His remoteness and his sadness and his before-dinner drinking made sudden and complete sense to her. So many almosts and what ifs riddled the story. What if my father had been able to meet Anna? What if Anna herself had mustered the courage to finish her way up the drive, arriving at the house? What if Anna's mother had accepted my grandfather's offer and gone to college? What if my grandfather had never met my eventual grandmother? What if, at three years old, my father's little sister had not died, sending my grandfather into years of unresolved grief?

When people write to tell me that my book has made them weep or has touched their lives, I am of course deeply gratified. What else but connection does one aspire to throughout those years of work, those days and days at the desk with nothing yet to show for it but fatigue? I hope my readers weep because for a moment they think of how fragile all lives are, of how easy it is to judge, and how much harder to feel compassion. I don't know anything, really, about why my readers feel moved, except that it has little to do with me or with my own family's story. Reading is always an act of the imagination, and when a story moves us, it does so because of something in our own lives that connects us to those words. We come to care about characters because they represent facets of ourselves, of our own experience.

Months have passed since I first began work on this epilogue. A semester of teaching, another harvest. As I write the last words, we are heading toward 2009 and the shock is still reverberating from the largest financial upheaval my generation has ever seen. Change. Change for the better, change for the worse. Change that crept up on us and change dreamed and fought for. Change so fast we can't seem to adjust before the next wave hits. And in the midst of it all, a yellow house still standing, barns, and the land, etched like some great rune with centuries of agriculture, which for almost a hundred years now has been the language of apples, pears, plums. A Hudson Valley farm; three centuries, five wars, one family.

The author about 1977, riding Peter

Family Tree

ADMIRAL AERD VAN NESS: earliest Dutch ancestor

WILLIAM VAN NESS (1711–1790): 1732, purchased tract from John
I. Van Rensselear, dated on Pennfield map; married GERTRUDE
HOGEBOOM of Claverack; seven children, including Petrus Van
Ness and William W. Van Ness

PETRUS VAN NESS: son of William Van Ness

WILLIAM W. VAN NESS (1775–1823): son of William Van Ness;
1807, appointed justice, New York Supreme Court; 1807–1812,
built Talavera

GENERAL JOHN P. VAN NESS (1770–1846): son of Petrus Van
Ness; 1802, married MARCIA BURNES (1782–1832); 1805, portrait painted by Gilbert Stuart; 1830, elected mayor of Washington, D.C.

ANALIZA VAN NESS: daughter of William W. Van Ness; 1816, married HENRY LIVINGSTON; eight children; lived at Talavera until
Henry Livingston's death in 1827

GERTRUDE VAN NESS: daughter of General John P. Van Ness;
married MARTIN HOFFMAN

CATHERINE DUOW HOFFMAN (1797–1866): daughter of Gertrude Van Ness and Martin Hoffman; 1821, married COLONEL
HENRY G. PHILIP (1763–1829); three sons

LIEUTENANT JOHN VAN NESS PHILIP (1823–1862): son of Catherine Duow Hoffman and Colonel Henry G. Philip

COLONEL WILLIAM HENRY PHILIP (1824–1881): son of Catherine Duow Hoffman and Colonel Henry G. Philip; 1864, married ELIZA WORTHINGTON (1842–1896); seven children

MARTINUS HOFFMAN PHILIP (1826–1888): son of Catherine Duow Hoffmann and Colonel Henry G. Philip

MAJOR JOHN VAN NESS PHILIP (1866–1949): son of Colonel William Henry Philip and Eliza Worthington; 1921, married HELEN MUNROE STOTT (1883–1973) (grandmother); three children

CHARLES WORTHINGTON PHILIP (1867–1875): son of Colonel William Henry Philip and Eliza Worthington

WILLIAM HENRY PHILIP (1869) (died as infant): son of Colonel William Henry Philip and Eliza Worthington

HERMAN HOFFMAN PHILIP (1872–1951) (great uncle): son of Colonel William Henry Philip and Eliza Worthington

GASTON PEARSON PHILIP (1874–1913) (great uncle); son of Colonel William Henry Philip and Eliza Worthington

298

ELIZABETH "BESSIE" WORTHINGTON PHILIP (1876–1967) (great aunt): daughter of Colonel William Henry Philip and Eliza Worthington

WILLIAM HOUSTON PHILIP (1877) (died as infant): son of Colonel William Henry Philip and Eliza Worthington

LEILA VANDERBILT STOTT (1880–1969) (Aunt Lee): sister of Helen Munroe Stott

JOHN VAN NESS PHILIP JR. (1922–1992) (father): son of Major John Van Ness Philip and Helen Munroe Stott; 1951, married JULIA WILLIS (1924–) (mother); five children

LEILA STOTT PHILIP (1924–1927): daughter of Major John Van Ness Philip and Helen Munroe Stott

NICHOLAS WORTHINGTON PHILIP (1926–1975): son of Major John Van Ness Philip and Helen Munroe Stott

LEILA STOTT PHILIP (born 1961): daughter of John Van Ness Philip Jr. and Julia Willis

Sources

RESEARCH FOR THIS BOOK BEGAN IN 1995 with the discovery of a cache of unsorted family and farm papers located in the house and barns at Talavera. Systematically removing, cleaning, stabilizing, then sorting these papers to create an archive took two years. The resulting collection, now called the "Philip Farm and Family Papers," includes photographs, correspondence, genealogies, farm and house ledgers, journals, accounts, assorted business papers and agricultural literature. Together with a collection of family papers that had been removed from the house in 1975 and acquired by the New-York Historical Society in 1980, these papers tell the story of the Van Ness and Philip families in the early political, social and economic life of New York. The two collections also describe the continuous ownership of one farm by one family for almost three centuries, making them a unique case study of agriculture in the Hudson Valley.

Within the text, these primary materials are indicated by quotation marks rather than traditional footnotes. Most of the letters and diaries of Lieutenant John Van Ness, William Henry, Martin Hoffman, Catherine Douw, Eliza Worthington, Herman Hoffman (Hoffman), Elizabeth Stark (Bessie), Gaston Pearson and the early letters of John Van Ness (1866–1949) cited in this book are located in the "Philip–Van Ness" collection in the New-York Historical Society. Most of the later correspondence of John Van Ness Philip (1866–1949), along with farm journals and my father's letters and papers, is drawn from the private collection "Philip Farm and Family papers."

One of the most difficult areas of research was the story of Tom, Thomas W. Johnson, the freed slave who fought with Lieutenant John Van Ness in the Civil War. Not surprisingly, family correspondence that mentioned Tom never mentioned his full name. I assumed that the will of John Van Ness's father-in-law might deliver some information about Tom, but my first task was to find it. I fi-

299

SOURCES

nally tracked down the name of Laura's father, John Johnson, by looking in Maryland newspapers on the day of his death, October 6, 1856. I then discovered that he had died intestate. Through perseverance, luck and with the help of a particularly knowledgeable staff researcher in the Maryland State Archives, I was able to uncover letters of administration that his widow, Mary Johnson, had received on April 6, 1858. Checking the administration accounts for that date revealed the inventory of John Johnson's estate. There, under household accounts, I found Tom's listing: "Negro man Tom slave for life 21 years of age." He was valued at $850.

Once I had verified Tom's identity, I was even more determined to find out, if I could, what had happened to him. He was not listed among family members and servants in the1865 population census for Claverack. I began to look through the U.S. naval records of the Civil War. There I finally found his full name, Thomas W. Johnson. He was listed as one of the "landsmen" wounded in a skirmish with the *Wilder* in an official report filed by the captain of the USS *Cuyler*, Captain Winslow. *Official Records of the Union of the Confederate Navies in the War of the Rebellion*, Series I, volume 17 (Washington, D.C.: Government Printing Office).

Other key sources of primary materials included: Columbia County Historical Society, Kinderhook, New York; Columbia County Agricultural Society, Kinderhook, New York; Columbia County Surrogates Court, Hudson, New York; Columbia County Clerk's Office, Hudson, New York; Hudson City Clerk's Office, Hudson, New York; Hudson City Library, Hudson, New York; Library of Congress, Washington, D.C.; Maryland State Archives, Annapolis, Maryland; Municipal Archives of the City of New York, New York City; National Archives, College Park, Maryland and Washington, D.C.; New-York Historical Society, New York City; New York State Library, Albany, New York; private papers of Anna Post; private papers of Julia Philip.

In addition to the primary research sites listed above, a book of this nature requires broad reading in a number of areas. While this book was not written to stand as a definitive family or farm history, through the writing of it I was soon propelled into the following subjects and fields: American history, landscape studies and cultural geography, African-American history, landscape gardening and architecture, art history, pomology, agricultural history, horticulture, fruit growing, the women's suffrage movement and beekeeping. It was particularly important to read widely about the Dutch history of the Hudson Valley, the role of Columbia County in the founding of the new republic, the intricacies of the manorial system in colonial New York and the complex land transactions between the Mohicans and early Europeans in the valley. Luckily, some excellent research has been done on the Livingston and Van Ness families in early New York, which provided me with critical background.

ADDITIONAL SOURCES

Three excellent references for readings in the meaning of landscape:

Jackson, John Brinckerhoff, *Discovering the Vernacular Landscape*, New Haven: Yale University Press, 1984.

Miller, Angela L., *Empire of the Eye: Landscape Representation and American Cultural Politics, 1825–1875*, Ithaca: Cornell University Press, 1993.

Tuan, Yi-Fu, *Topophilia: A Study of Environmental Perception, Attitudes and Values*, Princeton: Princeton University Press, 1974.

Five imporant sources on memory and identity:

Halwbwachs, Maurice., *On Collective Memory*. Chicago: University of Chicago Press, 1992.

Kammen, Michael G., *Mystic Chords of Memory: The Transformation of Tradition in American Culture*, New York: Alfred A. Knopf, 1991.

Lowenthal, David, *The Past is a Foreign Country*. Cambridge, 1985.

Spence, Donald P., *Narrative Truth and Historical Truth: Meaning and Interpretation in Psychoanalysis*, New York: Norton, 1982.

Pierre, Nora, "Between Memory and History: Les Lieux de Memoire," *Representations* 26 (1989): 7-25.

For information about landscape and landscape gardening, particularly during the romantic era in the Hudson Valley:

Anderson, Jean Bradley, *Carolinian on the Hudson: The Life of Robert Donaldson*, Raleigh: The Historic Preservation Foundation of North Carolina, 1996.

Downing, Andrew Jackson, *A Treatise on the Theory and Practice of Landscape Gardening adapted to North America with a view to the improvement of Country Residences*, New York: Wiley and Putnam, 1844.

Nygren, Edward J. with Bruce Robertson, *Views and Visions: American Landscape before 1830*, Washington, D.C.: Corcoran Gallery of Art, 1986.

Major, Judith K., *To live in the new world: A.J. Downing and American Landscape Gardening*, Cambridge: MIT Press, 1997.

Three excellent sources on architecture:

Ackerman, James S., *The Villa: Form and Ideology of Country Houses*, Princeton: Princeton University Press, 1990.

Bachelard, Gaston, *The Poetics of Space*, New York: Orion, 1964.

Piwonka, Ruth and Blackburn Roderic A., *A Visible Heritage: Columbia County, NY, A History in Art and Architecture*, Hensonville: Black Dome Press, 1996.

SOURCES

Three excellent sources on the social and economic history of Columbia County and New York State:

Huston, John R., *The Anti-Rent Wars: Jacksonian Politics and The Contest Over Free Labor in New York, 1785–1865.* (PhD dissertation, Yale University, 1994).

Stott, Peter H., *Industrial Archeology in Columbia County, New York,* Kinderhook: Columbia County Historical Society, 2001.

Taylor, Alan, *William Cooper's Town: Power and Persuasion on the Frontier of the Early American Republic,* New York: Alfred Knopf, 1995.

Four key sources on the manorial system in New York State:

Breugel, Martin, *The Rise of a Market Society in the Rural Hudson Valley, 1780–1860,* PhD dissertation, Cornell University, 1994.

Breugel, Martin, "Unrest: Manorial Society and the Market in the Hudson Valley 1780-1850, *The Journal of American History,* March 1996.

Ellis, David Maldwyn, *Landlords and Farmers in the Hudson-Mohawk Region 1790–1850,* Ithaca: Cornell University Press, 1946.

Kim, Sung Bok, *Landlord and Tenant in Colonial New York: Manorial Society 1664-1775,* Chapel Hill: The University of North Carolina Press, 1978.

For background on Van Ness Family history:

Bonney, Catharina V.R. (compiled and arranged by), *Legacy of Historical Gleanings: with illustrations and autographs in two volumes,* Albany: J. Munsell, 1875.

Denman, Peter Van Ness, *From Deference to Democracy: The Van Ness Family and Their Times, 1759 to 1844.* (Volumes I and II), PhD dissertation, The University of Michigan, 1977.

Two excellent books on early African American history in New York:

Hodges, Graham Russell, *Root and Branch: African Americans in New York and East Jersey, 1613–1863,* Chapel Hill: University of North Carolina Press, 1999.

Litwack, Leon F., *North of Slavery: The Negro in the Free States, 1790-1860,* Chicago: The University of Chicago Press, 1993.

For background on the Livingstons:

Kierner, Cynthia A., *Traders and Gentlefolk: The Livingstons of New York, 1675–1790,* Ithaca: Cornell University Press, 1992

SOURCES

For general history of the Hudson Valley:

Dunn, Shirley W., *The Mohicans and Their Land 1609-1730*, Fleischmanns: Purple Mountain Press, 1994.

Ellis, Franklin Captain, *History of Columbia County, New York: Some of Its Prominent Men and Pioneers*, Philadelphia: Everts and Ensign, 1878.

Sources of colorful local history for Claverack:

Gebhard, Elizabeth L., *The Parsonage Between Two Manors: Annals of Clover-Reach*, Hudson, NY: Bryan Printing Company, 1910.

Webb, F.H., *Claverack, Clover-Reach*, Claverack, December 1892.

Two excellent sources on the Paris art world of the 1890's:

Merrill, Linda, *The Peacock Room: A Cultural Biography*, New Haven: Yale University Press, 1998.

Weinberg, Barbara H., *The Lure of Paris: Nineteenth Century American Painters and Their French Teachers*, New York: Abbeville Press, 1991.

For background on New York State agricultural history:

Hedrick, Ulysses Prentiss, *A History of Agriculture in the State of New York*, New York: Hill and Wang, 1933.

Willard Wesley, Cochrane, *The Development of American Agriculture: A Historical Analysis,* Minneapolis: University of Minnesota Press, 1979.

An excellent source of apple history was the beautiful classic:

Beach, S.A., *The Apples of New York: Report of the New York Agricultural Experiment Station for the Year 1903*, volumes I and II, Albany: J.B. Lyon Company Printers, 1905.

Acknowledgments

FUNDING FOR RESEARCH ON THIS BOOK was received from the American Association of University Women and the Colgate University Research Council, Furthermore, the publishing program of the J. M. Kaplan Fund and the National Endowment for the Humanities. In 1999, the Columbia County Historical Society served as a sponsor for this project.

For help creating the archives, I am indebted to Helen McLallan of the Columbia County Historical Society, Carl Peterson of Case Library at Colgate University and to my sister, Katherine Philip Chansky, a professional archivist. I am grateful to Margaret Heilbrun, the director of the library at the New-York Historical Society, for help tracking down acquisition records for the "Philip–Van Ness" collection. For help in researching the often shadowy and incomplete history of eighteenth-century land holdings in Claverack, I am indebted to the work of Ruth Piwonka, a consulting researcher who specializes in Columbia County. Maryland State Archives researcher Rob Barnes helped to find the missing clue that connected the pieces of Tom's life. Colgate reference librarian David Hughs helped track down Johnson genealogies.

Several individuals allowed me to interview them. I want to thank Mrs. Nancy Testa and Captain Ronald B. Moser USN–RET, for many great conversations and for help researching Lieutenant John Van Ness. Special thanks go to Anna Post for deciding that "it was time" and for generously allowing me to use her story. I learned a great deal from conversations with spray representative Gil Lasher and Steve McKay, educator at the Cornell Cooperative Extension Service of Columbia County. Thanks also to Dr. Jan Nyrop and Peter J. Jentsch, researchers active with the exciting "*T. pyri* Project," which aims to achieve biological control of European red mites in the Hudson Valley.

A number of people read my work at various stages along the

way and their encouragement and insight were golden. Thank you: Bobbie Bristol, Teresa Carbone, Jenna Laslocky, Angela Miller, Susan Packer, Kirk Savage, Christine Stansell. My great friend, Elizabeth Thomas, generously read my work with her famed red pen in hand. Wonderful support came from Joan Davidson and Mike Gladstone. Thanks go to my agent, Kim Witherspoon, who never had any doubts and to my editor at Viking, Ray Roberts, for believing in this book from the first pages on.

I would like to acknowledge the dedicated individuals and organizations, working with energy and vision to ensure that the rural landscape of the Hudson Valley endures for future generations.

My mother deserves all praise, not just for keeping the farm going, but also for her generosity and patience. I want to thank my brothers and sister for their trust as I poked around in our shared past. Finally, it would never have been possible to write this book without the great love, courage and unwavering support of my husband, Garth Evans. Along the way, our son Rhys, kept us both laughing.

For the most part, the portraits and photographs reproduced in this new edition of the book are in the possession of the author's family. Thanks to the Connecticut Historical Society for permission to reprint images of the Ammi Phillips portraits of Colonel Henry G. Philip and Mrs. Henry G. Philip. Thanks to the New York Historical Society for permission to reproduce the photograph of Colonel William Henry and Eliza Worthington Philip around the time of their marriage. Thanks to the Columbia County Historical Society for permission to reprint the 1858 map of Columbia County. Thanks to Valerie King, for loaning the beautiful picture of Anna Van Ness for inclusion in the book. Thanks to photographer Carlos Loret de Mola for permission to reprint the 2008 photograph of my mother. Thanks to Ann Drumm for sharing her memories of Anna. Thanks to my agent, Miriam Altshuler, ever astute and encouraging.

Huge thanks to the State University of New York Press, especially Associate Director James Peltz and Senior Production Editor Laurie Searl, whose work has brought this book to life again in a new incarnation.

As always, and forever, thanks to my husband Garth and to Rhys, the ongoing joy of our lives.